THE
LIE IN OUR
MARRIAGE

BOOKS BY ANNA-LOU WEATHERLEY

The Night of the Party

The Woman Inside

The Stranger's Wife

The Couple on Cedar Close

Pleasure Island

Black Heart

Vengeful Wives

Wicked Wives

THE
LIE IN OUR MARRIAGE

ANNA-LOU WEATHERLEY

bookouture

Published by Bookouture in 2023

An imprint of Storyfire Ltd.
Carmelite House
50 Victoria Embankment
London EC4Y 0DZ

www.bookouture.com

ISBN: 978-1-80314-968-4
eBook ISBN: 978-1-80314-967-7

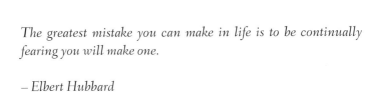

The greatest mistake you can make in life is to be continually fearing you will make one.

– Elbert Hubbard

For Claire Bord, with much love.

1

Greeted by a rush of cold and fetid air as she unlocks the hatch to the loft, Maggie Wendover slips off her sparkly silver Jimmy Choo sandals with one hand and hoists her silky wrap dress up around her thighs.

Climbing the ladder with a sense of careful purpose, she enters the loft bottom first, swinging her legs up behind her. It's chilly and a little creepy up here, and she feels for the light string and pulls it, illuminating the space with a welcome, warm orange glow.

Barefoot, she begins to navigate her way through the boxes that are piled high like giant bricks, their dusty cardboard lids half-open like mouths waiting to be fed. Lofts are the graveyard of a home, she supposes, the place where items you once loved and treasured have been laid to rest.

Maggie peers inside one of the boxes. It's filled with old toys from when the kids were little: loose stickle bricks and a broken Etch A Sketch, Barbie dolls with shaven heads and biro-covered limbs. There's schoolbooks and scrapbooks too, leather-look photo albums piled high and an old suitcase that was almost certainly for the rubbish tip but which, if she remembers rightly, was a wedding gift, someone from Len's side, though she can't recall who anymore. *Bloody brain fog* – she's convinced it's getting worse.

Anyway, now she thinks of it, she was sure there had been two of them, a matching pair, because she distinctly remembers feeling terribly sophisticated as she and Len had wheeled them through the airport on the way to their honeymoon in the Costa del Sol all those years ago.

Maggie stoops, picks up a teddy bear peeping out from an old black sack and smiles as a wave of nostalgia washes over her. Bongo! *Ahhh*, Bongo had been her son Lewis's favourite toy as a tot. He never went anywhere without Bongo Bear right up until he was about six or seven if she remembers rightly.

Poor careworn old Bongo looks a little unloved now with his patchy, balding fur and a missing eye. She replaces him carefully back into the sack with half a thought of restoring him, make him all new again to pass down to the little life that's growing inside Casey's tummy.

A sliver of joy ripples through Maggie once again. She's going to be a grandmother!

Light with excitement and anticipation, Maggie hears the muted sound of her guests outside in the marquee below, their voices rising up through the floorboards, punctuated by joyful laughter. From a distance, she can just about make out the singer, and her heart drops as she hears the familiar melody of Rod Stewart's 'Maggie May'. Len will almost certainly be looking for her now. It's one of 'their' songs and he will want to dance. *Bloody hell*. She'll need to get a wiggle on.

She crouches down to open the door to one of the eaves where she's stashed her secret laptop. For months she's been creeping up here to the cold, damp and stale-smelling loft – usually while Len's working or fiddling around on one of his vintage car projects in the garage – to prepare tonight's surprise: a twenty-minute spectacular visual presentation of their life together so far. She's spent weeks sifting through hundreds, probably thousands, of old photographs, cards, mementos, keepsakes and old video footage of them all throughout the years, carefully selecting the best, the funniest and the most poignant to splice them all together in a short film she plans to project onto a giant screen for tonight's grand finale. She's hoping to impress Len, hopes he'll be pleased by the fact that she still wants to.

She places her hand inside the eave and feels around for the laptop, her fingers searching in the dark for where she last left it. Tutting – it's usually easy to locate – she reaches for her phone and turns on the torch app.

Oh, thank goodness. She spots it wedged against something up against the back wall and... *what's that?* She feels a softness against her fingertips... fabric of some sort.

Grunting with exertion, she grabs it, dislodging the laptop so that it falls flat with a loud smack against the floorboards.

'*Shit!*' She pulls the two items out of the eave and sits back on her haunches with a heavy sigh, her heartbeat accelerating.

It's a scarf – a woman's scarf, though she doesn't recognise it as her own. Doesn't recognise it at all in fact.

Curious, she instinctively brings it up to her face.

Perfume. It smells of perfume, sweet and pungent, very distinctive and... familiar somehow. Is she imagining it or is it a similar smell to the perfume her neighbour, Brenda, is wearing tonight?

She feels a strange fluttering sensation in her chest. Well, whoever it belongs to, it's been worn recently – had to have been for it to still smell of perfume, surely?

She studies it closely... it's patterned pink with skulls – little black skulls – printed all over, and it's stained with spots, random dark-brown splashes like paint. It was definitely not there the last time she was up here, just the day before yesterday. The small eave where she's been hiding her laptop is always empty save for a few damp boxes marked 'Len's Bits and Bobs' written in faded black marker pen. She would've noticed it.

She rubs the thin fabric between her fingers. It looks and feels expensive. She checks for a label, locates one on the corner and holds it up to the light, squinting. Alex... Alexander... McQueen. It's designer.

Maggie stares at it, perplexed. The patterned brown splashes seem a bit too abstract now that she inspects it closely and...

A bolt of unease suddenly strikes right through her. Tendrils of fear begin to snake their way through her lower intestines, causing her hands to lightly tremble. Is that... *blood*? Are those *bloodstains* she can see on it?

Maggie blinks, stands statue still as she holds the scarf up to the light. It'll be engine oil. It must be one of Len's old oil rags he uses on his cars. Yes, that'll be it. But her attempts at reassuring herself feel strangely flimsy and ephemeral. Why would Len use an expensive designer scarf on one of his old cars? It's definitely not her daughter's either – Remy would have made a real song and dance about buying something from Alexander McQueen. Besides, she could never afford it anyway, not on her student budget, and what if it's... maybe it *is* Brenda's scarf – she's sure it's the same perfume she's smelled on her tonight. *Oh God*, is Brenda having an affair with her husband?

Maggie shakes her head in a bid to erase such a thought, like she would that broken old Etch A Sketch in the box behind her. It's an absurd idea and she knows it. And anyway, even if Brenda *was* having an affair with Len – which she isn't – then what on earth would her bloodstained scarf be doing up in their loft?

2

Unsettled, Maggie almost drops the scarf like a hot stone, then rolls it into a ball and throws it back into the eave before closing the door. It was nothing, just an old scarf. It was probably one of hers, one she's forgotten all about. Her memory really has been so foggy lately. Clutching her laptop, she makes her way precariously backward down the loft ladder.

'Brenda!' She almost drops the laptop in surprise when she sees her standing there, on the landing. She'd been outside in the marquee just a couple of minutes ago, chatting animatedly to her brother-in-law, Bob, and his wife, Julie. What is she doing skulking around upstairs in her house? She gets a waft of that distinctive perfume again as Brenda blinks at her in alarm.

'I... I was looking for the bathroom. Got a bit disorientated.' She rolls her eyes in a show of self-deprecation.

'There's one downstairs,' Maggie says, careful to conceal the hint of tightness in her voice, 'next to the kitchen.' She'd made a point of telling guests where to find it on their arrival.

Brenda looks awkward, her face flushing red. 'Yes, but there was a bit of a queue and I was desperate – too many bubbles.'

She waggles her empty glass and laughs a little too loudly. 'The champagne is delicious by the way, creamy.'

She's blathering, Maggie thinks. *Probably came upstairs to be nosey and has been caught out.*

'You have a very beautiful home, I have to say,' she adds, looking around her. 'Wonderful taste. Anyway, terrible news about the girl, isn't it?'

'The girl?'

'Haven't you heard? They've found a body in the river. It's all over the news.'

Maggie looks at her blankly. She hasn't seen the news – funnily enough she's been somewhat distracted by the hundred or so guests she currently has outside in her garden.

'Wonder if it was suicide?' Brenda says, her voice trailing off. 'If she threw herself off the bridge maybe?'

The word 'suicide' feels like a short, sharp slap around Maggie's face, instantly conjuring up an image of her mother inside her head.

'A body, really? Oh, that's terrible,' she says, getting a waft of that perfume once more. 'Dreadful,' she adds, shaking her head and trying not to think about the scarf, how it had smelled.

'Mags!' She hears her husband's voice rising from downstairs. 'Where are you, chickadee? The singer's doing "Maggie May" and we're missing it!'

She gives an endearing inward eye roll. She's never really liked the song, though she's never had the heart to tell him as much.

'It's such a shame,' Brenda continues sagely. 'Such a beautiful place. Seems sad that it's become synonymous with sui—'

'It's down the hall, second on the left – the bathroom,' Maggie cuts in, not wanting her to say *that* word again.

'Oh right. Brilliant, thanks.' Brenda's face is still a little rosy as she sashays off, empty champagne glass still raised in the air like a trophy.

'*There* you are, chickadee!' Len is halfway up the stairs, coming towards her. 'I've been looking for you. Come on – the guests are waiting and I'm about to make a speech.'

Maggie briefly turns back to see Brenda slip into the bathroom.

'Coming, darling,' she says.

The mellifluous ding of a knife tapping against glass causes the animated conversation inside the marquee to lull into a gentle hush, and Maggie is forced to smile out at her onlooking guests. She swallows back her nerves with a swig of champagne, tries not to think about wherever her son and Casey have got to, tries not to think about the scarf.

'They'll be here – stop fretting!' Her friend, Christine, squeezes her elbow reassuringly. 'There's been some sort of incident down at Riverdown Park apparently,' she whispers. 'The police have cordoned the whole area off.'

'Yes,' Maggie hisses back, 'Brenda just said something about some poor girl being pulled from the river?' She tries not to think about who she might be, or the grief that's about to descend on the lives of those she's left behind. Regrettably, she knows what that feels like only too well.

Christine gives her arm a little pat. 'They'll be stuck in traffic is all.'

Len stands now, clears his throat theatrically before tapping the microphone in front of him with his forefinger. 'Unlucky for you lot, it seems to be working! Ahem... Ladies and gentlemen, girls and boys, those among us who identify as either, neither or both – and yes, I'm looking at you, Mike Bowden!' Len nods at his friend – a tall hulk of a man with a full bushy black beard – and the place erupts into laughter, right on cue.

'We all know why we're gathered here this evening with our

dearest family and many, many wonderful friends – *plus a few we felt obliged to invite...'*

There's more laughter tinged with mock outrage.

'And the reason is' – he turns towards his wife – 'this amazing, beautiful woman sitting here next to me.'

Maggie feels her face flush as she looks up at her husband, aware that all eyes are upon her, although in this moment she only has eyes for him. Len always gives such emotive speeches.

'It's all in the timing,' he always tells her. 'Knowing precisely where to place a pause, a sigh, a joke...' *Good timing* – it was everything when you really thought about it.

'Twenty-five years ago to the day, this incredible lady took my breath away as she walked down the aisle, a vision in white – *well, we won't say too much about the whole virginal white thing...'*

More of the guests' laughter rises up through the marquee like helium.

'... and did me the greatest honour of my life by becoming my wife.'

A collective harmony of 'ahhs' rings out across the lawn and Maggie feels herself tearing up, the faces of her guests blurring round the edges like watercolours left in the rain. She doesn't dare blink. She's had her make-up professionally applied tonight and she doesn't want fifty quid of it running down her cheeks.

'All I can say is the angels must've been smiling down upon me that day as it was undoubtedly the best decision I've made in my entire life...'

One of those carefully placed pauses ensues.

'And here we are, a quarter of a century later, and she's still as beautiful – no, *more* in fact – than she was the day I met her, a day that changed my life forever and certainly for the better.'

Maggie can't imagine ever giving such a captivating speech herself, or any speech at all to be fair; she's never been great at public speaking, and besides, these days she couldn't guarantee that her pelvic floor wouldn't collapse with nerves. Still, she can't wait to see Len's face later, when he watches the compilation video she's made. If she pulls it off without a glitch, there won't be a dry eye in the house. She feels a ripple of anticipation just thinking about it.

'I want to thank my wife,' Len continues, 'my darling, *darling* Mags, for putting up with me and sticking by me these past two and half decades – well, over three if you count from when we first met – for better for worse, in sickness and health, and most definitely for richer and – after what tonight has cost me – for poorer, and of course, forsaking all others, *though there was this one time on a weekend away in Amsterdam with the lads in 199—* Oh, never mind, we won't talk about that.'

Raucous laughter chimes throughout the marquee as Maggie playfully slaps her husband's thigh and mouths, 'What is he like?' to the onlooking guests.

A wasp suddenly begins to buzz around the champagne on the table and she quickly waves it away with a hand.

'Shoo!' Len ducks down as it passes over his head. 'Damn bloody things... Mags!' He looks to her, mild panic in his eyes, and she reaches into her handbag on the table, pulls out an EpiPen and waggles it at him reassuringly. Len's allergic to wasps – one sting could kill him, send him into anaphylactic shock. Terrifyingly, it's happened once before, when they were newly courting. The date had ended with Len being carted off in an ambulance, blue lights and sirens screaming as he was rushed to Thorton General.

'It was a good thing you called an ambulance when you did,' the doctor had advised her sagely. 'Any longer and his organs would've started to shut down – it could've been fatal.'

Swatting the pest away again and satisfied it's gone, Maggie spots her daughter, Remy, at the back of the marquee and waves at her enthusiastically, but she's busy taking selfies on her phone, pouting provocatively into the camera, and doesn't see her.

A little frisson of pride flutters inside her belly. Remy looks so beautiful tonight – the epitome of blossoming womanhood – her long dark hair cascading in waves down her shoulders, and the dress! A strapless pink tulle creation that offset her colouring and accentuates her décolletage and prominent curves. She's probably texting that Whatshisface, the boy she's clearly smitten with whose name Maggie can't remember now.

She casts her eyes over the crowd again, searching for her son Lewis and his girlfriend Casey. They're missing Len's speech. A tiny part of her had even hoped Lewis might make one himself, though admittedly it had been such a tiny hope that it barely existed at all. Her son had been so outgoing once, just like his father, but that was before—

Now, now, Maggie, don't start getting all maudlin.

'Joking aside' – Len's voice drops down an octave – 'I think you'll all agree she's an incredible wife, mother and friend, and I cannot wait to spend the next twenty-five years of my life by her side if the man upstairs allows. Maggie Wendover, I love you, my chickadee!'

Len stoops down swiftly to kiss his wife on the lips, but in his exuberance, his mouth bumps against hers painfully and her eyes begin to water. *Brilliant* – that's another twenty quid's worth of eyeliner down the drain. Her guests are thrilled by the gesture at least, and the marquee erupts to the sound of chairs scraping as people stand, clapping, cheering and whistling, their champagne glasses collectively chiming like bells.

'To Len and Maggie!' someone in the crowd – she can't tell who – calls out.

'Len and Maggie!'

3

Round the side of their sprawling house, somewhat set back from the marquee, Maggie leans against the apple tree and lightly sips on a mimosa. The smooth, dulcet tones of the singer they've hired for this evening's entertainment ring out through the temperate evening air, perfumed by the freshly cut blooms that have been carefully positioned in huge decorative bunches throughout the garden.

She observes her guests drinking and laughing as they converse and sway to the music, helping themselves to the lavish buffet whose 'around the world' theme represents cuisine from every country she and Len have ever visited throughout the last twenty-five years. She hopes it'll all get eaten – she does hate to see good food go to waste.

She's a little surprised to see that their new neighbour, Clive, has turned up tonight though. He's hovering awkwardly next to the DJ stand, nursing a glass of something – probably the rum punch (a nod to their tenth anniversary in the Caribbean). She can't help thinking that there's something a little creepy about him, though perhaps it's how he presents, all arms and legs somehow. She's only met Clive once – just yesterday in fact – and admittedly he'd been something of a last-minute invite.

Maggie wonders what his story is – she's seen no wife or family since he moved in a couple of weeks earlier. Seems a little odd him rattling around in that big house on his own.

She smiles in wry amusement as Len's older brother Bob twirls his newish – and notably much younger – wife Julie around on the makeshift dance floor. She hopes he isn't going to keel over, the silly old sod; he only had a pacemaker fitted last year.

Taking in the merriment before her, Maggie's proud smile gradually begins to fade along with the waning light. How she wishes in this moment her own mother could be here to see this – to witness how far she's come in her life – twenty-five years happily married, a successful business, two wonderful kids – though they were all grown up now of course – a beautiful, well-kept home and impressive garden... She wonders if she would be proud of her. She'd certainly like to think so. As it was, her mother never even got to meet Len, let alone her grandchildren and—

Her greying complexion, eyes wide and bulbous, her tan-coloured summer sandals tied up around her ankles, swaying some distance above the floor. The grim line of her mouth and her tongue, exposed and purple...

The image flashes up in front of her vividly, bright and blinding, like someone flicked the switch on a floodlight. It's a mild late May evening – no need for a cardigan even – yet a chill sweeps through her like fire and she wraps her arms around herself protectively as she involuntarily shudders a little. *For goodness' sake, Maggie, this is a happy occasion.* It's been such a long time since she's experienced this flashback. It feels like a bad omen somehow.

The feel of hands sliding around her waist from behind startles her, violently pulling the plug on her thoughts.

'Jesus, Len, you made me jump!'

He laughs, nuzzling the back of her neck as he pulls her body into his.

'Caught ya! What you doing hiding away round here anyway? I've been looking for you. Why aren't you down there enjoying the fun with everyone else? It's your big night. I think we might've run out of tonic already.'

'Already? No way! I bought ten bloody crates of that Bay Tree stuff!' She can smell warm alcohol on his breath though it's not unpleasant as such. 'And I wasn't *hiding*,' she corrects him. 'I was... *observing* – taking a private moment to appreciate everything.'

'Mmm, I know what *I* would appreciate right now,' he says, nibbling at her earlobe.

'Stop it.' She pulls her chin into her neck. 'That tickles.'

'I can't help it – you look so bloody gorgeous in that dress.' Len slides a soft, warm hand down the front of her wrap dress onto her breast. For a man who's spent most of his life grafting with them, her husband has surprisingly smooth hands.

'Len! You soppy old sod.' She smacks it away playfully. 'You're drunk!'

'Less of the old, and I most certainly am not,' he says, mock indignant. 'OK... well, maybe a teeny tiny bit. Champagne always goes straight to my head.'

He nuzzles the back of her neck again. She doesn't tell him about the flashback – doesn't want to kill his buzz.

'I tell you where that dress would look even more amazing, shall I?'

'Oh yeah?' She rests the back of her head onto his chest with a small sigh. 'And where's that?'

'On our bedroom floor,' he says, wrapping his hands tighter around her waist; a waist she feels is thickening by the second thanks to her age and the onset of the dreaded menopause. Miserably, she remembers a time when he'd been able to put both hands around it with his fingers touching, and that was without even squeezing. She supposes it was thirty-two years ago now though.

'Well, play your cards right and you might get lucky later,' she says, indulging him, though in all honesty she imagines she'll be too exhausted to do much more than hastily take off her make-up and fall into bed, and in truth probably just the latter.

'Why wait till later,' he says provocatively, pausing to look around him.

'You're not serious, Len. What here, now, outside... *out in the open?*'

'C'mon – you only live once.' He grins lasciviously, starts to tug at the belt of her wrap dress.

Oh God, he's not joking!

'Don't be daft, Len,' she says, careful not to sound as horrified as she feels. 'There's an entire party full of people just a few metres away!'

'So?'

'*So?* So they'd see us!'

'Yes, well, that's half the thrill, my little chickadee.' He's still tugging at her belt. 'Anyway, what's wrong with a little spontaneity? We haven't done it outdoors in... well, I can't even remember when the last time was.'

'Ibiza 1984,' she reminds him sniffily, mock indignant at his lack of recall – she remembers it vividly herself. She hadn't enjoyed it, even back then when she really had been young and lithe and toned. Oh how youth was wasted on the young. By the time you realised what you once had, it was long gone. 'On Salinas beach underneath a parasol. I was still brushing sand out of intimate places for days afterwards... Anyway, I have a surprise for you.' She looks at her husband, his eyes a little glassy from all that cheap champagne they'd bought in bulk from Costco.

'A surprise?'

She tries to prise his fingers from around her waist.

'Yes, I'll go and get it now.' It'll give her an excuse to look for her son and Casey. They still haven't made an appearance yet and her worry is beginning to slide into full-blown panic. *Some sort of incident... police have cordoned the whole area off...*

'Oi-oi!' Christine suddenly appears from around the corner of the house with a wide-eyed expression.

Guiltily, Maggie is almost relieved to see her.

'What are you two love doves up to skulking away in the shadows, eh?' she says, her tone sitting somewhere between accusation and amusement. 'Blimey, twenty-five years and you *still* can't keep your hands off each other.' Her laughter rings out like gunfire across the lawn.

'We were just standing back and appreciating the moment,' Maggie feels compelled to explain, slightly flustered. 'And I'm just about to go and sort out Len's surprise.' She gives Christine a conspiratorial wink.

'I hope it's a stripper,' Len calls out to them, and she turns to poke her tongue out at him as she links arms with Christine and they make their way down the steps.

'Speaking of strippers,' Christine murmurs as Brenda sashays past them in a fugue of that strong, sweet and distinctive-smelling perfume, her ample chest wobbling like a pair of blancmanges as she does that half-walk, half-dance thing that people only ever seem to do at parties.

'Stop it.' Maggie elbows her with smile.

'Everyone knows that when you get to our age, it's either tits or legs, never both,' Christine says, as if Brenda has committed the ultimate cardinal sin. 'Anyway' – her voice lowers to a conspiratorial whisper – 'you know people say that her and Ron have an open marriage – that they're swingers apparently?'

Maggie pulls her chin into her chest.

'I'm serious,' Christine says sagely. 'Worst-kept secret in Thorton Vale apparently. You know, car keys thrown in the middle of the table, pampas grass in their front lawn and all of that...'

Maggie laughs. 'Pampas grass?'

'It's a sign apparently, that you're into swinging.'

'Oh, come on, Chris! If that's the case then Mrs Easton up the road must be at it as she has some in hers – and she's eighty-four!'

Christine raises her eyebrows comedically. 'Blimey, eighty-four and she's getting more than me!'

They both collapse into laughter as they simultaneously turn back to look in Brenda's direction.

Realising that their glancing has slipped into gawping, Maggie quickly looks away. 'Anyway, just because Brenda's sartorial choices lean towards the short and low-cut variety doesn't mean she's at it with all the neighbours.'

Len has rejoined the guests now and Brenda has seemingly made a beeline for him, her jiggling boobs a hair's breadth away from becoming a bona fide wardrobe malfunction as she greets him with an exaggerated embrace.

'See.' Christine nods with a sardonic smirk, as though this were some sort of confirmation.

Maggie shrugs. 'Well, whatever floats your boat.'

'Yeah, well, she'd never sink with a pair like that, would she?'

'You are awful, Christine Langford, you know that.' She pushes her playfully, but her mind is already wandering elsewhere as her eyes instinctively search the marquee for her son and Casey.

Oh God, where the hell are they? Maybe it's the baby. Casey's only just past the three-month danger zone – what if something's happened? Or what if Lewis has had one of his 'episodes'? She'd really hoped all that is long behind him now. He's been doing so well ever since the doctor prescribed him new medication and—

Stop it, Maggie – you're doing it again! Christine's right – they've probably just been held up in traffic. It's murder coming through town at the weekends at the best of times, let alone if there's been an incident.

'Mum!'

Oh thank God! Warm relief floods through her as she sees Lewis – closely followed by Casey – hurrying across the lawn towards her.

'Jesus, we're *so* sorry we're late.' He looks harried, his face a detectable red in colour, even in the receding light.

Maggie embraces him warmly, breathes him in. He smells faintly of sweet sweat and the outdoors, like he did as a child.

'Oh my darlings!' she says, clutching her face instinctively. 'I was worried... Chris said there's been an incident, down at Riverdown Park? I wondered where you were, the pair of you. You missed your father's speech, you know!' She's careful to keep the disappointment from her voice – Lewis is such a sensitive boy and she doesn't want to trigger him.

'No matter.' She waves a hand dismissively. 'You're here now, and you're just in time for my big surprise, thank God.'

She leans in and kisses Casey on both cheeks, resists placing a hand on her belly. She isn't showing yet, but in all honesty, Maggie can't wait until she is – there's no greater privilege in life than watching a growing baby belly swell.

'Ah, so you've finally graced us with your presence, brother dearest!' Remy struts across the lawn to join them, a vision in pink tulle. 'We were going to send out a search party!' She kisses her brother on both cheeks, hugs Casey warmly.

'We were stuck, just a few miles back, down by Thorton Bridge, near Riverdown Park, you know?' Casey explains, handing Maggie a beautiful gift box.

Casey must've wrapped it, she thinks – her Lewis couldn't wrap himself in a blanket.

'They cordoned the whole area off,' she says, a little breathless with excitement. 'Tailbacks for miles. There was police tape and cars *everywhere*.' Casey's eyes are wide. 'And there was a forensic van and dogs and everything, so I knew it must be serious,' she adds sagely, though clearly thrilled by the drama.

'Oh dear,' Maggie says as Christine heads off towards the marquee. 'Does anyone know what happened yet?'

Lewis and Casey exchange a brief glance.

'Didn't you see it on the news, Mum?' he says. 'It's all they're talking about…'

'See what on the news?' Remy looks at her brother expectantly and takes a generous slurp of her champagne. 'Don't tell me something exciting has happened in Thorton Vale because I won't believe it.'

'No, I haven't seen anything on the news yet…'

Out of the corner of her eye, Maggie spots Len dancing with Brenda to 'Oops Up Side Your Head' alongside his brother Bob and his young wife Julie who, despite making a consolidated effort, she simply can't warm to. Perhaps it's because she was once so close to Bob's former wife, Heather, who was sadly taken by breast cancer a couple of years earlier, or maybe it was the fact that despite her overall attractiveness, Julie's eyes were a little too close set, which – perhaps unfairly – gave her a sense of untrustworthiness.

'So?' Maggie turns her attention back to her son, though she's sure she can see Brenda's boobs bouncing about in time to the music in her peripheral vision.

'A woman – they pulled a woman's body from the river,' Lewis says. 'She's been murdered.'

4 DAN

Like the scent of the earth following rain, the zesty zing of freshly cut grass or the perfumed purity of a newborn baby's skin, death has its own unique smell, an indescribable yet unmistakable aroma that I have the regrettable suspicion I'm about to become imminently reacquainted with.

I'm not the first on the scene. Forensics are already milling around with purpose in full PPE, placing things into plastic ziplock bags with purple latex-gloved hands. Uniform is here in numbers too, their high-vis vests glowing like beacons as they set about sealing everything off with yellow tape, not a minute too soon either as I suspect it won't be long before the press gets wind of the good news and turns up like a shiver of sharks smelling blood; their long lenses and cumbersome media trucks compensating for their shortcomings on integrity. They love a dead body, do the press, especially a young, beautiful one.

I spot two police divers standing on the riverbank and two more in the water, their glossy wetsuits reflecting the early light as they bob simultaneously up and down in the river like a pair of seals. It's early, around 6 a.m. I'd guess. I can tell by the hint of the sun breaking through the hazy gossamer layer of grey that blankets everything, getting set for another day's work – much like everyone here I suppose.

I'm suddenly reminded of something my recently deceased father used to say to me: *'There are three things in life you can be sure of, Danny Boy – the sun, the moon and the truth!'* Already convinced by the former two, I wonder just how long it'll take me to get to the latter in this case.

My trusted colleague, DS Lucy Davis, who I endearingly refer to – much to her dismay – as my 'number two' is down by the riverbank, walking in circles as she speaks on her phone, and I spot DC Parker, a relative newbie and most promising protégé, deep in conversation with a couple of uniform not too far behind her. Their familiar faces bring me a modicum of comfort – at least I know that our Jane Doe, whoever she is, is in capable hands.

Riverdown Nature Park is an impressive expanse of space, all one thousand plus acres of it. Surrounded by woodland and fields, it's a local beauty spot connected by pathways that all somehow lead back to the majestic river that runs through it. It's not tricky to see why it's so popular with the local residents from Eden Gorge and neighbouring areas. People flock here to walk, run and cycle, and make use of the vast picnic and BBQ areas in the summertime – weather permitting of course. Though part of it is rural, further in, it's a spectacular monument to nature and wildlife; a tranquil, peaceful place – or at least it was.

I feel it as I move closer, careful not to slip in the morning dew on the grass bank – a touch more than I would expect for this time of year – the impending horror, the disgust and sorrow I know I'm about to experience, and I brace myself, pull at the collar of my light jacket in that way people do when they're about to assert themselves, though I have no idea how it's supposed to help. I take an audible breath and go in.

'Gov! You're here!' Davis breaks off her phone conversation

as I approach. She looks pleased to see me. I don't bother with the niceties though, the 'good morning' because it isn't one. There can be nothing good about this morning now.

'Any idea who she is?' I ask.

'No ID on her, boss – nothing at all in fact. She was found naked, no possessions... divers are searching the river now, but we suspect her name is Amelie Fox, twenty-two, reported missing yesterday by a' – she flicks open her notebook – 'Holly Redwood, her flatmate. Says she never showed up for an important photoshoot she was due to attend – claims she'd never have missed it – and again that evening when she'd been expected to meet friends and was a no-show there too. Says it's completely out of character for her to go off-grid without letting anyone know where she is, and to not be able to get hold of her.'

'Her parents?'

'Haven't been able to make contact, boss. Both numbers going straight to voicemail. I'll keep trying.'

I detect the emotion in her inflection. In our game, you learn to leave the feels at the door, to approach a potential murder scene and victim with a pragmatic, logical head, but sometimes in a situation like this, where you're looking at the untimely demise of someone so young, their life cut short by another human being – and I use the term 'human' loosely – then the struggle becomes all too real.

Twenty-two. I repeat the number silently in my head. Twenty-two is a live forever kind of age. Twenty-two is your whole life in front of you. No one contemplates death at twenty-two, least of all their own. At twenty-two you don't see the Grim Reaper coming.

'Who found her?'

'Dog walker, sir.'

I hear Parker coming up behind me.

'Sorry, sir— I mean, sorry, *boss*.' Parker has remembered that I hate to be called sir as much as I don't need to be. It reminds me of my former headmaster, Mr Wallace, a tall, stern and unforgiving man whose breath perennially smelled of strong coffee and cigarettes. He was particularly spiteful around a plastic ruler.

'Annie Simpson, sixty-two, lives up on Primrose Avenue. She went out early for a walk with her new puppy because she was a bit excitable – the puppy I mean,' he clarifies, without necessity. 'She says she saw something in the river, down by the bank, partially caught up in the reeds and branches there. She thought it was a mannequin at first, a tailor's dummy or something she said, but when she got closer... Anyway, she's over there.' He points in the direction of an older lady being comforted by two female uniform up near the pathway. 'She's pretty distressed.'

I'm starting to become concerned that Parker may have a slight penchant for stating the obvious. Anger prickles at my skin because I know that what Annie Simpson has witnessed this morning will leave an indelible still frame of horror imprinted on her memory forever. Killers rarely contemplate the ripple effect their crimes have. I suppose it's this lack of regard, an absence of conscience, that allows them to commit them in the first place. Annie Simpson is simply another victim in the story, little more than collateral damage.

'What time was that?'

'Around 5.10 a.m.,' Parker says.

'Right, well, I want everything sealed off, the whole park, entrances, exits, no one in or out.'

'The *whole* park?' He blinks at me, and I nod sagely.

'It's a crime scene, Parker. We need to preserve any and all evidence carefully. So get onto the council immediately, advise them of the situation and call in any surrounding CCTV – I've got a feeling we're going to earn our wages on this one.'

'Boss.'

'And let's find out where her phone last pinged, what time

and where. Let's get a stick search started as soon as possible, start combing the fields and park, see if anything turns up.'

I nod at Davis.

'We're checking ID now, gov, but I think it's our girl. She matches the description – young, white, blonde, slim... it's not looking good.'

Not for Amelie Fox's family, that's for sure.

'She's an influencer apparently. Bit of a social-media star by all accounts, an Instagram model and vlogger, promotes cosmetics, fashion, health-food supplements, that kind of thing. Very popular – has over 500,000 followers on her IG account.'

'Great,' I say flatly. 'That'll narrow down any list of suspects.'

Davis sighs gently, her breath hitting the chilly early morning air like cigarette smoke.

'Best I take a look then.'

I step inside the white tent that's been erected around her body, offering her a modicum of dignity in her death at least. I crouch down and see that my hands are shaking as I pull back the light plastic sheeting that's covering her.

The smell hits me like a wall – decay followed by an uppercut of stagnant water. I feel my empty stomach somersault as I look down. She's bloated, indicative of being immersed in water for a period of time, and her eyes are bulbous, giving her face a ghoulish mask of horror and surprise. She's covered in dirt and debris from the river, her hair fanning out behind her and hanging in reeds like the ones she was entangled in. She looks almost mythical somehow, like a creature from the deep – a mermaid. A *murdered* mermaid. Her fingernails, though coated in filth and a couple broken, are long and visibly painted in an arty kind of design, bitterly reminding me of her recent humanity, just a regular young woman who liked to take care of herself.

Despite the condition of her skin, which has begun to

wrinkle and peel off in ugly, fleshy layers, the marks around her neck – the purple, angry bruising – are still visible. I suspect she's been strangled, that she was maybe already dead by the time she was deposited into the river, thrown away like an old shopping trolly. I can only hope that this tragic young woman's death was mercifully quick and that her suffering was short. I'll know more once Vic Leyton, my favourite pathologist, arrives to give her preliminaries. She's on her way, and I can already hear her clipped Home Counties inflection pre-emptively in my head. '*Always a pleasure to see you, DCI Riley, though alas never in pleasurable circumstances...*'

I take her hand in mine, feel the need to touch her, to comfort her somehow. I brush some debris and hair from her face, feel an overwhelming need to protect her, like she's my own child. Because she *is* someone's child, a treasured and loved child no doubt.

And I think of my own girl then, my Juno – or Pip as I call her. She's only just turned three, but I imagine that it's her lying dead underneath a clinical plastic sheet, her bloated, lifeless corpse decaying with each passing second, and it takes every bit of willpower I possess not to allow the tears forming behind my eyes to fall.

Got to keep the feels at the door, Dan.

My wife, Fiona, is currently expecting our second 'happy accident' as she likes to refer to it. She's a few weeks off giving birth and we're both jiggling with anticipation to meet our new addition. I already love them, and it's this feeling, this overwhelming feeling of love and the need to protect, that's tugging painfully at my guts now, because I know this young woman's parents no doubt feel exactly the same about their child – their now deceased child – a child they would happily exchange places with so she could live another day. When I think about it, if loving someone is in direct correlation to how painful it would feel to lose them, it's a wonder any of us has the courage ever to procreate at all.

I stare down at her body once again. *Come on, sweetheart, tell me who did this to you – talk to me.*

I know she can't actually speak obviously, but the dead do have their own silent language. If you know what to look for, they tell you things from beyond the grave, offering up mute clues as to what happened to them. Regrettably, I've become fluent in the linguistics of the dead – *die*-lingual you could call it, though I don't mean this as a mockery. I'm deadly serious.

I notice something on the inside of her left wrist – it's just visible beneath the dirt and debris. I brush that away, attempt to get a better look. It's a tattoo of an angel, a tiny angel with wings...

The rustle of the tent flap causes me to gather myself and turn round. Ah, Dr Victoria Leyton.

'Hello, Detective Chief Inspector.' She gives me that enigmatic smile of hers, one that never quite seems to reach fruition.

'Dr Leyton.' I nod graciously though I feel more like embracing her. I wonder if she senses this because she pushes her glasses further up her nose in a gesture I've come to recognise as something between endearment and embarrassment. 'It's been a while.'

'Though I suspect not long enough given the circumstances,' she says.

Hey, I was close.

'Well, regrettably I'd never get the pleasure of your company at all otherwise,' I reply.

'Every cloud, Detective. So,' she says, signalling that the banter is over and it's down to business, 'what have you got for me?'

'How long do you think she's been dead?'

'Notoriously difficult to tell with the water babies, I'm afraid,' she says as she starts examining the body. 'Decomposition in a wet environment differs from that of other settings, both the changes and the rate at which they occur...'

Uh-oh, I can feel one of her educational explanations coming on.

'Typical decomposition changes proceed more slowly in water due to the cooler temperatures, and the anaerobic environment of course.'

'Of course,' I agree, and she glances sideways at me, a brief look that tells me she's well aware I haven't got a clue what she's talking about.

'Insect and animal species feeding on the remains are different for submerged bodies; temperature and current and obstacles and structures play a part too...'

'But at a glance?' I blink at her, hopeful.

She sighs. 'You know I'd have to do a full post-mortem to give you optimum accuracy,' she says, half chastising me. 'But if I must... well then I'd say a couple of days, no more than three.'

'She was reported missing on Friday.'

She nods. 'Makes sense. Though I'll know more once I get her in the mortuary, which incidentally we'll need to do as soon as possible. Putrefaction will be accelerated now that she's been taken from the water.'

I inwardly grimace.

'The gasses are what brought her to the surface most probably – sulphate and...'

I find myself tuning out again.

'Anyway, she was lucky really.'

'Lucky?' It's hardly an adjective I would use to describe this young woman and her fate.

'Yes, if she hadn't become entangled in the reeds and branches then she may have been taken out further by the current, swallowed up by the water and disappeared forever. Undiscovered watery graves,' she says, her voice trailing off slightly, 'the world must be full of them, Detective Riley.'

'The marks around her neck... do you think she was dead before she hit the water?'

'Difficult to tell without a full examination I'm afraid, but they suggest something may have been used to restrict her breathing, a ligature of some sort, so it's a distinct possibility. What's also interesting is the abrasion to the back of her head...'

'Abrasion?'

'Yes.' She lifts up the girl's head, angles it in such a way so as I can – albeit with some reluctance – see. 'There's an abrasion, some contusion also, to the back of the skull. It's possible it could've been sustained by the elements, her body hitting obstacles and structures, dragging against rocks, that sort of thing, but equally she could have been struck with something.'

A picture begins to form in my head of the way this young woman met her end. She was struck on the head first, rendered unconscious perhaps, then strangled and her body dumped in the river. It's a very basic first assumption but if it's correct then I suspect this isn't the scene of her murder and that it took place elsewhere, which also means someone had to have transported her body.

'Any sign of sexual assault?'

'Not outwardly. Again, I'll be able to give you more clarity once she's on the table. But...' She pauses for a moment.

'But what?'

She glances up at me briefly. 'I don't know,' she says. 'Something's telling me that it may have been sexually motivated.'

Her summation mirrors my own.

'Because she's naked?'

'Not just that, no,' Vic says, which is uncharacteristic of her. Unlike me, she doesn't usually deal in intuition or conjecture – facts and science are her remit. 'It feels... personal.'

Tell me something I don't know. Statistics show that well over half the people who're murdered are known to their killers – a former spouse or partner, a family member or friend, an employee or a neighbour. It begs the uncomfortable question, do any of us ever *really* know those closest to us?

'Gov?' Davis pokes her head through the tent and I excuse myself.

'Positive ID, gov.' She holds up her phone, shows me a photograph of a young, blonde and exceptionally beautiful young woman who's smiling seductively for the camera with full glossy lips. I read the caption below.

> The Pout is real, huns! Check out PussyPout Lip Plump, the revolutionary new pout in a pot from Lulu's Cosmetics Company. Instantly delivers nourishment, hydration and volume for lips for that 'has she or hasn't she?' alternative to injectables. Get 10% off your first purchase today with my discount ANGELFOX10! Link in bio.

'A recent picture she posted on Instagram – looks like the last in fact,' Davis says. 'She has a tattoo, on her left wrist doesn't she, an angel?'

I nod, barely able to take my eyes from the captivating image.

Davis audibly exhales. 'It's her, gov. It's Amelie Fox – also known among her followers as Angel.'

The irony isn't lost on either of us and we're both silent for a moment. I feel like screaming, to try to expel some of the emotion that's lodged inside my chest like trapped wind.

'Do you want to do the honours, gov,' Davis asks eventually, 'or shall Parker and I go?'

By 'do the honours' she means inform the parents. It may sound like a glib way to describe such a horrendous task but actually in fact there *is* something very honourable about having to impart such tragic news to a victim's nearest and dearest, because with it comes great responsibility. I imagine the Foxes to be a good-looking couple in their late forties, no doubt concerned about their daughter's absence but never believing, not truly, that something like this could've happened to her – not their beautiful, precious, beloved daughter. I can hear her mother's screams in my head already, the sound of her father's fist smashing down on the table in grief-stricken rage and disbelief.

I look at her photograph again, so young, so vibrant, *so alive*.

'I'll do it.' My voice sounds flat, a deliberate attempt to disguise my own rage.

Davis nods, lowers her eyes. She doesn't need to say anything – her expression does the talking for her.

'The last picture you say?'

'Yes, on her personal IG account.'

I take the phone from her, look at the time stamp on it. It was posted on Thursday at 3.07 p.m., got 157,000 likes and over 118 comments and... hang on. This picture is dated two days ago, which would mean, if Vic Leyton is right in her – albeit preliminary – assessment of time of death, and she usually is, then Amelie Fox was probably already dead when this was posted.

5 MAGGIE

'I'm telling you, it's the absolute gospel truth!' Lorraine holds her hands up in earnest. 'She came home unexpectedly early one morning from work and there he was, sitting on the couch, bold as brass, watching *Judge Judy* wearing the whole get-up. I'm talking underwear, dress, make-up, wig – the full nine yards!'

Jackie clutches her face in shock. 'You've *got* be kidding me!'

'I *swear* I'm not!' Lorraine is emphatic. 'Forty years married the pair of them, *forty years,* and she's adamant that she didn't have an inkling, not even a whiff.' She sits back in the banquette, clearly chuffed to have imparted such salacious gossip.

'What, not old Les whatshisname and his wife? Not the pair who used to live on Mulberry Avenue surely? The one with the slight hunch? But he's got to be in his mid-sixties if he's a day – they both have!' Linda's mouth has formed an exaggerated O shape.

'Yup.' Lorraine nods slowly. 'Les and Maureen Bateman.'

Jackie is shaking her head in disbelief. 'You're telling me

that they've been married for forty years, all that time, and she had no idea whatsoever that he liked to dress up in women's clothes? Nah, I don't buy it.'

Lorraine rolls her eyes. 'Well, don't then, but I'm not lying.'

'And you know this *how* exactly?' Christine asks, narrowing her eyes with the hint of a smile.

'Lyzette, my hairdresser told me.'

The narrowing quickly becomes a roll. 'Oh, well, in that case, it *must* be true then.'

'She's been doing Maureen's set and blow for the past fifteen years – says she just came out with it one day.'

'Does she do him a set and blow too?' Linda collapses into a fit of giggles, sloshing a little of her mimosa onto the table.

Maggie joins in though in reality she feels more pity than she does amusement. Assuming it's true – this has come from Lorraine after all, a total sweetheart but the planet's greatest monument to gossip – then it must've been an absolutely dreadful shock for the poor woman.

Maggie hadn't much felt like attending tonight's Power Pilates class and even less like the ritual mimosas in Jazz's wine bar afterwards. She was still feeling a touch weary from the weekend. These days her hangovers last in direct correlation to the number of drinks she's consumed, so by her own calculations she should be feeling normal again – whatever that means; she isn't sure these days – a week on Tuesday. Still, it had been worth it – the party had been a resounding success. If it hadn't been for that scarf – that *bloodstained* scarf – she'd discovered in the eaves and that dreadful news about the murder, then it might even have been perfect.

She'd thought about the woman they'd pulled from the river ever since, hoped that maybe they'd somehow got it all wrong, the police, and that it had simply been a tragic accident. She'd wondered what the victim's story was, who she was, how old she was, if she was married with children, or little more than a child herself?

Paradoxically, Maggie has done her utmost *not* to think about the scarf she found in the loft, has made a conscious effort to dismiss it from her thoughts – it was nothing, *right?* But it was akin to when you decide to go on a diet and food is subsequently all you can think about because it keeps flashing up in your consciousness like a bloody Belisha beacon. Were they really bloodstains she'd seen on it? It had certainly looked like it. And that scent of fresh perfume... the one she's convinced Brenda was wearing at the party.

Suddenly a vision of her neighbour's ample cleavage threatening to escape the quarantine of her tight dress as she'd danced with her husband flashes up in her mind. *'You know people say that her and Ron have an open marriage – that they're swingers...'* Christine's voice resonates in her head. She'd caught Brenda prowling around upstairs in her house as well. Had she really been looking for the bathroom or was it something else she'd been doing?

Enough, Maggie, you're being ridiculous.

Deep down, she knows it's a preposterous idea. Really, *Brenda and Len?* And yet she visualises it with such clarity that it feels as if it's already happened, her husband and neighbour together in uncompromising positions, the sounds of their clandestine carnal betrayal amplified in her ears. She knows she's giving her imagination a free run, but in the absence of any explanation for the scarf, it's all she seems capable of doing.

Over the years, Maggie has seen many friends through the bitter heartbreak of betrayal and divorce – sometimes more than once – endless tears shed over equally endless bottles of Pinot Grigio. She's witnessed first-hand how adultery can turn the most gentle, loving souls into bitter, resentful cynics; has seen how it can destroy hearts and minds, cripple people financially and mess up the kids in the process; and despite being there to hand out tissues and advice respectively, secretly, *guiltily* she knows she's thought, *Thank the stars this isn't me.* With Len she'd got something right at least.

Despite the self-deprecating 'you'd get less time for murder' jokes, she's genuinely proud of their lengthy marriage and unblemished record. They were Len and Maggie after all, a blueprint of how to get it right. Len would never do that to her, would he, not his *chickadee?*

Perhaps she should've taken that damn scarf with her from the loft, gone downstairs to the marquee and asked him about it. She honestly isn't sure why she didn't now. She'd dismissed it as nothing, had tried to convince herself that it must be one of hers that she'd long forgotten about, but her subconscious mind had other ideas because deep down she knows it doesn't belong to her. She'd never seen it before that night and she's pretty sure, *absolutely sure,* she'd remember buying something from Alexander McQueen.

The smell of *that perfume* wafts into her consciousness once more, strong and sweet... It has really left a bad taste in her mouth. She swallows some of her cocktail in a futile bid to wash it away, but the thoughts press on.

Miserably, she wonders if it's her recent lack of interest in the bedroom department that has potentially driven her husband directly into the open arms – and legs – of the local resident femme fatale. Why hadn't she let Len make love to her that night? She really wishes she had now. As she'd predicted, once the last of the party stragglers had left, she'd collapsed, exhausted, into bed, face still on and fully clothed. Len hadn't been too far behind her.

'I've brought you up some of your peppermint tea, chick-adee, plus some Alka-Seltzer for the morning, one of those evening primrose capsules you take for your *women's things* – and of course, a Hershey's Kiss – you didn't think I'd forget, did you?'

Maggie had inwardly smiled. A Hershey's Kiss, every single night without fail. It was a ritual that had started back when they were first courting and Len had gone away on a pre-planned trip to America with his brother. Upon his much awaited return, he'd presented her with a huge bag of 'candies' called Hershey's Kisses. She'd never seen them before, not in the UK anyway, these cute little silver-wrapped chocolate drops of love. He'd left one by her bedside every night since. She dreads to think how many calories that amounted to after thirty-odd years!

That night Len had placed her stash on the bedside table next to her and sneaked in beside her, spooning into her, something she has come to recognise over the years as a precursor to sex. She'd groaned, pretended to be asleep already. Sleep, that's what she'd really wanted – *all* she'd wanted.

She'd lain there, unresponsive, as he'd begun to kiss the back of her neck and attempted to untie her wrap dress. She'd even feigned little snoring noises for goodness' sake!

After a few moments, she'd heard him softly sigh and roll over. Her poor Len. Now she feels guilty rejecting him like that, and on their anniversary night as well, but she can't explain how she feels to her husband, can't really even explain it to herself in all truth. She doesn't want it to sound like a cringeworthy cliche, that whole 'it's not you, it's me', even if it is true. She knows Len – he's a sensitive softy underneath all the bluster and she doesn't want there to be an elephant in the (bed)room, even if she feels she's rapidly *becoming* the elephant.

The truth is, she hasn't felt like herself since she started going through the change, isn't sure who Maggie Wendover really is now, her likes and dislikes. She doesn't even know how to dress anymore. These days all the fashion is geared up for either tiny teenage supermodels or frumpy, austere mother-of-the-bride types, and she doesn't feel as if she fits into either of these categories.

Her friend's words echo in her head. '*Everyone knows that when you get to our age, it's either tits or legs, never both.*'

How old is too old to wear a bikini? She's no longer sure of the rules. Who bloody well makes them anyway? Recently though, her diminishing libido seemed to be in direct opposition to her husband's, or perhaps it's simply her lack of sex drive that's highlighting his, but either way, Len has never seemed more amorous towards her. Hardly the behaviour of a man who's at it behind her back, is it? Or perhaps it's *because* he's doing the dirty on her. Maybe his interest is simply a smoke-screen, an attempt to put her off the scent. She's sure she's read somewhere – probably in one of those insufferable women's magazines designed to make you feel inadequate – that men often become more interested in their wives sexually when embarking on an extra-marital affair – that it reawakens their passions and desires.

Maggie's head begins to throb. She's overanalysing all of this into paralysis. She must go and see her GP soon, she really must.

'What would you do, Chris,' Lorraine asks, 'if you came home and found Gary in a pair of your leggings and a blonde wig, throwing some shapes around the kitchen to Gloria Gaynor's "I Will Survive"?' She breaks into song dramatically. Even Maggie manages to raise a laugh.

'Well, I'd be pretty pissed off if my leggings fitted him in the first place to be honest,' she quips, 'and I can't see Gary as a blonde myself... more of a brunette,' she muses. 'Anyway he *hates* that song, but thanks for that image 'Raine. I'm going to need another cocktail now.'

'Apparently' – Lorraine leans forward in her seat once more – 'now she's over the shock of it all, Maureen goes clothes shopping with him, dressed in drag and everything. They've been seen in the underwear section at M&S together.'

Christine is shaking her head, incredulous. 'You don't half talk some bullshit, Lorraine Masters, do you know that?'

'I swear to *God* it's true,' she says through laughter.

'Well, if it is then she's a better woman than I am,' Jackie cuts in. 'I couldn't do it. I mean, how could she still *fancy* him for one thing, knowing that he's a closet cock in a frock?'

'Doesn't mean that he's gay, Jackie,' Linda tuts. 'Just that he likes dressing up in women's clothing.'

'Well, exactly! It's weird! I couldn't look at my other half the same way ever again! Makes me glad I'm currently single.' She snorts. 'They're all bloody deceitful, men, in some way, shape or form – not that I'm bitter or anything.'

Twice-divorced Jackie's latest partner, 'Pete the Perv' as he's now fondly referred to by them, was recently given the elbow after she'd discovered he'd been sending lewd text messages to a woman at work.

'Anyway, I'd be straight down the solicitor's asking them to draft a decree nisi,' Jackie says, slapping the table.

Lorraine sighs. 'I don't know, it's always men, isn't it, when you hear about this kind of thing? Having another secret family on the sly for years, murderers, rapists, paedophiles, warmongers, tyrants – historically always men!'

'Careful, Lorraine,' Christine warns her. 'You'll be lynched by the woke brigade if you carry on!'

'Oh, bloody well let them cancel me if they like, I'm only telling the truth. It's always... OK, OK, *mostly* men who do this kind of thing. They're all wired wrong, the bloody lot of them.'

'Yeah, but how could you *not* know if your husband was a serial killer or a child molester, or that he's had another wife and kids on the go for the past twenty years? Surely you'd suspect *something*?' Linda says. 'Maybe they're in denial, those women.'

Christine snorts. 'You'd be surprised. Some people are exceptionally good at hiding things, compartmentalising different parts of their lives.'

'Yeah, you think you know someone...'

Maggie really wishes they'd talk about something else. The conversation is sending her anxiety off the grid.

'Traffic is still dreadful down by the park,' she says in a bid to steer the topic elsewhere, 'where that poor woman's body was found in the river. Police have sealed off half the area and—'

'Another mimosa all round?' Linda throws her hands up. It's more of a statement than a question though as she's already heading towards the bar.

'Do they know who she is yet? Have they identified the body?' Jackie asks. 'Can't believe she was murdered – *murdered!* So close to home as well. Doesn't bear thinking about. Have they said what happened to her – how she was killed?'

There's a commotion at the bar and suddenly Linda is hurrying back to the table, sans mimosas, indicating it's serious. The grave expression on her face causes a flicker of fear to ignite inside Maggie's solar plexus.

'Oh my God, oh my *God! You're not going to believe this!*'

'What?' Lorraine is almost up out of her seat. 'What is it? What's happened?'

Linda looks like she's about to burst into tears. 'The girl – the murdered girl down at Riverdown Park. It's only... Oh no.' She's hyperventilating and can barely get the words from her lips. 'It's only... it's only Helen Fox's daughter, Amelie.' She immediately takes her phone from her handbag and begins tapping on it.

'Amelie... not Amelie Fox surely?'

'Turn the telly up will you, Harry?' Christine calls over to the barman as they all look up at the screen on the wall above them.

'... the body of a young woman murdered and pulled from the river at Riverdown Park on Saturday has been named as former local resident, Amelie Fox, police have confirmed earlier today.' The news anchor, a woman with a severe black bob and red lipstick, addresses the camera with gravitas. 'Amelie Fox, twenty-two, was discovered by a dog walker in the early hours of Saturday morning. Police believe the social-media influencer, a successful Instagram model and blogger who promoted various celebrity-endorsed brands including cosmetics and fashion, had been strangled...'

Lorraine gasps, covers her mouth with both hands as Linda starts crying.

'No... I can't believe it.' Jackie is shaking her head.

'Oh my God, poor Helen,' Christine says, unable to take her eyes from the screen. 'You remember her, don't you, Mags, from the school?'

Maggie struggles to think through the shock that is beginning to fizz up through her stomach into her chest. Helen... Helen Fox? The name rings a bell. Valley Primary School was where she first met Christine and Lorraine. Christine's son Billy had been in Remy's class, and Lorraine had Esme in another class in the same year. Most of the 'playground mums' she'd made friends with back then, when the kids had been small, had naturally fallen by the wayside once they'd left for big school, but the three of them – her and Chris in particular – had remained close.

'You do,' Christine prompts her. 'Helen... small blonde woman, always glamorous, drove an Evoque, lives up by Eden Gorge. Amelie was a couple of years older than our girls, but she also had a boy... can't think of his name now, in Lewis's year.'

Maggie's mind has gone blank. She can't picture the woman in her head, but she can feel her pain real enough already.

'I see her at the gym all the time,' Linda says tearfully. 'We grab a protein shake together sometimes. Christ, this is *awful, just awful.*'

An image of Amelie Fox flashes up on screen then and they all simultaneously look up. She's smiling for the camera, her lips parted to expose a cosmetically enhanced white smile.

Maggie stares at the screen solemnly. Suddenly she feels stupid, guilty even. Here she is getting herself all in a tizzy about some stupid scarf she found in her loft and the ridiculous, absurd idea that her husband might be having an affair with their neighbour, while this poor young girl has been found dead, *murdered* – and one of their own as well, a local girl who her own children had once been at school with.

It could've been her own daughter; it could've been Remy.

Panic races through her, causing her heart rate to gallop.

The news anchor's voice brings Maggie's thoughts back into focus.

'... reported missing on Friday by her flatmate...'

Another picture flashes up on screen, this time of Amelie in a bikini, exotic white cabanas, blue sea and sand in the background, her model figure tanned and toned as she sips on a coconut through a straw. Maggie can barely watch.

'She was so incredibly beautiful as well,' Lorraine says wistfully, as though this somehow makes it worse. 'Police are appealing for witnesses to come forward.'

A third image appears: Amelie in a black leather jacket, her long ice-white hair cascading down her shoulders, a wide smile on her face and—

Hang on. Suddenly everything else disappears in Maggie's peripheral vision. The image pans in towards her closely, quickly, like the cliffhanger from a TV drama. Instinctively her hand goes up to her chest. She can feel the rapid acceleration of her heartbeat beneath her fingers. *Is that...?*

She grabs the edge of the table instinctively, almost upending the remaining mimosas with the momentum. Her pelvic floor muscles threaten to collapse as a rush of adrenalin smashes into her bloodstream, slipping like mercury into every cell in her body. Silently, she starts to shake. No, *it can't be...*

She stares at the image on screen, too afraid to blink. It's draped loosely around her neck, almost intertwined with her long blonde hair, but she recognises it almost instantly – the pink, silky fabric, and those horrible tiny black skulls...

She's wearing the scarf.

6

'Mags... Mags...'

Christine's voice comes back into focus as Maggie stares, unblinking, at the TV. The image has disappeared now but she can still see it in front of her, like it's been indelibly inked onto her eyeballs. She needs to leave – she needs to leave right *now*.

'Are you OK?' Christine's looking at her, concerned.

'What? Sorry, yes, yeah I'm fine.' Her attempt at convincing her is a pathetic one – she doesn't even believe it herself. 'It's a shock that's all. It's just horrible, that poor girl... up the road as well. Look, I'm sorry, Chris, I've really got to run.' She thinks on her feet. 'Remy's car's playing up. Len said he was going to look at it today, and I've just remembered I said I'd give her a lift into town tonight if he hadn't got round to it. Lucky I only had one drink.' It's only half a lie – Remy's car really has been playing up but Len has already managed to sort it.

Christine nods. 'Better not let the girls out on their own after this.' She looks spooked. 'There could be some nutter on the loose.'

The news footage is still playing on the TV in front of them but she can't bring herself to turn and look at it – she's too frightened of seeing the scarf again.

'Place is going to be awash with TV crews now I suppose,' Jackie laments, her tone a mix of anger tinged with excitement. 'I mean how can someone be murdered *here*, in Thorton Vale? This is a nice area, for God's sake!'

'Oh look.' Lorraine is pointing animatedly at the TV. 'The reporter, she's outside the library. Oh, and that's Gill Patterson's house just behind it! She won't be pleased. Looks like her windows could do with a clean.'

Christine looks at Maggie and gives a little eye roll that quickly morphs into a frown. 'You sure you're all right?'

Maggie attempts to put her running jacket back on, but it suddenly feels as if she's grown another pair of arms.

'I'm fine. I'll call you tomorrow.'

She can see that Christine is still watching her in the reflection of the glass window as she leaves the bar.

The spiteful crunch of the gearbox as she attempts to put her car into first causes her to wince and she has to slam the brakes on hard as she pulls out, narrowly missing an oncoming Audi. *Shit!* She's not concentrating. Her hands are violently shaking.

The scarf... It couldn't possibly be the same scarf, the *exact same* scarf, that was around that poor girl's neck, could it? Because that would mean... *What would it mean? Come on, Maggie – keep breathing. In through the nose, out through the mouth.*

She needs to stay calm, to think rationally, but she can feel a hot flash coming on and opens the window a touch in a bid to get some air circulating inside the car. It *had* to be a coincidence, didn't it? Of course it was. No doubt hundreds, possibly even thousands, of people owned that very same scarf. Maybe it wasn't even really the same pattern and she's got it wrong.

Those little black skulls though, so distinctive...

Suddenly she wishes, hopes, that it does in fact belong to Brenda after all, because the other alternative is just too horrific to entertain.

In through the nose, out through the mouth. That's it...

As soon as she gets home, she'll go up into the loft and retrieve it, put her mind at rest. It won't be the scarf and she'll have just let that overactive imagination of hers run amok. She'll have a stiff vodka afterwards, give herself a good telling off, maybe even have a little laugh at her own ridiculousness. She pre-empts her impending relief, looks forward to it.

Maggie switches on the radio in an attempt to try and distract herself from her racing thoughts but the news is full of it.

'... formally identified today. Her body was discovered early on Saturday morning. Police believe Amelie, a model and social-media influencer, had been missing since Wednesday evening after friends expressed their concern that she'd failed to meet them for drinks as planned and went on to miss an important photoshoot. They are appealing for any witnesses to come forward...'

Maggie closes her eyes for a few seconds longer than could be deemed safe while driving. *This is a nightmare.* That poor girl's parents, poor Helen.

She tries again to picture Helen Fox's face in her mind but draws another blank.

Traffic begins to slow up in front of her as she approaches the junction towards Eden Gorge. There's a police cordon up in front, large marked vans parked either side of the road. She turns to her left to see the rows of unformed police officers in the field in the distance, their high-vis vests glowing in the diminishing evening light. They're combing the fields, searching the parkland for evidence she assumes.

Are they looking for the scarf?

Maggie dismisses the idea as soon as it enters her head. Maybe her father had been right all along – something she's loath to admit – that she is 'histrionic', always thinking the worst, always making more out of something than it really is.

'*Mental-health issues run in the family you know, Margaret,*' her father's compassionless voice amplifies in her ears.

She hears her phone beep suddenly, alerting her that she has a new voice message. She clicks on it, grateful for the distraction.

'Hello, this is a message for Margaret Wendover... this is Elisa Constantinople from St Smithen's College. I'm the resident student counsellor and safeguarding officer and I wondered if I could speak to you regarding your daughter, Re—'

A sudden tap on her window causes her to shriek in alarm, almost causing her to drop the phone.

'You startled me!' She ends the message playback, clutches her chest, opens the window a touch more.

'I'm afraid you'll have to take an alternative route, madam,' a police officer informs her flatly. She's probably had to say the same thing to hundreds of other motorists this evening, probably had enough of it all to be fair. 'We've closed the road off. You'll need to double back round...'

'Yes,' Maggie says, 'I know the route. What's going on?' she finds herself asking, though obviously it must have something to do with Amelie Fox's murder. 'Is it the girl – the body that was found in the river?'

'If you could just turn around,' the police officer says without looking at her.

Maggie nods, does her window up and puts the car into reverse, the gears crunching loudly once more, causing the officer to give her a brief backward glance. She winces again; holds an apologetic hand up, embarrassed.

She swallows dryly. Why does she suddenly have a sickening sense of guilt, like she's done something wrong?

7

The garage light is on as she pulls up into the driveway of their home at last. *Thank God.* She can see a thin outline of light around the door which means Len's still in there, working on his car.

Snatching up her gym bag, she locks the car door with a beep, doesn't initially see him standing at the end of the driveway until she's halfway to the front door.

'Evening, Maggie.'

'Oh! You made me jump!' That's twice in quick succession tonight – her nerves are hanging in rags. 'Hello, Clive.'

Her attempt at gathering herself lacks conviction, she's sure. Her creepy neighbour is standing at the end of her driveway, looking all arms and legs, like he had at the party.

'Sorry, I didn't mean to scare you.' He takes a step backward, embarrassed. 'Lovely evening, isn't it?'

It isn't, not particularly anyway – if anything it's a touch windy. It strikes her as an odd thing to say. *She's paranoid as hell.*

'Yes, lovely,' she agrees for argument's sake. She just wants to get inside, get up to the loft and locate that scarf. She honestly can't focus, can't think about anything else right in this moment.

'I see he's got it up and running then.' Clive grins amiably.

Small talk is the last thing she needs right now, but she doesn't want to be impolite.

'Got what up and running?' She smiles at him, has no idea what he's talking about.

'The car... the Cadillac.' He nods towards the garage. She realises it's become dark all of a sudden.

'Oh! The car, yes... no,' she corrects herself awkwardly. 'He'll be in there for a fair few months more, trust me.' She rolls her eyes, mostly for effect. The last vintage car Len had restored – an old American 1950s Mustang – had been a real commitment. He'd spent months fitting it with a new engine and restoring it back to its former glory. There had been a big fanfare the day it became roadworthy. He'd bought champagne so that they could toast its 'maiden voyage' as he'd called it, had even wrapped the bloody thing in a red bow.

Clive blinks at her curiously. 'Oh, it's just that I thought... No... doesn't matter.' He shakes his head, laughs it off with a wave.

She hasn't got time for this, but now she wants to know what it is that 'doesn't matter'.

'Thought what?'

'Well, I thought... could've sworn I saw it last week, out for a late-night spin... or early morning really, if you want to be pedantic.' He chuckles awkwardly.

'Really?' He's mistaken surely? She would've absolutely known about it if Len had got the car up and running, let alone driven it for the first time. He wouldn't have shut up about it. It would've been a very big deal, a cause for celebration.

'I... yes, Wednesday night. Though like I say, it was more like early Thursday morning to be exact. I looked out of the window – I'm a terrible insomniac you see,' he explains, clearly feeling the need to do so, 'and I could've sworn I saw...' He shakes his head, looks all arms and legs again. 'Anyway, must be my bad.' He dismisses it again with another apologetic shake of his head.

Maggie nods, forces a smile. He's got to be mistaken. Len was away for the day on Wednesday with his brother, Bob, attending the vintage car fair. The pair of them were staying at the Platinum Inn Hotel down in Eden Gorge for the night. Yes, she's sure of it, isn't she? Oh anyway, right now, all she can concentrate on is getting inside and up into the loft – she's already halfway up the stairs in her head.

'Dreadful news about that girl, isn't it?' he says sagely. 'Strangled and dumped in the river.' He tuts three times in quick succession. 'Just a few miles from here as well. I go walking in Riverdown Park all the time and—'

'Yes,' she agrees, 'yes, it's tragic, absolutely awful. Sorry, Clive, but I'm—'

'Did you know her? The girl – Amelie somebody?'

'Fox,' she says. 'Amelie Fox, and yes – no – well, I knew her mother – knew *of* her mother I mean.' The urge to get inside has become overwhelming – she's almost dancing on the spot.

'Gosh, how awful... it's all over the news and—'

'I'm so sorry, Clive, I'm really in a rush.' She shoots him a look of apology as she clenches her car keys in her hand and turns towards the front door.

'Great party the other night by the way,' he calls out to her. 'Thanks for inviting me. It was great to meet some of the rest of the neighbours and your friends, Brenda and...'

Brenda. Out of everyone at the party he mentions her! Well, there was a surprise. What was it with these men? They were just a pair of tits for goodness' sake! Maggie rolls her eyes, but she has her back to him so he doesn't see.

'You'll have to pop over soon,' she says, wincing at her own disingenuousness, 'have a glass of wine with me and Len. You can grill him about the car. I'm sure he'd be thrilled to bore you with all the details – you'd be doing me a favour...'

'I'd like tha—' She's already closed the front door behind her.

After throwing her keys into the dish on the console table with a clatter and kicking off her trainers in haste, Maggie pads through to the kitchen. She needs a glass of water, though in truth a stiff vodka would probably be better.

Remy is sitting at the kitchen table, her eyes glued to her phone. She doesn't even look up as Maggie enters the room.

'Oh! Darling!' She's surprised to see her daughter – she thought she was heading back up to London today. 'You're still here.'

'Hmmm?' Remy is tapping away on her phone, engrossed.

Maggie pauses, grabs a glass from the kitchen cabinet and takes some iced water from the fridge. That reminds her: she didn't finish listening to the voicemail message that woman from Remy's college left her. She'll do it later, once she's been up to the loft.

'You're still here,' she says again.

'What? Oh, yeah. I thought I'd say on for a while longer if that's OK?'

'Of course it is,' she says. 'Stay as long as you like, darling – you know you're very welcome.'

'I've got some reports to write for my coursework, some studying to do, and it's less distracting here. You don't mind, do you?'

'Like you have to even ask! Have you eaten?' Maggie enquires, automatically beginning to busy herself. She's vibrating with nervous energy, needs to expel some of it.

'I made a chowder earlier, your dad's favourite – I can heat some up for you. I got some of that crusty tiger bread from the bakery this morning that'll go nicely with it.'

She'll put the chowder on a low heat, go upstairs on the

pretext of taking a shower, then she'll slip up into the loft. *She's got to get up into that loft.*

She glances at her daughter; she's still looking at her phone, her expression grave – no, not grave... upset... angry even. 'Is everything OK, sweetheart?'

Her daughter is unresponsive, continues staring intensely at her phone.

'Remy?' She focuses on her for a moment longer. 'Is everything OK? What are you reading?'

There's another pause. 'Rems?'

'What? Oh sorry, Mum.'

'Are you texting Whatshisname?'

Remy finally looks up at her, her expression softening. 'He says he's missing me, can't wait to see me.' She gives a small squeal, clearly chuffed.

'Ah well, that's nice, darling, and why wouldn't he, eh?' Maggie smiles warmly at her, cocks her head. 'You really like this one, don't you?'

'He says I'm the most beautiful girl on Instagram,' Remy gushes, 'and that he wants to take me to Santorini.'

'Santorini! Oh, wow! It's beautiful – your dad and I have been there, before you were born. Very romantic, lots of little white houses with blue roofs and stunning sunsets...'

'Maybe he's going to propose,' Remy says, her expression animated. 'Can you *even* imagine? I mean, the photographs for one thing!'

Maggie raises an eyebrow. 'Yes, well, let's meet him first at least, before you walk up the aisle together!'

She turns, smiles. It's lovely to see her daughter so happy. She remembers that feeling so well, the nervous exhilaration of falling in love for the first time, those heady initial hot flushes of a blossoming romance. Now all she has are hot *flashes*.

'Alex not coming over today? You're not studying together?'

But Remy is back busy tapping on her phone again. 'Huh?'

'Alex. You remember, your flatmate – small girl, lovely hair, you go to college together...'

'Yes, har har, very funny. And no, she's, uh... I think she's busy or something – gone shopping with her mum.'

'We could hit town together later this week if you want? I need to get—'

Maggie suddenly spies a couple of black plastic refuge sacks, tied up by the back door.

'What are those?' She points at them.

Remy glances over at them, shrugs. 'Dad's I think.'

'Dad's what?'

'Dunno. Old clothes or something, for recycling, I think. I said I'd take them up to the plant for him now that my car's fixed.'

'Your dad's cleared out his old clothes? Well, that's a first!' Maggie blinks in surprise. She can't remember the last time Len sorted his old cast-offs to be recycled. In fact, she can't remember *any* time. He's always left all that sort of thing to her.

Distracted, she switches the gas on, places the large pot of chowder onto the hob.

'I suppose you've seen the TV today – the dreadful news about that murdered girl, Amelie Fox?'

The chowder quickly begins to spit and splutter aggressively in the pan and she turns the heat down.

'Yeah,' Remy says, 'it's awful, isn't it? Sexual assault or something they reckon.'

Maggie's stomach lurches so violently that she drops the spoon into the chowder. *Sexual assault?* She hadn't heard any mention of sexual assault on the radio, and they hadn't said anything like that on TV. She swallows dryly, gulps a little water.

'They said that, the police?'

'She was naked when they found her apparently, so I figured... Anyway, it's so sad. Like, who would even do that to her? She was so pretty... and she had so many followers on Insta.'

Maggie turns round, looks at her daughter.

'You know she's a bikini model, Mum – or was anyway. Check out her Instagram page – she had over half a million followers. I've only got 9,000 so far, but I'm working on it and—'

'Did they say she'd been sexually assaulted, the police? Did they *actually* say that?'

Remy shrugs again. 'Why else would she be naked when they found her?'

Maggie's guts are lurching. She doesn't want to believe it. Suddenly she wishes she still smoked. She gave it up long ago, before the kids were born, but every now and again the urge for a Marlborough Light still grips her.

'Do you remember her, from school? I've been trying to think what her mother looks like – Helen Fox. Christine reckons I know her, but I just can't picture her.'

'She was a couple of years above me I think,' Remy replies casually. 'Can't say I do really.'

'It's just awful...' Maggie feels like crying. 'Her poor family. I mean, she's only a little older than you, Rems. To lose her life like that, murdered, in such a horrible way. I can't think about it, and so close to home, it's frightening.'

She continues to stir the chowder manically, the fishy aroma reaching her nostrils.

'Promise me you'll not go out alone. Take the car if you go anywhere, and make sure you've got your phone charged and—'

'Yes, yes... don't fuss, Mother. I'll be careful.'

'I mean it, Remy.' Maggie's voice hardens. 'There could be a killer on the loose, someone local even. It's absolutely terrifying.'

Remy rolls her eyes, abandons her phone finally. 'I highly doubt it, Mum. This is Thorton Vale, remember? Nothing exciting happens here.'

'I hardly call a young woman being murdered exciting!'

Typical Remy – nothing ever seems to phase her. The beauty of youth she supposes. At that age, you never think anything bad will happen to you. Until it does. No doubt poor Amelie Fox thought the same thing.

'You know what I mean,' she retorts. 'Anyway, it was probably someone stalking her, an obsessive fan or something. She had a lot of admirers, was super friendly...'

'I thought you said you didn't know her.'

'I don't. I just follow her on Insta.'

'I heard she was doing really well by all accounts, on the brink of celebrity.'

Remy stifles a yawn. 'Yeah... Think I might go upstairs and do some reading,' she says, making to stand.

'Oh, darling.' Maggie reacts quickly – she really doesn't want her to go upstairs. She'll hear her clambering into the loft, will want to know what she's doing. 'Would you mind staying down here and watching the chowder while I take a quick shower? I don't want it to stick... bit sweaty from Pilates.' She pulls at her T-shirt to demonstrate. 'I really won't be long.' She gives her a cocked smile of gratitude.

Remy sighs heavily. 'Oh all right... but be quick yeah? I've got a bit of studying I need to do.'

'Well, if you spent less time on that phone to Whatshisface...'

Maggie takes the stairs two at a time. Light with adrenalin, she marches into the bedroom and immediately switches the shower on in the en suite, grabbing a fresh towel from the rail. The sound of the water running will act as a decoy, allow her to do what she needs to do without alerting Remy downstairs.

The hatch to the loft opens with more ease than usual – or perhaps it's just her imagination – and catches her finger. There's a couple of seconds' delay before the pain registers.

'Shit!' She grimaces, looks down at the broken skin between her thumb and forefinger, shakes the pain out. *Bloody thing.*

Instinctively she sucks at it, the iron taste of blood tingling on her tongue.

Cursing as she climbs the stairs, Maggie's thoughts begin to swirl together in a diabolical soupy mix inside her head. *Sexual assault... found naked...* Ironically, she hasn't yet thought as far as what she'll do when she finds the scarf, if it turns out to be the same one that Amelie was wearing.

The image she'd seen earlier flashes up in her head again. Her beautiful face thrown back in laughter, her long glossy blonde hair intertwined in the scarf... those little black skulls. What will she do? She should first check that it doesn't belong to Brenda, shouldn't she? That was her initial thought after all, that the scarf must be hers because it smelled strongly of perfume – the same, or similar at least, to what she was wearing at the party. If it turns out to be hers then she can at least put her troubled mind at some level of rest. She'd deal with the aftermath later – there would be a rational explanation no doubt.

But what if there isn't? What if it *is* Amelie's scarf. The marks on it that she thought looked like bloodstains... how could they be explained? Who had put it there in the first place? Because she sure as hell knows she didn't, and in truth, that only really left one other person who could've, *didn't it*?

She thinks of Len then, suddenly terrified that he'll smell that bloody chowder and come in from the garage. It's his favourite.

In through the nose and out through the mouth, Maggie. That's it.

But she's hyperventilating by the time she's standing, and the loft hatch closes behind her with a nasty clunk.

She walks past the dusty boxes, the pair of suitcases... Hang on. She blinks at them both. *Pair?* Yes, there had always been a pair of them, but she's sure she only saw one suitcase when she was up here on Saturday night. Maybe she was a little drunk and missed it... maybe she's just losing it.

Aware of the pivotal moment in front of her, Maggie almost doesn't want to open the door to the eave. Instinctively, she knows that by doing so it may well be akin to opening Pandora's box. But she has no choice. She *has* to know.

Still, hope remains that she's made a mistake, that she's been scaring herself witless over absolutely nothing, as she pulls at the light string.

Maggie crouches down, opens the torch app on her phone. That familiar musty stench hits her nostrils as a gush of fetid air rushes to greet her. Shaking, she shines the torch inside the small eave. The sealed boxes are still there, unmoved just as before, but... *it's empty.*

She shines the torch again in every corner, scans the dusty floorboards carefully, once, twice, a third time, every inch of the small space – nothing.

Exhaling loudly with adrenalin, she shifts the two boxes, wondering if the scarf had somehow fallen between them when she'd screwed it up into a ball and thrown it back into the eave on Saturday night.

It's not here. *Oh no. Oh no, no, no.*

She holds herself still for a moment, wonders if in fact she really *is* losing her mind, that she's somehow imagined all of it, and there was never any scarf in the first place, because it doesn't make any sense, no sense whatsoever.

Confusion and panic struggle for pole position inside her, and her earlier fantasy of being mistaken, of realising she's got it all so wrong, evaporates like condensation in a morning sunrise.

The scarf is gone.

8 DAN

'So...' Vic Leyton removes the sheet from the body in that way she always does, unveiling the corpse like a magician revealing a trick. 'I was correct in my initial preliminaries,' she states unapologetically. 'She suffered a blow to the back of the head first, blunt-force trauma, possibly inflicted with some type of glass object – an ashtray or bottle maybe, something with an edge sharp enough to pierce the scalp and cause bleeding anyway. It would've rendered her unconscious or semi-conscious at best.'

For once I'm hoping for the worst – that she was unconscious, so she didn't unduly suffer.

'And then she was strangled,' Vic concludes. 'There's bruising to the neck, as one would expect, abrasions from the compression, which incidentally was quite forceful, enough to fracture her carotid artery. There's petechiae on both eyes and—'

'Petechiae?'

'Little red spots, Detective.' She glances at me, gives me a look that suggests I should know this by now. 'And the capillaries in her eyes were broken, bloodshot... all indicative of strangulation. It would've been over fairly quickly, mercifully.'

I nod solemnly. It's scant compensation.

'Did he use his hands to strangle her – manually I mean?'

'No,' she says quickly. 'No, no bruises consistent with finger marks. A thin ligature of some sort,' she explains. 'A pair of tights maybe, a scarf, dressing-gown tie, a bra, something soft... Still,' she adds, almost brightly, 'in terms of evidence, she's been something of a marvel, you'll be no doubt pleased to know.'

I thought of the moment I'd first seen Amelie Fox's bloated and disfigured corpse, freshly pulled from the river, and silently pleaded with her to talk to me, to tell me what I needed to know to catch whoever committed these atrocities. Maybe she'd heard me after all.

'Oh?' I look at her hopefully.

'All in good time, Detective.' Vic gives one of her enigmatic smiles.

'The other good news, if you can call it that, is that the divers managed to recover Amelie's clothes from the river – though no personal possessions that you might have expected her to have on her – phone, handbag and the like. A pair of jean shorts with a designer belt and a sparkly shirt, a matching nude underwear set, a cropped denim jacket and a pair of expensive, so I'm informed, Nike Air Jordan trainers – all of which are currently with forensics. The killer didn't really take much trouble to hide her clothing, by burning them for example – they simply threw them in the river after her, dumped them like trash, like they did her body.

'There are fibres underneath her fingernails as well as all the dirt and debris from the river of course. I suspect they may originate from the boot of a car, a rug or a carpet perhaps. I'm certain she was already dead before she hit the water, perhaps only by a matter of hours, so I suspect the murder scene was elsewhere and that she was transported not too long after death. We found traces of engine oil—'

'Engine oil?'

'Yes. You'd think it would've been washed away by the river water, but Amelie wore extensions and some of it was found in the adhesive used to tape them to her hair – something of a lucky result really,' she adds. 'Not sure of the name or grade yet, but forensics will know more once they've completed their examinations.'

I scribble the words 'engine oil' into my notebook. This is good. If we find out the name and type of oil, it'll give us a possible identification of the type of vehicle that may have been used to transport her body.

'There's DNA too.' She glances sideways at me, awaiting my reaction because she knows that in our game, this is the equivalent of Willy Wonka's golden ticket to a sugar addict. Plus, knowing Vic as I do, she does like to always leave the best until last.

'Underneath her fingernails. There's not much of it, trace at best, but it could just be enough.'

I say a silent prayer.

'Her stomach was pretty much empty, some partially digested matter, putting her last meal around midday, but there was a little alcohol in her blood, probably ingested the previous evening. Her liver shows no permanent damage though, as one would expect from a woman of her age, even if she were a moderate drinker. Not a smoker either, and no traces of drugs in her blood, prescription or recreational, aside from the contraceptive pill.'

'Anything else?'

Vic gives me a look as if to imply, *Isn't that enough?*

'As a matter of fact, Detective, there is.'

'Oh?'

She pauses – deliberately, I'm sure.

'We found semen, in her vagina.'

I feel my adrenalin kick in. 'Semen... so you think she *was* sexually assaulted then?'

She opens her palms. 'I'm afraid I can't say one way or another. There are no obvious signs of assault, no bruising or tearing to the vaginal or anal walls, no internal injuries or contusions. It tells us that she had sex recently, though whether it was consensual or not is another matter. The sperm was still alive for some time even after her death, and of course this gives us definitive DNA.'

'*Still alive?*'

'Oh come, come, Dan – didn't you pay attention in biology class at school?'

My expression causes her to sigh. 'No wonder both your wife's pregnancies were such a shock to you!'

I smile, wondering how she even knows Fiona is pregnant again as I'm sure I haven't mentioned it to her.

'Human sperm can live in the female uterus between three and five days after intercourse.' She glances at me. 'It's a marvel isn't it, nature? Anyway, she could've had sex up to a working week before she was found, though my professional opinion would suggest that it was more recent than that, more like a day or so.'

'So you do think this was a sexually motivated crime?' I push her.

I'm aware that it's not in Vic Leyton's remit to make assumptions, but her trained eye and unparalleled expertise is something I've come to trust implicitly.

'You know I deal solely in factual, scientific evidence, DCI Riley,' she chastises me, albeit with the lightest breath of good humour.

'Yes, but in your *opinion,* Ms Leyton?'

I sense that she senses I'm attempting to use my charm on her, assuming I possess any that is. Fiona tells me I can 'turn it on when I want to'. I suppose it must've worked on at least two occasions.

She pushes her glasses a little further up her nose, begins removing her latex gloves with a snap before heading to the sink.

'In my *opinion*...' She sighs resignedly. 'Well, strangulation is one of the most common methods used in domestic violence homicides – as you *should* well know. It's a power thing, control, and power and control are generally two factors that regularly feature in sexually motivated crimes – which you also should well know, Detective.'

'I do.' I nod. 'I just wanted to hear you say it.'

She doesn't turn back to look at me, and I feel a little frisson at the idea she may be embarrassed.

'Time of death is a bit trickier, and you know how meticulous I like to be about this, Dan.' She uses my Christian name to denote her sincerity. 'But all things considered, I conclude that she was killed some time on Wednesday afternoon, somewhere between 3 p.m. and 6 p.m.'

I stare down at Amelie's body. She's been cleaned up, the dirt and debris washed away to reveal her perfectly unblemished skin. It feels bittersweet somehow.

As far as apartment buildings go, from the outside, the one Amelie Fox shared with her flatmate, Holly Redwood, with its gleaming, ergonomic glass frontage, reminiscent of the shape of a ship's sail, is nothing short of impressive, not least for such a young woman.

'Oh to be young, beautiful and rich!' Davis comments with a sigh as we call the elevator. Yeah, young, beautiful, rich and dead. None of it was any good to Amelie Fox now.

Situated in the heart of Chelsea, with balconies overlooking the river – the most salubrious of vistas to boot – my initial thought, aside from the fact that I've clearly been in the wrong profession all these years – is that it goes without saying that a plush-looking building like this must have the most sophisticated CCTV – and that thought is a serendipitous one in what is otherwise a dire, depressing situation, not least following Amelie's bittersweet post-mortem.

'Blimey, gov,' Davis says as we take the glass-fronted elevator up to the sixteenth floor. 'Imagine living in a gaff like this at twenty-two. Talk about living your best life!'

I can't disagree with her.

'What do you reckon it costs to live here a month?'

'More than our combined salary,' I say, pretty sure I'm not even joking.

The inside of the elevator is entirely mirrored, and no matter how hard I try, I can't avoid my own reflection staring four ways back at me. I've been awake for almost forty-eight hours straight and it shows. I've got more luggage underneath my eyes than a footballer's wife at an airport, and my hair is sticking out in directions that defy science. I look – and feel – as if I've been tasered. I run a hand through my hair in a futile bid to tame it – I suppose I should be at least grateful I still have some left – and I catch Davis, who incidentally, annoyingly still looks fresh as the proverbial daisy, watching me.

'Ready for your close-up, gov?' she mocks me with a cheeky smile.

'As I'll ever be,' I reply as we ring the bell to apartment 16B.

'Will I get that back? It's Louis Vuitton,' Holly Redwood is saying to someone as we enter.

She looks like a watered-down imitation of her former flat-mate. Striking but definitely not as beautiful, though I guess that's subjective. Anyway, she doesn't look happy and I'm unsure if that's because forensics are currently going over her incredibly pristine apartment with a fine-toothed comb, or if it's because her – I assume – close friend has been brutally murdered. Both would be enough to piss most people off, I'm sure. I introduce myself.

'DCI Dan Riley.' I offer her my hand, which she takes without making eye contact and shakes loosely. 'And this is DS Lucy Davis.'

'Pleased to meet you,' Davis says.

Holly musters up a small smile, but it does little to mask her distress.

'How long are these people going to be in my apartment?' she asks miserably. 'Are they going to clean up the mess?'

'We're sorry for the inconvenience, Holly,' Davis says a little tightly. 'But in light of what's happened... we're sure you understand.'

Holly nods resignedly, looks on the verge of tears. I can't help feeling empathy for her, her flatmate and friend murdered and now a bunch of strangers turning her apartment over...

'Tell me about her, Holly – about Amelie.' I cut to the chase, careful to keep my voice soft – she looks nervous enough as it is.

'What do you want to know?' She wraps a soft cardigan around her small frame and suddenly looks young and naïve.

'Everything,' I say, nodding to the large squishy grey couch. 'Shall we sit down? Nice apartment. You lived here long?'

She sniffs. 'About eighteen months. We rented it together, though Angel took care of the first couple of months' rent as I'd not long started a new job and needed to play catch-up. She was generous like that...'

'What do you do? For a living I mean?'

'I work in PR,' she says, falling back into the sofa and running her hands through her long, honey-blonde hair. 'The beauty industry.'

It figures. Despite what Holly must be going through right now, she still looks like she should be wearing a T-shirt that says 'I woke up like this'.

'I met Amelie through work a couple of years ago, through her modelling contracts. She was doing a shoot with a tanning company I promoted at the time. We hit it off immediately.' She lights a cigarette, a pink cocktail one from the packet on the table, with shaking hands. 'I can't believe she's dead, that she's *actually* dead,' she says. 'Who the hell would want to kill Angel?'

'I was hoping you might be able to tell me, Holly.'

She blows smoke forcibly from her full lips. 'Me?' She tucks her slim legs up underneath her. 'Look, all I know is that Angel's name suited her. She never upset no one, never had no enemies, none that I knew of anyway.'

I'm suddenly aware of her accent – London, south-east, or possibly Essex.

'She was… well, she was just so… *lovely*, and she was doing so well an' all, was really starting to make a name for herself.'

She absentmindedly picks at some skin by a manicured nail. 'She'd applied for a few reality TV shows recently, you know – *Sex Text Ur Ex* and *Date Your Best Mate.* Have you watched them?' She looks at me expectantly. 'She'd been shortlisted and everything.' She sighs heavily. 'She had so much to look forward to…'

'A boyfriend?' I say. 'Was she seeing someone – anyone?' I need to get as much information as possible, as quickly as possible. I've got a bad feeling about this case, something off about it, can't yet put my finger on it.

She blinks at me, like it's a ridiculous question. 'You've seen her, right?' She uses the present tense. I suspect it hasn't quite hit home yet. 'Angel was a dude magnet. Blokes went crazy for her.'

She rubs her eyes with her forefingers carefully. I stay silent – it's a neat psychological trick to get people to open up. Silence unnerves most people, makes them feel obligated to try and fill the blank spaces.

'I dunno.' She shrugs again. 'There were a few guys on the scene, nothing serious – flings, friends with benefits if that's what you want to call them, a reality TV star here and there… We used to laugh about it,' she says, throwing her hair back, visibly distressed. 'The better-looking the dude, the worse he was in—' She stops herself short, suddenly looks coy. 'You know… *bed*.'

Davis raises an eyebrow. I can't help wondering where that might put me on the spectrum in that particular equation. On second thoughts, I'd rather not know.

'These flings – any names?'

'Look, I didn't keep tabs on her love life. I mean, we chatted about it of course, but Angel was her own person. I don't get involved in other people's relationships – make it my business not to.'

'Wise,' I say. 'But you really can't think of anyone – a name, anything?'

She rubs her temples, flicks her ash in the glass ashtray in front of her on the trendy white Perspex coffee table. *Glass ash tray.* I'm reminded of Vic Leyton's post-mortem findings and nod at one of the forensics.

'Bag that up, will you?'

'*What the—* Hang on, that's vintage.' She makes to stop them but relents, sits back in the sofa with a soft sigh.

'When was the last time you saw Amelie, Holly?' Davis cuts in.

'Wednesday,' she says, allowing her ash to fall onto the marble tiled granite flooring in absence of the ashtray. 'She was supposed to meet some friends that night, but no one thought much of it when she didn't show – they just figured something had come up. But she was supposed to be doing a photoshoot the next day, a big one, an important one for Beachbabes, the swimwear brand. Have you heard of them?' She looks me up and down, decides I probably haven't. 'Kim Kardashian endorsed them once. *Kim Kardashian,*' she says again. 'I knew something was up when the toggie phoned me on Friday morning, said she'd been a no-show the day before. And then when I discovered she hadn't turned up to meet friends that evening too I... I thought it was odd, not like her, you know, she was always pretty reliable.'

'Toggie?'

'Photographer.' She gives me a look as if to say I must be an imbecile who lives under a rock somewhere. 'Kinsman, you know, the famous dude?'

I don't.

'The one who shoots all the celebs. We're friends,' she says, unable to mask her delight at sharing this blatant name-drop. 'I've shot with him a few times on various campaigns. I couldn't believe it. I mean, no one doesn't show up to a Kinsman shoot.' She sits up straight, unfurls her long legs.

'Amelie was found in Riverdown Park, near Thorton Vale. We're not sure how she got there. We know her parents live close to the area, but they were away from Thursday to Sunday and said that Amelie knew this. Did she mention that she might be visiting someone up near there? A friend, a relative perhaps?'

It had been yet another terrible blow when uniform had turned up at the Foxes' address to inform them of the abhorrent news about their daughter only to discover that they were enjoying a long weekend in the remote Welsh countryside. As if fate hadn't already dealt them such an egregious blow, they'd learned of Amelie's death as they were just about to tuck into room service in a posh hotel room. They hadn't even been aware their daughter was missing when uniform tracked them down. Her mother, Helen, had been so shocked and distressed by the terrible news that she'd collapsed, hitting her head on a table in the process and had needed hospital treatment.

'Could she have been visiting a friend, a boyfriend... one of those friends with benefits?' I address Holly once more.

The Foxes didn't seem to have thought so, said that Amelie's life was now firmly London-based and that she only really ever returned to the suburb where she grew up to see family.

'No idea,' Holly says. 'If she was planning to, then she never mentioned it to me. I know she didn't much like the place, only ever went there to visit her parents. She said it was boring, nothing going on, not like here in Chelsea. She loved her mum and dad though, got on well with them. Her mum was a model herself once, you know – Helen. She's really nice.'

I nod my agreement. Amelie was very much a carbon copy of her mother, a younger version of course, but the physical resemblance was striking nonetheless. It's a cruel twist of fate that she'll be reminded of her daughter's face each time she looks in a mirror. Seems like there's no end to certain people's suffering sometimes.

'Can you show us her bedroom?'

Holly lights another cigarette, an aqua blue one this time, from the packet on the table. She's chain-smoking, which seems incongruous for someone who works in the beauty industry. It doesn't suit her.

'It's through here,' she says, reluctant. 'I haven't been able to go in there since I found out – don't want to.'

'It's OK – I'll be with you,' I reassure her.

Davis, who's been in the kitchen talking to forensics, rejoins us.

'Could Amelie have had a stalker, Holly?' she asks. 'Did she ever mention anything to you? An admirer, any unwanted attention, someone she couldn't get rid of, wouldn't take no for an answer?'

Holly blows smoke in Davis's direction. Looks her up and down, though more in curiosity than contempt.

'There's no such thing as "unwanted attention" is there?'

'You tell me, Holly,' Davis says. 'She had a lot of male followers.'

She shrugs. 'Blokes messaged her constantly. Like I said, you saw her, right? Men loved her. She made a lot of money out of her OnlyFans account.'

'OnlyFans? She was on OnlyFans?'

'Yeah.' Holly's sudden wide-eyed expression implies she's realised she may have said something she shouldn't have. 'She had tons of subscribers. How else do you think she afforded to live here, drove the car she did and bought all that designer drip – working in Tesco's?'

I look at Davis and our eyes meet. Thanks to Amelie being something of a social-media sensation, the team has really got their work cut out. With followers running well into six figures on her IG account alone, and now no doubt a whole load more on OnlyFans, they'll have to check out each and every one of them, unless we get a lucky break early, which intuition tells me isn't going to happen – not that I'm being especially negative, but the phrase 'needle in a haystack' springs to mind. I'm hopeful about CCTV though, have already requested it from the owner of the building. I can only pray that throws something up because so far, we have very little to go on and no obvious suspects.

'Did she use her real name on OnlyFans?'

Holly's eyebrows rise. She thinks I'm a complete dinosaur.

'Er, no, she called herself AngelFox, like on her IG. She got a lot of traffic to her OF account through her IG.'

Well, OMFG, LOL, IDK, silly old me.

'I'll let tech know,' Davis says, pre-empting my instruction and making the call on her mobile.

'But she didn't do porno or nothing,' Holly quickly adds. 'It was just lingerie and bikini stuff, some imposed nudes, pretty tame by some people's standards. And no, to answer your question, she never said nothing to me about no unwanted attention, though I know there's a lot of pervs out there... some of them are even my ex-boyfriends.' She laughs a little then, which all things considered could be deemed somewhat inappropriate, but in this profession I've come to learn that people's response to death varies drastically. Laughing and humour is actually quite a common reaction, a human one.

She schleps through the state-of-the-art modern kitchen, which looks like something out of a TV advert – immaculate, though a touch soulless in my opinion. I doubt they cooked in it much – no doubt it was Uber Eats all the way.

A strange sensation grips me as I enter Amelie's bedroom, a sixth sense perhaps, and my adrenalin quickens. Did something happen to her inside this room? On first glance there's no reason to suggest it did – it looks pristine, nothing out of place, but my intuition is nagging at me like the onset of toothache.

'Feels really weird being in here.' Holly visibly shudders. 'To think she was just here a few days ago, doing her hair and make-up...'

A large faux-fur throw covers the bed, and giant pink-and-grey matching cushions are precisely placed against the plush pillows, like you see in five-star hotels. The white shutters, plantation style, are a touch open, which, assuming they haven't been moved, suggests it might've still been light when she was here last. A soft, geometrically patterned grey rug sits at the end of the king-size bed, a large ornate dressing table to the right. The pink fur stool is positioned a little way behind it, suggesting someone may have moved it after they'd been sitting on it.

The pink neon sign above it reads: 'Ready for your close-up', and I wonder if Davis can add being psychic to her list of attributes. She'd said the exact same thing to me in the elevator on the way up.

'She took a lot of her IG stuff here, in this room,' Holly says flatly. She looks uncomfortable, like she doesn't want to be here as she wraps her cardigan tighter around herself.

I inspect the dressing-table contents. It's filled with make-up and beauty products, perfume bottles and lotions, all expensive looking. I glove up, start looking through it, though I'm unsure for what. I pick up a pot of something.

'Creme de la Mer,' Holly says, watching me. 'All the celebrities use it – costs over £150 a pop.'

I put it back, pick up a large glass perfume bottle, blue, in the shape of a star with a silver lid. It says 'Angel' on the front of it.

'She had her own perfume brand?'

Holly looks at me curiously. 'Thierry Mugler, the French fashion designer,' she says, like I should absolutely know this. 'Angel – it was her signature scent, one of the reasons she adopted the name. She'd have loved to have had her own perfume though, like Britney or Kim,' she adds, her slim shoulders sagging slightly. 'I'm sure she would've an' all. She was destined for big things.'

Instinctively, I spray a little onto my shirtsleeve. It smells sweet, almost reminiscent of chocolate, indicative of youth somehow, very strong and distinctive – the kind that would linger on your memory and bed sheets.

'She got through bottles of the stuff.' She blinks back tears. 'Says she was nose blind to it in the end.'

I nod to a passing forensic, tell them to bag it up.

'You say you last saw Amelie on Wednesday?'

'Uh-huh.' She nods. 'In the afternoon, about 12.30 p.m. I was working from home that morning. I went to the gym around 11 a.m. and then had a meeting with a client for lunch. She was sitting there' – she points to the dressing table – 'getting ready when I left.'

'Ready for what?' Or who?

She shrugs. 'Dunno. She didn't say, but she never went anywhere without looking her best. That was her job.'

'What was she wearing, when you last saw her?' Davis goes over towards a set of double doors, opens them. 'Bloody hell,' she curses. 'Check out this lot!'

The doors open into a huge walk-in closet of the like I've never seen before – not that I've seen many walk-in wardrobes or, in fact, any. There are rails containing hundreds, even thousands, of colour co-ordinated items – dresses, shirts, trousers, coats... The in-built shelves are piled high with folded T-shirts, with a separate one for jeans. And her shoe collection is nothing short of impressive – neatly stacked clear plastic boxes one on top of the other.

'A veritable Imelda Marcos,' Davis remarks.

'Yeah, she loves her drip, does Angel.' Holly smiles thinly. 'I was always borrowing her stuff.' She looks up. 'She never minded though. Oh God.' Her face drops to her hands. 'I can't believe I'm never going to see her again.'

I watch her as reality continues its harsh journey towards acceptance.

'Can you remember, Holly? Her clothes?'

She shakes her head, visibly straining to recall. 'I... I think she was wearing shorts, denim shorts, with her Gucci belt and a shirt maybe, yeah... her new Jordans and a cut-off jacket, her Alexander McQueen scarf and—'

'A scarf?'

She's accurately described the items that were recovered from the river, but I don't recall there being any scarf. Davis and I exchange glances. 'Can you describe it – the scarf?'

'Ummm.' Her face is a mask of anguish and concentration. 'Yeah, it was her current favourite – a McQueen one. She loved fashion; that girl could certainly shop. Anyway, it was pink, with little black skulls on it, signature McQueen,' she says, as though everyone should know what 'signature McQueen' looks like.

'Would this be the same outfit?' Davis produces her phone from her pocket, shows Holly a photograph. 'It was posted on Instagram on Thursday, the last known image of her.'

Holly gasps, taps the screen. 'Yeah! That's it!' She's almost dancing on the spot. 'That's what she was wearing when I see her last, the jacket and the scarf. She'd not long bought it – still got the bag, over there.' She points to a collection of designer carrier bags, neatly folded in a pile: Chanel, Dior, D&G, Hermès, Alexander McQueen...

Davis glances at me again. Had the frogmen missed the scarf or had the murderer taken it? A memento perhaps?

'Do you have access to Amelie's Instagram account, Holly? Or know anyone else who might?' Davis presses her.

She shakes her head. 'No. Not that I know of anyway – she rarely had her phone out of her hand to be fair, and... Why?'

'The time stamp,' I say, 'I'm sorry to say this, but the pathologist seems to think that Amelie was most likely already dead when the last photo of her was posted to her Instagram account.'

'What?' Holly looks up at me, her expression morphing into horror as the gradual realisation descends. 'It wasn't just scheduled to post then?'

'We're looking into that, but we don't think so.'

'But that means...'

I nod.

'That's just sick!' She shakes her head. 'Maybe it's still here, the scarf?' she says, beginning to manically rummage around her friend's wardrobe. 'She hangs all her accessories up in the—'

I move to prevent her.

'This may be a crime scene, Holly,' I say gently. 'We need to preserve as much evidence as we can.'

She nods, watches me as I lightly finger an array of scarves and ties and belts with a gloved hand.

'Actually, now I think of it, there was this one thing,' she says after a pause. 'It may be nothing. It probably *is* nothing...' She bites her lip anxiously.

'There's no such thing as nothing, Holly,' I tell her. 'Everything is always *something*.'

'She mentioned it again recently; it came up in conversation... something about some dude she'd been seeing on and off for some time. He'd...' She pauses. 'She said he'd' – her eyes lower – 'that he'd once filmed them having sex together and that he'd put it out on social media a while ago.'

'A sex tape?' Davis looks at Holly and then at me.

'Yeah... I suppose so.'

'And you've seen this video?'

'Yeah,' she says quietly. 'She showed it to me. I think it's still out there, you know, on the internet. She was a bit annoyed that he'd released it without her permission at the time – I mean, it was a private video – but anyway, she weren't even really that bothered about it; bit embarrassed about the idea of her parents getting wind of it, but it hadn't seemed to do her no harm or nothing. If anything, it drove more traffic to her IG and OF accounts she said.'

She's looking down at the floor when I turn to face her, abandoning my search. It's not here, the scarf. *It's missing.*

'Can you remember the name of this *gentleman* – the one in the video?'

She visibly swallows, and I can see she knows how potentially important this could be.

She tuts crossly at herself, shakes her head. 'I'm sorry, I dunno. If she did then I've forgotten. She just told me what he'd done.' She shakes her head apologetically. 'We joked about it really. I mean, it didn't do Paris Hilton or Kim Kardashian no harm, did it? The opposite in fact, so we was— Anyway' – she looks away, her face blooming pink; I'm almost old enough to be Holly's father so I imagine it's not an altogether comfortable subject for her to talk about – 'the reason I thought of it, well… it's probably nothing but…'

Davis re-enters the closet and I'm relieved, hoping a female presence might make her feel less self-conscious so she can tell us more.

'Go on,' I coax her.

'He tied her up, in the video… he tied her up with a scarf.'

10 MAGGIE

'Oh! You're home!'

Startled, Maggie drops the pan into the waste unit with a loud clatter.

'For fuck's sake, Len,' she snaps, her heart thudding against her ribs. 'Creeping up on me like that... you scared the crap out of me!'

Her husband's eyes widen. She doesn't often used the F word, doesn't like him to either.

He grins, chuckles a little. 'I love it when you talk dirty,' he says, going over to her and wrapping his hands around her waist. 'You OK, darling? How was Pilates?' He kisses the side of her neck, rests his head on her shoulder briefly.

Maggie inwardly flinches. She feels like she might burst into flames at any moment.

'Fine. Good. I burned the chowder,' she says miserably. 'I'm sorry.'

Len peers over her shoulder at the charred mess in the pan. He sighs, makes a little sign of the cross. 'Rest in peace,' he says, and she finds herself smiling for the first time that day.

'Never mind, chickadee,' he says, leaving her side and slapping himself on the chest with both hands. 'Let's be all millennial and get Uber Eats instead. I've worked up a real appetite tonight in the garage.'

'How's it coming along?' She hopes her voice doesn't sound stilted.

'Oh, you know, slowly, slowly, catchee monkey.'

'When do you think it'll be roadworthy?'

He blows air through his lips. 'Not for a while yet. I thought I might be able to recondition the engine that was already in there; didn't look so bad at a first shufty, but on secondary inspection...' He opens the fridge, pulls out a beer. She doesn't drink the stuff – it makes her gassy.

'Pour me a glass of wine, will you?'

Len glances at her.

'What?' she says, catching his expression.

'Nothing,' he says lightly. 'Just not like you to drink wine on a Monday night.'

'Got to live on the edge sometimes,' she says, suddenly reminded of what creepy Clive had said, about thinking he'd seen the Cadillac during the early hours on Thursday last week. It was such a strange thing to have said – to be mistaken about, surely? A dusting of unease settles lightly upon her stomach like fresh snow. Len was staying at the Platinum Inn hotel the previous night, with his brother, Bob. The pair of them had attended the annual vintage car fair that Wednesday like they did every year. Perhaps she'll go-online and look at their joint bank statement, double check she's got the dates right.

'So it's not drivable as it currently is then, the car?'

'What?' Len's at the table now, checking his phone. 'Oh, no. Well, technically yes, it is drivable... I mean it *goes*, but I wouldn't want to drive it, not in its current condition anyway. Too risky – anything could go on that engine. It's on its last knockings.'

Maggie nods, squirts some more washing-up liquid into the

ruined pan and fills it with hot water. 'So you haven't taken it out for a little spin then, just to see?'

'God no. Like I say, I wouldn't want to risk it.' He pauses. 'Why the sudden interest? You're not usually so inquisitive about my cars.' He narrows his eyes at her playfully. 'What are you after, lady?'

She laughs through her nose a little, shakes her head. 'I'm not after anything,' she objects. 'Just showing an interest, that's all.'

'No Rems?' Len's gone back to looking at his phone.

'No, I think she's— That reminds me, did you bag up some of your old clothes for her to take to the recycling centre? I saw a couple of old sacks by the door when I got in.'

She takes a large gulp of wine. The gubbins have all but come off the pan now, but she continues to scrub – doesn't want to turn round and have to face him.

He doesn't answer her.

'Len!' she prompts him, but then the doorbell rings and he heads off to answer it.

She hears them in the hallway, the low baseline of voices vibrating through to the kitchen. There's a woman's voice... Her heart rate begins to accelerate. *Is that...?*

Len enters the kitchen and she's following close behind him.

'Brenda's here to see us, darling,' he says, looking as surprised as she is.

'Helloooo, Mags!'

Maggie is drying her hands with a tea towel at the sink, almost drops it in haste. *Mags?* Did she just address her as *Mags?* Bit overfamiliar, isn't it? Only Len and her close friends call her that. She inwardly bristles. How bizarre though – she was only just thinking about going over to Brenda's house to ask her about the scarf and now suddenly she's here, standing in her kitchen in front of her. She's never called round before, and certainly not unannounced. '*Speak of the devil and he shall call.*' That's what her old Nanny P always used to say, adding, '*Just make sure you don't invite him in!*' Bit late for that now.

'She wanted to drop by to say thank you for the party. Look – she's brought you some flowers! How lovely!'

Is it her or is Len fawning a little? *You're being paranoid.*

'I thought I'd pop in and give you these.' Brenda comes towards her. Instinctively, Maggie takes a step backward. She feels flustered, unprepared.

'To say thank you, both of you.' She glances back at Len. 'For the other night. I had *such* a good time!'

Yes, I remember. She blinks at her neighbour, manages a smile. Brenda is wearing a low-cut camisole top and a pair of jeans that look as if she's been piped into them.

'How *lovely* of you.' She takes the bouquet from her – pink roses and lilies, quite beautiful in fact – and sniffs them, but all she gets is a waft of that perfume again, the strong, distinctively sweet one that Brenda was wearing at the party. The same smell that was on the scarf.

'They're gorgeous – you didn't need to do that.'

Suddenly she feels helpless, like her life is a farce that she's playing along with. Why is Brenda here *really*?

'Well, it's just a small token. I thought about popping over on Sunday to see if you needed a hand, you know, with the clearing up and all of that, must've been a bit of a job, but then there was that awful business with the girl... the body down at Riverdown Park. It really threw me. Ron and I have been terribly upset by it.' She shakes her head. 'Darling-looking little thing she was as well... no wonder she was known as "Angel".

Maggie swallows dryly, takes another gulp of wine. Would it not have been as dreadful if it had been a plain Jane who'd been murdered?

'Bloody awful,' Len agrees. 'Just bloody awful. Not much older than our Rems as well, and right on our doorstep. Sit down will you, Brenda,' he says, gesturing at the kitchen table. 'Would you like a glass of wine?'

'Ooh, yes please!'

Maggie feels her heart sink as she goes to the fridge and takes out an opened bottle of Pinot.

'It's all over the news again today,' Brenda says, accepting the glass with both hands, mouthing a thank you to Maggie. 'And there's still a huge police presence down by Eden Gorge. Crawling all over the place they are. Looks like they're searching for something in the fields and parkland.'

Maggie surreptitiously watches Len's reaction. Is she imagining it or is he staring at Brenda's cleavage? Hard not to really, she supposes, it was just so... *there*, in your face. It's a job not to stare herself.

'My Ron was going to ask if they wanted any help. Get a few local bodies together – you know, a little search party.'

'But we don't know what it is they're searching for though,' Maggie finds herself saying.

Brenda looks at her. 'No, I suppose not, but anyway, it was just a thought, you know, support in the community and all of that. Everyone's upset about it. It was strange though,' she says, her eyes glazing over. 'I had a premonition about it – about the murder.'

'A premonition?'

Brenda shakes her hair out a little, affording Maggie another waft of that perfume. 'Oh, didn't you know? I thought it was common knowledge.'

'What's common knowledge?' That she and Ron are swingers?

'I'm a practising psychic,' she announces. 'I've had the gift ever since I can remember.'

'*Psychic?*' Did she just hear her right?

'Uh-huh.' Brenda nods sagely. 'And I had this terrible premonition last week, kept getting these horrible visions, the sensation of being asphyxiated.' She brings her hands up to her neck. 'Kept getting short of breath and everything.' She sits back in the chair. 'It was no surprise to learn that's how she was murdered.'

Maggie is stunned into silence. Surely she can't expect people to actually believe this? Brenda, psychic? Wait until she tells Christine!

'Oh,' Maggie manages to say. 'I had no idea.'

'Yes, well, it comes and goes, you know,' she explains. 'It's a blessing but also a burden sometimes, although it's very rewarding to give people messages of comfort from their loved ones who've passed over.'

Maggie hopes the incredulity isn't showing on her face. 'You *see* dead people?' She glances at Len, but he appears to be fixated with something on his phone and doesn't seem to be listening. Probably just as well as she's pretty sure he wouldn't be able to keep a straight face.

'Hear them really more than see them,' Brenda explains, 'but sometimes I'll get a vision – usually when there's been some kind of unrest, you know?'

No, she absolutely doesn't. She blinks at Brenda. *Attention*, this is all for attention, she feels sure of it. She's no more psychic than she is demure. She suddenly feels a little sorry for her.

'Well then, perhaps you'll hear something from her – from Amelie. Maybe you can help solve her murder.' Surely Brenda can't expect her to take this seriously?

'If only it worked like that,' she sighs. 'I'd be more than happy to help if it did, but I'm afraid I don't get to choose – the spirits choose me, you see, not the other way round.'

Of course they do.

'Actually, she went to school with Remy,' Maggie says. 'Amelie Fox.'

Len looks up from his phone suddenly. 'Did she? You didn't say, darling,' he says, clearly surprised. 'I didn't know that.'

'Yes.' Maggie's voice sounds thin and unlike her own. 'Valley Primary School, though they weren't in the same year – Amelie was two years above her. I knew her mum, Helen.'

She doesn't know why she's saying this because she didn't – doesn't – know Helen, not really; she still can't picture what she looks like in her head.

'Oh my God!' Brenda looks aghast, clutches at her ample chest. 'How awful, you poor thing.' She leans forward again. 'How is she taking it? The mum I mean?'

Maggie has to stifle a sarcastic reply. *Oh you know, really well, in her stride...*

'Stupid question really,' Brenda adds.

Perhaps she is psychic after all.

'I heard that they think it might be someone local, you know – the killer.'

'Do they?' Maggie glances at Len but his expression hasn't changed. She's sure he's still slyly copping a look at Brenda's tits. 'How do you know that?'

She shrugs a little. 'Just what I heard,' she says, leading Maggie to conclude that it's probably no more than hearsay with no foundation.

'Scary to think though, that we could have a killer in our midst, someone we know to say hello to, someone we could walk past every day.' Frankly, she looks positively thrilled by the idea, Maggie thinks. 'I was only saying the same thing to Clive yesterday...'

Clive. Is there any man on this street Brenda *isn't* friendly with?

'How's Ron?' Maggie deliberately changes the subject. But really she wants to ask Brenda about the scarf, wishes she could just come right out with it and ask her straight up if it belongs to her, but she can't bring herself to. Besides, she no longer has it to give back to her even if it *is* hers.

'My Ron?'

'Yes, we didn't see him at the party, did we, Len? Come to think of it, I haven't seen him at all for a while...'

She turns to her husband, but he's gone back to reading something on his phone again. She feels irritated. He could at least help her out with the conversation – he can see she's struggling.

'What? Oh... sorry,' Len says. 'Yes – no, we didn't see him at the party.'

'Oh, he's fine.' Brenda flaps a hand. 'He fell off a stepladder last week while painting the downstairs bathroom, hurt his back, the daft sod. He's been laid up for a while, grumbling his demands at me from the bedroom.' She laughs and shakes her auburn hair out again, the movement making her breasts jiggle in her flimsy top.

'Well, send him our best, won't you?' Maggie realises that this statement sounds like the prelude to a goodbye and suddenly feels embarrassed – she honestly hadn't meant to sound rude. *Anything but rude.*

Len stands suddenly. 'Right, I'll leave you two ladies to your chit-chat. Got a bit of work to do in the office.'

'Have you?' Maggie looks up at him, wishes she hadn't sounded as surprised as she is. Perhaps Brenda has come here to spy, to see how they interact together, pick up on any cracks in their relationship.

'Won't be too long, darling.' He kisses the top of her head. 'We'll order in when I'm done...' He smiles at Brenda and she giggles girlishly, almost melts on the spot.

Maggie's skin suddenly prickles.

'Lovely to see you, Len!' Brenda gushes, her voice rising an octave.

'Lovely to see you too, Brenda. Thanks again for the flowers.'

'They reckon it happened on Wednesday night,' Brenda says conspiratorially once Len has left the room, 'and then her body was dumped in the river.'

'Oh, do they?' She polishes off her wine, hopes it might help wash away the internal struggle that's taking place within her.

'Actually, before I forget,' Maggie says, the alcohol giving her some Dutch courage, 'you didn't leave anything here on Saturday by chance, did you?'

'Leave something?' Brenda pulls her head into her chin. 'No, I don't think so. Like what?'

She doesn't want to answer but can see no other way around it. 'A... a scarf maybe.'

'A scarf?' Brenda says. 'Hmmm, no. What did it look like?'

It was a yes or no answer. She either left it or she didn't. Maggie watches Brenda carefully, studies her reaction intricately for anything unusual, any signs of awkwardness or guilt. She doesn't look particularly phased though. Maybe she's a practised liar. God, her head really hurts.

'Oh, just... I thought I would check, see if you'd lost one. Doesn't matter – it must belong to someone else.'

'Where did you find it?'

Maggie inwardly exhales. Can't she just drop it now?

'Back of a chair, in the marquee,' she says quickly, standing.

'I'll put those in some water.' She picks up the bouquet. 'Thank you again – they're really pretty.'

'You're welcome,' Brenda says, standing herself. She's taken the bait, or maybe her psychic powers have kicked in. Anyway, it looks as if she's got the message, thank God.

'Must get going now. Don't want to miss *Naked Attraction*.' She glances at the kitchen clock. 'It's on soon. Ron and I love it! We have such a laugh,' she adds, chuckling. 'Anyway, thanks for the wine, and thanks again for Saturday night – you guys sure know how to have a bun fight!'

For a second, Maggie thinks she has misheard her say 'bum fight'.

She walks her to the front door.

'You're so lucky you know,' Brenda says in a low voice.

'Lucky?'

'To have a husband like Len. That speech he gave at the party... and the way he looks at you. He clearly worships the ground you walk on.'

She sighs, and Maggie suddenly thinks she's been utterly ridiculous to even consider that Len would ever...

'Yeah, I put up with him.' She smiles, and Brenda laughs a little, embraces her suddenly, catching her off guard and overwhelming her with *that* perfume again, and once more her thoughts are taken from comfort to confusion.

'What is that perfume you're wearing?' she finds herself asking. 'I smelled it on you on Saturday night. It's very distinctive, unusual.'

Brenda looks pleased, pulls at her barely there camisole top. 'Oh this... it's called Angel, by Thierry Mugler. I'm so glad you like it! I get a lot of people commenting on it,' she says, swishing her hair again. 'Angel...' she says, her voice trailing off. 'So sad isn't it... poor little love. Her whole life ahead of her... and on the precipice of such big things too... I've no doubt she would've gone on to become super famous, just got that feeling you know. Anyway, *ciao bella*,' she says with a little wave.

11

Len has left her peppermint tea, oil of evening primrose capsules and a Hershey's Kiss on her bedside table, just as he does every night.

'I feel stuffed,' she says, swallowing one of the capsules with a mouthful of tea. 'We shouldn't have eaten so late – it always gives me such terrible indigestion.'

'The peppermint tea will help with that.'

She's aware of him watching her undress, can see that certain look in his eye that she's become so familiar with over the years, the one that silently informs her that her husband is feeling ardent. Maggie inwardly sighs with resignation. She knows she's not going to be able to get out of it, not this time – she's used up all her excuses and he'll definitely think something is up if she rebuffs him yet again. Better to get it over with. Hell, she might even enjoy it, if only she could relax for a second and stop all these crazy thoughts she's having – thoughts about affairs and bloodied scarves, about a murdered young woman and her husband not being home on the night Amelie was killed. Maggie used to enjoy making love to Len once –

surely she can again, *if she can only just bloody well relax and switch off.*

'Just going to brush the pegs,' she says, slipping into the en suite.

'Hurry back,' he replies, pulling the covers back to display his naked body, which is clearly ready for action. He still looks good – better than ever in fact – he's taken care of himself over the years. She supposes his profession has played a part in keeping the pounds off, all that manual work, carrying and lifting. For a man pushing sixty, he could easily pass for twenty years younger.

Suddenly she feels like crying. It's her hormones again, she's sure of it. She wishes she could turn the clock back, even as little as a year ago, before the menopause had gripped her and turned her into a dried-up, sexless, anxious wreck whose waistline seemed to be expanding as her husband's was shrinking. She used to like herself then.

Maggie shuts the door behind her and picks up her toothbrush, squirts some toothpaste on it haphazardly and begins to brush. Why does she feel like something terrible has happened – this nagging, sick sensation in her lower intestines that won't seem to soften? Why had Brenda turned up like that out of the blue uninvited? Had it really been to say thank you for the party or was it a smokescreen for something else? She hadn't sensed anything unusual in Brenda's demeanour, and Len had seemed otherwise distracted and—

Her greying complexion, eyes wide and bulbous, popping out of her skull manically. Her feet swinging above the floor, her brown summer sandals and painted toes... her mouth open, her purple tongue exposed...

Maggie drops her toothbrush in alarm. *Oh no, not again.* What's happening to her? This is twice in the space of a couple of days she's had the flashback of her mother's death – twice in quick succession after decades of nothing. Why now?

'You OK in there, chickadee?' Len calls out to her from the bedroom.

Bent over the sink, gripping it for support, Maggie attempts to control her breathing. Oh God, she can't deal with this.

Maybe it's her hormones that are sending her doolally and paranoid as hell?

'Mags? What you doing in there?'

Len is calling her again and she groans, rolls her eyes and takes another few deep breaths before entering the bedroom.

Maggie watches the red illuminated numbers on the alarm clock change in real time: 2:48... 49... 50... 51... She's been staring at it, unblinking, for what feels like hours now as Len makes soft snoring noises next to her.

Breaking her gaze from the clock finally, she glances at him. He looks so peaceful lying next to her, his chest gently rising and falling in time with his breath. She almost thinks to prod him awake – it doesn't seem fair him sleeping with such blissful ease while she's wracked with insomnia and her own increasingly disturbing thoughts.

The sex hadn't been so bad in the end, though perhaps a touch different than usual. A little rougher maybe. No, not rougher, more... *urgent,* yes, urgent was more accurate. Maybe she's just looking for it, overanalysing everything in minute detail and making her own head spin.

'*You look into everything too much, Margaret, ask too many questions.*' Her father's stern voice is like a trapped bug in her ear.

Len has always been a gentle, considerate lover, or so she thinks – the truth is she hasn't got much to go on by way of comparison. She's only slept with one other man her whole life – and even that had been a bone of contention between them. Len had been disappointed not to have been her first. That particular accolade had gone to a boy named Nigel Walters, a friend of the family – well, of her father's wife, Marietta, who he'd gone on to marry – almost immediately – after her mother had died. He didn't even have the good grace to wait six months. *Callous bastard.*

Her first time had been awkward and over very quickly, leaving a bemused Maggie to wonder just exactly what all the fuss was about. Of course, a couple of years later, once she'd met Len, she slowly began to realise...

She watches her husband sleeping soundly, his mouth slightly open, eyelids flickering, and feels the sudden urge to kiss him. She's loved him for so long she can't remember a time when she didn't. Maybe there never was one.

It's no good though – she can't sleep, not with her racing thoughts on top of the night sweats and heart palpitations. Maybe she'll take a Valium. She's sure she still has some in the medicine cabinet from years ago.

Slipping out of bed carefully, Maggie pads barefoot down the stairs. Len had been distracted this evening during Brenda's visit, engrossed on his phone. Should she look through it? The thought – a first throughout their marriage – deeply depresses her. She'll go into the office, read up on Amelie Fox, see what else she can find out about her, locate the image of her wearing that scarf. Maybe she'll begin searching for it again. It had to be *somewhere.*

It's a little cool in the office, causing her to wrap her thin robe around herself. Len's left the fan on. She switches it off, feels the room warming almost instantly.

Taking a seat on the leather swivel chair behind the desk, Maggie opens her husband's laptop, the screen illuminating in the dark. Although she has her own laptop, which she usually uses for doing the accounts and sending emails, very occasion- ally she uses this one, ostensibly to send e-mails on Len's behalf to clients, or to bring up spreadsheets and invoices. Len leaves most of the admin side of things to her; rarely uses it as far as she knows.

Maggie suddenly gets an attack of the guilts as the screen unlocks. She's snooping and it feels wrong.

She taps Amelie Fox's name into Google, watches as a list of news stories comes up. She clicks on the first one, begins reading.

Amelie Fox, 22, a successful social-media star and Instagram model, was found murdered on Saturday...

She skim reads the rest. Nothing she hasn't already seen or heard on the news.

She clicks on another link. The same... a bit of background on who she modelled for, some quotes from 'devastated' friends and family.

Sighing she scrolls up, clicks on 'images'. A montage of Amelie's face fills the screen, her beautiful bright smile and ash-white hair and— *Oh shit, it's there!*

Maggie clicks on the image, brings it up full screen. Her skin feels instantly cold again, and she can feel her heart rate increase, the sound of her own breathing as she leans in close. It's the same image of her she'd seen at Jazz's wine bar earlier that evening – Amelie smiling, the scarf draped around her slim neck.

Maggie studies it, cocks her head from side to side. She feels her chest deflate. There's no ambiguity, no mistaking it; it's definitely the same as the one she found in the loft – pink and silky, sheer almost, with those horrible little black skulls on it...

She moves the image to the side of the screen, remembering that she was going to check the bank statement, cross-reference the payment Len must have made for the hotel he and Bob had stayed at last Wednesday, the night of the vintage car fair at Riverdown.

Rubbing her eyes, Maggie stifles a yawn, puts her glasses on and logs on to her and Len's joint account.

Suddenly she feels foolish. If Len is hiding anything from her, he wouldn't be stupid enough to run the risk of her checking, would he? Of course he wouldn't. They share everything from their bed to their passwords – no secrets, none that she knows of anyway.

She scrolls down the pages of statements: £187.30 at Party-Wares Supplies – it was a lot of money to spend on balloons; £1850 at Costco – the not-so-cheap-after-all champagne and some ready-made canapes for the party; £98 at MAC – well, the eyeliner flick alone had been worth it...

She continues to scroll down until she reaches Wednesday last week, the twentieth. An ATM withdrawal at Eden Gorge petrol station – that was hers; she'd needed cash to pay the window cleaner, who came fortnightly on Thursdays; £75 in Tesco – again, definitely hers; £25 to Flock and Cattle, their local butcher – she'd bought short ribs for a slow-cooked supper, made a rich red wine sauce to go with them, one of her specialties that was always a big hit with Len.

She scrolls some more. Small payments: a direct debit to Len's mobile-phone provider, another transaction in M&S – a new cushion and some support knickers, if she remembers rightly – but there's nothing listed for the Platinum Inn.

Maggie scrolls up, rereads each transaction in case she's missed something. Nope, nothing: no booking, no payment, no reference number, zip.

She closes her eyes for a second, steadies her breathing once again. Why is it not showing up on the bloody bank statement? She categorically remembers the conversation they'd had between them about it. She'd ribbed him. 'Ooh, the Platinum Inn, and there I was feeling jealous!'

'It's local, just a bed to fall into for the night... I'll be in no state to drive home – you know what it's like when Bob and I get together for the car fair.'

'I've heard the all-you-can-eat breakfast is pretty good,' she'd continued to humour him. 'Unlimited sausages and everything.'

'Well, it was Bob's choice anyway.'

'Figures,' she'd remarked.

It was something of a running joke that Len's brother had 'very deep pockets... and very short arms!' He wasn't known for his generosity, especially when it involved anything of the fiscal variety. Not that he couldn't afford it mind. Though hardly on the bones of his backside, Bob had never quite mimicked Len's success in business, and therefore she and Len usually picked up the tab whenever they went out for dinners together – or at least they had when Heather had been alive. They've been out as a foursome just once since he married Julie – to a terrible and tacky themed Mexican restaurant of Julie's choice – and that had been tricky enough without the added awkwardness of bartering over the bill. Better just to pay it and avoid any red faces.

She can't imagine Bob picked up the hotel tab, but stranger things have happened she supposes. She wonders how to bring the subject up with Len without making it look as though she's been snooping. Maybe she'll simply ask Bob instead.

Maggie stares at Amelie Fox's photograph again, rubs her tired eyes. It's inconceivable that her Len could've ever had anything to do with the poor girl's death, isn't it? She almost laughs out loud. She hadn't really believed for a second...

She'll close the laptop, get herself off to bed and stop with all this nonsense. She'll make herself ill carrying on like this.

Maggie makes to shut the laptop down, but hang on, maybe she'll just check Len's internet browsing history, have a little squiz at whatever he's been looking at – more vintage cars no doubt – and... Maggie feels heat run the length of her body as she clicks on 'search history' and a list appears.

Hot Insta chicks uncensored

Dirty sluts on Instagram reveal all

Insta model's sex tape uncensored

Images of AngelFox Insta sensation

AngelFox gets fucked on camera

Suddenly she can't breathe, has to remind herself how. *In through the nose, out through the mouth. That's it.*

She feels lightheaded, like she might pass out or be sick, maybe both at the same time. *Oh no... oh no, no, no.* She squeezes her eyes shut, but when she opens them again, the list continues.

How to dispose of a dead body, the most effective methods

The five stages of decomposition in water

Asphyxiation: A painful death?

Her eyes are reading the words, but she doesn't see them, has to reread each of them over again to believe that she's really seeing what she's seeing, that she's not imagining it, not hallucinating, that it's *actually* real.

12

Maggie isn't sure if it's the sound of the laptop whirring that's penetrating through the silent darkness or her own laboured breathing. She clutches her chest through the thin cotton fabric of her robe. A strange sound escapes her lips – a low, desperate whine she's never heard herself make before.

Her first instinct is to slam the laptop shut, but her hands are frozen above the keyboard, and she's convinced that if she moves them, they'll disintegrate into dust. But what choice does she have but to investigate further? She *has* to see, to know.

Her finger hovers over the return key, and after two aborted attempts, she finally clicks on one of the links. Instinctively, her body moves backward in the chair, as if she's bracing herself – distancing herself – while she watches the little circle rotate round and round...

A few seconds pass before the screen lights up with a plethora of bright moving images that cause her to blink in quick succession, naked bodies in various uncompromising positions, jiggling across the screen in a vulgar montage.

'Unlimited Free Porn!' one of the banners screams out at

her in garish colours. 'Watch your favourite OnlyFans chicks getting fucked on camera – no subscription!'

'Live anal action with Lucy Lips.'

'Webcam girls in your area want to suck your—'

She closes her eyes, covers her mouth to catch the gasp. She can feel her breath, hot and heavy, on the palm of her hand, which is shaking so violently that she has to put the other on top of it to steady it. Her entire body beings to vibrate. If she wasn't already seated, she's pretty sure she would collapse.

In through the nose, Maggie. Breathe...

Her eyes lock on to the screen.

OnlyFans sensation AngelFox as you've *never* seen her before – 1 hour 17 minutes of pure filth, *only* and exclusively available on Porn Farm! Sign in now or click here to register for unlimited access for only £19.99 per month!

Despite every molecule in her body screaming at her not to – she knows what's coming and doesn't want to have to see it – Maggie, her chest heavy with adrenalin, clicks on the thumbnail image. It takes her to a sign-in page, asks for an email address and password.

Shit.

She clicks on the address box and the keychain notification appears. The details – username and password – have been saved to the computer already.

She stabs at the return key like it's a nuclear button.

Another box appears in the middle of the screen and begins to play. The footage is dark, shadowy – there's nothing in focus for the first few seconds. The camera wobbles, like someone is positioning it on something. It's apparent that this isn't going to be a slick production.

She opens the desk drawer, keeping her eyes firmly fixed on

the computer screen. Len keeps a spare pair of glasses in it, more than one pair probably. She blindly searches with her fingers until she finds them and puts them on. They're a little on the big side though, and annoyingly keep sliding down her nose.

She hears music playing in the background of the footage, barely audible behind the low hiss of the rudimentary recording, though she thinks she recognises this song... Chris Isaak's 'Wicked Games' maybe?

Amelie appears on screen first, her skin illuminated in the darkness as her torso comes into focus. She's wearing a neon-pink lacy bra and knickers, her long blonde hair hanging in waves around her slim shoulders. She shakes it out, positions herself on the bed. She's not looking directly at the camera, doesn't appear to be aware of it even as she moves unconsciously in various poses on the bed, then takes a sip of something from a glass that's out of shot.

Maggie makes that strange, low whining noise again, one she doesn't recognise as coming from her. She feels like she's spying on an intimate private moment, no better than a peeping Tom looking through a keyhole, a voyeur. She gets the distinct – and sickening – impression that Amelie isn't, wasn't, even aware that she's being filmed.

Maggie's hand is clutching at her chest again, her nails clawing at the skin on her clavicle until it's sore, but still she can't avert her eyes. Amelie's face, even in the dim light of the recording, is recognisable, the ice-white luminous smile, those gravity-defying cheekbones.

She's just so young and beautiful...

Tears forming behind Maggie's eyes start to blur the edges of her vision, and she presses her thumb and forefinger on them underneath the lenses, squeezes them together tightly.

He enters left of screen, the boy – man – it's difficult to tell his age as the footage is so poor. It's as if someone has smeared the lens with a layer of Vaseline. He speaks, but it's little more than an inaudible low hum.

She leans in closer towards the screen – she doesn't want to turn the sound up, can't bear to, and she certainly doesn't want to wake Len.

He positions himself behind her, his torso in view of the camera. He has well-defined abdominal muscles, a six pack, and muscular arms with visible tattoos, though the image isn't sharp enough to know exactly what of. He's holding something, a rope... no... oh God, it's *a scarf*.

Maggie leaps up in her seat so suddenly that the glasses she's wearing slip clean off her face.

Shit!

She scrabbles to retrieve them from the floor. Is that... is that *the* scarf? She can't tell – it's too dark, too grainy, the quality too poor.

He loops it around Amelie's neck. Maggie swallows, blinks rapidly. She really wants to look away but it's like a pair of invisible hands have her in a chokehold. She needs to know if that's the same scarf she found in her loft; she needs to see what her husband has clearly been watching in secret.

Amelie is talking to him, turning her head behind her to say something, but it's impossible to know what.

He begins to have sex with her.

Maggie recoils in shock as he slaps her on the backside with one hand and pulls at the scarf around her neck with the other, like she's an animal on a lead and—

No, no, that's enough!

She snaps the laptop shut, sits motionless in the dark for a moment, the sound of her breathing amplified as she tries to absorb what she's just seen, to process it all. How *could* Len, how could *her* Len, have been secretly viewing this kind of filth? *Pornography.* Low-grade, grubby amateur pornography featuring these young people, people his own daughter's age?

Suddenly she feels dirty herself, sullied, like she needs to scrub herself clean in the shower. Why has Len been watching this particular video? By all accounts, there's certainly enough better quality free porn available to watch – why this one of Amelie Fox? Why had he googled 'asphyxiation', 'how to dispose of a dead body effectively' and 'the five stages of decomposition in water'? Why, why, *why*?

Panic ignites around her like she's been set on fire. And it burns. She *knows* there can only really be one explanation, but she's struggling to allow herself to even entertain it for a second – it simply won't form as a genuine solid truth in her mind and instead shapeshifts into uncomfortable cognitive dissonance.

Maggie realises she's whimpering again – primal, guttural sounds that are pushing their way up her diaphragm through to her larynx.

She holds her throat, feels the low vibrations against her fingertips as she tries to keep the anguish from exploding out of her mouth. Yet despite all of this, in spite of what this is all increasingly beginning to look and feel like, she still hopes that somehow she's got it all wrong, that she *must* have, that she's putting two and two together and making thirteen, that she's being overdramatic, looking for things that can appear one way but can be explained away. She's been here before after all, after her mother died.

Suicide they'd called it, but as time passed, and she'd begun to comprehend the dynamics of her parents' volatile relationship, Maggie had started to experience a crippling sense of doubt as to what had *really* happened. As she'd grown older, she'd become more and more convinced that her father had something to do with her mother's death. That he was responsible for it. She found it hard to believe her mother would ever have willingly chosen to leave her then ten-year-old only daughter without a mother, and this feeling had only increased with time, not least when she became a mother herself.

'*She was mad as a two-bob watch.*' That's how her father had insensitively put it whenever she'd tentatively questioned him about her mother, about who she really was and why she'd done what she did.

'*She wasn't a well woman,*' he would simply tell her with a breathtaking absence of compassion. '*She was mentally ill, unhinged, suffered from all sorts of issues: depression, bipolar, personality disorders – you name it – and it grew worse after you were born,*' he'd added coldly, a statement that had only compounded her sense of guilt that it was somehow all her fault.

Her father was a serial adulterer and had been conducting an affair with her mother's best friend, Marietta, at the time of her supposed suicide. Marietta had been one in a long line of mistresses though, and Maggie had wondered if it had been this final straw – or perhaps even something more egregious – that had led her mother to make such a fatal decision. Had he driven her to it? Had he driven her to such despair by his consistent betrayals that it had sent her mad in the end and she'd seen no other way out of her misery? Or had he actually – and not just metaphorically – given her the rope himself?

She'd even put it to him once, asked him outright when she'd been a defiant fifteen-year-old. It's the one and only time she can recall her father ever hitting her, slapping her hard across the face with the back of his hand. She can still feel the sting on her cheek now as she recollects, the hot salty tears that had followed, burning against her raw angry skin. He'd blamed the therapist she'd been seeing at the time for 'putting ridiculous ideas' in her head and had swiftly recruited a new one.

She'd left home at the earliest opportunity after that incident, unable to tolerate her father's lack of empathy any longer, which had been far more damaging than any slap could've ever been.

'*You're just like her,*' he'd said as she'd thrown her suitcases in the back of her old VW beetle. *'It's hereditary, you know, madness – passed down through the genes!'*

Bipolar, manic depressive, HPD, that callous bastard could call it what he wanted. To Maggie's knowledge, her mother had never been professionally diagnosed with any of those things – but she certainly hadn't been imagining her father's myriad affairs, that much she did know. He'd hardly even bothered to hide them throughout his marriage. If he hadn't physically handed her mother that rope, then he'd as good as killed her with his psychological torment.

Maggie had been seventeen when she'd finally turned her back on him and his deceitful, jealous, money-grabbing wife.

She wonders again why she's suddenly begun experiencing flashbacks of her mother's death after so long. She's sure it's a sign somehow, a bad omen.

She looks down at the closed laptop. The happy little apple on the lid seems so incongruous to how she feels, and she places a hand over it. She wonders when Len started watching porn – pornography featuring dead murdered young women, women young enough to be his own daughter. A couple of years ago? Five? Ten? More? Has he always been into this kind of degrading filth and she just hasn't known about it? That just can't be possible, can it?

But then she's reminded of the conversation she'd had with the girls last night at Jazz's, the one about old Whatshisface and his wife, the bloke who'd been dressing up in her clothes for the past forty years without her having had even the slightest inkling – well, according to Lorraine anyway. Has she been in denial all this time? Has she seen it but *not* seen it, ignored the red flags? Has she really been living with a pervert, a misogynist, *a cold-bloodied murderer*?

Maggie suddenly stands with purpose. She needs more. She needs more evidence, something concrete.

Still shaking, she attempts to get a grasp on her thoughts as she makes her way from the office, but they're slippery like mercury, and keep sliding back and forth inside her head. Then it strikes her: *the garage.* If Len's going to hide anything – like that wretched scarf – she's pretty sure that's where he would stash it. She never goes in the garage, and if she does, it's only ever briefly to tell him something like 'dinner's ready'.

She sees him in her mind's eye, sliding out from underneath whatever vintage car he's working on, his grey overalls oily, that distinct smell of petrol and metal and testosterone in the air. *'Be right with you, chickadee!'*

She tightens her thin robe around herself, as much for protection as anything, and makes her way through the house, down the hallway, through the kitchen and out onto the patio. The internal door to the garage is locked as it usually is of a night – it contains Len's most prized possession after all – and she punches in the security code – 1999, a nod to Prince, one of their favourite artists of the nineties.

Glancing behind her, she gingerly pushes the door open.

13 DAN

'Bring me up to speed on the Fox case, Riley,' my formidable boss Gwendoline Archer says abruptly without looking up at me from her pristine desk, where she's busying herself on her laptop. 'I hope you've some good news for me.'

Good news for *her*? I was thinking more along the lines of good news for Amelie's parents, Helen and Tony, but I'm not about to argue with her. I get the distinct impression she's not in the brightest of moods.

'Have you seen the news?' she says, her voice rising an octave. 'Bloody press scaremongering everyone, riling up the local community, suggesting there's a killer on the loose, a killer in their midst who may strike again. And it hasn't helped that the girl was somewhat of a media sensation already. I mean, look at her – her picture is everywhere, absolutely everywhere.' She spits the words out crossly.

'Maybe that's a good thing, ma'am?' I suggest, though I know I'm playing devil's advocate by verbalising it. She's right though – the press have gone wild for Amelie Fox. Nothing like a pretty face I suppose.

'We'll need to organise a press conference,' she says. 'Try

and put the locals' minds at rest. I've been hearing reports that they're organising a meeting among themselves. Goodness only knows why or what for – we found the body after all. They should just let us do our bloody jobs – we don't want a mutiny on our hands.'

Yep, she's definitely pissed off. And yep, it's all about *her*. Again.

I bite my tongue so hard that my left eye begins to water.

'Well, we can't really give any assurances at this stage, ma'am,' I say, quickly adding, 'about a killer being on the loose I mean. Because there *is* a killer on the loose.'

She looks up at me so sharply that I feel a stab of adrenalin in my solar plexus.

'Yes, and it's your *job* to catch them,' she adds, clearly not impressed by my response. 'So... what have we got?'

'DNA,' I say brightly in an attempt to lift her spirits. It's three letters every copper worth their badge likes to hear in a murder case. 'Semen.'

'Do we know whose yet?'

'Not yet, but it'll be run through the database of course, so here's hoping that there's a mat—'

'I'm not interested in *hope*, Dan,' she interrupts, unblinking. 'I'm interested in facts and findings. What about a murder weapon?'

I detect a note of urgency in her voice, like there's something I don't yet know but am about to. It's disconcerting.

'Nothing yet. Preliminaries suggest she was struck with a sharp object first and that a ligature was used to strangle her, an item of clothing most probably. We retrieved her clothing from the river: a pair of shorts, shirt, jacket, pair of trainers, under-wear... it's all been confirmed as being Amelie's.'

'By the parents?'

'Yes, and the flatmate, Holly Redwood – she says it was

what she was wearing the last time she saw her on the Wednesday she was killed. But—'

'But?'

'But there was a scarf, a designer scarf.' The designer's name has completely escaped me. I'm hardly what you'd call a fashion maven after all, so perhaps I can be forgiven for this oversight 'And it's missing. Holly Redwood says she was definitely wearing it when she last saw her, but it hasn't been recovered.'

'And you think it might've been used to kill her?'

'Yes,' I say, surprising myself with the clarity in which I answer because as yet I have no evidence of this. 'Actually I do.'

'You think the killer took it? Disposed of it?'

'Possibly, ma'am.' In actual fact however, my instincts are telling me that whoever killed Amelie kept hold of it, as a memento perhaps. But Archer wants facts, not intuition, so I keep my mouth shut, sensing it may irritate her further.

'Keep looking for it,' she says. 'Find it.'

'Well, that's the idea, ma'am...'

She gives me that sharp look again.

'They've dredged the river – twice in fact.'

Archer sighs. 'And what about the photograph... the one she posted on Instagram on Thursday?'

'Tech are looking into it, and we've been in touch with Meta... Instagram... to see if they can shed any more light – if it might have been scheduled or not – but they're notoriously slow and somewhat unhelpful.'

'Tell them they'll be penalised if they don't act quick sharp – we'll do them for obstructing a murder inquiry.'

Blimey, her feathers really are ruffled.

'I mean it, Dan. I want all hands on deck on this – no slip-ups, no procrastinating...'

Procrastinating? I'm mildly affronted. Perhaps it shows

because her tone softens somewhat. 'Look,' she says, glancing over my shoulder. 'Shut the door, will you?'

I nod, do as I'm told. It seems she wants to tell me something in private.

She begins rearranging the pens on her desk, placing them onto the table one next to the other with precise equidistance in between. She fiddles around with them until she appears satisfied. Aside from her raging OCD, Archer is something of an enigma really – I still don't know much about her other than the usual salacious nick rumours, like she's supposed to have killed both her ex-husbands for example, who, it appears, respectively died rather unexpectedly. I doubt it's true of course – that my super is a double murderer – in which case it's rather sad all told. Clearly she's no stranger to loss.

'This is... well, this is somewhat delicate, Dan.'

She actually looks nervous, something of a first, and this makes me feel nervous by proxy.

'I need you to be... well... I need you to be *discreet*.'

'It's my middle name, ma'am,' I say.

'It can't go any further than this office, you understand?'

Now I *am* intrigued. 'Of course, ma'am.'

'I have a connection to Amelie Fox – a personal one.' She speaks quickly, avoids eye contact. 'I know Tony Fox.'

'Oh,' I say, trying to keep the surprise from registering on my face. 'You know the Foxes?'

'That's not what I said. I know *Tony* Fox.' She clears her throat slightly, adding, 'Personally.'

'Personally? I...' The penny drops. Good Lord! Archer... *and Tony Fox*? I try not to look stunned but I fear my body language may be leaking. I open my mouth to speak but nothing comes out.

'Look, it's all rather... *embarrassing*.'

She's practically squirming in her swivel chair, and while I hate to admit it, I do get the slightest frisson of satisfaction watching her discomfort.

'We... we sometimes play golf together,' she explains, still averting her gaze.

Well, I've certainly never heard it called that before!

'We occasionally share a drink... in the clubhouse after a game. I never met the girl,' she adds, 'Amelie, just so you know, and I'm not familiar with his wife either...'

'Helen,' I say, and she finally glances at me. At least she has the good grace to appear somewhat ashamed I suppose, unless I'm simply imagining it. But Gwendoline Archer and Tony Fox? It's an unusual pairing by anyone's standards. I've only met Tony Fox once and in terrible circumstances to boot. But first impressions are everything in this game, rightly or wrongly. To me he presented as a man's man, a bit rough around the edges I suppose, despite the slick, monied appearance, but he seemed devoted to his family. It's a bit of a stretch of the imagination to put him together with the fragrant Gwendoline Archer. The words 'chalk' and 'cheese' spring to mind, but each to their own I suppose.

'I'm telling you about it now, about my association with Tony Fox, because I suspect you would've found out anyway given how thorough you are.'

I'll take that as a compliment.

'I'd... he'd – we'd both – rather it wasn't something that was made public. We don't want people to think that there's any nepotism involved, any special treatment in the investigation because of our rela— our *friendship*.'

I nod, though I suspect nepotism is the least of her concerns in truth. It would be an absolute scandal if the press got wind that the super has been knocking off the murder victim's father in a clandestine affair, and I've no doubt she knows this as well as I do.

'Obviously, my main concern is for the Foxes – Helen Fox in particular,' she says, briefly looking down at her pens.

I can tell this is excruciating for her.

'She's just lost her daughter after all and...' She sighs, meets my eye. 'And well, the thing is, Dan, I couldn't possibly have known that this was going to happen, that Amelie was going to end up murdered, dumped in a river somewhere, you understand... just all terrible bad luck.'

Luck. There it is again. It works both ways I suppose.

'Your secret is safe with me, ma'am,' I say with as little emotion as I can manage.

She visibly bristles, clearly loath that she's been forced to impart such personal information.

'Listen, Dan, it wasn't... well, it was never – it isn't—'

I watch her struggle to get the words out with a guilty sense of schadenfreude.

'It wasn't anything serious, you know?'

Ah, so it was just about sex then. I'm not sure if that makes it better or worse, but I suppose it's nothing if not honest.

'Yes, ma'am, thank you for giving me the... heads-up,' I say, clearing my throat.

She smiles at me thinly. 'So, any idea of what the motive could be? And before you ask, I have no idea, no insider information – we've never spoken about our respective personal lives at any length.'

I'm guessing talking wasn't high on their agenda then.

Motive in murder is everything. If you think about it, take away the words 'in murder' and it's still a true enough statement. Everything we do in life is driven by motive and purpose.

'You said something about semen... you think she was raped?'

'Inconclusive I'm afraid.'

'But you think it was a sexually motivated crime?'

I suppose it would be fairly reasonable to draw this conclusion, just as I did initially. After all, Amelie Fox was a young, beautiful model, and she was found stripped naked with semen in her vagina. It stands to reason that this could be the case. And yet... I don't know.

'I think she knew her assailant,' I say, non-committal. 'It feels very personal.'

'Tell me about it!' She rolls her eyes, affording me a brief flash of authenticity.

She clears her throat again. 'A stalker or an ex-boyfriend?'

I shrug. 'We're looking into it.'

'Yes, but not some random killer – you don't think some stranger just plucked her from nowhere... wrong place, wrong time and all of that?'

'No,' I say. 'I don't think it was random at all. And I think she was killed in her apartment.'

Once again I'm shocked that I've verbalised my suspicion because as of yet we have no evidence whatsoever to support this.

'There were no signs of a break-in, no robbery, which is why I'm almost certain she knew whoever killed her, or was certainly not afraid of them – initially anyway.'

Out of my peripheral vision, I can see Davis standing outside Archer's office on her tiptoes, her head bobbing up and down over the frosted glass. She knocks on the door.

'Come in,' Archer says.

Davis pops her head around the door. She's holding what looks like a half-eaten sandwich. 'Sorry to interrupt, ma'am. Gov, I need to see you.'

'What is it, DS Davis?' Archer says. She clearly has a vested interest in this case which isn't great for me personally – or the team incidentally. It means she's going to be even more up my backside than usual. *Great.*

'Sex tape, boss,' Davis says.

Archers' eyes widen and she stands suddenly, the momentum sending her pens rolling across the desk.

'Oh Jesus *Christ!*' She runs her hand through her immaculate hairstyle. 'How on earth have they got hold of that?'

Davis and I exchange a look of curious confusion.

'Umm... Amelie Fox's sex tape,' she says gingerly, glancing at myself and Archer simultaneously. 'The one Holly told us about – we've found it online.'

Archer sits down, immediately composes herself. Only the red blotches creeping up from her neck gives away her panic.

'I'll be right there, Lucy,' I say, standing. 'Ma'am.'

She waves me away with a hand, doesn't look up at me as she begins repositioning her pens.

'What in God's name was all *that* about?' Davis asks as we make our way back towards the incident room. 'Archer looked like she was about to spontaneously combust just then!'

I glance at her. 'Honestly,' I say, watching as she hastily chomps on her ham-and-pickle sandwich, 'you really *don't* want to know.'

14 MAGGIE

The light is beginning to change outside as the night slowly gives way to morning, gradient layers casting a gunmetal ombre hue across the lawn of her garden. The birds will start with the first of their morning song soon – she thinks she can hear a chirrup or two already. A rush of cold air causes an intake of breath as the door opens.

'Bloody hell,' she whispers to herself, wrapping her arms around herself. She wishes she'd worn her fluffy slippers now – the pink ones Len had bought her for Christmas last year – the concrete is so cold it burns her bare feet.

There's a light in here somewhere, next to the security alarm. She feels for it in the dark, presses it. It turns on with a hum, the UV tubes flickering noisily to life.

The garage is Len's domain, his 'secret place' as he calls it, which somehow now, for the first time, strikes her as sinister. Her eyes scan the room as she breathes in the strong smell of oil or diesel, or maybe it's petrol – she's not sure what the difference is, though no doubt Len could tell her in detail.

He keeps it neat and tidy at least. There's a workbench towards the rear, a vice attached to it. Tools – most of which she can't identify – hang neatly on a rail above. The shelves are stacked with clear plastic boxes all clearly labelled with black marker pen. A collection of cloths – shammy leathers and old tea towels that she recognises have disappeared from her kitchen over the years – hang on hooks beneath them. Cans of oil are lined up on an adjacent shelf. Len's trusty, rusty, battered old metal toolbox – Christ, it's got to be older than their daughter – takes pride of place on the workbench.

She stares at the huge, magnificent vintage car, eyes it cautiously. It almost seems to be breathing somehow, like it's alive. 'A moving masterpiece' as Len had proudly proclaimed it – a pale pink Cadillac Eldorado 1959 Biarritz model. She only knows this because she's heard him repeat the make and model a hundred times now. He's even named it 'The Pink Lady'. She supposes it *is* quite a showstopper with its sleek long body and plethora of chrome finishings.

She bends down to open a cabinet. It's full of junk, odd metal objects that again she can't identify but assumes are car-related; rusty, scratched old tobacco tins filled with tacks and nails; faded newspapers; some old garden shoes; a dustpan and brush; some WD-40; turps and paintbrushes...

She closes it again, walks around in small circles, her body seemingly on autopilot.

Pulling open some drawers, she quickly realises there's nothing to be found in them, just bric-a-brac, car stuff, old papers, garage receipts and car manuals that she thumbs through like a pack of cards before discarding...

A pair of Len's overalls are hanging on the back of the door and she checks the pockets – they're empty save for a bit of fluff and some sweet wrappers. She wonders where that fluff that you always seem to find in old pockets comes from.

Fishing through some battered cardboard boxes, she finds old vintage-car magazine subscriptions – she sorts through them briefly but nothing, *nada*. She's exhausted everywhere – there's nowhere else to look.

Maggie exhales loudly, her whole body visibly deflating. Suddenly she feels like she could curl up right here on the concrete floor and go to sleep, but how can she sleep? The scarf, the pornography, what creepy Clive had said about seeing the car when Len shouldn't have been home in the first place, the missing hotel transaction, *the whole bloody lot of it...* much as she wants to, she can't simply deny these things to herself, can she? On their own, they don't mean so much, but put them all together...

The birds are beginning to wake up outside now, their earlier sporadic chirps turning into a melodic soprano chorus—

The car! She almost smacks her own forehead. How stupid of her! She'll check inside the car.

She makes to open the door but it's locked. Keys. Where are the keys?

With a renewed sense of purpose, she scans the garage, turning 360 degrees. Were they in one of the drawers? Has she missed them? She'll have to go back and look through them all again now.

She opens one, sorts through it – more junk, but hang on! There, underneath the alarm, a set of hooks, bunches of keys...

She goes to them. There's more than one set. Which ones open the Cadillac?

She removes them from the hooks with shaking fingers and they jiggle with the momentum like they're alive. Immediately she begins to try and test them in the lock on the driver's side. No good, she'll try another... and another... and another.

They slip between her fingers as she attempts to find a match, tells herself to keep going, keep trying and eventually... bingo! The lock makes a loud clicking noise as it releases, sending such a rush of adrenalin through her that she thinks –

her pelvic floor not being what it used to – that she might pee herself right here on the floor.

Inside, the car smells old, like it's somehow retained the odour of its past owners, and she detects the faintest hint of tobacco – real tobacco, sweet and moist, like the old stuff you could buy in a tin once upon a time.

The interior of the Cadillac is undeniably impressive: cream leather, chrome, glass, bespoke finishes... Beautiful really, she supposes, now that she looks at it properly. The craftsman-ship and attention to detail is incredible – none of the mass-produced plastic crap that you saw today.

Len's voice resonates in her head. *'They don't make 'em like they used to, chickadee.'*

She checks the glovebox first – it makes sense to. It squeaks loudly as it opens, and she winces.

It's empty.

She checks underneath the seats, between them, in the side pockets... No scarf – no nothing. She even lifts the carpets in the footwell, runs her fingers underneath them in case it's hidden there.

Shaking her head, Maggie sits still for a moment and tries to filter her thoughts. Her head feels like a lead balloon on her shoulders, cumbersome and heavy.

It's no good. She leans forward, rests her forehead on the large thin steering wheel and: *'Beeeeeep!'* The sudden loud noise, amplified in the cold dark garage, causes her to yelp in shock and jump backward in the seat. Her heart starts pounding painfully, rapidly, in her chest.

'Oh Jesus...' She's only gone and leaned on the bloody horn.

You stupid, stupid woman! Will Len have heard it? Their bedroom is all the way at the back of the house, but still...

She needs to get out of here quickly.

Maggie makes to open the door, but then she remembers

she hasn't checked the boot – or the 'trunk' as Len often corrects her in a bad American accent.

Exiting with haste, she closes the car door as quietly as possible and runs to the back of the vehicle.

Shit. It's locked.

She rakes her hands through her hair. *Shit, shit, shit.*

She looks at the internal door of the garage, listens out for anyone coming, praying no one's heard her. Remy sleeps like the dead, but Len's a sporadically light sleeper. She sometimes jokes that a sparrow's fart could wake him.

Her adrenalin is in overdrive as she fiddles with the keys again, jiggling them in the lock as she simultaneously looks behind her.

It won't open.

Nooo, please, she doesn't have time for this. Surely the same bloody key opens the trunk, doesn't it? And if not, why not?

She releases a low, frustrated growl between clenched teeth as she forces the key into the lock.

No good. It's not the right one. *Bloody hell!*

Exhaling heavily, Maggie, exhausted, her heart like a water balloon in her chest, slumps down over the trunk and— Pop!

Immediately, she stands upright and presses the lid. A warm rush of satisfaction floods through her as she watches it lift slowly. Suddenly she wants to laugh out loud at the absurdity of it all. 'Oh thank God...'

She peers inside, gets a waft of that same smell – sweet tobacco and faded memories – but her euphoria is quickly extinguished when she sees that it's empty, save for the carpet it's lined with.

Every ounce of oxygen in her lungs is lost as she exhales again, but she runs her fingers around the edges of the carpet, up underneath the sides and... Her eyes flick to the internal door again as she attempts to peel it back carefully. Len no doubt knows every single inch of his 'other wife' and she doesn't want him to start asking questions.

She's met with a little resistance though and begins to tug at the carpet a little harder. Still mindful of causing damage, she unwraps it like it's a fragile piece of china, peeling it back from the metal and—

Maggie gasps, takes a step or two backward, her hand flying up to her mouth again. *Oh my God!* She sees a corner of something, *something pink.* She recognises it instantly.

Her heart banging against the thin fabric of her robe, light fingers shaking with adrenalin, she tentatively steps forward and quickly but gently pulls it out from underneath the carpet like a magician revealing a trick from a sleeve. Holding it between her thumb and forefinger, she reminds herself to breathe.

She's found it, she's found the scarf and—

The sound of the internal garage door opening startles her so much that she drops it, before swiftly scooping it up again and shoving it into her robe pocket.

'Mags... *Maggie*, is that... is that *you*?' Len is standing in the doorway, the outline of his body highlighted against the darkness. He's in his paisley pyjama bottoms, naked from the waist up, and his hair is sticking up on end. He rubs his eyes. 'What the bloody hell are you doing in *here*?'

15

The image of Len as he'd stood in the doorway to the garage, blinking at her with surprise and confusion, flashes up in her head.

'What the hell are you doing in here, Maggie? It's 3.30 in the morning!'

She'd been paralysed to the spot, unable to move her feet, like they'd been superglued to the cold concrete beneath her. She'd noticed that the tip of the scarf was hanging out of her robe pocket and had hastily stuffed it back in.

'I... I thought I heard something – something woke me. I... I couldn't sleep.' Well the last part had been true at least. 'I came down to look – thought I heard someone,' she'd repeated, 'In here. I thought maybe it was you...'

He'd looked at her curiously, taken a step towards her.

Instinctively she'd recoiled from him.

'Heard something? Heard what? Mags... are you OK? You look terrified.'

He'd been right: she was terrified... of him, of what he'd been looking at, of what he might have done.

'You should have woken me if you thought you'd heard something. Why didn't you wake me?'

She'd opened her mouth to speak, but nothing had come out. She'd stared at him like she was seeing him for the very first time. He'd looked almost unrecognisable, like a stranger.

'You were fast asleep. I didn't want to disturb you. Just thought I'd come down and see...'

'In the garage? But no one can get in here, Mags,' he'd said, taking hold of her wrists lightly with his hands. 'It's alarmed up to the hilt, daftie.'

'I know...' She'd nodded. His touch had made her feel like bursting into tears, but she hadn't been able to pull her hands away. He'd have sensed something was wrong, *really wrong*. 'I just thought... well, I – maybe it was a rat... probably just a rat.' It had sounded so pathetic that even she hadn't been convinced. How would she have heard a rat in the garage all the way from their bedroom? Did he suspect something? Did he believe her? she'd wondered.

'You're shaking,' he'd said, frowning. 'Mags, you're scaring me.'

She was scaring *him*? Oh, the irony!

'I'm just cold,' she'd squeaked back, her larynx tight with panic. 'It's nothing. I'm... I'm just imagining things.'

'I'll go and check the house again, put your mind at rest eh,' he'd said gently, looking past her at the car. 'She's still in one piece at least.' He'd smiled at her, then kissed her on the top of the head, and she'd tried not to stiffen, kept her hand balled in a tight fist inside her robe pocket, clutching the scarf.

'You go and wait for me in the kitchen while I have a quick look around, make sure there are no *masked intruders*.'

He'd been making light of it a little then, which was good – it signalled he wasn't overly suspicious.

As instructed, she'd gone to the kitchen and slid, exhausted, into one of the dining chairs and placed her head into her hands. She'd have to sit on them if she couldn't get the damn things to stop shaking.

The few minutes he'd been gone had felt like an eternity. She'd wanted to go back to bed, to curl up in a ball and sleep, wake up in the morning realising it was all a dream – just an ugly, abhorrent nightmare.

'Coast is clear,' he'd said, eventually rejoining her. 'You scared the bloody shit out of me you know! I thought you'd been abducted or something when I realised you weren't in bed and I couldn't find you downstairs.'

'I'm sorry,' she'd said without looking at him. She *couldn't* look at him. She'd seen enough already for one night.

'Let me make you a peppermint tea, chickadee, hmm?' He'd cocked his head to the side. 'Then we'll get off back to bed. You look a little peaky, you know... I hope you're not sickening for something.'

He'd looked at her with an expression of such concern that she'd almost fallen apart, bits of her dropping off – an arm, a foot, an ear – hitting the kitchen tiles until she was just a pile of broken appendages. She'd certainly felt sick all right, absolutely sick to the pit of her stomach.

She'd watched him as he'd filled the kettle with cold water from the tap, the images from his computer flashing up in her mind like angry final demands: *her long blonde hair, the scarf around her neck as the man had pulled at it like a dog lead...* She'd shaken her head to try and dissolve them, but they couldn't be unseen and she'd felt it coming, the big question that her conscious mind had been refusing to ask her – to even entertain, it was that preposterous – but was now gaining strength and building momentum.

'We'll take these upstairs,' he'd said, holding the steaming mugs carefully in both hands. She hadn't wanted any bloody peppermint tea and had suddenly imagined herself throwing the burning hot liquid all over his face, envisaged his shock and pain as the boiling water made impact with his skin.

'Did you have your Hershey's Kiss tonight?' he'd asked her as he'd snuggled next to her in bed. She'd been sure to have her back to him.

'Of course,' she'd answered, willing herself not to break down crying, because that's what she'd felt like doing – crying and screaming herself hoarse until there was not a drop of moisture left in her.

Did he know? Did he suspect she'd been snooping, that she'd found the scarf and was starting to put two and two together? Was he going to kill her too? In that moment, part of her had even hoped that he might just to release her from her torment.

'Get some sleep now,' he'd said. 'The drama's over.'

Only she'd had a dreadful sinking sensation that it had only really just begun.

That morning, when Len had left for work – he was doing some construction inspection or another down at that new building site in Eden Place – she'd replaced the scarf back where she'd found it; in the trunk of Len's Cadillac before heading off in her car to Bob and Julie's. She couldn't run the risk of him discovering it was missing. He would know that she'd found it, that it was the reason she'd been snooping around in the garage. What would he do if he knew that she knew his terrible secret? A man capable of strangling and killing a young woman and dumping her body in a river was capable of anything, wasn't he? Killing a stranger was one thing, but murdering his own wife? His chickadee?

She hadn't had a second's peace the rest of the night, had lain awake for hours, rigid with fear and paranoia, with disgust and nausea. The few times he'd touched her, his skin making contact with her body, she'd flinched, like she was shrinking, attempting to make herself smaller, invisible, to disappear. And yet still she couldn't believe that Len would ever hurt her. In over three decades, he'd never so much as laid a finger on her – he'd hardly even raised his voice for Christ's sake.

When she'd finally given in to her body's demand for rest, it had been shallow and fitful, hovering precariously somewhere between sleep and consciousness, her thoughts slipping into terrifying dream-like visions of his hands snaking around her throat, choking her; paralysed by panic as she struggled to retain oxygen, desperately trying to prise his fingers from the soft flesh of her neck.

'You should have just left well alone, Maggie. Now look what you've gone and made me do…'

Maggie's phone rings, startling her so violently that she yelps. She's an absolute train wreck, a tangled ball of jangling nerve endings.

'Hey, Mum,' her son's voice rings out from the loudspeaker, and it gives her an instant and much welcome lift. She automatically clicks into 'mum' mode.

'Darling, how are you?' Is it just her, or does she detect the lightest hint of concern in his inflection? Panic spikes through her sharply. 'Is everything OK?' she asks measuredly, careful not to allow it to show in her voice. 'Everything's OK, isn't it? Is Casey OK, and that little growing grandchild of mine?'

Maggie realises she's been so preoccupied with everything else going on in her crowded mind that she's taken her usual close eye off the ball elsewhere in her family. Generally, she's on high alert where her son is concerned due to his track record. She'd missed it all once before and isn't about to make the same mistake twice. He's only twenty-four after all, young to be a father, by today's standards at least, and she worries if the thought of impending fatherhood is all a bit overwhelming for him after all. It wasn't a planned pregnancy, despite them all being over the moon about it. She needs to keep a close eye on him, make sure his anxiety levels are in check and that he stays on an even keel. Anxiety, such a dreadful affliction, and she should know – she's suffered with it as long as she can remember, and no less after her mother's death. Who wouldn't? she supposes, though she can't help wondering if it's simply a family trait on her side, one she's regrettably passed on to her sensitive, emotionally delicate son.

'Yeah, yeah, all good. The morning sickness has passed now, pretty much. She reckons she can already feel the baby moving inside her, but I'm not so sure. It's a little early, isn't it? Probably just wind or something!'

He laughs and she joins in, though she's only a breath away from it sliding into a manic, hysterical scream.

She should take the scarf straight to the police station, shouldn't she? She knows that this would absolutely, unequivocally be the right thing to do, the morally correct course of action to take. She should explain to the police where she found it and what she's seen on her husband's laptop. She should tell them that Len was away the night of Amelie's murder, yet he'd been seen driving the Cadillac in the early hours of the next morning by a neighbour and that he'd got rid of some old clothes – more evidence possibly – very soon after, which was highly uncharacteristic, not to mention suspicious.

But... but how *can* she do that? It's all hearsay really, isn't it – circumstantial? Though of course the scarf would be forensically examined and if it did turn out to be Amelie's then how could Len explain it being in the boot of his car?

'She's going for a scan tomorrow, sixteen weeks. I'm... I'm...'

'You're what, darling?' Maggie's spike of panic begins to spread throughout her body. 'What is it? *Talk to me.*'

Lewis pauses. 'I'm... *nervous,*' he says quietly. 'What if... there's something wrong with the baby?'

Maggie exhales. 'Oh, darling,' she says, a touch relieved, 'it's perfectly normal to feel nervous when you go for a scan. Lord knows I was when I went for both yours, and your sister's too.

It's all part and parcel of being a parent I'm afraid, sweetheart. The worry begins in the womb, and the truth is, you never stop worrying, no matter how old they are.'

'Great,' Lewis says flatly. 'I can't wait.'

Maggie swallows dryly. He really doesn't sound himself.

'It'll all be fine, darling,' she reassures him, trying not to convey her concern. 'You don't think there's anything wrong, do you? With the baby I mean?'

He sighs down the line. 'No... yes. Oh, I don't know. It's just that... I can't help thinking the worst, the what-ifs, you know? What if they find something, some abnormality? What if there's no heartbeat? I just... I don't think I could handle it, Mum, I really don't.'

Maggie's in half a mind to pull over.

'I get these dark thoughts sometimes, like I'm always imagining everything to be bad when really, I should be feeling happy. I worry that with all these negative thoughts running through me that I'll somehow call it on and something bad actually *will* happen. I don't know why I'm like this, Mum...' His voice trails off into a miserable whisper.

Maggie feels a stab of pain her chest. She knows why. She hears her own father's cold, accusatory voice taunting her once more, '*It's hereditary, you know... passed down through the genes...*'

'Listen to me, Lew: every expectant parent has concerns – you wouldn't be normal if you didn't. Try not to think the worst. Remember what your counsellor said about controlling your negative thinking, how to release those sorts of thoughts like letting go of a helium balloon and watching it float away? Even if you can't stop the thoughts from entering your head, you can decide how long they stay there, how to let them go and not to dwell on them.' Maggie bites her lip. She hasn't heard her son sound like this in a long time and is gripped by worry – he's been doing so well these last couple of years.

'Which hospital are you going to – to have the scan? Thorton General?' She hopes it won't be a dreadful reminder for him. He'd spent a couple of weeks there, in the psychiatric unit, a few years ago now, following *the episode*. Surely that was yet another reason not to go to the authorities with her suspicions? Her son's mental health hadn't always been what you'd call stable, though he was on medication now and there had been no incident in years. Something like this coming to light could absolutely undo all the good progress he's made, send him plunging back into depression, tip him over the edge – an edge she feels dangerously close to herself.

Lewis's depression had seemingly come out of the blue, at least to her anyway. Her son had always been such a happy, spirited child, a bit of a handful at times she supposed and certainly very sensitive, but she'd never had any real cause for concern until it was staring her in the face. His mental-health breakdown had blindsided her, though now, blessed with perfect hindsight of course, she supposes the signs had always been there. The manic behaviour she'd mistaken for garrulous teenage enthusiasm, the soaring highs when he'd seemed on top of the world – funny, witty, and energetic, consumed by life – followed by the crashing lows when he became withdrawn, sullen and hid himself away like he had the weight of the world on his shoulders. She'd honestly just put his pendulum-swinging moods down to his personality, his age, lack of direction, *something*. Lewis had always been sweet and salty in retrospect, light and shade, but she hadn't realised how negatively it was impacting on him, hadn't identified it as a problem.

It was far more complex than just a few simple mood swings though, as she's since come to learn. He'd hidden it all so well too, from himself as much as his family, but then he'd gone and got himself arrested one night, drunk and disorderly the police had said, though he'd never been a big drinker, even as an experimental teenager. It had shocked her badly.

'He was rambling incoherently when we found him,' the police officer had informed her when she'd turned up at the station, worried out of her wits. 'We think he needs to be assessed by a mental-health professional.'

Maggie had burst into tears – not her son, her Lew. Where had all of this come from? Why hadn't she noticed?

She'd blamed herself of course. What had upset her the most was the idea that her father had been right all along, that it *was* in his genes, passed down from her mother through her, skipping a generation. Had he inherited his maternal grandmother's precarious mental-health issues, ones that had resulted in her doing the unspeakable and taking her own life? The possibility of this left her feeling consumed with guilt.

How could she, of her own volition, annihilate her entire family and their happy existence by dropping this atom bomb on them? They were all doing so well: Lewis was back on track and soon to be a father, and Remy was seemingly surpassing herself at fashion college.

Oh bloody hell! Maggie smacks her forehead – she still hasn't replied to the message that woman from St Smithen's left her. She really must call her back, find out what she wanted. First though, she'll speak to Bob and Julie. Bob's somehow got to be the lynchpin in all of this. If Len genuinely was with his brother on Wednesday night, then that would mean he couldn't possibly have killed Amelie Fox and all of this... well, she'll have to come to terms with the porn stuff somehow, but that will be the worst of it.

Won't it?

16

She presses the doorbell with a shaking finger, takes a deep breath.

'Blimey, you're a bit keen aren't yo— Oh!' Julie swings open the front door wearing a silky semi-sheer chemise and a matching robe, her hair wrapped in a bath towel. She almost jumps back in surprise or maybe shock, perhaps both. 'Maggie!'

Clearly she isn't expecting her – which was the whole point after all, to catch her and Bob off guard – though it's obvious she's expecting *someone*. She wraps her robe around herself, looks confused, embarrassed. 'Were we... did you... I didn't know you were coming over.' She glances behind her, clearly expecting to see Len with her.

'Hi, Julie!' Maggie says with as much enthusiasm as she can muster. 'I was just in the area and thought, do you know what, I'll drop by my dearest brother-in-law and his wife, see how you're both doing!'

Evidently, it's not a good time.

'I'm sorry,' Maggie says, 'I really should've called first, shouldn't I?' She wrinkles her nose. 'Shall I come back another time?' She pulls an apologetic face, bites her lip. Maybe she's overdoing it a little.

'Um, no – no, not at all,' Julie stammers, looking flustered. 'I thought you were— Bob and I are having some friends over later. I thought it was them come early.' She smiles, and Maggie smiles back expectantly. There's a moment's pause. 'Oh God, sorry. Please – please come in...' Julie steps back from the front door.

'Only if you're sure, if it's not too much trouble.'

Maggie realises that this is the first time she's been inside Bob and Julie's house since they moved in, must be coming on for a year now. Bob had sold the home he'd owned with Heather not even six months after she'd passed away, which incidentally – and in her opinion, understandably – had caused a real stink with his kids, Catherine and Robert Junior.

'You'd have thought he might've waited a couple of years at least,' she'd remarked to Len, barely able to conceal her disapproval. 'No wonder Catherine and Robert aren't happy.'

'They're all grown up now though, Mags, got their own lives and families. Robert lives in Australia and Catherine's in Bristol. It's not as though he's made them homeless, is it?'

'That's not the point,' she'd argued. 'It was their family home, where they grew up, with their mother.'

Len had sighed. He was sticking up for his brother, which she supposed was only natural, but still.

'Bit insensitive though, don't you think, especially since he just went ahead and sold it without even discussing it with either of them first.'

'Yes, well, I think he found it difficult, you know, living there with all those memories. I'm sure Heather wouldn't have wanted him to be unhappy.'

No, and she's pretty sure she wouldn't have wanted him to almost instantly shack up with someone half his age and sell off her entire legacy either, though she'd thought it prudent not to say as much.

Len was close to his older brother, and she hadn't wanted to sound like she was judging, even though she thought the whole thing had been in very bad taste. Poor Heather hadn't even been cold in the ground before Bob had started parading Julie around on his arm. Within six months, he'd sold off their lovely old Victorian house near Eden Gorge and had married her within twelve. It had felt to her like Heather had been erased, almost like she'd never existed at all.

Perhaps she was being unfair. Grief affected people in different ways after all, and everyone deserves happiness, she supposed. She'd kill Len if he did that to her though, replaced her with a younger model so soon after her death – if he hadn't killed her first that is.

Funny, but now that she thinks about it, Maggie can't remember how Bob even met Julie. She's sure Len must've told her, but it's escaped her increasingly sketchy memory. Still, she now wonders if perhaps they'd already been 'acquainted' long before his wife's sad demise.

Maggie slips her espadrilles off her feet and places them by the door. 'You know, I don't think I've ever been here, to the new place.'

'No?' Julie is walking her through the hallway. 'Really, have you not? I can't believe that!'

She's pretty sure she can though because they've never actually been invited, or at least she hasn't.

Maggie glances around the place. It couldn't be more different from Bob and Heather's former home, which had boasted some gloriously stylish period features, subtle tasteful furnishings and sympathetic colour schemes. She blinks at the garish, patterned wallpaper with its bright red, yellow and green giant flowers. There's lots of crystal, chrome and glass furniture, giant mirrors and bold chenille rugs, all expensive no doubt, but horribly tacky and not to her taste at all.

Her eye is drawn to a large black-and-white photograph on the wall of a naked woman's torso, lying on her side, her breasts and pubic hair exposed. Maggie imagines that Julie thinks it's provocative and 'arty', though it looks vulgar and almost porno-graphic to her, not least when greeted by it in the hallway, there for everyone to see the moment they enter the house.

'Interesting artwork,' she remarks, unable to take her eyes from it.

Julie laughs. 'Oh, that... Yes, well, I was a lot younger then. Come through to the kitchen. I'll get us a drink. Bob's getting showered upstairs. I'll give him a shout, let him know you're here.'

Maggie prays she doesn't look as shocked as she feels. She's joking surely? Julie has a giant naked photograph of her own vagina in her hallway? She feels her face flush, turns away from it.

'What? Oh yes, a drink would be... great, thank you.'

'Coffee, tea or something a little stronger?' Julie smiles widely, though it looks a little strained at the edges. 'I was just about to have a vodka and orange myself, get the party started. Is it vodka o'clock yet?' She's already pouring herself one as she checks the kitchen clock.

'Coffee would be great,' Maggie says. 'I'd join you but I'm driving.' She hears the stiffness in her own voice. 'Though any time of day is vodka o'clock,' she adds in a bid to sound less of a bore.

Julie laughs. 'Atta girl, Mags!'

She inwardly bristles. She really hates it when people she hardly knows call her that – it's so overfamiliar and conde-scending somehow.

'So, what brings you over this way then?' Julie takes a slurp of her vodka and orange, pops another cube of ice in the glass and places a hand on her slim hip.

Maggie isn't sure how to answer Julie's question as to why she's turned up unannounced. With all her addled, anxious thoughts and the worrying conversation with Lewis, she hadn't settled upon a definitive story in the end and had instead decided to wing it, to trust herself to come up with something plausible. Luckily though, Julie answers her own question for her.

'Don't tell me you've come all the way here to go to the new Savacentre at the retail park, have you? Everyone's raving about it. You can get everything there from your weekly shop to a lawnmower and just about everything else in between. Some fantastic bargains.' She knocks back more vodka and orange. 'And the homeware section is to die for! It's where we got our wallpaper from,' she says proudly, 'though you'd never have guessed.'

Well, that was debatable, Maggie thinks.

'One pound fifty a roll – *one fifty*! – I'm such a sucker for a bargain. Bob loves that about me,' she says, her close-set eyes twinkling a little, which suddenly makes Maggie wonder if she's just being cynical and that it really is a love match between her and Bob after all.

'Yes!' she says enthusiastically. 'That's exactly why I'm here. My friend Christine told me it had recently opened and that I should definitely check it out, so here I am!'

'Christine? Your friend from the party you mean? The one in the red dress?'

'The red dress...' Maggie feels a ripple of irritation. Oh, she means Brenda, *of course!*

'I liked her – she was really nice. Up for it, you know?'

Maggie nods, smiles thinly, but she can't be bothered to correct her. There's a much bigger reason – a more important reason – why she's here.

'Must be your own wedding anniversary soon mustn't it, yours and Bob's? How long has it been now? A year? Two?' In fact, Maggie knows full well that Bob and Julie's anniversary had already been and gone last month and that it's been two years – she's good with remembering dates at least – but she wants to get the conversation flowing, try to get Julie to open up a little, to soften the discomfort she's pretty sure they're both feeling.

'It was last month actually.' Julie smiles. 'And it was two years. Cotton,' she says. 'Bob splashed out on some 800-thread-count Egyptian sheets for our new super-king-sized bed. They're absolutely div*iiiii*ine.' She exaggerates the word theatrically, rolls her eyes.

'Two years... Gosh, time waits for no man, does it? Do you know, I can't remember how you and Bob even met now. I'm sure Len told me once but... well, my memory's not so great these days.' She rolls her own eyes in a self-deprecating fashion, taps her temple. 'Brain fog.'

'Really.' Julie cocks her head to one side and sticks out her bottom lip in what appears to be sympathy. 'That's supposed to be one of the symptoms, isn't it?'

'Yeah, symptoms of madness!' Maggie forces a laugh but already she's regretting having come here. The conversation feels stilted and awkward, and Julie's house is giving her the heebie-jeebies. Perhaps it was just a big mistake, all of it.

Suddenly she feels stupid, ridiculous, like she's taken everything way too far and has lost her marbles. Surely a phone call would've sufficed instead of coming all this way, of having to think up lies to explain her impromptu visit. The Savacentre, *really*?

'Maggie!' Bob's familiar voice causes her to turn round.

'Bob!' She stands, embraces him warmly. She's known Bob almost as long as she's known her husband and has always had a bit of a soft spot for him, had been genuinely upset and concerned when he'd had a heart attack last year and had needed to have a pacemaker fitted. He wasn't too unlike Len really, aesthetically at least, though Bob perhaps hadn't aged quite as well as his younger sibling, and they certainly shared the same interests and passions. Miserably Maggie suddenly wonders if Bob secretly watches porn too. Pornography featuring murdered young women.

'How are you, Bobby? You look really well.'

He smells of strong aftershave, is clean-shaven and dressed in a smart polo shirt and jeans. He looks well turned out, if a little like he might be trying a bit too hard. She supposes this goes in tandem with having a much younger wife.

'What an unexpected surprise!' He glances over at Julie.

'I literally just popped in to say hi,' Maggie explains, catching the exchange between them. 'I won't be stopping... Julie says you're having guests over.'

He smiles at her, glances at his wife again. Maggie's sure she sees Julie shaking her head.

'Is everything OK?' Bob says with the lightest hint of concern. She'd pre-empted this question though. After all, she's never just turned up on their doorstep alone before. 'Is Len OK?'

Len, oh, you mean your perverted, porn-watching, murdering brother?

'Len's... he's good thanks, yes, all good. You know Len. Can't keep him out of that garage...'

Bob chuckles. 'Good ol' Fidel *Castrol*,' he jokes. 'It's a play on words – Castrol/Casto. You know, the oil, GTX and the Cuban leader... oh, never mind.' It really hadn't needed an explanation.

'You've recovered from the party then? Great night, wasn't it, Jules? We had an absolute blast, didn't we, babes?'

Babes? He'd never referred to Heather as 'babes' when she'd been alive, at least never publicly. It sounded wrong somehow coming from a man in his sixties.

Julie nods. 'God yeah, it was a right laugh. You've got some great friends I have to say, especially that Whatshername...'

'Brenda?'

'Yeah!' She's already forgotten that she'd confused her with Christine. 'She was hilarious, and so friendly. In fact, Bob and I were going to ask you for her number.'

Really? Why was that?

'Oh,' she says, trying to disguise her irritation. 'I'm afraid I don't have it. I don't actually know her all that well to be honest.'

'Well, she certainly made an impression with us, didn't she, BB?' Julie looks at Bob, giggles girlishly.

BB? It was clearly her pet name for Bob, though what it stood for she has no idea. In fact, thinking about it, she'd rather not know.

'We didn't get to chat too much at the party, did we?' Bob says, 'what with you being the hostess with the mostest and all of that. Cracking video you did at the end of the night though. Brought a tear to my eye, I can't deny it. Some of that old footage, blimey, did it bring back some memories or what... That clip from the eighties of us lot down in Southend, you remember? That weekend we all went on where we stayed in that hotel that had an outdoor swimming pool that looked like a lagoon in the brochure but was as green as the Thames when we got there... rooms were like something out of *Rising Damp*...' Bob's booming laugh bounces off the kitchen walls.

'*Rising Damp?*' Jules looks at them both blankly.

'It was a comedy sitcom in the seventies, bit before your time, Julie,' Maggie says, unable to help herself. Good ol' Bob – he's unwittingly given her an in, bringing up the Southend hotel.

'Bit like the Platinum Inn you and Len stayed in last week I'm sure.' She laughs. 'I've heard that one down near Eden is atrocious! Like the Bates Motel!'

Bob glances sideways at Julie again. There's a pause, yes, a definite pause, as the laughter stops. Is she imagining it, or do they both seem a bit shifty?

'No, actually...' Bob clears his throat. 'I didn't end up staying there in the end, did I, Jules?'

'Oh?'

'Long story but I ended up coming back here, left Len to the polyester sheets at the Platinum. Didn't he tell you?' The chuckle that follows sounds forced and disingenuous.

She blinks at him, signalling for him to elaborate. He knows her well enough to read her body language by now.

'No,' she says flatly. 'He didn't.'

'We had a leak, in the kit—'

'Bathroom,' Julie says simultaneously.

So which was it, the kitchen or bathroom? *Oh my God, they're lying.*

'Really? Oh, Len never said anything. Sounds like a nightmare,' Maggie says. 'Hope it didn't cause too much damage.'

Julies face blooms red. 'Think I'll have another vodka,' she says, standing.

'Think I'll join you, babes,' Bob says. 'One for you too, Mags?'

'Not for me, Bob – I'm driving.' Though what she wouldn't give for a double vodka tonic right now was anyone's business.

'Well, it started in the bathroom – the leak I mean,' Bob clarifies, 'and ended up coming through the ceiling, flooding the kitchen. Jules rang me and I had to get a cab all the way back from Riverdown.'

'Yes,' Julie confirms. 'I spent the whole night mopping it all up.'

Maggie looks up at the pristine kitchen ceiling.

'We had it repainted,' Julie quickly adds.

'Len didn't mention anything,' Maggie says again.

'Well, he was a bit piss— a bit worse for wear. We all were to be fair... always gets a bit messy when we all get together for the fair – you know how it is.'

Bob is jabbering now, which only serves to compound Maggie's suspicion that the story is a tall one.

'You girls really should come next time,' he adds, swigging at his drink. 'You'd enjoy it.'

An awkward pause ensues.

'How are the kids?' Bob changes the subject.

'Good, good thanks, yeah. Remy's down from fashion college' – *she must remember to ring that woman back* – 'and Lewis, well, I'm sure you already know he's going to be a father!'

But she can tell by Bob's expression that he doesn't.

'Did Len not mention it?' This too was strange. She's sure he'd have confided the good news to his brother by now.

'Um, no, he didn't... but we haven't spoken since the party. That's fantastic news, Maggie! Well I never, a new addition to the Wendover crew! Congratulations!' He raises his glass.

Maggie can't help beaming with pride. Right now, her future grandchild is the only thing holding her sanity together.

'You'll have to come over,' Maggie says, 'for a celebration, you and Julie.'

'God, yeah, we'd love that, wouldn't we, Jules? Maggie's an excellent cook and an impeccable hostess, as you already know!'

'Oh yes, yes, just say when.' Julie nods enthusiastically, looks at the clock nervously. 'I can burn toast me.' She glances back at Maggie. 'I'm not much of a cook – guess it comes with age and practice, like most things.'

Maggie smiles thinly.

'Well,' she says, draining her coffee cup, 'I guess I'll be off then, just a flying visit – and you've got guests coming...'

She's sure she can see the respective relief on their faces.

Bob comes towards her, gives her a hug. He even feels a little like Len, warm and familiar somehow; it makes her chest pang. *Bob will be a victim in all of this too.*

17 DAN

I'm just about to bite into a bacon sandwich – the first bit of sustenance that's passed my lips in far too long – when Parker comes racing into the incident room waving a piece of paper in his hand like it's one of Willie Wonka's golden tickets. For a moment I think he might actually be about to break into song.

'Luminol!' he says, a little breathless. 'Forensics found minute traces of Amelie Fox's blood in her apartment, in the bedroom near the dressing table! Luminol picked it up.'

I hastily put my sandwich down. 'Well, that *is* good news, Parker.' And boy could we use some of that right now because currently we have the princely sum of nada.

'Yeah, but it gets even better, gov.'

I look at Parker like he's suddenly my favourite person on the planet. 'Indulge me.'

'Traces of blood and a partial fingerprint were found on a perfume bottle... on Amelie's dressing table.'

Perfume bottle...

'Angel... the star-shaped glass bottle?'

'Exactly the one, boss.'

I recall picking it up when Davis and I were at the crime scene.

'Looks like that's what she was hit with. The abrasion on the back of her head – forensics say it's in keeping with the shape of the bottle. The killer attempted to clean it afterwards and replaced it but didn't quite make a good enough job of it.'

He looks so chuffed with himself that a wave of almost fatherly endearment washes over me, along with a slight sense of gratification, because I *sensed* something had happened in that bedroom from the moment I set foot inside it. There was nothing out of place, nothing immediately unusual that jumped out at me, but that in itself was what had given me pause – that and my intuition anyway.

'It looks like she was killed in her bedroom.'

'It certainly does, Parker,' I say, picking my sandwich up from the table again. I'm about to take a celebratory bite when Harding pipes up.

'Bad news I'm afraid, gov.'

I immediately put the sandwich back down on the desk. 'Go ahead, Harding – kill my buzz.'

'Sorry, boss, but you're not going to like this. CCTV from Amelie's apartment block – a new system was being installed from Tuesday through Thursday. There's nothing on the footage… there's no footage at all – and we're still going through the surrounding CCTV footage from Riverdown Park. Nothing yet though, boss, and what we do have is of pretty poor quality.'

I feel my chest deflate. *You've got to be kidding me.* I'd been relying on CCTV picking something up. It would have been impossible not to have, which is what makes this crime so perplexing. Amelie's apartment building is top-notch accommodation, state-of-the-art London living at its finest. How could the killer have been sure they wouldn't be seen? Was it possible they hadn't even thought to check for CCTV?

'Sorry, gov.' Harding looks at me sheepishly. 'The whole system was out of operation until Friday.'

'Well, that's just great,' I snap, frustration prickling the surface of my skin. Was the killer aware of this fact or had it all just been down to that four-letter word 'luck' again? Perhaps someone in the building knew that a new system was being installed and had seen it as an opportunity to strike undetected?

'Let's check out the building's maintenance company, see who might've been aware that there would be no CCTV that day. Could be an inside job.'

'Boss.'

I pick up the sandwich again. 'Right, people, listen up.'

The team look up from their desks and I'm met with a collection of tired eyes. The first forty-eight hours – the golden period – has long passed already and we've no obvious suspect, motive or murder weapon, though the perfume bottle and partial print are a definite boost. The problem with a partial print is that you need a body to match it to, and unless our killer has previous, it's about as much use as an ashtray on a speedboat right now. We've cleared the immediate family and the flatmate as suspects, only a few hundred thousand IG and OnlyFans followers to go. Mindful of a dip in morale – especially now with the lack of CCTV – I kick off with what we *do* know first.

'So, it now appears Amelie was most likely killed in the bedroom of her apartment, the blow to the head with a perfume bottle incapacitating her before she was strangled with what I believe to be her own scarf – which incidentally is still missing. No sign of forced entry, no sign of a robbery and no real signs of a struggle.'

'She knew them, boss,' Harding says. 'Someone she was familiar with, saw everyday perhaps, or certainly felt comfortable about giving access to her apartment, someone like a maintenance guy. It would make sense.'

I nod. Yes, it would. So why doesn't it? Why do I not get that feeling, that sense of being on the right track?

'This wasn't a random killing, though perhaps it wasn't as well thought through as it could've been.'

'What makes you say that, gov?' Harding says. 'They clearly attempted a clean-up job.'

I go to take a bite of the sandwich again but don't quite make it as my brain kicks into overdrive. 'Something... something at the scene. Whoever killed Amelie would've had to remove her body from the apartment complex without anyone witnessing them.'

'You think there may have been two of them – that the killer had an accomplice?'

Parker looks almost excited by this prospect, which I put down to the exuberance of youth and him being relatively new to homicide. One killer is more than enough. I suppose an accomplice would indeed answer some questions, but yet again, my instincts are telling me that this was a one-man job, a pretty amateur affair that saw the killer luck out.

'It's possible,' I say, because theoretically it is. 'Any joy with witnesses yet?'

Parker shakes his head. 'Nothing, gov. Slater and I did door to door. No one saw anything, no one heard anything – no screams, no unusual sounds – and no sightings.'

'So how did the killer get the body out of the building?'

'She wasn't a big person – tiny in fact, around 110lbs. They could've easily carried her,' DC Lauren Slater, a new addition to my burgeoning team of brilliance, suggests. She's young and tenacious, like Parker, which is why I've paired them together on this one, a kind of dynamic duo. Slater is the salt to Parker's sweet, and as anyone who's ordered popcorn at the cinema knows, it's a winning combination – works even when in theory it sounds like it shouldn't. Perhaps this is the key to Davis and I – she's the method and I'm the madness.

Anyway, if it works, it works, and right now that's all I care about.

'True but then why didn't anyone see anything? It would've been late afternoon/early evening, rush hour – there were people coming in and out of that building all the time. I'm pretty sure someone would've noticed someone carrying a dead body.' Someone must've seen something surely? Someone somewhere always does.

'Waited until the coast was clear?'

'Possibly.' Though once again I have a horrible suspicion that it may have been down to good fortune and timing yet again.

'*Success in life is a mix of preparation and luck, Danny Boy!*' I hear him again, the old man, in my earhole. Since his passing, I've heard his voice in my head much more than ever before, like a parrot on my shoulder. It's a comfort though, even when it sounds like he's telling me off.

Had the killer really been that prepared? Something – I can't be sure what – tells me they weren't, that this was an amateur attempt that miraculously seemed to go their way. Maybe they only decided to kill Amelie on the spur of the moment – the opportunity presented itself and they simply took it.

'The killer went back for her,' I say. 'She was transported by car before they dumped her in the river. He's local. He knew the area. Traces of engine oil was found in her hair extensions. I'd say she was in the boot of a car at a guess.'

'Ah yes, the oil!' Mitchell says, smiling. 'This'll cheer you up, gov.'

I feel a flutter of excitement dance inside my empty guts.

Mitchell flicks through her notes. 'It's a dexos-certified synthetic motor oil,' she states, like this is supposed to mean something to me.

I'm not really a car person. As long as it gets me from A to B and has a steering wheel then I'm pretty much happy. 'Is dexos a brand?'

'No, gov, it's a designation given to a special synthetic motor oil—'

'In English please, Mitchell.'

'It's specifically designed for Cadillacs and other GM vehicles, boss.'

Now this really is music to my ears! I'm so elated I almost offer to share my sandwich with her. 'Cadillacs?'

'Yup.'

'The vintage car fair... the one that took place on the Wednesday and Thursday down at Riverdown Park... we need to trace all the names of owners with MGs and Cadillacs who attended.'

'I'm already all over it, boss.'

I'm sure she is. Mitchell's a machine when it comes to intelligence work. Like a dog with a juicy bone, she'll not stop digging until she strikes gold.

'So what about surrounding CCTV from the area? ANPR?'

'Collating it now, boss.'

'How are tech coming along?' This is also Mitchell's remit. She has an unrivalled analytical mind that seems to naturally be adept at translating information of this particular variety. It's like Mandarin to me if I'm honest. Sometimes I wonder how I've even managed to climb to the lofty heights that I have. Maybe it's been down to that four-letter word again.

'They're sifting through phone and social-media messages, photos and records for any red flags, anything unusual or anyone prolific – a stalker perhaps, an overzealous fan. Problem is, there's just so many of them,' she clarifies. 'Amelie made a living out of selling live video and images, and she was good at it too. Last month alone she made in excess of £15,000 on her OnlyFans site.'

Whistles resound through the incident room.

Harding snorts. 'Bloody hell, I'm in the wrong game.'

'You'd be lucky to make fifteen pounds a month, let alone fifteen grand,' Baylis remarks.

'Bloody cheek!'

'OK, OK, settle down...' I'm not in the mood for banter, which admittedly is uncharacteristic. But I just can't shake the feeling that our killer has somehow already slipped into the ether undetected and it's largely, frustratingly, been down to little more than good timing and... well, I don't need to say *that* word again.

'Ex-boyfriend, or boyfriends plural... maybe someone she was seeing got the hump about her flashing her fan— flaunting herself online, gov?'

I shake my head. It would be perhaps the most feasible explanation – a disgruntled ex, an obsessed stalker – but as yet we've found no evidence to suggest this, nothing and no one to lead us down this particular path.

'We're looking into the identity of the guy in the video, the... sex tape. The press has made a big deal out of it – it's all over the papers and the internet. Can you believe the video has had over a million hits? And that's just since the news of her murder.'

I shake my head. *One million hits*. It's deeply depressing to imagine that people would actually choose to download an explicit video of a murder victim. Seems as though Amelie got the fame she craved for all the wrong reasons in the end.

'There's a few names in the running as to who the guy is. A couple of names keep cropping up, and we're looking into those, but it's all speculation right now, and no one has come forward as yet.'

It had made for difficult viewing, the short, unprofessional clip of Amelie and a lover in various uncompromising positions. Davis and I had watched it together, which even given the professional context still sounds wrong.

'Terrible lighting,' Davis had commented, cocking her head to the side. 'You can't see anything properly.'

'Is that a hint of disappointment I hear in your voice, Lucy?'

'Gov!' She'd laughed. She knows full well I'm ribbing her due to my own sense of discomfort. It's no laughing matter, and yet sometimes in this profession, you simply have to use humour as a barrier to protect yourself – and others – or else you'd crack under the strain, under the weight of all that horror and muck.

'John and I made a home video once,' she'd felt compelled to tell me.

I'd glanced sideways at her. 'Way too much information, Davis.'

'No, honestly, we did. When we were young and happy anyway, you know, before the divorce.'

'I'm glad it was *before* the divorce, Davis,' I'd said, and she'd laughed again.

'We thought it would be a bit of fun, you know, a bit sexy, a bit risqué and all of that. We watched it back together and...'

I'd pulled a face at her, one I'd hoped would be translated as an unambiguous red stop sign.

'... I signed myself up to Weight Watchers the next day.'

It had been my turn to laugh.

'It was like something off a David Attenborough programme.'

It was an image I'd rather not have been given. Anyway, the clip doesn't give us much to go on. Just over a minute long, dark and grainy, if we didn't know it featured Amelie Fox then it wouldn't have been immediately easy to identify her, and even harder to identify the male, given his face is never actually in shot throughout and as yet there's no such thing as 'penis recognition' – at least not that I'm aware of. Whoever he is though, he'd better bloody have a watertight alibi, because right now he's all we've got.

The fact that he'd tied a scarf around her neck in the video was a definite cause for concern, but yet again, watching it through, I didn't get a sense of anything overtly sinister having taken place, and while distasteful and a bit seedy – not least I imagine to Amelie's poor family – it all appeared consensual.

I'm about to take a bite of that sandwich finally when Davis enters the incident room. To the untrained eye, her poker-faced expression gives nothing away, but I detect the subtlest hint of disappointment on her even features. I suppose this comes with working so closely with someone for so many years. My heart sinks and I resignedly replace my sandwich back onto the napkin. I get the nagging feeling it's not going to get eaten any time soon.

'Don't tell me,' I address her. 'It's not good news.'

Davis blinks at me, gives me a look that suggests she knows that I know what she's about to say.

'We ran the sperm DNA through the database.'

I nod. I know what's coming.

'Sorry, gov,' she says, as if she's personally responsible for the lack of a match.

Well, this is just getting better and better. We've interviewed Amelie's closest friends and family, all of whom state that she wasn't in a relationship with anyone, to their knowledge at least. Whoever deposited the sperm inside her wasn't a 'boyfriend' and she hadn't confessed to having had any sexual encounters with anyone prior to her death to anyone.

It could, of course, belong to the killer, but something tells me otherwise. This case has been deemed sexually motivated from the outset – Amelie's looks and profession – the fact she was stripped naked, all of which would certainly point in that direction, and while I agree that it appears to be a very personal crime, I can't make my mind up. Any sexual assault taking place has thus far proved inconclusive, which begs the question, if it wasn't a sexually motivated crime, then what was it? A crime of passion? A consensual sexual encounter gone wrong? A crime that was made to appear sexually motivated in a bid to lead us down the wrong path?

The press attention hasn't helped either. A dead young model and a widely circulating sex tape – it's like all their Christmases have come at once. The fact that the male in the video hasn't yet come forward of his own volition could suggest he has something to hide, but equally it could simply suggest that he's simply embarrassed or scared.

Her friends and family and at least one of her former boyfriends have all said that Amelie wasn't into anything 'kinky' – BDSM, role play, domination, all that sort of caper – and looking at her OnlyFans account, there's nothing there to support that she was either. Her photos, which some might describe as risqué, were little more than highly stylised bikini and lingerie shots, some imposed nudity, common or garden porn-lite, and even that's pushing it. You can see far raunchier on *Love Island* – or so I'm told.

Phone records haven't thrown up much either. Her call log running up to the day she was murdered consisted of a few friends, some business contacts and her parents. The last text she sent was to a friend she was due to meet with later that evening, briefly making plans. She didn't take drugs, though she enjoyed a drink now and again like most young people her age, and there was alcohol in her system when she died, but there's nothing to suggest she was involved in anything untoward or illegal which could potentially have put her in harm's way.

And then there's the mystery of the photograph that was posted after she was killed, the picture where she was wearing the missing scarf. We know now it wasn't a scheduled post, so clearly she didn't post it herself – the killer must've thoughtfully done that for her.

'The picture,' I say, 'the photo posted on her IG account on the Thursday…'

Davis nods.

'It came from her phone. The killer most likely posted it, perhaps to make it look as though she was still alive, put people off the scent, make sure no one was unduly worried.'

The phone is still missing. I look up at the board, at that last final photograph of Amelie and I study it, look at her happy, beautiful smiling face, her head thrown back with a sense of ease, not a care in the world, not one iota of what was about to happen to her.

'They took it – the killer took the scarf,' I say aloud. 'They strangled her with it and took it as a memento, maybe her phone too, though I imagine they probably discarded that somewhere.'

'Well, the divers never recovered it from the river, it isn't in the apartment or at the Foxes' house, and it went off-grid the day after she was killed, last pinged at the tower local to River-down, just south of Eden Gorge, so there's a strong indication you're right, gov.'

Forget indications, I *know* I am.

I pick up my sandwich again and take a bite, finally. It's stone cold and the bacon has congealed.

'We find that scarf and we find our killer,' I say, giving up and throwing it in the bin.

18 MAGGIE

It's a stiflingly warm late afternoon, close and sultry, and Maggie pulls at her shirt dress irritably as she walks through the automatic doors of Savacentre. It's sticking to her skin. *At least it's cooler in here*, she thinks as she picks up a basket on autopilot and aimlessly makes her way down the first aisle.

Brightly coloured packets and tins jump out at her, ugly neon signs screaming '20% off' and 'three for two' hurt her sore eyes, and the smell of the nearby fish counter makes her feel nauseous. This is the bloody last place she wants to be, a busy discount hypermarket, but she can't go home empty-handed. She'll need to buy a few bits to make the journey look authentic and worthwhile to Len.

She wonders if Bob has been on the phone to him already, informing him of her impromptu visit. Will it make him even more suspicious on top of finding her snooping around the garage? She's pretty sure it will, which is why she needs to have her story straight, back it up with some bargains that they neither want nor need.

She heads for the homeware department, passing the deli on the way – Julie had been right, this place is a one-stop-shop-fits-all. She might as well get something for dinner while she's here. She stares down at the selection of cold meats and various tapas behind the counter.

'I'll have some of the chorizo, some of the meatballs and some of those herby artichokes in oil please?' The words come out of her mouth on autopilot, like someone else has said them on her behalf.

The young girl behind the counter nods back at her, begins to fill a selection of little plastic pots.

Maggie swallows dryly. The place is packed full of thrifty shoppers hungry for a bargain and suddenly she feels claustrophobic, like she wants to abandon her basket and run screaming towards the nearest exit.

In through the nose, Maggie...

She places a hand on the glass counter in a bid to support herself and is suddenly conscious of a pair of eyes upon her, a woman standing in the queue to the left of her. She recognises her and... it's Alex's mum, isn't it?

Yes, the girl who Remy shares a flat with in London. She doesn't really know Alex's mum, not *know her* know her anyway, not on a personal level, though she has seen her around town enough times to exchange a nod, a smile, or a brief 'hello', but that's as far as it's ever gone. Still, they have another common denominator now that their daughters are living together. She feels obliged to acknowledge her.

'Hi!' Maggie says with as much of a smile as her facial muscles will allow. God, she doesn't even know the woman's name, although she's sure she does know it and just can't remember it. Since the onset of her menopause, it's as if the part of her brain that retains those sorts of details has been lobotomised.

The woman looks directly at her and Maggie sees the flicker of recognition in her eyes before she quickly turns away, begins to look down at the produce in the counter.

Maggie feels her stomach muscle twitch. She glances at her quickly again, but the woman has turned her whole body away from her now and has her back to her. Clearly she can't have recognised her. But surely she does, *she must*? They've been acknowledging each other since she can remember. In fact, just a couple of weeks ago, she'd seen her in Boots on the high street, in the pharmacy line, and she'd given her a small wave and mouthed the word 'hello'. Why on earth would she ignore her now?

Maybe she's short-sighted, maybe she hasn't seen her properly – that's got to be it.

Maggie thinks to tap her on the arm but decides against it. Besides, she's moved too far away from her now.

Feeling slighted, she rubs her forehead – it feels warm and a little sticky.

A wasp suddenly begins to buzz around her face, whirring like a helicopter in her ear, causing her to shriek in alarm and waft her hand around manically in a bid to swat it away. Damn things – so many of them around at the moment. Must be the heat.

Irritated and embarrassed, Maggie grabs the deli pots from the counter assistant with a harried 'thanks' and scurries off, turning round briefly only to see Alex's mum do just the same.

What in the hell was all that about?

Maybe she's just being paranoid again. She no doubt recognised her too late and felt too embarrassed to say hello – she's done it herself once or twice. Everyone has, haven't they?

Maggie leaves Savacentre with a bag of groceries and a large bottle of vodka – a last-minute purchase – and throws the items into the boot of the car. The conversation she had with Bob and Julie about the Platinum Inn is spinning like a hamster's wheel in her mind.

'No... I didn't end up staying there in the end... left Len to the polyester sheets.'

Why hadn't Len told her that Bob had headed home? Why hadn't he mentioned the leak to her? She can only think of one reason.

19

It takes longer than it should for the bored-looking woman behind the reception desk at the Platinum Inn hotel to look up at her. Hardly what you'd call 'service with a smile'.

'Can I help you?' she asks without conviction.

Oh, yes, yes please, please help me. I think my husband has murdered someone, that beautiful young woman that's all over the telly, the one they pulled from the river at the weekend, you know, and I just need to know if he was here, where he said he was, on Wednesday last week, because if he wasn't then my life is over, my family's lives are over and I don't know what I'll do...

'Yes, sorry to bother you...'

The woman stares at her blankly.

'My husband stayed here last week, on Wednesday evening,' she says, almost unable to draw enough breath to expel the words. 'The twentieth,' she adds, suddenly fighting back tears. 'Wednesday the twentieth...'

The woman is still staring at her blankly, and she feels like screaming in her nonchalant face.

'He, um... he thinks he may have left something in the room, some… some cufflinks, silver cufflinks, and I wondered if you could check – if you'd check to see if anyone's found them.'

'Oh right, OK,' the woman says, shifting her large frame on the stool. 'Can I have his name?'

'Yes. Yes, it's Len Wendover, Mr Len Wendover. He checked in here last—'

'Wednesday, yeah, you said.'

Maggie exhales, but her chest feels so tight it's like her lungs are a pair of old paper bags.

The woman begins to tap on the keyboard in front of her. She appears so disinterested that Maggie half expects her to sigh and roll her eyes.

'Wendover you say?'

'Yes, Mr Len Wendover.'

Her bottom lip protrudes as she shakes her head. 'Sorry, that name's not coming up.'

'Are you sure?'

The woman looks up at her slowly, like it's an effort just to raise her head.

'No one of that name checked in here last Wednesday.'

'You're absolutely *positive*? Are you spelling it correctly? It's W-e-n—'

The woman blinks at her like she just came down with the last shower. 'Yeah, I'm spelling it right. No Len Wendover.'

'Try Lennard maybe? He may've used his full name.' It's a long shot but she checks anyway. Len never uses his full birth name – says it makes him sound like an undertaker. 'How about Bob – Robert Wendover?'

The woman looks at her, clearly impassive.

'It could have been booked in his brother's name instead.'

'No one called Wendover was booked in here last Wednesday – no Len, Lenny, Lennard, Bob, Bobby, Robert, Rob, Bert, Bertie… or any other abbreviation I'm afraid.'

Maggie suddenly feels like leaning over the desk and slapping the woman in her facetious face.

'Are you sure you've got the date right?'

'Yes,' Maggie spits back, 'absolutely – Wednesday the twentieth.' She hears the desperation in her own voice. The woman has no idea how important this is, how much is riding on it.

'Can you check again?'

The woman looks up at her again.

'Please?' Maggie adds, imploring her. 'It's terribly important, they were an... anniversary present.'

The woman finally sighs. Taps on her keyboard again.

'Look, I'm sorry,' she says, 'I can't magic it up. Whoever he is, he never checked in here last Wednesday – look for yourself if you don't believe me.' She turns the computer system round to show her the screen. 'No one by that name – no one called Wendover was here last Wednesday.'

She can't hold it together any longer. Maggie bursts into tears. This confirms it – her worst fear has become a reality. Len wasn't with Bob on Wednesday night. He never stayed at the Platinum Inn like he'd told her. He's lied to her. He's lied about where he was and who he was with. He has no alibi for the night of Amelie Fox's murder. He has her bloodstained scarf in the boot of his car. He's been viewing pornography on his computer that features her in it, and he's been researching asphyxiation and how to dispose of a dead body. *Len has murdered Amelie Fox.* He's killed another human being, a young woman who could be his own daughter. Maybe he raped her as well.

Oh Jesus, what did he do to that poor girl?

Maggie thinks she's going to throw up – she can feel it travelling up from her stomach and her mouth is full of saliva.

The woman behind the desk stares at her in shock.

'I need to use the bathroom,' she manages to croak through her tight throat.

'Just down the corridor to the left, though they're really for guests only, and—'

But Maggie is already en route.

She pushes the toilet door open with such force that it bangs loudly against the wall and promptly throws up in the cubicle, guttural sounds echoing throughout the bathroom as she retches violently into the bowl. Her nose begins to run and she grabs some toilet paper from the roll, wipes it. She's hyperventilating, she feels dizzy.

In through the nose, out through the mouth. That's it – keep breathing, Maggie, keep breathing.

She isn't sure how she's got here – she must've driven her car on autopilot because she can't remember anything of the journey, save for the local news on the radio, news that was still full of the Amelie Fox murder. The host from Thorton Vale Radio, a vociferous woman called Hilary, who clearly liked the sound of her own voice yet often spoke a lot of sense, had been waxing lyrical about 'personal safety', advising local female residents not to go out at night or travel alone. It had also come to light that a sex tape of Amelie was circulating – surely the same one she'd found in Len's search history – and listeners had phoned in to discuss the case, local residents mostly.

'Well, she was obviously into the seedier side of life, wasn't she? Little more than a sex worker really,' one particularly well-spoken lady had called in to say.

'Doesn't mean she deserved to be murdered though, does it?' Hilary had bluntly replied.

'He's local,' a man had rung in to say. 'The area where she was dumped was not accidental in my opinion. That part of the river is particularly secluded and only someone with knowledge of Riverdown Park would know that, wouldn't they?'

Hilary had agreed with gravitas. 'Maybe the police should

ask for all the local men aged over eighteen to offer a voluntary DNA sample,' she'd gone on to say.

This suggestion had only exacerbated Maggie's burgeoning sick terror. *It won't be long before the police come knocking, will it? Evidence will surely, eventually, lead them to Len. If she's managed to work it out herself then it's only a matter of time before the authorities do too. No one gets away with murder these days – it's nigh on impossible. Even if they don't get their killer straight away, invariably it catches up with them. Everything always does in the end.*

Maggie looks to her right at the Thorton Police Station sign that she's parked in front of. *Should she jump before she's pushed? She'll just go in there and ask to speak to someone, tell them everything. Maybe she could do it anonymously – maybe Len would never have to know that she shopped him and the kids wouldn't have to find out.*

Maggie's phone rings suddenly, and she jumps in alarm. *This is how she will be forever more unless she confesses to what she knows – a paranoid, tortured nervous wreck. She'll spend her life looking over her shoulder. It will eat her away – she'll get cancer, she'll—*

'Mags?' Len's voice rings crisply out of the speaker. He sounds concerned. 'Where are you, chickadee?'

She winces. She's always loved him calling her by her pet name; it's become second nature after so many years, but now it makes her feel physically sick.

I'm outside the police station, Len, just about to go inside and tell them that you're a murderer, responsible for killing Amelie Fox. Put the kettle on, sweetheart – I won't be long!

'I'm... I'm on my way home,' Maggie says, though she's not sure how she's managing to get the words out. It feels like her throat has closed up, like her voice box has been brutally torn from her body.

'Lew and Casey are here,' Len says. 'They've come to show

us the scan pictures of the new Wendover addition!' He sounds elated, happy, like he hasn't a care in the world.

Silent tears fall from her eyes.

'Oh, that's lovely,' she says, wiping one away.

'They're dying for you to see them,' he says. 'They're both cock-a-hoop. What time will you be back? Where have you been anyway?'

'To Westhill. I... I went to that new Savacentre place.' Her voice sounds thin and broken – she can hear the cracks in it. Surely he can hear them too?

'What, that place down near Bob and Julie, at the retail park?'

'Yes. I dropped in to see them actually. Didn't stay long, just to say hello.'

There's a pause on the line.

'Oh,' he says eventually.

She detects a hint of surprise in his voice

'And how were they?'

'Good, yes, all good... they were having friends over so I didn't—'

'He didn't mention anything then?'

Maggie feels her heartbeat accelerate so quickly that she's forced to grip the steering wheel. She'll surely have a heart attack at this rate.

'Mention what?'

There's another slight pause.

'Oh nothing, it's nothing really... we just had a little falling out that's all.'

'Fall-falling out? You and Bob? Why? Over what?'

'Didn't you notice anything at the party?'

'No,' she says truthfully.

'Well, we weren't really speaking.'

'Why?' she asks again.

'Oh, something and nothing, you know what Bob's like – what he can be like anyway.'

It's hardly an answer.

'It'll blow over,' he says dismissive. 'Anyway, are you coming home?'

Maggie stares at the police sign until her vision begins to blur.

'Mags?'

'Yes,' she says, turning the key in the ignition. 'I'm on my way now.'

20

She observes them all from a crack behind the door, huddled together as they look at the pictures. She can hear Casey cooing and Lewis's animated excitement filling the kitchen, the throbbing heartbeat of her home.

'Casey reckons she's got my nose already,' Lewis says, pointing with one hand and squeezing Casey's waist with the other. 'I can't even tell what way is up, let alone where her nose is!'

Her. Hang on, they said 'her', didn't they? *Oh my goodness, it's a girl!* Maggie covers her mouth with both hands in a bid to stifle the scream that's threatening to escape from it and blow her cover. A baby girl!

She feels her heart expand inside her aching chest. For a nanosecond, this joyful news overrides all other thoughts in her crowded mind – and it feels wonderful – but it's painfully short-lived. Silent tears slip from the corners of her eyes, and she wipes them away as quickly as they're falling. Were they tears of joy or anguish? It's difficult to tell – she feels so conflicted, so confused, a hybrid mix of disbelief and joy, horror and elation, love and hatred, disgust and delight all at the same time, and frankly it's *unbearable*.

Remy is studying the scan picture now, pointing at something as her dad looks on.

'Absolutely amazing what they can do nowadays,' Len's voice resonates through the room. 'All this 3D high-definition business. You can practically see her eyelashes – incredible! Not like it was when we were expecting you two – you just looked like a grey blob on a screen to me. Your mother's going to be over the moon when she sees this.'

'I want to be the one to tell her that we're having a girl,' Lewis says as Len hugs his son proudly.

Maggie catches her breath. Their baby boy was going to become a father.

'We're having a little girl!'

'A granddaughter!' Len booms triumphantly. 'We'll crack the champagne open when your mum's back... whenever that will be. You can have one glass, can't you, Casey? I'm sure I stashed a bottle behind from the party somewhere.'

Remy begins to take some flutes from the glass cabinet. 'Where is Mum anyway?'

Maggie flattens herself against the wall. She doesn't want them to see her, not just yet.

'Oh... I don't know. Said she was up near Westhill, went to that new Savacentre place in the retail park or something... Anyway, what about names – little-girl names? Your mother likes floral names: Rosie, Daisey, Fern... you were going to be called Fleur at one stage,' Len tells Remy. 'Can't think why we didn't call you it now.'

Maggie can't help smiling. They had hotly debated what to call their little girl when she'd finally arrived, almost two weeks overdue. Due to Maggie's blood loss during the tricky and protracted birth, which had resulted in her being in a coma for a couple of days, Remy's first forty-eight or so hours had been nameless.

'I wanted to wait until you woke up,' Len had said as he'd squeezed her hand. 'So we could name her together.'

Fleur had been the frontrunner throughout her pregnancy, but when Maggie had finally got to look at her precious daughter for the first time, it hadn't suited her somehow, so they'd come up with Remy instead. She forgets who thought of it first now.

Maggie watches her family as they celebrate, a warm happy glow around them, and a wave of anguish hits her like a tsunami in the chest. The very things that have kept her grounded in her life, things she's taken for granted like truth and morality, shared integrity and values, respect, trust, and honesty have all but vanished, and she feels weightless, like gravity no longer exists in her world and that she might just float away into the ether. The people standing in her kitchen right now are her entire life, her true loves; they – her family – are what keep her going day after day. How can she destroy them all with the terrible, ugly truth? How can she deliberately detonate a bomb in all their lives by telling the police what she knows about her husband, their father, that new little life's grandfather-to-be? She can't. She just can't do it to them, to her own children and grandchild – *a granddaughter*. It would ruin them all, maybe even cause Casey and Lewis to split up, or Lewis to sink back into depression or, God forbid, worse. Her beloved son has never been happier, never been more focused and upbeat. This would be like handing him a loaded gun, wouldn't it?

But if she can't go to the authorities with what she knows, if she mustn't, then what *can* she do? How can she live with what she suspects is true? How can she function normally knowing that she's hiding Len's abhorrent, unthinkable secret?

She studies her husband from her clandestine viewpoint

behind the kitchen door, observes his large slender frame that has always made her feel so safe and secure, his strong arms that have comforted and protected her for all these years, his once dark thatch of hair, now slightly receding and more salt and pepper (*It's hanging on in there, chickadee!*) the familiarity of his gait, no inch of him unexplored, untouched, unloved a thousand, a million times over.

Does she still love him? Maggie asks herself the question, though in truth, the real question is: *can* she still love him? She doesn't know how to stop loving him – love isn't a light switch that you can turn on and off, is it? Yet she's repulsed, sickened to her core by what he's done. She's disgusted by the things she found on his laptop, his secret sexual perversions.

In that moment, she realises that it is absolutely possible to love and despise someone at the same time and how egregious such a feeling is, how such cognitive dissonance is like a fracture to the soul, enough to drive a person crazy.

'Just like your mother, Margaret.'

Maggie screams internally. Will this torture and torment that she's feeling ever end? Will it ease with every passing day? Will she learn to live alongside it? She'll have to, won't she? The alternative would be far worse. This way, by harbouring Len's secret, only *she* suffers day-to-day, only *she* will have to carry such a burden, not her children, not her future grandchild. She will sacrifice herself for them.

Of course, she realises, the decision may be taken out of all of their hands – that somehow the police may catch up with him. She wonders how she can find out what, if anything, they've got, the police. She looks at Len again, can't quite get her head around just how normal he's presenting as. Perhaps he's a psychopath...

Momentarily distracted by her thoughts, Maggie leans on the kitchen door and it creaks.

'Mags! Is that you?'

Immediately, Maggie composes herself. She takes a deep breath and walks with purpose through the kitchen door.

'Hello, my darlings,' she says brightly. 'I'm home.'

21 DAN

The still silence in the incident room reminds me that I'm alone, for now at least.

I stand, move over to the window and pull at the cheap, dusty Venetian blind, open it a crack between my fingers. It's dark outside, somewhere just gone midnight I'd say.

I check my watch: 12.11 a.m. Well, at least I'm on the money in one respect. It's hot and stuffy thanks to the sudden hot spell that has descended upon the UK, a gift from the Gulf of Mexico apparently. Unsurprisingly, the air con has packed up in the office and the smell of toil and sweat lingers heavy in the thick air.

I pull at the collar of my shirt, unbutton it as I rub my eyes – they feel gritty and sore, like they've shrunk back into their sockets. I can feel my body shutting down. My head feels tight, like it's stuck in a vice, and my feet are like two barking dogs. I know I should go home, get some rest like I've instructed the team to do, but my brain won't allow it, won't wind down like my body is actively doing, and the internal battle taking place between the two is only compounding my fatigue.

I think of Fiona, my heavily pregnant wife. She's only a few weeks off her due date now – theoretically she could go into labour at any time. I know I should be with her instead of pacing up and down here like a fart in a fixture, turning in circles and getting nowhere. I know she needs me; that I should be in our poky flat placing pillows underneath her bump and rubbing *her* aching feet. She'll have been running around after Juno all day no doubt, and I say running in the literal sense. I swear my daughter has wheels instead of feet. Who needs the gym when you have an inquisitive three-year-old firecracker with seemingly boundless energy to keep up with? I think about stopping off at the takeaway on the way home, picking up some of that tom yum soup Fiona keeps craving in a bid to assuage some of the guilt I feel.

'I thought the cravings stopped after the first few months,' I'd said one night after my second trip up to our local takeaway – the amusingly named Wok This Way.

'Have *you* ever been pregnant?' she'd shot back, the lid already off the polystyrene pot. I'd wisely not answered her, just handed her a spoon instead.

And so it's here that I find myself, faced with many questions and few answers, which isn't the equation I'd hoped for. A burning sense of responsibility towards Amelie Fox and her parents, Helen and Tony, is what's keeping me here, shattered and alone in the incident room in the early hours of the morning. I owe it to them all to get to the truth, to give them the answers they so desperately need to allow them to begin the arduous, mountainous climb towards acceptance of their daughter's murder. In my experience as a homicide detective, it's always the not knowing, the unanswered questions, the lingering whys and hows that torment and torture those left behind. My burden to fill these empty gaps feels, in this moment, overwhelming.

I suppose a murder case is much like completing a jigsaw puzzle: providing you have all the pieces, you just need to fit them together to create the whole picture. The problems arise when there are pieces missing, a bit like buying a second-hand jigsaw from a charity shop and realising it's incomplete.

My father used to do jigsaws, great big ones, 2,000 pieces plus, especially after my mum died. I suppose it gave him something to do, kept his mind occupied and distanced from the painful finality of his loneliness. He'd spend weeks, sometimes months, painstakingly fitting them together, tiny piece by tiny piece. He'd start by building the framework and then gradually fill in the body. It had always looked like a lot of hard work to me.

'How on earth do you know where each piece goes?' I'd asked him once, looking at the front of the box of the particular picture he was hoping to recreate: 'The Great Wave off Kanagawa'.

'You don't even like water,' I'd remarked, wondering why he'd chosen such an image. 'And you've always said you've never fancied Japan.'

'That's really not the point, Daniel,' he'd replied brusquely. 'It's not the final image that gives me the pleasure – it's all in the construction, the creation.'

I'd picked a random piece up in my fingers. 'So you know, just by looking at it, where this piece goes?'

'I have a fair idea,' he'd said, glancing at it. 'That piece you're holding is a floater.'

'A floater?' It had sounded ominous.

'Yes, it means it's neither a corner piece nor an edge – it fits in around other pieces. A floater.'

'I see,' I'd said, replacing it among the thousands of other identical-looking pieces.

'Time and practice and patience, Danny Boy!' he'd said, picking it up and almost instantly placing it into the puzzle correctly. 'You come to recognise them after a while, get a feel for where they sit in the bigger picture.'

I stare up at the incident board in front of me. It covers the entire back wall of the room. Tiny pieces of information that need to be fitted together to create the final image – to provide the bigger picture.

I get the sense that we have all the pieces of this particular puzzle, but that as yet I haven't managed to complete the outer framework somehow.

I hear my father's voice in my head. *'You can't start a jigsaw from the inside out – you must begin with the outer workings, the frame.'*

I blink at the myriad pictures of Amelie Fox in front of me, of the last photograph of her ever taken, her smile wide and easy, juxtaposed next to the one of her bloated corpse. I glance at the maps and routes, at the names scrawled on the whiteboard with black marker pen. The words 'sex tape, male identity?' jump out at me, swiftly followed by 'missing scarf – Alexander McQueen'. There's a picture of it next to them, pale pink with little black skulls...

I feel frustration rise up through me, prickling my skin. By rights this case should've been solved by now – after all, we have a wealth of evidence in our possession. We have a body that's given us DNA, semen, and as yet untested DNA from underneath Amelie's fingernails and a partial fingerprint. We have her clothes, minus the scarf, and we've identified the perfume bottle that was used to hit her on the back of the head. We also have a sex tape featuring an unidentified male who's yet to make himself known to us. Archer has convinced herself that this individual is paramount in the case, largely because I believe he's the closest thing we've got to a prime suspect – the only thing in fact. But there *is* something missing, something important, something integral to unravelling the mystery of Amelie Fox's murder: motive. I can't seem to find one, and the pieces of the jigsaw puzzle in front of me offer no real explanation.

Why was she killed? Who could've wanted her dead? By all accounts, she had no enemies, wasn't involved in anything untoward or illegal, there's no evidence of blackmail or coercion, and nothing to suggest she was being stalked or harassed. Her family loved her, adored her; she had plenty of friends – all of whom spoke well of her. The amateur sex video, which no doubt caused her family some embarrassment, hadn't seemed to affect her in an overtly negative way when she'd been alive. She'd made no complaint to the police, no request to have it removed from the porn sites it originally appeared on.

I pick up a biro from my desk, tap it against my lips as I stare at the jigsaw pieces in front of me, attempt to build that all important framework my father swore by.

Amelie was at home the day she was murdered. Someone came to see her at her apartment in Chelsea, someone who knew where she lived, someone she didn't feel threatened by, at least not at first. The killer took her by surprise, I feel sure. She didn't see the blow to the back of head coming. They'd left her there, dead in her bedroom, and come back for her body sometime later. How did the killer know that she would be alone by the time they returned? How could they've known that her flatmate Holly Redwood wouldn't return home and find her body before they'd had the chance to dispose of it? Was it simply luck? Chance? Had Amelie told her perpetrator that Holly would be out all day and evening? What's making me believe that this wasn't a sexually motivated crime yet was made to look like one?

There's someone in this equation that we don't yet know about and it's not simply a case of putting these pieces together, it's a case of *finding* them.

My phone rings, dragging me away from my nagging thoughts.

'Dr Livingstone, I presume?' my wife's dulcet tones greet

me from down the receiver. 'Are you planning on paying us – you know, your family – a visit, any time soon?'

She doesn't sound angry, more... resigned, I suppose. Fiona knows what I do, who I am, *how* I am, and for the most part she accepts this – the long absences, my lack of presence even when I'm present, my burning need to find justice for the victims I encounter, and their families. She's cut from a similar cloth, has that compulsive desire to chip, chip, chip away until you uncover the truth, to provide the answers, to give closure. Her own profession, journalism, isn't so dissimilar to my own. Her current condition, however, is.

'I know, I know,' I say, my voice heavy with apology. 'I'm sorry. Are you OK? How are Pip and Leo? How's our bean?'

She sighs heavily. 'Bean is wriggly,' she says, 'keeps turning and moving, kicking... I think they're trying to make a break for freedom.'

'You're not...?'

'No, no,' she says, 'I'm not in labour yet. But I think I've had some Braxton Hicks.'

'Braxton what?'

'Hicks,' she reiterates. 'They're like trial-run labour pains, contractions.'

I feel myself turn cold, try not to recall the screams I remember her making during her contractions with Juno. 'Unearthly' is the word I would use.

'Oh, Fi...'

'They're named after the doctor that discovered them in 1872 – John Braxton Hicks.'

She's nothing if not a wealth of information, and a wave of guilt hits me square in the stomach again. I should be at home – I should be with her now.

'Anyway, it's nothing to worry about, just my body preparing me for what's coming, even though I *know* what's coming, God help me.'

'I'll be home soon,' I say.

Her response is a barely audible sigh and I realise in that moment how much I love her, how lucky I am to have found this woman, the mother of my children, my accidental family. 'Shall I bring you some of your soup?'

I think I hear her smiling.

'The takeaway will be shut now,' she says. 'And anyway, Leo ordered me some on Uber Eats earlier. If I don't birth a wanton, frankly I'll be shocked.'

I smile. Leo, her son from a previous encounter some ten years ago now, is the man of the house when I'm not around, which admittedly is often. It's a role he appears to enjoy – and excel at – but I'm painfully aware that a nine-year-old boy shouldn't really be expected to fill my shoes.

'How's Pip?'

'She's not happy.'

'No? Why?'

'Oh, something or other that happened at nursery,' she says. 'She's becoming a right little diva.'

'What happened?'

'She's jealous I think, of her little friend, Edie. There's a boy, Milano – I think she likes him but he's quite attached to Edie. She was upset that he likes Edie's curly hair, says she wants curly hair just like Edie's so that Milano will like her too.'

'Jealous, but she's only three! And who calls their son Milano anyway?'

Fiona laughs. 'Trust me, it starts young, Dan.'

I exhale, incredulous. But it triggers something inside me, I don't know what, a thought...

'I'll be home soon,' I say again. And again, she says nothing.

I hang up the phone still staring at the wall in front of me.

The door to the incident room opens and it startles me.

I sit up, gather myself. 'Davis?'

She's in the doorway, holding two coffee cups and a piece of paper.

'What in God's name are you still doing here? I thought I told you to go home hours ago.'

'You did,' she says, placing the cup onto my desk. 'And as usual I ignored you.'

She perches against my desk, opens the lid of her coffee cup.

'Lucy, why are you still here?' I look at her affectionately. 'Haven't you got a home to go to?'

'Nope,' she says bluntly. 'I haven't really, unlike *you!*'

I stare at her, my trusted number two, and feel a pang of sadness. It's not been long since her divorce and I suspect she's probably right – perhaps she doesn't have any reason to go home. This job can sometimes destroy lives, families and most certainly marriages. It takes a certain kind of selfless, independent spouse to understand the job we do, and not everyone is cut out to be the other half of a homicide detective, to understand such a calling. I know I'm lucky. Ah! There it is again, *that word.*

'What's that you've got?' I say, nodding at the papers in her hand.

'Starbucks' finest,' she replies, 'a double espresso macchiato, chai latte something or other.'

She's playing games and I cast her a look.

'Names,' she says, placing the papers onto the desk. 'Of everyone in the area who owns a GM, more specifically, a Cadillac.'

I feel myself perk up and I haven't even had a sip of my coffee yet.

'Ah, really!'

Davis nods slowly, sagely. 'We've requested a list of every single Cadillac and GM owner who attended the vintage-car fest last week too. It'll take time for the organisers to give us all the registered owners' details, but for now...' She taps the papers on my desk. 'Over 300 of them locally.'

I pick up the papers, read the names on them. 'Jonathan Reginald, Carey Sanderson, William Thackeray, Ravinda Vinod, Len Wendover...'

I place them back onto the desk, take a sip of the coffee she's thoughtfully bought me. It hits my empty stomach almost instantly and, with it, an idea.

'DNA,' I say, and Davis looks at me, shaking her head, a gesture that asks me to elaborate on my thinking.

'We'll put a request out locally, ask all the men in the area to give a voluntary DNA sample, see if we get a match.'

'It's worth a try, gov. Got to eliminate to accumulate.'

Davis's eyebrows rise and I feel a slight rise in momentum alongside them.

'I'll get onto it,' she says efficiently. 'Why don't you go home now, gov?' she asks, though it sounds like more of an instruction than a question.

I smile at her, my wonderful colleague and friend who I respect, even love, though I'd never tell her that.

'I am home,' I say.

22 MAGGIE

It's just so ridiculously, stiflingly hot, Maggie thinks as she opens the duplex doors in her kitchen and is hit in the face by a backdraft of warm, dry air. As well as Amelie Fox's murder, the news was full of the 'rare and unprecedented' heatwave that was currently sweeping across the UK like fire, prompting experts to proclaim it the 'hottest May ever on British record' and causing the Met office to issue an amber weather warning.

Lewis and Casey have dropped by unexpectedly this morning to show her the new baby purchases they'd picked up at a trip to the local shopping centre. It's a welcome distraction for Maggie but even as she lightly fingers the beautiful soft knitted blanket and coos over the tiny bibs and booties, she can't stop her racing thoughts, can't focus on anything other than the terrible conflict inside her aching head.

'We've all been invited to attend a candlelit vigil for Amelie Fox tonight,' she says. 'Eight p.m. at Riverdown Park. Christine phoned me earlier, said all the locals are going to pay their respects.'

She tries surreptitiously to gauge Len's reaction as she imparts the news with a sideways glance. He's been in the garage all morning, working on that bloody car, a car she's convinced he used to transport Amelie's body to where they're going to be standing tonight to pay their respects.

Maggie vividly imagines herself looking down at the riverbank, at the expanse of dark inky water, and sees Len as he grunts and huffs and puffs, dragging Amelie's lifeless, naked body from the trunk of the Cadillac before rolling it into the river like an old carpet. She hears the sound the body makes as it impacts with the water, the splashing and popping, the ugly glug-glug noises as Amelie's body is swallowed up in its black jaws. She stifles a shudder.

'I really think we should all go, pay our respects,' she says, finally brave enough to briefly turn and face him. Sweat is dripping into her eyes, causing them to sting and her vision to blur. She wipes them with a tea towel, looks at him. Len has splashes of oil on his overalls, and his hands—

Oh God, his hands are covered in blood! Maggie gasps in shock and her own shoot up to her face in horror, causing her to drop the tea towel.

'What?' Clocking her expression, Len looks down at himself, wide-eyed. 'What's the matter, Mags?'

She blinks at his hands, tries to focus... A warm jet of relief rushes through her system. It's just oil, just grease from the car, yet for a minute she'd really thought... She must be hallucinating in this unbearable heat. She's properly losing it.

'Nothing, I... sorry. I said I think we should go, you know, as a family – show our support.'

'Yes... yes of course we should go,' he agrees, busying himself with the ice machine on the fridge. 'Though we'll need to take plenty of water along – it's like the bloody Sahara desert out there today.'

He switches the machine on and it begins to whir into action. She detected nothing from him, not even the slightest flinch at the mention of Amelie's name.

'Yes,' she agreed, turning to look at Casey, who was still busy sweetly inspecting her nursery purchases. 'You must make sure you stay hydrated in this weather, sweetheart – we don't want you passing out.'

Casey looks up and nods with a bright, wide smile. Her cheeks have a rosy bloom to them and she looks so happy it breaks Maggie's heart.

'I'll look after her, Mum, don't worry,' Lewis says protectively.

Maggie glances at him, wonders if he seems a little subdued today or maybe she's just looking for it. Her paranoia is off the chart.

She's reminded of their last telephone conversation, where he'd confessed to her how he was feeling, of being nervous about the scan, about impending fatherhood. She needs to watch out for any red flags, any signs of anxiety or depression, a decline in his mental health. She really wants to ask him if he's taking his medication but doesn't want to do it in front of Casey, doesn't want to worry her too, not in her condition.

'Who the *fuck* has been using my phone?' Remy suddenly bursts through the kitchen door, causing everyone to look up. Her face is a sweaty red mass of anger.

'Remy!' Maggie says, shocked. 'Language, please!'

'Someone's been using it!' she says, her voice a hard, high-pitched shriek of accusation as she waggles her iPhone at them. 'Someone's been messing with my phone.' She glares at everyone around the kitchen, her eyes narrowing into slits.

Len holds his hands up. 'Don't look at me, sweetie chops,' he says, seemingly unperturbed by his daughter's use of expletives. 'I've been in the garage all morning, working on the Pink Lady.'

'You then!' She turns to Lewis. 'Have you been looking through my phone?'

Lewis rolls his eyes. 'I borrowed it, OK. Mine's run out of juice. I needed to make a quick—'

'How dare you!' Remy rears up like a startled stallion.

Maggie can see her daughter is hyperventilating, her chest heaving with rage.

'How fucking dare you!'

They all stop still in shock.

'Why were you looking on my phone?' she demands. 'It's MINE! I don't go through your phone, do I?' Spittle flecks from her mouth with the force of her projection. 'What gives YOU the right to start—'

'Hey, chill out!' Lewis protests. 'I didn't *look* through your phone. I just borrowed it to make a quick call, OK? Calm the fuck down.'

'Calm the fuck down? CALM THE FUCK DOWN?' Remy moves right up in Lewis's face then as if she's about to strike him.

Maggie gasps.

'I suppose you went through all my messages as well, my personal stuff, looking at my pictures...' She looks him up and down in disdain. 'Nosey, sick bastard.'

'Remy!' Maggie's mouth falls open. 'What the... for goodness' sake.' She instinctively glances at Len, looks to him urgently for support. 'Don't speak to your brother like that! Apologise immediately. He said he borrowed it to make a call that's all. He wasn't snooping – why on earth would he?'

Remy's focus is still on Lewis. 'I don't go poking down your phone, do I? You didn't even ask to use it. And it's typical of *you*, Mum' – she spins round towards Maggie – 'taking his side all the bloody time.'

Maggie turns away from her daughter, dumbfounded. She doesn't want to deal with this now – she really can't.

'Did you read my messages? Did you look through them?' Remy throws her phone down onto the kitchen table so hard that the screen breaks with a sharp crack, causing Casey to wince in alarm.

'Jesus, what is this?' Lewis stands, abandons the baby clothes he and Casey had been looking through. 'Are you off your head?'

'Ha!' Remy sneers, a defiant hand on her hip as she faces off with her brother. 'I think *that* particular accolade belongs to you in this family, doesn't it?'

A look of hurt, swiftly followed by anger, flashes across Lewis's face. 'You spiteful little—'

'That's ENOUGH,' Maggie snaps, unable to take any more.

Frowning, she turns to her daughter. 'What the hell is wrong with you? Why are you behaving like this?'

'I'll tell you why,' Lewis says, suddenly looking on the verge of tears. He hates any kind of confrontation, and Remy knows this.

'Leave it, Lew,' Casey says softly. 'It's not worth it.'

'It's because of this bloke she's wrapped round, isn't it? This... dickhead she's gone all soft over. Had an argument with him, have you? Is that why you're so pissed off, overreacting like some sort of lunatic?'

'Oh fuck off, will you?' Remy hisses, snatching her phone from the table and inspecting it. 'Oh for— It's broken!' She glares at Lewis. 'Look what you made me do!'

Lewis is looking at Maggie, shaking his head in disbelief. 'I borrowed it for a few seconds, that's all,' he says miserably. 'You're not right in the head, you know, kicking off like that.'

Shaking, Maggie folds her arms tightly around her chest. 'Stop this,' she begs, 'please. I hate it when you two fall out. It's only a phone for God's sake.' She turns to Remy. 'I'm sure your brother wasn't snooping, Rems. You need to calm down. Sit down,' she says softly, trying to defuse the situation. She glances at Len, widens her eyes, silently requesting he step in.

'Yes, sit down, Rems, you're getting your knickers in a twist over nothing, sweetheart. He just borrowed it to make a phone call, that's all.'

'Must be some shit on there that you don't want anyone seeing,' Lewis remarks sardonically. 'Why else have such a fucking meltdown? And why aren't you back at college anyway? Term started ages ago.'

'Oh please.' Maggie bangs her fist onto the table. 'Enough now, both of you. It's too hot for this... and I want us to put on a united front for tonight.'

'Tonight? Why, what's happening tonight?' Remy falls into one of the chairs and immediately begins looking at something on her phone like nothing has happened. She grabs a biscuit from a plate on the table and takes a bite.

'Amelie Fox.'

'What about her?' she murmurs with a mouthful of custard cream.

'Jesus, it's so hot today.' She pulls at her cropped T-shirt and puffs. 'I could barely sleep last night. We seriously need air con, or a swimming pool or something. Alex's family have one, you know, in their garden, and they're not even as well off as we are.'

Lewis and Casey are silent, the buoyant mood of earlier all but evaporated.

'We're going to go and pay our respects tonight for Amelie Fox, down at the park. All the locals are going... it's a candlelit vigil. You'll come, won't you?'

Remy doesn't look up from her phone. 'Oh that, yeah I saw. It's all over Insta – everyone's going to be there.'

'Yes, and so should we, as a family, show our support to the Foxes. Show that we *care*.'

'Well, actually, I was thinking I might go and get my hair done in town later – this weather turns it into a frizz ball... and I'll need to get this screen fixed now thanks to old beak-nose here.' She briefly looks over at Lewis, but her blind anger seems to have dissipated now. 'I'm not sure I'll be able to make it.'

Maggie swings round. 'Yes, well it's not a bloody catwalk, Remy, it's a remembrance vigil for a local girl that's been murdered and you *will* be there. We all will.'

Remy still doesn't look up from her phone. Maggie feels a flourish of irritation prickle her skin. 'Can't you put that bloody thing down for five minutes? It's caused enough trouble as it is. Surely you can go a few minutes without talking to What-shisface!'

Remy finally looks up at her then, her mouth a little open. She glances over at her father.

'Jesus, *someone* got out of the wrong side of bed this morning!'

'Just make sure you're ready for 7.30 p.m.,' she says, willing her own anger to dissipate. It's not like her to snap. They'll think something's wrong.

Everything's wrong.

'OK, OK, keep your bloody wig on.' Remy stomps from the kitchen, tutting loudly before slamming the door behind her.

The room is silent for a moment.

'I think we'd better be off,' Casey says, eventually breaking it. 'We'll see you tonight, at the vigil.'

'See you tonight, Mum,' Lewis says, standing.

Maggie detects deflation in his inflection. Remy's temper tantrum has clearly killed his earlier happy disposition.

'Don't worry about Remy, darling.' She looks at him apologetically. 'You know what she's like sometimes.' But even as she says it, she thinks how over the top her daughter's outburst had been.

'She's not bloody right in the head,' he grumbles miserably. 'Anyway, later, Mum, Dad...'

Len was staring at her as they left the room.

'What?'

'Nothing,' he says quickly, adding, 'Are you OK?'

'Me?' she says defensively. 'I'm fine… just a bit taken aback by Remy's outburst that's all. I don't know what's wrong with her sometimes.'

His head is cocked; he's looking at her curiously.

'Oh, give the girl a break,' he says dismissively. 'She's in the first flushes of love – you remember what that's like, don't you? I certainly do – hormones all over the place, all hot and heavy, every minute spent thinking about that person, wanting to talk to them, see them… surely you haven't forgotten what it's like? You wouldn't want your brother looking through your private messages either, would you?'

'I don't have a brother,' she replies flatly, 'and he *wasn't* looking through her private messages.'

He seems so cool and calm it's all she can do not to come at him with the knife she's been washing in the sink, plunge it into his chest over and over again until he collapses in a lifeless bloody heap on the tiles. It would be no less than he deserved.

'And yes, of course I remember what it was like in the beginning,' she adds miserably with an ache in her chest. 'I'm just hot… hot and tired, that's all.' She turns her back to him once more. She felt like she might unravel at any moment, like a loose thread on an old sweater.

Hold it together, Maggie. Please just try and hold it the hell together.

'I'll make you a peppermint tea,' Len says, pouring some hot water onto a teabag.

'Here you go.' He places a mug down next to her by the sink. 'It'll cool you down, relax you.'

Relax? How can she *relax*?

She glances down at it. She's never even liked peppermint tea all that much, though Len insists on making her a cup of it every evening to take up to bed, but now she can no longer stand the smell of it, the bitter taste of it on her tongue. Maybe she should tell him this, tell him that she hates peppermint tea, and she hates Rod Stewart's 'Maggie May' as well come to think of it, but above all that she hates the fact that *he's a murderer*. Maybe she should just come clean, tell him that she knows everything, about the porn, his internet search history, about him lying about where he was last Wednesday and creepy Clive's sighting in the early hours of Thursday morning... She'll tell him that despite knowing all of this, she's not going to go to the police and that she isn't going to turn him in but instead will keep his sordid secrets, not for his sake, but for the sake of their family, for their children – their innocent children – and their grandchild on the way.

Maggie realises in that moment that she's never kept a secret from her husband throughout their entire marriage, not until now anyway, and it wasn't even her secret to keep.

Maggie sighs. He comes up behind her then, wraps his arms around her waist, and she feels her body stiffen like the onset of rigor mortis.

'We could always have an "afternoon nap" together, if you fancy it?' he whispers into her ear, nuzzling the back of her neck. 'Remember those early days when we first met and couldn't keep our hands off each other, like Rems and this guy she's taken with? I've worked up quite an *appetite* this morning, and you look hot in those gym shorts I have to say...'

He squeezes her backside, gives it a playful little slap. She thinks she might throw up in the sink, has to grip it for support.

'I would if I didn't have so much to do today... darling,' she adds for authenticity, moving out of his clutches and placing the spotlessly clean knife into the kitchen drawer. 'Got a shop to do, and I'm getting my nails done in town.' The first part was true at least.

'A woman's work, eh?' he says, sighing. 'It's never done.'

'I'd hug you but I'm literally a hot sweaty mess!' Christine's familiar voice reaches Maggie's ears as she approaches. She leans in, kisses both her cheeks warmly and does the same to Len before greeting Lewis and Casey and Remy.

Maggie feels herself tearing up as a plethora of conflicting emotions rises up within her. On one hand she's happy to see her friend, relieved, comforted by the familiarity of her – oh, how she needs some comfort right now. Yet she can barely look her in the eye because she realises it's not just the police she'll be lying to, it's not just Amelie Fox's family she'll be keeping the awful truth hidden from, it's everybody, isn't it? She wonders what Christine would say, what advice she would give her if she was to confide in her, tell her everything.

'All the gang's over here...'

She looks over Christine's shoulder, sees Lorraine and Linda and Jackie standing together. Jackie is fanning Linda's face with what looks like a magazine in a bid to cool her down. Gary, Christine's husband, is here too. Len has gone over to join him already, chatting animatedly, incredulously, like it's a social event.

'And look who else has shown up... *together*.' Christine links a sticky arm through her own.

Maggie feels grateful for the support. She's honestly not sure how she's managing to stay upright, and this unbearable heat isn't helping. Drinking half that small bottle of vodka in secret before leaving the house probably hasn't helped either, but she'd needed something to get through the evening.

'Who?' Maggie asks. Her reactions feel sluggish, impaired. Christine raises an eyebrow, points in another direction.

She turns to look, sees busty Brenda and creepy Clive, standing a little further down to the left of them. Brenda is wearing a translucent strapless summer dress that leaves little to the imagination, not least because her infamous chest is spilling over the top of it like pizza dough. She and Clive are looking down at something in Brenda's hand. It looks like a remembrance card; other people seem to have them too, small laminates with Amelie's photograph in an oval shape in the middle with words around it – a poem, or a eulogy perhaps.

'Here you go, Mum,' Lewis says, handing her one along with an ice-cold bottle of water. 'I got one for you, and you, Rems.'

He gives one to his sister. The earlier tension between them, thankfully, seems to have passed and she looks down at it, takes a photo of it on her phone.

'Remy!' Maggie hisses at her.

'What?'

'Don't do that – it's inappropriate!'

Remy rolls her eyes. 'But I was just going to put it on Insta!'

Christine gives her a little eyebrow raise. 'They can't fart, kids these days, without letting everyone know about it on social media. My Billy's the same. He'd be here tonight only he's up in Manchester with his girlfriend – lovely little thing she is... Anyway, that dress!' She looks over in Brenda and Clive's direction once more. 'I mean, I know it's a heatwave and everything but still… you can practically see what she had for lunch!'

'Brave,' Maggie manages to say, adding, 'but I suppose if you've got it, you may as well flaunt it.'

Christine will suspect something if she doesn't do her best work to appear normal. She's an emotionally astute woman who picks up on other people's vibrations easily. If Maggie's not careful, she'll get the third degree.

'Brave or *brazen*?' Christine says, though without her usual acerbic edge. 'It's a fine line.'

'Maybe she had a premonition that it was going to be such a hot evening?' Maggie says, but the humour she's attempted to inject into her voice falls woefully flat.

'A premonition?'

'Apparently she's psychic,' Maggie says, recalling the conversation she'd had with Brenda the day she had turned up at their house impromptu and had brought flowers, after the party.

'She's *what*?' Christine's head spins round. 'Nooo! Shut *uuup*!'

Maggie nods. She feels like she's on autopilot, like another entity is wirelessly operating her from the inside out. 'Reckons she has "the gift".'

'Yeah, right.' Christine snorts. '*Two* of them! Anyway, it's lovely that the kids came along tonight. I thought Remy would be back up in London by now, back up to college?'

'She wants to stick around a bit longer,' Maggie says. 'She says it's easier to study at home, fewer distractions and— Shit!' Maggie curses suddenly.

'What?'

'Oh, it's nothing.' She shakes her head. 'Just that I forgot to make a phone call today,' she says, remembering that she *still* hasn't got round to returning the voice message that woman from Remy's college had left her. She supposes she could be forgiven for the oversight, all things considered.

'Brain fog,' she says, tapping the side of her temple. 'I'd forget my own head if it wasn't attached to my neck.'

'Hmm, you need to get yourself down to see that GP of yours, pronto,' Christine says with her usual sisterly concern. 'The moment I went on HRT, all those horrible symptoms like forgetfulness, hot flashes and the dreaded *dry vagina*' – she says the words from the corner of her mouth – 'they vanished – poof! – I'm telling you. It's like a little patch of magic!'

Maggie tries to smile, gulps some water. If only there were a patch available on the NHS that erased time and memory. She'd give her house for one if it existed, swap it for the symptoms of a hundred thousand menopausal women collectively.

This time last week, she'd been gearing up for the party, run ragged with last-minute preparations, the extent of her worries amounting to whether or not she should opt for pink-and-white ribbon to decorate the cake she'd ordered or go for the sugar-paste flowers instead. She wants so much to be that woman again, the one from last week who was happy and content, bliss-fully unaware, but she knows now that she's gone forever, that she'll never be that person again. How can she be?

Lorraine taps her on the arm by way of acknowledgement. 'Fancy a bit of light refreshment in Jazz's after, Mags?' she whispers underneath her breath. 'We're all heading up there later for a few mimosas…'

The crowd noise lulls to a hush. Someone is about to speak.

'Thank you all for being here, especially in this heat, to cele-brate my sister's life, to mourn her tragic death. It means so much to our family to see so many of you turn out to pay your respects tonight, to say goodbye to our beautiful Angel.'

Maggie looks up at the handsome young man who's a male version of his sister, young and ridiculously good-looking. Guilt flushes through her like a virus.

He continues to speak about his little sister, shares some anecdotes from their childhood that raise a few melancholy laughs from the crowd, but she can't listen to it, begins to hum a tune inside her head in a bid to block out his voice.

She glances sideways at Len – he's staring straight ahead, expressionless, and she wonders what he's thinking in this moment, how he's even able to physically stand here among Amelie's friends and family. How has he got the front, the gall, the *nerve* to have turned up tonight, bold as brass, to face them all, knowing... *knowing* that he's the reason they're all gathered here in the stifling muggy heat, *knowing* that it's because of him that people are crying, holding lit candles with their heads bowed, comforting each other in their grief and loss?

They can do that though, can't they, psychopaths? She's seen it on these true-crime documentaries that had seemed so shockingly far removed from her own existence before any of this happened.

Maggie looks down at the grass underneath her flip-flops. She feels such hatred and loathing towards her husband in that moment that she wants to scream out loud and point. 'He did it! This evil bastard standing next to me! He killed your sister, your daughter, your friend! He's a sick, twisted, monster that needs to be locked up for all eternity!'

'... my mum and dad want to say a few words...' The brother has finished his speech and now it's Helen and Tony Fox's turn.

She watches as they walk in tandem, solemnly onto the grass verge. She can see in her peripheral vision that Jackie is clutching her chest, biting her lip, and Linda is already fighting back tears before she's even opened her mouth.

Helen Fox is wearing a T-shirt with Amelie's face on it. She recognises the image, the last one ever taken of Helen's only daughter, her head thrown back in careless abandon, her long blonde hair, her perfectly neat teeth and that scarf... that wretched scarf.

Hot candle wax is dripping down onto Maggie's fingers now, but she doesn't move them – the sharp burst of pain is almost a relief.

'My daughter, Amelie Letitia Fox, was known to most people as "Angel".'

Helen Fox's voice sounds thin and strained. Maggie hears the anguish in it, the raw pain tangible, like she could reach out and catch it in her hands. She closes her eyes for a moment in a bid to prevent – or at least delay – the tears from forming behind them. Even if she might have recognised Helen Fox under ordinary circumstances – as Christine had insisted she would – she certainly can't now. The woman looks like all the air and blood has been drained from her body. She looks fragile and diaphanous, like a light wind would blow her clean over. Liquid is running down her thin face – she isn't sure if it's tears or sweat or a mixture of both.

'God, she's aged ten years since I last saw her,' Linda remarks, 'and that was only a few weeks ago. That poor, poor woman. My heart absolutely breaks for her.'

'It was a childhood nickname that not only befitted her but became her in the end,' Helen continues.

Her voice is breaking, cracking like the embers of a fire. She's on the verge of breaking down, Maggie can sense it, but she knows, somehow, that – like her – she can't, that she must be strong for her daughter, her murdered dead daughter, just like she must be strong for her family too.

'The day Amelie was born, twelfth April 2000, Tony and I were gifted a millennium miracle, an angel. From day one she was a head turner, stopped passers-by in their tracks with that face of hers. "Isn't she an angel?" Strangers would look into the pram, and she'd smile right back up at them...' Helen's own smile reflects the pain of the memory. 'She lived up to her nick-name – she blessed everyone she met, bringing kindness and joy and love to all the many, many lives she touched in her young life before it was brutally snatched from her, from us all...'

She falters then, stumbles slightly, and her husband brings his other arm onto hers for support.

'I still can't believe she's never coming home, that I'll never again see her beautiful face as she breezes through the front door, full of life, full of stories, full of laughter and energy and hope... I can still smell her everywhere, the perfume she wore and...'

Maggie's heart jumps in her chest. The perfume, sweet and pungent, the same perfume Brenda wore, one that asked – demanded – that you notice the person wearing it. She'd been right – it was the same smell that had been on the scarf, that was *still* on the scarf hidden in the trunk of Len's Cadillac.

'... we ask you, our friends, our family, Amelie's friends, our neighbours and strangers alike, we implore you, *beg you* to help us find the person who took our beautiful girl away. She didn't deserve to die, she didn't deserve to die in such a cruel, brutal way...'

Helen pauses – she's swaying slightly on her feet, like she's about to pass out. It's just so damned hot.

'We've spent our whole lives protecting our children, as every good parent does, and we're tortured by the thought that in the end, when she needed us most, we weren't there to help her, to save her from the monster who snuffed out her life and threw her away like a piece of rubbish, a—' Helen stops, drops her head, and her husband gestures to their son to help his distraught mother.

'This is awful,' Casey says, rubbing her belly, visibly upset. 'We'll have a daughter ourselves soon and...'

Lewis puts a protective arm around her, draws her into him.

A camera flash pops in the night sky like a firework.

'The press.' Christine leans in towards Maggie. 'There are cameras everywhere... they say they're trying to raise awareness of the case, but, well, if you ask me, they're just bloody ghoul-ish... and they've done a great job of making her out to be some kind of slut, what with that home video circulating everywhere. It's so wrong, so unfair. I'd sue the bloody bastards!'

'Please' – Tony Fox takes the microphone from his wife – 'please help us find who did this to Amelie. If anyone knows anything, if anyone remembers anything, however insignificant you may think it is, however trivial, please speak to Detective Riley of the Met Police...' He gestures to a tall man with dark hair standing a little way to his right.

Maggie's eyes shoot towards him. The police – the police are here, at the vigil!

Adrenalin explodes in her stomach like a mushroom cloud, and more camera pops illuminate the sky. She briefly glances at Len, expecting to see something on his face, a flicker of fear perhaps, a dip of the head, guilt, remorse, *anything*, but he looks the same as he always does, his face, though beaded with perspi-ration, gives nothing away.

The detective takes the microphone from Tony Fox, comes to the forefront. 'It's with great sadness and regret that we are gathered here today, as much to celebrate Amelie's life as to mourn her untimely and truly abhorrent death.'

Pop, pop, pop. The sound of the cameras, the flash of the lights are triggering her, setting her off. Suddenly, she's besieged by a primeval urge to run, to kick off her flip-flops and sprint away. How is Len managing to remain so bloody calm, so normal and unaffected when she feels like this, like *she* is the one who's committed murder, the one experiencing all the fear and panic and guilt and remorse, like *she* is the guilty party?

'I ask, on behalf of Amelie's devastated parents, her family, friends and loved ones, for anyone to come forward with any information, reiterating what Tony has said, however insignifi-cant they feel it may or may not be, anonymously if needs be. We believe that Amelie's killer is local, and I say this not to alarm you but to arm you with knowledge and power... which is why we're asking you, voluntarily, to give a DNA sample, to help us eliminate you from our ongoing enquiries.'

'Jesus Christ!' Lorraine's whisper reaches Maggie from down the line. 'He could be here, tonight, the killer, standing next to us!'

Oh, the irony!

'You'll do it, won't you, Gary?' Christine nudges her husband. 'You'll give a voluntary DNA sample.'

'Too right,' he says. 'I hope they catch the bastard and quick.'

Silent tears are streaming down Maggie's cheeks now, and as fast as she attempts to brush them away, she can't keep up with them. *Oh God,* they'll want Len's DNA sample too, won't they? He can't be seen not to give one – it would look suspicious, would draw attention to him, *to them.*

Maggie can taste the vodka she consumed earlier – it's threatening to make a reappearance, burning the back of her throat. She thinks she's going to be sick right here, right now on the grass. She can't stay here a moment longer.

Helen Fox is making her way through the crowd now and— Oh no – no, no, no, she's heading towards them!

'Helen, we're all so, so sorry.' Lorraine, typically, commandeers her first, grabs her hand as she's passing.

Helen stops momentarily, nods her thanks with tired, red-rimmed eyes. 'Thanks... thank you all for coming.'

Linda lurches forward and hugs her tightly, says something into her ear, and Helen smiles as she releases herself from her embrace before looking directly at Maggie.

'Thank you so much for being here,' she addresses her. 'Amelie would be so touched.'

Maggie can't speak – she's too afraid of what will come out of her mouth if she opens it. She tries to say something, but her voice box feels like it's been superglued shut, bonded by a viscous layer of guilt.

'She went to school with some of you, didn't she?' Helen looks at Remy.

'Yeah,' Remy says, 'she was in a couple of classes above me... I didn't know her or anything, but I always thought she was kinda cool. I'm so sorry for your loss – I really am.'

Maggie hears a catch of emotion in her daughter's voice, like she's about to burst into tears.

Helen touches Remy's face affectionately. 'Bless you, sweetheart.'

'Our hearts go out to you,' Len suddenly says. 'As the father of a daughter myself, I can only imagine...'

'Thank you,' Helen says again. 'It means so much that you came.'

She moves away from them, continues her solemn parade through the crowd, words of condolence ringing out through the thick humid air as she passes.

Maggie feels as if she's turned to stone. She can't move; she tries to breathe but it feels like the hot air is burning her lungs. How can he do this? How can he look Helen Fox in the eyes and say those words like he means them? It's inhuman, so cold and calculated, so *evil*.

Len grabs her hand then, squeezes it, and instinctively she snatches it away. He looks visibly stunned by her reaction.

'Mags? Are you OK?'

She shakes her head violently. 'I... I think I'm going to be sick.'

24 DAN

The killer is close. They're here, tonight, in among the crowd, hiding in plain sight. I sense it, can feel it all around me, oppressive in the atmosphere, a dark cloud descending, like impending rain. My empty guts are churning manically as I look out into the crowd of people gathered together to pay tribute to Amelie Fox, a sea of solemn eyes blinking back at me.

The crowd is a mixed bag of men and women, young, old, all ages, genders and race. Amelie moved in trendy circles, was on the peripheries of celebrity culture, a model and influencer, and tonight's attendees for her candlelit remembrance include the young, attractive millennials she preferred to associate with, but there's also people she grew up with too, the parents of the people she knew from childhood, neighbours, old schoolteachers, local shopkeepers... ordinary, everyday people, *local* people.

I'm acutely aware that my decision to mention a request for voluntary DNA samples tonight is something of a gamble. And no one more than my dearest number two makes this patently clear to me.

'That was a bold move, boss,' she says, rapidly blinking at

me like I've had a full frontal lobotomy. 'You do realise it could give our killer the heads-up, especially if it *is* a local guy we're looking for. He could get scared and do a bunk. I mean, he could be here, tonight, in the crowd.'

'Innocent people don't usually run, Davis.' I give her my wisest smile but she's right of course. 'A man with nothing to hide hides nothing. And if he does abscond, then it will be *him* giving *us* the heads-up, don't you think?'

'If you say so, boss.' She's shaking her head – the method to my madness.

'And the killer *is* a local, Davis,' I say unequivocally, 'and they *are* here tonight, right under our noses, no doubt verbalising their condolences, hugging the Foxes, even speaking to the bloody press... which is why I need you and Parker to be extra vigilant.'

'How do you know they're here tonight, gov?'

I cast her a sideways look furnished by the lightest brow raise. She knows better than to ask me that question, so much so that she doesn't even bother to wait for an answer.

'Where is Parker by the way?'

I've requested his presence tonight because he's got an exceptionally keen eye. He's an unassuming sort, doesn't say much, but when he does, it's usually worth listening to – a rare quality – and something of a gift, not least in this game. Parker seems to possess an innate ability to read people correctly, qualities that if used correctly could see him go far in this business.

I spot him, beckon him over.

'Boss?' he addresses me keenly, his youthful exuberance somewhat infectious, giving my increasing exhaustion a little lift.

'I want both you and Davis to be extra vigilant tonight. Keep an eye out for any unusual behaviour, and any *usual* behaviour too, come to think of it. Watch out for body language, engage all your senses – eyes, ears and most importantly your gut. Talk to people but, more importantly, let *them* talk to *you*.'

In my experience, which is somewhat seasoned, compared to Parker's anyway, guilty parties are often wont to give themselves away – involuntarily of course. If you think about it, we all do. Watch closely enough and people often give off vital silent clues, subtle nuances that trigger a gut feeling or reaction that something is off. It's a proven scientific fact that whenever we tell a lie, our heartbeat and breathing quickens, our blink reflex becomes more rapid, our adrenalin increases, triggering our fight-or-flight response, perhaps our face flushes a little, our toes tap or our palms sweat – though in this heat anyone's would to be fair. Inauthenticity can be difficult to detect, but in my experience, the body almost always betrays us in some way, leaking information subconsciously. You just need to learn what to look out for.

'Detective... Riley, isn't it?'

A man approaches me with a sense of purpose, his hand outstretched.

'Yes, DCI Riley – Dan Riley.' I nod at him and he shakes my hand firmly.

'Len,' he says, 'Len Wendover, and this is my wife, Maggie.'

She's standing two paces behind him, her face a little pale, illuminated by the candle she's holding.

'We – I mean my wife and I – well, we just wanted to say how grateful we are to the police, for all the hard work you're doing trying to apprehend Amelie's killer, and if there's anything we can do to help...'

'That's very good of you, sir,' I say. 'We're doing everything we can to keep the local community safe.'

He nods sagely. 'Absolutely, yes – yes, of course. I mean, it's incredibly worrying, there being a killer in our midst, what with me being a father and all. I have a daughter a similar age to Amelie, you see. They went to school together actually, not in the same class or anything, but still, bit close to home and all that... Dreadful business. We're all very upset – everyone is.'

'Yes... er, Len, isn't it?'

'Len Wendover, yes, and this is Maggie, my wife; my daughter, Remy; and my son, Lewis; and his partner, Casey.'

I look over at his wife again, an attractive woman with dark hair that's sticking to her face. She's swaying a little from foot to foot.

'Hello, Maggie,' I say, smiling at her.

'Hel—' She coughs slightly, smiles politely. 'Hello.' She tentatively steps forward to shake my hand.

'We live up in Thorton Heath. We've been coming here to Riverdown for decades, haven't we, chickadee? We've been married twenty-five years,' he explains, 'just celebrated our anniversary... get less for murder these days.' He starts to laugh and then stops himself, shakes his head. 'God how insensitive of me!'

I smile politely back at him. 'Twenty-five years is indeed a long time – congratulations. And I understand your concerns; I'm a father myself. I can assure you we're doing all we can to find the person responsible, bring them to justice.'

'That's wonderful to hear... wonderful,' he says. 'Well, it was fantastic to meet you, Detective Riley.'

'Yes, you too, Mr Wendover, Mrs Wendover...'

She nods quickly, flashes me a coquettish smile.

'I can count on you offering a voluntary DNA sample, can I? We're setting up a room at Eden Gorge police station in the next day or so.'

'Yes... yes, absolutely,' he says.

'Great, that's great, thank you – we really appreciate it. The more people we can eliminate at this stage, the better.'

'Not at all,' he replies robustly. 'Both my son and I would be happy to help.'

I watch them as they leave, Len and Maggie Wendover,

together with their family. The daughter drops something as she walks away – the small, laminated remembrance card that the Foxes have been giving out all evening with their daughter's picture on the front.

'Hey! You dropped—' But they're too far in front of me now and I have neither the time nor the energy to run after them, not least in this unbearable heat.

I'm struck by an odd sensation as I bend down to pick up the card. The name... *Wendover*. It sounds familiar somehow. I know it from somewhere. I've heard it before, haven't I, recently? I'm sure of it, but where?

Come on, Dan. Think, man, think!

I stare down at the laminate in my hand, at Amelie's image, the last one of her ever taken. She smiles back up at me, her beauty almost three dimensional as it leaps out at me, the scarf I've still to find loosely draped around her slim neck, taunting me. I read the florid printed script that surrounds her picture.

> *'Our Angel's Wings'*
> *In life she was our angel,*
> *In death she remains one still,*
> *Only now for all eternity,*
> *Her death the bitterest pill*
> *Our beautiful baby girl, Amelie,*
> *Taken against her will*
> *Fly, fly with those angel wings of yours*
> *Know how much you are loved and adored*
> *Make heaven your home now,*
> *No longer in pain*
> *Fly, fly our darling with those angel wings,*
> *Until we meet again.*
>
> *Amelie 'Angel' Fox, 12/4/2000–23/5/2022*

I daren't swallow for fear of dislodging the tears that are pricking the backs of my eyes, look up to the sky and curse underneath my breath.

25 MAGGIE

'I'm off down the hairdressers, that new one in town,' Remy says as she breezes into the kitchen, grabs a piece of leftover toast from the table and places it between her teeth. 'I'm going for a new look, something different,' she says, taking a bite.

'That's nice, darling,' Maggie replies, hearing the flatness in her own tone. It breaks her heart to hear her daughter – *their* daughter – so upbeat, not a care in the world, her whole life stretched out ahead of her. More than anything she wants it to be a happy and successful one, a *normal* one.

'Yeah, I fancy a change,' Remy explains, ruffling her long dark hair. 'Reinvent myself, you know – a whole new me!'

'What's wrong with the old one?'

Maggie stands in front of the sink. She's been rinsing the same mug out for the past ten minutes now. She desperately wishes she could share her daughter's joie de vivre. What she wouldn't give just to be thinking about a new hairdo. Her body feels so heavy, even taking a few steps feels like a consolidated effort, like she's dragging one club foot in front of the other.

'Nothing,' Remy says. 'Well, actually, *everything*...'

There's a moment's pause.

'Are you OK, Mum? Is everything all right?'

'Yes, darling, I'm fine. Why do you ask?' The question almost undoes her completely and she swallows back the granite lump that's lodged at the back of her throat, continues to scrub the mug without looking round at her daughter.

'I dunno. You don't... you don't seem yourself.'

Was it that obvious? Her family know her intrinsically – they can sense when she's not on her A game. She'll need to make more of an effort. She doesn't want them asking questions.

Ask me no questions and I'll tell you no lies. Only lies are all that she's heard recently, one after the other like lemmings, not least the ones she's been telling herself. Her whole life with Len has been one great big lie.

'I'm just tired,' she says softly, wondering how much more mileage she can get out of this excuse before it wears painfully thin and shatters. 'And this damned heat's not helping. When do you think you'll be going back up to London? Don't you have classes to attend?'

She hadn't meant that how it sounded, like her daughter has overstayed her welcome. But Remy being here, right under her nose, is simply another person to act out this ridiculous charade in front of, and besides, nothing usually gets past her astute daughter.

'You need to chill out, Mum. Why don't you sit in the garden and read a book or something? Or maybe you and Pops should have a weekend break away somewhere together, take some time out, relax?'

'Oh, there's no time for that at the moment, sweetheart – got things to do around the house and...' Maggie can't think of anything worse than spending a weekend in a hotel room with Len. How is she going to get through potentially the next thirty years if the idea of spending just a couple of days alone with her husband terrifies and repels her? Maggie's mind snaps sharply back to last night's vigil again and how Len had so readily – so brazenly – offered to come forward and give a voluntary DNA sample. How on earth was he going to get round that? Would he secretly use someone else's, or had it just been a verbal diversion tactic and he had no intention of providing one?

'Anyway, your dad's busy with his car at the moment. We'll think about that kind of thing once he's finished it perhaps.'

'OK... laters, Mum!' Remy breezes out of the kitchen as quickly as she'd entered it, her trainers squeaking against the tiles.

Hearing the front door close behind her, Maggie starts to cry as she continues manically washing the mug. She's scrubbed the damn thing so hard that some of the pattern has started to peel off.

Through blurred vision, she looks through the kitchen window out onto her beautifully kept garden, tries to appreciate the flowers that are in full bloom, pink roses that have opened up like a loving embrace and daffodils with their happy little yellow faces, so incongruous to how she feels. She needs to keep busy, try to keep her mind occupied on other things because right now it feels as if it's going to explode out of her cranium and splatter across the ceiling. Vacuuming. She'll vacuum the hallway and the stairs, clean the whole house from top to bottom, anything to divert her thoughts and prevent her from pacing up and down the kitchen and brooding, which is what she knows she'd be otherwise doing. She hurries off to the utility room, grabs the cordless vacuum cleaner, the fancy one Len had bought her and that she'd been so pleased with. "No cumbersome cord to trip over chickadee!" She plugs it in and begins vacuuming with purpose, scours every inch of the large kitchen, careful to include the woodwork and the corners until she's worked up a sweat – not that it's difficult in this heat – before tackling the stairs.

If only she had a mother herself to talk to, to turn to. It's been in moments like this, whenever she's felt alone, bereft, frightened and unsure that she feels most robbed of her mother's presence, of a soothing, reassuring voice, a wise word born of experience passed on.

She's long since stopped being angry at her mother for leaving her, but it's taken years to learn how to consciously let that anger go. It had burned inside of her for so many years, a painful black void, asking herself why her mother hadn't loved her enough to stay with her, her own pain and inner turmoil outweighing the love for her only child.

'*She was always a selfish, self-absorbed woman,*' her father's dispassionate voice resonates in her mind.

But there's a sad truth to his words that she's struggled to accept throughout her whole life. Like any child, she'd *needed* her mother, the warmth of her touch, the unconditional love only a mother can have for their offspring. She'd needed her protection, her wisdom, her advice and guidance. As a result of this being so brutally denied her, Maggie had sworn that if and when she ever became a mother herself, she would always be there for her children, put them first, no matter what she may have to endure herself.

Her mother's suicide had left her fearful as a child, without the cloak of protection, without security, without a supportive voice, confirmation that she was doing the right thing, making the right choices, that she wasn't *alone*. She'd been left to her own devices, to navigate her way through life without a reassuring maternal compass. The fear of bad things happening became a preoccupation because she'd learned in the most painful way that they could and did.

But that fear had also propelled her somehow – it had made her vigilant and determined, self-sufficient. She had felt safe and warm and loved when her mother was alive, never having had an inkling that anything might be wrong, that her mother was ill or suffering with her mental health. She'd missed it then just as she'd missed it now. How, after everything, has she done that? All her life, she's been left with unanswered questions about her mother's suicide, which perhaps had been the most painful part, trying to comprehend the incomprehensible, too afraid to ask the questions that may have helped her to heal sooner.

Maggie inhales deeply. It's no good. She needs to know. She needs to understand why Len has done this, needs to confront him, look him directly in the eyes and demand answers.

Suddenly angry, Maggie decides she must do it now. She'll go down to the garage right this minute and tell him she needs to speak to him urgently. She'll just have to find the words somehow, summon up the courage and overcome the fear.

Maggie stands on the landing, the noise of the state-of-the-art vacuum cleaner whirring in her ears, and looks out onto her beautiful, flourishing garden again from the upstairs window as she mentally prepares herself to confront her husband. Switching the vacuum off, she carries it downstairs, practically throwing it back into the utility room before returning to the kitchen where she begins to scrub her hands.

A loud noise startles her so suddenly then that she knocks the mug that's on the drainer back into the sink, where it cracks in half.

'Shit!' What the hell was that...? She stands statue still for a second, listens. It sounded like something falling to the floor, a loud crash...

'Mag... Magg... *Maaaaaggggiiiiiiie...*'

It's... is that Len? His voice is faint but she hears the urgency in his cries and gasps as fear hits her square in the chest like a lump hammer.

Abandoning the sink, she rushes from the kitchen, the sweat in her sandals almost causing her feet to slide out of them as she runs down the hallway towards the internal garage door.

'Len? LEN!' she calls out to him in panic.

Cool air greets her as she swings the garage door open in

haste and that unique smell, the scent of petrol and testosterone, immediately hits her nostrils. He's lying on the floor, the top half of his overall-clad body exposed, but his legs are still positioned underneath the Cadillac.

'Oh my God!' Her hands cover her mouth as she gasps. His eyes are swollen shut, just slits on his face, like two thin pencil-drawn lines. His face is bloated, his skin red and blotchy, angry hives appearing with each passing second.

'*Help... meeee!*' His hands are outstretched towards her, and his voice, barely audible, is a horrible wheezy rattle.

'Oh my God, Len!' She drops down onto her knees instinctively, takes his hand.

'A... a...'

She leans in closer to him, touches his forehead. He's burning up.

'Wa... wasp.'

'A what? Oh Jesus Christ!'

He's been stung and he's gone into anaphylactic shock! She's seen this before, all those years ago when they'd first started dating. The picnic that had ended with him taken away in an ambulance, the scream of the sirens drowning out her own as it had raced him to Thorton General.

'*It was a good thing you called an ambulance when you did. Any longer and his organs would've started to shut down – it could've been fatal.*'

The doctor's words echo all around her as her heart rate accelerates, pulsing loudly in her ears. He needs epinephrine! He needs an ambulance!

Maggie springs into action.

'Just hang on, Len – hang on, OK?'

An influx of adrenalin makes her feel giddy, like she's stood up too quickly. The EpiPen, yes! There's one here somewhere... she's seen it recently, when she was searching for that bloody scarf...

Maggie rushes over towards Len's work bench, opens the cabinet drawer underneath it, her fingers violently shaking as she begins to rifle through it in blind panic, the contents coming alive with her haste.

'*Oh Godddddd...*' Where is the damn thing?

The doctor's words filter through her thoughts again. '*Good thing you called an ambulance when you did... his organs would've started to shut down... it could've been fatal.*'

A terrible thought sprints through her consciousness as she continues searching the drawer. *What if... what if Len died?* If he was dead then no one would know his sordid secret, would they? He'd take it with him to his grave. There would be no police investigation, no knock at the door. No one would ever have to discover the truth – she'd destroy the evidence just like she'd planned to do, have him cremated before they had a chance to obtain his DNA.

No, Maggie, stop – stop this now. This is your husband, the father of your children—

Her children... they'd be devastated by their father's death of course, but this way their lives wouldn't be obliterated by his evil actions. There would be no protracted and very public court case, their loving memories of him would remain forever intact, their names never dragged through the mud, vilified, treated like pariahs, the children of a murderer. People's parents die all the time – her own mother for one – they would grieve him of course, but if he was to die then they would all be spared the shame of his actions, the relentless press intrusion that would inevitably follow if it ever came to light, a lifetime of burden and guilt. If Len was no longer here, they could remain a happy family, lead a normal life. Their granddaughter would grow up never knowing who or what her grandfather really is, was, and they could all stay in this house, the house they grew up in, in a place where they were known and loved and respected, their reputations unscathed, untarnished, *safe*. If Len died, that would solve everything, *wouldn't it*?

'Epi... Ep...' Len's voice is a low, sickening rasp as his breathing becomes more laboured, more shallow, his hands still outstretched towards her, his fingers clenching as though he's reaching for something. He starts to convulse, his body juddering into short sharp spasms, and she sees saliva foaming at the corners of his mouth.

Her whole body violently vibrating, Maggie suddenly slams the drawer shut.

'It's not here – I can't find it!' she says. 'There's one in the kitchen... Hang on, Len – *just hang on!*'

She rushes from the garage, runs down the hallway, through the house towards the kitchen.

She struggles to turn the kitchen door handle, her hands are shaking so violently and slippery with sweat.

She sprints over to the drawer next to the sink and opens it, sees an EpiPen in among the various utensils, the odds and sods. She picks it up, stares at it, her chest heaving so manically that she can hardly retain oxygen in her lungs. She knows that if she doesn't act fast then Len's airways will become blocked, his tongue will swell, and his vital organs will begin shutting down. How long before that starts to happen? A minute or two? Five? Ten? She knows time is of the essence, that she should run back to the garage immediately and administer the shot of epinephrine, she knows this will save his life but... but she just can't move. Her feet feel as if they've been welded to the kitchen floor.

She listens out for him, thinks she can hear him faintly calling out to her, or maybe it's just her imagination. He'll be wondering what the hell she's doing, why she isn't in the garage with the EpiPen, why she isn't helping him, *trying to save his life*?

She looks up at the kitchen clock. How many minutes have passed? Two? Three?

She looks down at the EpiPen in her fingers.

Can you live with this, Maggie? Can you live with the knowledge that you didn't help your husband, that you deliberately stalled in administering him the life-saving medicine he needed? What would be worse, living with and harbouring a murderer's secret, a secret that will forever hang over you and your family, one that could be exposed at any time and that would detonate like a bomb in all your lives, or this way – a tragic, fluke accident that resulted in his accidental untimely death?

Len would die feeling loved by his wife and family, his reputation undamaged. What would be the least hard to live with? She'd still know the truth, but with Len gone, it would be easier, wouldn't it? She could live with his dark secret knowing that the wrong had somehow been righted by his passing. He'd no longer be able to cause any harm to anyone if he wasn't here.

Placing the EpiPen back into the kitchen drawer, Maggie sits down on the kitchen chair and closes her eyes.

Maggie goes over to the fridge, opens it and locates the small bottle of vodka she'd hidden there yesterday, half of it drunk last night so she could get through that awful vigil. She knocks it back straight from the bottle, savours the burn at the back of her throat.

Come on, Maggie – you can do this. You must do this before Remy gets back from the hairdressers.

Her daughter is going to arrive home to the sounds of sirens no doubt, to find that her beloved 'pops' has suffered a terrible fatal accident. She can hear Remy's screams in her ears already, high-pitched with shock and grief. She'll need to be strong for her, to comfort her. She's got to be strong for her children, for all of them.

Oh, Maggie, no... no, you can't do this. You mustn't. There's still time. What are you thinking? He's your husband, your Len – whatever he's done, for whatever reasons, you can't let him die this way. You're a good person, Maggie...

She takes another swig of vodka then snatches the EpiPen from the kitchen drawer and inhales deeply. This isn't the way

– it isn't right. She's not thinking straight. She's lost her bloody mind. All of this... it's wrong. It's all just so wrong.

Clutching the EpiPen, she abandons the vodka and sprints back to the garage, hyperventilating as she opens the internal door. It's still and silent as the cool air hits her, followed by that smell of petrol and testosterone. She sees him in her peripheral vision, can see his body as it was when she found him initially, half sticking out from underneath the Cadillac.

She rushes towards him, throws herself onto the floor next to him before pulling the cap off the EpiPen and stabbing it into his thigh.

He doesn't move, not even a flinch.

'Oh my God...' Her voice is a rattling whimper. 'Oh Christ.' Her hands instinctively cover her mouth. 'Len... LEN! Answer me, Len! LEN!'

He's not moving.

She edges closer towards him, her body vibrating with fear as she shuffles on her knees. One hand is down by his side, the other outstretched next to him, still reaching for something, for someone, *for her*. His face is swollen, puffy and bloated, his skin still red and blotchy. It doesn't look as if he's breathing. She's frozen, watches his chest to see if it's rising and falling. It doesn't appear to be. There's no sign of life.

She's too late.

'Len...' Her voice cracks like broken glass. '*Len.*'

He doesn't respond.

Maggie swallows. It feels airless in the garage, stifling. Her tongue is sticking to her teeth. She swallows again, but there's not a drop of moisture left in her.

'Oh, Len...'

She makes to touch his face with her shaking fingers but pulls away at the last second.

Fighting back fear and revulsion, she makes another attempt, lets her fingers lightly rest on his forehead. His skin still feels warm. Gritting her teeth, Maggie leans in closer towards the body, presses her fingers against his neck to check for a pulse.

There isn't one.

She grabs his wrist, tries to locate one there.

Again, nothing.

Len's wrist smacks against the concrete as she drops it with a gasp.

He's dead.

As the realisation hits her, Maggie stands, backs away from him, knocking something over in the process. Panic floods through her, and she begins crying – short, anguished noises escaping her lips.

'Oh no... no, no, no, no...' What has she done?

She stands for a moment, paralysed by horror. Her head is shaking from side to side, her hands covering her mouth as she continues to say the word no on repeat.

An ambulance. She needs to call the emergency services now!

Suddenly, her panic slips up a gear into self-preservation. The scarf – she needs to find that scarf and dispose of it right now.

Running to the back of the car, Maggie pops the trunk, roughly pulling back the carpet to locate the scarf underneath it.

But it's not there.

Frantic, she pulls the carpet back further, scours the boot. It's... it's gone. It's been moved. Someone... Len has moved it!

Maggie's hands fly up to her face and she claws at her skin with her fingertips. Why isn't it in here?

'What have you done with it?' she screams at Len's lifeless body. 'What have you done with it, you stupid, stupid man!'

Strange animalistic noises emanate from her as she walks in a circle, her hands on top of her head as she tries desperately to think. Forget it – she'll have to forget it, worry about it later. She must call an ambulance – quickly. It can't look like she left it too long before calling the emergency services from the time she found him. They can tell all of these things, can't they, those forensic people? She's seen it on TV. No one gets away with murder.

Running solely on adrenalin and shredded raw energy, Maggie makes her way back into the kitchen to make the call but... she turns back briefly to look at him. *Len.*

She blinks at his body, still and lifeless on the concrete floor, and it hits her like a swinging brick to the face. Her husband, her Len, the man she's been married to for twenty-five years, the man she has two children with, a lifetime of memories, of happy moments, the man she's loved and lived with for three decades, shared so much with, *is dead*, gone forever, and she knows that nothing after this moment will ever be the same again.

Tears are blurring the edges of her vision, slipping from her eyes and splashing down onto her feet. Her hands are slippery and shaking as she punches the numbers into her phone.

'Which emergency service do you require?'

'Yes. Please – please come quick. I need an ambulance – you need to send an ambulance quickly. It's my husband – he's not breathing.'

27 DAN

'It's great,' I say. 'I'll take it.'

The young estate agent looks at me as if I've just told him he's had a lottery win. We've been here less than five minutes.

'Really? That's fantastic, sir. I wish every client was as decisive as that – would make my job a lot easier! Are you sure you don't want to look round a little longer before you make up your mind?'

'Nope,' I say unequivocally. 'I've seen enough. I get a good feeling about the place, you know?' Frankly, the fact that it has more than two bedrooms and some outside space is enough to swing it. We've seriously outgrown my pokey two-bedroom apartment, and I promised Fiona I'd sort something out before our new addition arrives.

'Oh yes, yes,' he agrees emphatically. 'Three decent-sized bedrooms too, and of course, the pièce de résistance...' He opens the small set of patio doors that lead out from the kitchen onto the garden with a theatrical flourish. I can picture Pip out here already, dunking her dollies as she's splashing around in a paddling pool.

I take a sip of water, resist the urge to tip the remainder of it over my head. It's tipping thirty-eight degrees today, an all-time UK record for this time of year.

'When can we move in?'

The ecstatic young estate agent opens his mouth to speak but my phone rings.

'Davis...'

'Where are you, gov?'

'At home,' I say. It's not entirely a lie I suppose.

'Home?' I can tell she doesn't believe me. I'm never at home.

'What is it, Lucy?'

'We think we've found out who the bloke is – the bloke in Amelie's sex tape.'

This is turning into a good day. First a new home, and now a prime suspect.

'His name's been trending on Instagram – looks like he could be our man.'

'And you're sure about that how? It's not like we can identify him by his *face,* is it, Davis?'

I think I hear her smiling.

'Tattoos, gov. We cross-referenced the name with his IG account and he has the same – or at least very similar – tattoos as the guy on the tape has.'

'So, who is he?'

'Name's Graham, gov, Graham Benson – twenty-four from Putney, originally anyway, but—'

'But what? Bring him in!'

There's a slight pause on the line that I sincerely hope isn't a sign my ebullient mood is about to be extinguished.

'Well, he's been away in Marbella, boss, filming some reality TV show called *Sex Text Ur Ex.*'

'Wasn't that the name of the TV show Amelie was planning on appearing in? I'm sure Holly, her flatmate, said something about it.'

'Yeah, I think so, boss. Anyway, we've made contact, and he's back later today, so we'll bring him in then.'

'Good work, Lucy. I can't wait to meet him.'

Maggie chews her fingernails, watching from the window as the ambulance containing Len's dead body disappears from view. Some of the neighbours are out at their front doors, peering towards the house, wondering what's happened, why there's an ambulance, why there are police cars parked outside. She can't blame them – she's pretty sure she would be curtain twitching too if the boot were on the other foot.

She spots creepy Clive looking over, his gangly, awkward frame filling his doorway as Brenda hurriedly makes her way across the road towards him, dressed in a barely there bikini top and a sarong, raising her hands as if to ask 'what's going on?' She snaps the blind shut.

'I'm so sorry to have to ask you these questions at this stressful time, Mrs Wendover – you've had a terrible shock – but I'm afraid I have to. It's routine, you understand?' the policeman – DC Parker she thinks he'd introduced himself as – apologises gently. 'Can you tell me at what time did you enter the garage and find your husband on the floor?'

Maggie turns to face him. 'I don't know. About... 1.30 p.m., 1.45 p.m., I can't say exactly.' She wipes her face with a tissue.

She's sweating profusely, wants to open a window but decides against it. She doesn't want it to look like she's concerned about anything other than her dead husband in this moment.

'I... I'd been vacuuming upstairs, doing some housework. It was so hot. I... I was going to prepare some lunch, make some iced tea to cool off. Len was in the garage, working on his car. It's his hobby, you see – he likes to buy and restore old American vintage cars. His last one was a red Mustang... months he spent fixing it up – it was a real labour of love.'

Her sobs are genuine. She doesn't need to put on an act. *Len is dead. Her husband is really, actually dead.*

She recalls the face of the paramedic as he'd entered the garage, the look he'd given his colleague behind him, a sombre shake of the head.

'I was in the kitchen when I heard a noise—'

'A noise?'

'Yes, a crashing sound. It startled me. I wasn't sure what it was at first, but then he called my name...' Maggie coughs the words into her tissue. 'So I ran into the garage and that's when I saw him on the floor. His eyes were swollen and his skin was all red and blotchy. I went to him, panicked, you know... he said something about a wasp – so many of them about at the moment, especially in this heat. I don't know how long he'd been there like that... I knew he'd been stung, knew about his allergy, so I ran back to the kitchen, grabbed the EpiPen from the drawer. But by the time I reached him... by the time I administered it, I was... I was too late.'

Maggie's head drops into her hands, and she squeezes her eyes tightly shut, tries to erase the image of Len's bloated features flashing up in her head, his convulsing body as it twitched on the floor.

'It's OK, Mrs Wendover,' the DC says gently. 'You did all you could – you did the best you could.'

'But... but I could've saved him, couldn't I?' Maggie looks up at the detective with blurred vision, can feel the hysteria swelling inside of her, threatening to take over. She feels like laughing and screaming all at the same time. She feels *deranged*. 'If I'd just got to him a little earlier, a little sooner... he'd still be here, wouldn't he? He'd still be alive.'

DC Parker hands her a clean tissue, rests his hand on her vibrating arm. She wonders if she'll ever be still again. In this moment, she simply can't imagine it.

'There was nothing else you could've done. It was a tragic accident. I'm so sorry, Mrs Wendover... Maggie. Is there anyone that can be here with you? Anyone you can call?'

Maggie wipes her eyes, but the tears won't stop coming, and her nose is dripping, the new tissue is already soaked through with saline and mucus.

'My... my children. Oh God.' Maggie clenches the wet tissue in her hands. 'They love their dad so much... adore him. They're going to be devastated. It's all my fault... it's all my fault...'

She breaks down then, throws her head forward between her knees as she thinks of her son and daughter. What has she done? Remy will be back from the hairdressers soon and Maggie can imagine her daughter's reaction as she pulls up outside the house to see the police car out front, imagines her panic and confusion as she rushes through the front door to be greeted by the terrible news. And Lewis, her darling boy, so fragile and sensitive, what will it do to him? How will he cope with such a tragedy? Will it send him over the edge, trigger his depression?

You did it for them, Maggie, to save them, to prevent their lives from being ruined, to protect them from the truth. You did it for your children, for your children's children.

'It wasn't your fault, Maggie,' but DC Parker's attempts at reassuring her are no consolation as Maggie grapples with the overwhelming influx of guilt that's snaking its way around her neck, threatening to strangle her. 'It wasn't your fault.'

He pats her arm again, the young policeman who couldn't be much older than her Lew now that she looks at him properly.

'My friend... Christine... I could call her.'

Parker nods. 'We'll do that for you, OK – ask her to come over and be with you. You need someone to be with you.'

He pauses. 'Has your husband ever had a severe allergic reaction before now?'

An arrow of cold fear shoots through her. Why is he asking her that? Does he suspect something?

Calm down, Maggie – it's just a routine question. He's just doing his job.

'Yes, yes, it happened once before, a long time ago, when we were first courting – first going out,' she adds. She's showing her age. No one uses the word 'courting' anymore. 'Must be over thirty years ago now. We were on a picnic and he was stung by a wasp, went into anaphylactic shock, his eyes... all swollen. He couldn't breathe... I remember the doctor at the time told me it was a good job I called an ambulance when I did – any longer and his organs would've started to shut down. He would've died then, and I'd never have got to spend the next twenty-five years with him...'

She suddenly wonders in that moment what it would've been like if Len *had* died all those years ago, what her life would look like now. She would probably be married to someone else, living somewhere else, maybe with two different children, maybe more? But she *had* saved him, she *had* called an ambulance in time and saved his life. And look how he'd repaid her. If he'd died that day of the picnic all those years ago then none of this would've happened. Amelie Fox would still be alive. Maybe in some warped twist-of-fate kind of way she *is* somehow to blame for all of it.

'After that incident we were always so careful, took an

EpiPen wherever we went, two or three on holidays, and I keep one in every room of the house just in case,' Maggie feels compelled to say. 'I thought there was one in the garage – I was sure, but when I looked... I ran to the kitchen, knew there was one in the odds-and-sods drawer, so I ran back into the garage and gave him a shot in the leg...'

As her words trail off, she can feel the trauma taking hold like a cold black blanket smothering her, just like she'd felt that day she'd come home from school to find her mother's body hanging from the light fitting in the hallway. *Her feet in her summer sandals gently swaying above the wooden floor, her neck crooked to one side, eyes bulging from their sockets, her tongue purple and exposed.*

Another rasping sob escapes from her lips. It had all been a bad omen, the flashbacks she's recently been experiencing after so many years, her father's dispassionate voice taunting her... it was all leading to this, a warning that something terrible was going to happen, she's convinced of it. How will she come back from this? It's taken her years, decades, a lifetime to get over her mother's suicide. She isn't sure she has the strength for this, to make room for more dark, twisted visions, the distorted dead faces of the people she's loved returning to haunt her.

'Perhaps I can take a look' – DC Parker's voice is soft, almost melodic – 'in the garage.' He stands. 'You don't have to come with me – you can stay here with PC Slater.'

Maggie looks up then, sees a female officer standing behind her to the left of the door. She hadn't even noticed she was there the whole time.

'And we'll call your friend, Christine, OK?'

Maggie nods. She needs vodka. A cigarette – she'd kill for just a puff. *Kill.*

'The garage – can you access it internally?'

Maggie nods. 'Through the house, all the way down the hallway and to the left. I think the door's still open.'

DC Parker leaves the room, leaving her alone with the female officer.

She smiles at her. 'Can I get you anything? A cup of tea perhaps? You've had a terrible shock, Mrs Wendover.'

'I need a stiff drink,' she finds herself saying.

'A brandy perhaps?' the officer says.

'There's vodka in the kitchen.' Maggie's own voice sounds alien to her, a high-pitched squeak that she doesn't recognise.

'Of course. I'll get you a glass. And if you give me Christine's number, I'll call her now too.'

Maggie does and she disappears from the living room, leaving her alone. Questions sprint through her fragile mind as her knees jiggle up and down in a bid to expel some of the adrenalin that's coursing through her. Will there be a post-mortem, she wonders? They always do them when someone dies unexpectedly at home, don't they? Will she have to wait weeks before his body is released? And what about his DNA? If they do a post-mortem then it'll be on file, won't it?

'Here you go.' The police officer returns from the kitchen, hands her a small glass of vodka.

She takes it, knocks it back in one hit. Instantly she wants another.

'Maybe that will help. I've called Christine too, and she's on her way over.'

Maggie nods on autopilot, though she's sure nothing can help her right now.

'Mrs Wendover...'

He's back, the young detective. She searches his expression.

'Your husband... Len – is that his Cadillac in the garage? Was that the car he was working on when he... when he died?'

He's asking about the car. Why is he asking about that? Has he found something?

'Yes... yes, it was his latest project. He... he had it shipped over from the States, was reconditioning the engine. He talked about nothing else practically – it was his pride and joy, along with his children...' Maggie closes her eyes again.

Parker nods. 'How long has he had it, the car?'

A fresh burst of adrenalin smashes into her lower intestines. Now she's convinced he's found something. What did that have to do with him being stung by a bloody wasp and dying? She tries to think about the answer she should give. Whatever she says now could potentially trip her up later on, couldn't it? She thinks about creepy Clive, about what he'd said about seeing the Cadillac during the early hours of Thursday morning. Will the police speak to him? Will Clive drop her in it by telling them what he'd seen? No. Why would they even want to speak to Clive? Len's death isn't suspicious, is it? They'd have no reason to.

'A few weeks I suppose,' she says, 'although it doesn't actually go – doesn't run yet. He was reconditioning the engine like I said. He was hoping to make it roadworthy soon, was looking forward to it and...'

She remembers the conversation she'd had with Len in the kitchen a few days ago, after what Clive had told her. She'd asked him if he'd taken the car out for a spin yet and he'd told her that while it *did* run, he wouldn't want to risk it, that the engine wasn't sound. 'Why do you ask?'

The words have left her lips before she can stop them.

'Just curious.' DC Parker smiles at her gently, writes something down in his notebook, but he's too far away for her see what.

Maggie feels sick. She's sure Len used the car to transport Amelie Fox's body to Riverdown Park.

She hears the front door go and her heart drops like a rock. It's Remy – she's back from the hairdressers.

'Mum!' She hears the concern in her daughter's voice. 'Mum, are you here? Are you OK? What's going on? There's police cars out front and—'

She bursts into the living room, panic etched on her face as she sees the detective and police officer standing there. She turns to look at Maggie, her eyes wide with fear as she sees the state of her. 'Has... has something happened?'

Maggie blinks at her youngest child, tears staining her raw skin as they silently drip down her cheeks, and the words come out before she can think about them.

'Remy... what on earth have you done to your hair?'

29 DAN

Graham Benson possesses the kind of face that I could quite easily slap on repeat. He sits slumped back in the plastic chair, with one leg casually balanced over his knee. He is, undeniably, a good-looking young man with high cheekbones, a defined jaw and bright blue eyes offset by a deep bronze tan, but it's his demeanour that lets him down. His arrogance is almost as strong as the aftershave he's wearing, like it's oozing from every pore of him and bouncing off the four walls. He introduces himself to Davis and me as 'G' with a self-assured nod.

'Short for Graham, I take it?'

He bristles a little. 'No one calls me that. It's just G, you know, like the rappers.'

I smile thinly. There's nothing remotely 'gangster' about 'G'. In fact, Graham Benson looks like a walking aftershave advert whose mum secretly still does his washing with his perfectly styled, almost black bouffant, the tattoos on his well-built forearms and his outfit – white linen shorts, designer belt and a crisp white T-shirt with 'Gucci' emblazoned on repeat.

He clocks me looking at it. 'Picked it up at the airport. I never wear anything more than once.'

I open the top button of my shirt, which incidentally is probably older than 'G' is.

'Thanks for coming in, *Graham*,' I say. 'We really appreciate it. Especially since we know you've come straight from the airport.'

He sniffs, taps his defined calf with his fingers. 'No problem, boss – glad I can assist. When I heard the Feds were looking for me, I thought it best to come pay you a visit as soon as.'

I'm genuinely concerned that if his ego gets any bigger, small planets will start circling him.

'Well...' I smile again. 'You obviously know why you're here?'

He nods. 'Yeah, Amelie... ol' Foxy.' He's shaking his head. 'It's sad, man.'

He looks positively *heartbroken* by the news.

'So, you heard about her death then, about her murder?'

'Yeah, while I was in Marbella – it was all over Insta. And then my phone started blowing up... journalists asking questions about how I knew her and if I was her boyfriend and that. The paps were waiting for me at the airport too – loads of them, man! Waiting *for me*!'

Ah, so now the snazzy get-up makes sense. He knew they would be there with their cameras to greet him.

'I mean, it's a bit of a bummer though, you know. I liked Foxy.'

'Yes,' I agree tightly, *just a bit*. 'So, can you tell us how you knew Amelie, and in what capacity?'

He waggles his espadrille-clad foot. I notice he's also wearing a diamanté Rolex watch on his left wrist. I expect that was the whole idea – for me to notice.

'Treated myself after I did a stint on *Date Your Best Mate* – you know, the reality TV show. Did you see me on it?'

'Can't say I did, Graham,' I say, and he looks at me like this is nothing short of implausible.

'So, Amelie Fox,' Davis prompts him.

I imagine 'G' would be more than happy to discuss his first love – himself – all day long without pausing for breath if given the green light.

'I've known her on and off for a few years. I used to see her out and about on the circuit.'

'The circuit?'

'Club circuit mainly. We hung out at the same places. She was one of those chicks you always saw at all the cool parties, always in the VIP area, surrounded by guys, you know.'

'When did you start dating?' Davis says.

Graham's eyes widen slightly but I notice that his smooth forehead doesn't move an inch.

'I wouldn't say we "dated", man – like, we were never in a proper relationship.'

'And how would you define a "proper" relationship?'

I think the question catches him off guard, forcing him to actually think about the answer.

'Well, like... you know... exclusive I suppose. We were more like friends with benefits,' he says causally. 'I think she was more into me than I was into her though.'

Jesus, if he was an ice cream, I'm pretty sure he'd lick himself right about now.

'What makes you say that?'

He shrugs nonchalantly. 'It's always that way with chicks. They get too attached, you know, after you've fuc— after you've *slept* with them. Some are harder to get rid of than herpes, man. I mean, there was this one chick, I only slept with her once – hardly remember it to be fair – and she wouldn't leave me alone after that. Started bugging me big time, texting, calling, following me, telling everyone I was her boyfriend and that we were getting married and shit. A proper nutter. I had to—'

I think I see Davis give a little eye roll in my peripheral vision.

'Amelie,' she cuts in, prompting him again.

'Nah, Foxy was all right – she knew the score. We hooked up on and off for a couple of years pretty much, nothing regular, just every now and again. She was kind of like a go-to, you know, a fail-safe.'

Davis glances sideways at me. 'Lucky girl. Tell us about the video.'

'Oh, the sex tape, you mean? The one me and Foxy made?' He grins provocatively, like he's glad to have been asked about it.

'There're others?'

'Yeah, man, a few probably.' He looks at us both simultaneously. 'Ah, come on, don't tell me you both never have...'

I'm uncomfortably reminded of Davis's candid confession when we'd first watched Amelie's sex tape and pull at my collar again. *It's so bloody hot in here.*

He smirks. 'Look, *she* was smoking hot, *I'm* smoking hot... We weren't hurting anyone. It was just a bit of a laugh.'

Hilarious.

'You released it without her permission though, the video – isn't that right, Graham?'

He bristles at my use of his somewhat unhip Christian name. Admittedly, I'm doing it to rile him – can't help myself.

'You're kidding me, right? Is that why I'm here? You think I did some kind of revenge-porn thing on her? Man, that's not my bag.' He shakes his head.

'Look, I knew she wouldn't really care if I put it out there... she pretended to be a bit pissed about it at the time, but I'm telling you, she knew what those kind of videos did for the likes of Kim K and Paris Hilton, knew it wouldn't do her any harm. She started an OF account on the back of it, started making some serious cash. I did her a favour – got her name out there, among other parts.' He actually sniggers.

'Wow, how incredibly altruistic of you, Graham,' Davis says. But her irony is wasted on him, and he stares at her blankly.

'Yeah, well, it's a fucking media sensation now though, ain't it, since she was killed and that? It's got over two million hits since her death hit the news – can you believe that? *Two million*! My agent reckons it's come at just the right time as well, on the back of *Sext Text Ur Ex*. The show's producers are gassed about it, man.'

He's grinning like the cat who got the cream, and it's all I can do not to lean across the table and wipe that cosmetically enhanced smile clean off his smug face.

'It's going to send my profile through the ceiling and—'

'You tied her up in that video, isn't that right, Graham?'

'Yeah.' He shrugs. 'So? It was just a bit of fun – a bit kinky, that's all.'

'What did you use in the video – to tie her up with I mean?'

The question throws him. 'Fuck, man, I don't know, can hardly remember now. A scarf or a tie or something I think... We were loaded at the time. It was just a bit of fun, you know. Everybody does that kind of shit – makes videos and that.'

'Do they?'

'Yeah!' He looks at us like we're T. rex and stegosaurus respectively. 'It's a bit of a bummer that you can't really tell it's me in the footage though, because you can't really see my face... but that adds to the mystique, so my agent reckons. Plus you can see my ink so people know it's me... the lighting was pretty shit. Like I said, it was just a bit of a laugh really – I didn't plan on releasing it publicly when we made it. Once she started making a name for herself though, I thought it might... you know, help her career and that.'

'How very thoughtful of you, Graham,' I say. 'So, she wasn't angry? She was absolutely fine about you making that private, intimate moment between you public?'

He snorts, leans forward on the table. 'Yeah. I told you. I think she made out that she wasn't happy about it at first, but I saw her quite a few times after and she had no beef with me about it. Wouldn't have kept coming back for more otherwise, would she?'

I try to imagine his shock as my palm connects sharply with his smooth tanned skin.

'Was the scarf yours or hers?'

'What?'

'The scarf – in the video.'

'I dunno.' He pulls a face. 'Hers probably. Don't remember it. Why the interest in the scarf? I doubt anyone was looking at that when they watched the video. I mean, you've seen it, right?' He looks at Davis, grins. 'Yeah, you've definitely seen it – I can tell.'

'When was the last time you saw Amelie, *Graham*?'

He bristles again at the use of his full name. 'Before I flew out to Marbs. I was out there shooting this reality TV show called—'

'*Sext Text Your Ex*?' Davis interjects. 'Yes, so you've said, *a few times*.'

'She'd been shortlisted to come out there as well, was waiting for the green light from the producers. We'd been texting each other, kind of deliberately, so that the producers could see she was legit my ex, even though she wasn't, not really, but she knew how to play the game.'

'You said you saw her when exactly?'

He sips a little water from the plastic cup on the table, smacks his thick lips together loudly.

'Yeah, we hooked up again recently, had sex at her place, her Chelsea pad. Nice yard.'

'A date, Graham,' I say, my patience running thin.

He puffs, looks up at the ceiling as though trying to recall. 'Last Tuesday week I think.'

Davis and I exchange a look. That would've made it the day before Amelie died.

'Silly bitch put some cryptic message out about it on social media though... made some comment about how she'd been "more than sex texting an ex, one who'd hit the "G" spot!" I think she did it to get the TV producers' attention you know, make out that we were legit when really we were just shag buddies... Anyway, that post really messed it up for me with this other chick I've been circling, that Cindy Hannock from *Love Island*. You know the one I mean? Blonde, big tits, got a Geordie accent, but hey, you can't have it all, man, can you? Anyway, she put two and two together, you know, "G" spot? Talk about a cock block! But it was an open secret that we hooked up from time to time, so I think some people knew it was me in that video... and if they didn't then, they sure as shit do now.'

He sits back in the chair, affords me a waft of his strong, sweet aftershave, and I try not to imagine the abject horror that would run through me if, in fifteen years' time, any of my kids were ever to bring home someone like the delightful Graham Benson here – a vainglorious, narcissistic, misogynistic non-entity who's prepared to capitalise on the hideous death of an innocent friend just to raise his own profile.

'And how was Amelie when you last saw her? Did she seem OK? Did she strike you as worried about anything – or anyone? Did she mention any stalkers, any unwanted admirers, obsessive fans, ex boyfriends?'

He shakes his head. 'Nah, man, she was cool from what I remember. We had a few drinks, had some fun. If there was anything bothering her then she never said, but then again we didn't do much talking that night.' He grins again. 'She was desperate to get that gig on *STYE* with me, was well jel that I was jetting off to Marbs with a shedload of hotties the next day.

She wanted me all to herself, didn't she? Didn't want to share me, though like I always tell 'em: "Babes, there's more than enough of G to go round." Know what I'm saying?' He winks at Davis.

It's a pity the same the same can't be said of Graham's grey matter. If he grew another brain cell, I'm convinced the other would be 'well jel'.

'When did you fly out to Marbella, Graham?'

'Wednesday, the twentieth – early flight, 5 a.m., full of lashed-up mental cases who hadn't gone to bed the night before.'

'Including you?'

'Well, Foxy and I had been up all night, but we weren't drinking too much.'

I think he tries to raise his eyebrows. I suppose I feel a touch disappointed, though not nearly as much as Archer's going to be when she finds out that all the hopes she's pinned on Graham Benson being our prime suspect have been spectacularly dashed. There's no way lover boy here could've murdered Amelie, given that he would've been in a different country at the time, and I'm pretty sure there'll be a whole host of people who can corroborate this, given he isn't exactly the type to try to hide his light under a bushel.

'Would you be willing to give us a voluntary DNA sample, Graham?' Davis asks brightly. 'Just for elimination purposes you understand?'

He winks at her again. 'That's what all the girls say.' He chuckles at his own attempt at humour. 'I quite like a MILF – have had a few myself and they're always the most—'

'Yes, thank you, *Graham*,' I interject, 'we get the picture.'

He makes to open his mouth again, but I cut him off. 'Speaking of which, we're going to need your phone as well.'

He seems a tad nervous all of a sudden. 'Can you even do that? Don't you need a warrant or whatever?'

Davis smiles. 'Yes, Graham, and no... we don't.'

He sighs a little, shrugs. 'Yeah, OK, why not? I got nothing to hide.' He takes his state-of-the-art iPhone from the pocket of his skin-tight white shorts, opens it and slides it across the table.

'So what happened to her then – Foxy?' I thought he'd never ask. 'Said in the press that she was strangled and then dumped in some river, man.'

'Yes, we believe she was killed in her apartment, and her body disposed of in Riverdown Park.'

He shakes his head. 'Man, that's harsh.'

For a second, I think I see some genuine remorse flash across his features, but it's hard to tell underneath all the fake tan and Botox.

'Did someone break into her apartment? Was she like, you know... *raped and shit?*'

'Do you know of anyone who had any issues with Amelie? Anyone who might have wanted to harm her? Anyone she'd fallen out with or who had a grudge against her?'

He looks like he's trying to think, which I imagine is something of a struggle.

He shakes his head. 'Nah, man, Foxy was calm. Everyone liked her. She wasn't a troublemaker – didn't go out looking for agg. I can't think of anyone who didn't like her, let alone would've wanted her dead.'

He pauses, looks down at his Rolex. 'Listen, I'm not being funny or anything... but, like, are we going to be much longer here because I've got another appointment soon. *The Sun* want me to do an exclusive with them. My agent's set it up for 3 p.m. and—'

'We won't keep you too much longer, Graham,' I say, making a mental note to ask Mitchell to take her time down-loading the contents of his phone and taking his DNA sample. I can imagine the press article now, the myriad pictures of Graham's good-looking face, his expression – if he manages one

– forcibly sombre as he talks 'candidly' about his 'love' for Amelie Fox, about the video he made of her and graciously put on social media for all to see. And it saddens me, that this young man's sole priorities seem to be about chasing fame, about feeding his ego, gaining attention, adoration and money at the expense of Amelie Fox's untimely and brutal demise.

There's a knock at the door and Parker pokes his head around it. 'Boss, a word?'

'It's been an absolute pleasure, Graham,' I say, standing, leaving lucky old Davis to finish the interview. 'Don't leave the country, eh? We may well want to speak to you again soon.'

'Anything, boss?' Parker says as I close the door behind me.

I shake my head. 'Nothing, unless you want a lesson in why reality TV is the youth of today's complete undoing.' I sigh, adding, 'He wasn't even in the bloody country when she was killed.'

'Oh.' Parker looks at me apologetically, like it's somehow his fault.

'Anyway, we're taking a DNA sample to check against the samples taken from Amelie.' Miserably, I suspect that one – the semen – will be a match if Don Juan's statement is anything to go by, which, in some small way of consolation, at least may mean the sex she had before her death was consensual.

'Maybe the phone will throw something up?' Parker gives me his best youthful, hopeful look. He's probably around the same sort of age as Casanova in there and I'm struck by the marked difference between them. One has dedicated his life to helping others find justice, the other, a mirror.

'Anyway, you wanted to see me, Parker,' I exhale.

'Yes... I've just been to an incident, sir— sorry, boss, down at Thorton Vale – accidental death by the looks of it.'

'And?'

'Someone by the name of Wendover – Len Wendover. He was stung by a wasp, went into anaphylactic shock. The wife administered drugs through an EpiPen but it was too late, he was DOA.'

I'm still listening to him but my mind has taken a sharp right-hand turn somewhere else. *Wendover...* now why does that name ring a bell?

'OK. So why are you telling me, Parker? You think it's suspicious?'

'No, gov, looks like a legitimate tragic accident. The wife's in pieces. Body's down at the mortuary for a routine post-mortem as we speak.'

'OK, so...' My desperation is gnawing at my patience and I loosen my collar again. It's damp to touch in the heat. 'Get to the point, Parker.'

'Yes, boss. Well, he was in the garage of his home when it happened. He was something of a petrolhead, a mechanic in his spare time and—'

'Yes?' I'm almost dancing on the spot.

'And he was working on restoring a vintage car when he was stung, was underneath the vehicle by all accounts.'

I swallow back my frustration. 'Fascinating – and tragic – as this is, Parker, is it something I need to know?'

'Maybe, boss.' He pauses.

I roll my eyes. 'And do you care to tell me why exactly?'

'Because it was a GM, boss, the car Wendover was working on. It was a Cadillac.'

30 MAGGIE

She inspects herself closely in the mirror, pulls at the crêpey skin underneath her eyes, rubs some cream into her face. Sighing heavily, she pulls some items from her make-up bag: eyeliner, blush, mascara... She has to put her face on – *a brave one*. She can't fold, not now, *not today*. The limousine and horse-drawn carriage will be here soon, and the pallbearers.

Applying some concealer under her eyes, Maggie hears voices in the next room, the low vibrations of a conversation taking place between Christine and Bob.

'I just don't understand what the rush is, Chris, I really don't. He's not even been gone much more than a week. I know she'll give him a good send-off and everything, but it's all so... so quick. None of us has even had the chance to process any of it. And not only that, some people simply won't be able to make it today, what with it being such short notice.'

Bob's voice, so similar to Len's, causes Maggie to grip the sink with both hands. It's like he's in the next room, is going to walk through the door at any minute. *'Fancy a peppermint tea, chickadee!'*

'I don't know, Bob...' Christine's soothing tones reach her

ears. 'Honestly, I think she just really wants it all over with. She might act as if she's coping on the surface, holding it together for the sake of the kids, but I know her: she's in pieces inside. I mean, they were married, together, for so many years. Can you imagine the shock of it all, losing him so suddenly, so senselessly like that, out of the blue? A bloody wasp sting for God's sake!'

'Yes!' Bob says shrilly. 'Which is why it's even more odd. I mean, you know Maggie: she's an organiser; she likes to make sure everything's in its place. I remember when Heather died, it took me and the kids weeks to organise burying her, thinking about the wording on the invitations, choosing the flowers and the songs carefully, what type of coffin to have, writing the eulogies, where to hold the wake afterwards...'

Yeah, but it didn't take you long to replace her though, did it, Bob? Maggie raises her eyebrows in the mirror, thinks what a hypocrite he is.

'I think she's suffering with terrible guilt,' Christine says, 'that she didn't get to him in time, that she couldn't save him. I think she's torturing herself over it. Maybe once the funeral is over then she can start to grieve properly. It's different for different people – you know that, Bob.'

There's a pause.

'Yes, well, she really shouldn't blame herself.' Bob's voice is softer now. 'It wasn't her fault.' He sighs. 'It was just a terrible, tragic accident at the end of the day. Everyone knew about his allergy; she always kept an EpiPen handy... I blame this bloody heatwave personally, attracting those bastard things everywhere. The post-mortem said he died of asphyxiation due to an acute allergic reaction. It would've only taken a matter of minutes. She mustn't blame herself – she did all she could.'

'I think she's worried about the effect on the kids too, you know, what with Lewis's background – she's worried he'll slip back into depression again.'

'Yes, I know, I know,' Bob says. 'But honestly, Chris, she's not even giving a eulogy at the service – only Lew and Remy are speaking apparently – and then a low-key wake in the garden? I knew my brother: Len would've liked a good send-off, bit of fanfare, a knees-up. You know how he was: he loved a party, loved being the centre of attention, making speeches, entertaining people and all of that. It doesn't make sense that she wouldn't want to say a few words. And don't even get me bloody started on the cremation. I *know* my brother wanted to be buried because he told me – we'd talked about it once or twice, like you do. He clearly stated that he didn't want to be cremated after his death.'

'Shhh,' Christine says. 'Keep your voice down, Bob – she'll hear you! Look, I don't know... she's not herself. She probably isn't thinking straight – is still in shock.'

'All the more reason to have waited a while, come to terms with it all a little before making all these big decisions. This just doesn't feel like a fitting goodbye for my brother is all I'm saying.'

A fitting goodbye? Maggie wonders what that would entail. Dumping Len's naked body in a river perhaps? Well, it had been good enough for Amelie Fox. Bob has no idea. The quicker she burns that bastard's body, the better. Then they can all get on with their lives.

'You know she's never been a big public speaker, and maybe she's just needed something to keep busy, occupy her mind. I don't know. These things, they're very personal.'

Christine was definitely on the money about keeping her mind occupied though, because if she stops, even for a second, then the images come: ugly, frightening, grotesque visions of Len's swollen features as he lay dying on the garage floor, and the sound of her daughter's screams, high-pitched, piercing, as she'd learned of her father's death.

'No! Nooooo! You're lying! You're LYING! Dad's not dead – he's NOT.'

She can never forget the look Remy gave her, eyes wide with horror and disbelief, as though they were all playing some cruel, twisted joke on her.

'This isn't real!' Her daughter's shock had quickly morphed into blind rage as the news had started to sink in and she'd picked up the empty glass on the table and thrown it at the wall, where it had exploded, pieces of glass shooting off and shattering in all directions, causing Maggie to place her hands over her ears.

The glass had felt like a metaphor for her own heart. Like a priceless vase that had been dropped and smashed. Oh, you could mend the cracks all right, plaster over them, even repaint it, but if you looked closely enough, the damage would still be detectable. It would never be perfect again.

Maggie stares at her reflection once more. Perhaps if she looks hard enough, she might see herself looking back at her, who she'd been before all of this. Her life feels unrecognisable, like everything she once knew, everything that has defined her, has vanished, evaporated into the ether. Even her own daughter looks like a stranger to her now. Remy had returned home from the hairdressers that fateful afternoon almost unrecognisable, her long dark hair dyed a bright white blonde. It was certainly a change all right, but Maggie didn't like it – it didn't suit her.

Guilt feels like a monster growing inside her, chewing and slicing its way through her insides with its sharp teeth. Witnessing her children's acute shock and distress at the news of their father's unexpected death was perhaps the worst thing Maggie has ever experienced, each of their anguished cries and sobs a razor slash on her heart, but she forces herself to remember that this would be nothing compared to discovering the truth about who their dad *really* was and what he'd done.

You did the right thing, Maggie. You did the right thing by them.

It will all be over soon, Maggie attempts to silently reassure herself. Once today is over then they can all move forward, together as a family – her, Remy, Lewis, Casey and her future granddaughter. They can be happy again – they *will* be happy again in time. It's the greatest healer, isn't it? Or so they say. She just needs to be strong, stronger than she's ever had to be in her lifetime. She'd survived her own mother's untimely passing, didn't she? And so her children will survive too, perhaps not completely unscathed, but they'll survive nonetheless.

After dabbing some blush on her pale cheeks and applying some lipstick, Maggie slips into a simple black pencil dress and struggles with the zip. Len had always been on hand for this kind of thing and it's yet another painful reminder of her solitude. Len had been her safety blanket as long as she can remember. She'd never had to worry about anything with him around. Now she was on her own, walking a tightrope without a security net, no one to catch her if she fell.

She realises in this moment how privileged she's been to have had that kind of protection for all those years, someone to absorb and share the stresses, the problems, ride the rollercoaster of life with. Len had wrapped her in cotton wool for the past thirty-odd years; he'd made life easy for her, manageable, *bearable*. The prospect of being alone is frightening, the concept alien. How will she cope on her own? Losing Len is akin to losing a limb, a vital part of her missing, but he'd been a diseased limb, hadn't he? A limb that needed to be amputated or else the disease would've spread. For all her husband had represented to her, at the end of the day, she'd learned that he was nothing but a predator, a covert monster, a wolf in sheep's clothing. As terrifying as the thought of navigating life on her own is, it's more terrifying to think of spending the rest of it with a cold-blooded killer.

'Mum!' Remy knocks on the bedroom door. 'Dad's arrived – the hearse is here, the coach and horses.'

'OK, sweetheart,' she says, looking at her daughter in the mirror. 'I'm nearly ready. Are you all set?'

Remy nods sombrely. 'Lew and Casey are downstairs with Bob and Julie. Christine and Gary are going to come with us in the limousine if that's OK with you.'

'Of course it is. No Whatshisface then – this boyfriend of yours? I thought he might be here to support you today, finally get to meet him at last.'

'Well, it's hardly the best occasion to introduce him to the family, is it?' Remy says miserably. 'And he's away at the moment, working – wouldn't have been able to make it anyway, not with such short notice.'

Maggie inwardly sighs. None of them can possibly understand why she's burying – or rather cremating – her husband in such haste, and she intends to keep it that way for all their sakes. It was a miracle she'd even be able to in all fairness.

She'd told the pathologist at the mortuary where Len's postmortem had taken place that she needed his body returned as soon as possible, in keeping with his religious beliefs. It was yet another lie to add to the increasing collection surrounding her husband. A lifetime of lies – what difference would one more make?

Once the coffin has gone through that curtain then maybe, just maybe, she can start the long, slow and arduous process of rebuilding her life. Right now though, it seems an impossible task, what with the night terrors and the visions that are constantly haunting her every waking and sleeping moment, the eternal threat of exposure, of Len's secret – *of her own* – coming to light, fear and worry incessantly lurking over her shoulder, a persistent black shadow of doom that feels as if it's physically pulling her downwards, like gravity.

She tells herself not to worry, to take one small step at a time, keep upright. *Just keep upright, Maggie.* The police haven't been here sniffing around, Len's death has already been officially classed as an accident, which theoretically it was. No one suspects he had any involvement in Amelie Fox's death, nothing's been said, no suspicions raised. She just needs to hold her nerve. Once today is over, she can concentrate on tying up any loose ends.

She's already destroyed Len's laptop, the one with all those incriminating searches on it. She'd poured boiling-hot water over it then taken a hammer to it, one she'd found in Len's garage, smashed the bloody thing to pieces before sweeping it all up and distributing it into separate little ziplock bags that she'd flushed – all ten of them – one by one, down the toilet. The car was next on the list. Bob has agreed to help her with that particular problem, says he knows someone who might take it off her hands, a contact from the car fair, another vintage-motor buff.

'He'll do it justice,' Bob had assured her, 'will finish what Len started. He would've wanted it to go to a good home, to someone who shared his passion.'

She'd ripped the carpet out of the boot and burned it in the fire pit in the garden, given the whole damned thing a complete thorough clean inside and out, just to be on the safe side, in case the police did come sniffing around.

The scarf, however – that wretched, hateful thing that had started all of this – is still missing.

Maggie tries not to think about it. Those horrible little black skulls, the sweet smell of that perfume... She'd searched every inch of the entire house, even the garden and outhouse with precision, acutely aware of its importance. She can only hope that Len had destroyed it after all, that he'd done something right at least.

Maggie looks out of her bedroom window, sees the stately Victorian carriage, the casket containing her husband's body visible through the glass, the words 'Len' and 'Pops' written in white flowers adorning either side. The black horses, with their impressive feathered plumage, are standing perfectly still, and she marvels at their obedience, almost as if they know somehow, can sense the sombre occasion.

'Mum?' Remy is hovering by her bedroom door. She looks pale in the face – the blonde really washes her out.

'Yes, darling, I'll be right down. Have the caterers turned up yet?'

'I think so,' Remy says. 'Christine's dealing with it.'

Maggie nods. Good old Christine – she really has been an exemplary friend, a port in a storm. She wonders if she still would be if she knew the whole truth.

'Mum, do you believe in karma?' Remy looks down at the carpet, visibly upset. She supposes it's only to be expected – she was so close to her beloved 'pops'.

'Karma?' Maggie spritzes herself with a little perfume – Nina Ricci's L'Air du Temps. It was always Len's favourite. He said it smelled like 'sunshine'.

'Yeah, you know, like, if you do something bad then something bad will happen to you in return? An eye for an eye, that kind of thing...'

Maggie looks over at her. 'Why are you asking me that, sweetheart?'

Remy shrugs. 'I dunno. I just wondered if you believe in that kind of thing?'

In truth, Maggie has never had much cause to think about karma up until recently.

'Life has a strange way of righting wrongs, Remy,' she says. 'The truth will always out in the end, will always catch up with you however much you keep running from it. No one can run from their mistakes forever – I believe the law of the cosmos makes sure of it somehow.'

Remy nods, still looking at her feet. Maggie thinks she's crying softly, thinks she sees a tear fall onto the carpet.

'It's OK, my darling.' She goes to her daughter then, holds her in an embrace. 'It's all going to be OK – trust me.'

'Will it, Mum?' Remy looks up at her with a tear-stained face. 'Will it really?'

She squeezes her tightly, strokes her hair like she used to when she was a child. 'I promise.'

31

The last of the mourners are leaving now, having helped themselves to the generous buffet and limitless alcohol all after-noon. She supposes it's been a decent turnout all things consid-ered, especially given the short notice. Family, friends old and new, colleagues, people Len worked for and with over the years, his car buddies, neighbours – of course Brenda had turned up with the biggest bouquet of flowers, dressed in an extremely low-cut black minidress which had prompted Christine to comment acerbically that, 'She can't even do demure at a funeral, that one.' Creepy Clive had been with her, his tall gangly frame an almost comedic juxtaposition beside Brenda's short curvy one. Brenda had thrown herself theatrically around Maggie the moment she'd seen her, crying her condolences into her neck. She could smell that damned perfume on her again and had pulled away. It repulsed her.

'It's just so awful, Mags,' Brenda had spluttered as Maggie had released herself from her embrace. 'If there's anything I can do, anything at all.'

Yes, she could let her go and leave her alone.

Clive had rubbed her shoulder with a large sweaty hand. 'I'm so sorry, Maggie' he'd said awkwardly. 'I'm just so sorry.'

They had all gathered to pay their respects, share their memories, and say their last goodbyes to the 'marvellous and magnificent man that was my brother, Len Wendover' as Bob had emotionally referred to him during his eulogy. He'd omitted the word 'murderer', Maggie had thought bitterly.

The day had been a strange pendulum swing between tears and laughter, joy and anguish, celebration and commiseration. There was no doubting that Len had been a popular man, well liked and respected by everyone who knew or had ever known him. He'd be so loved.

Thanks to the Valium and vodka, Maggie had been on a numbed autopilot throughout the service, had barely heard the words the funeral director had said in praise and tribute to her late husband, and when Lewis and Remy had given their eulogies, she'd had to concentrate so hard on remaining upright that it had taken all the mental and physical strength she'd had left in her body, plus Christine's arm tightly wrapped around her waist.

She'd whispered words of support in her ear throughout the service. 'You can get through this, darling. I'm here, OK... I'm here.'

At the wake afterwards, she'd been caught in a whirlwind of people offering their condolences, what felt like a thousand lips had kissed her face, squeezed her arm, every one of them having something to say about her late husband, the kind of man he was, the memories they shared of him, how much he would be missed, how sorry they were, if there was anything they could do...

Maggie had smiled until her face muscles ached, must've said a polite 'thank you' a million times over, her emotions cushioned by drugs and alcohol. The fact that people were keen to verbalise their own personal memories and experiences of Len had been something of a blessing though, allowing her to listen more than she had to speak. She's sure everyone could tell that while she was attempting to put on a brave front, she was an emotional wreck inside – though they had no idea as to the real reasons why.

It wasn't Len's untimely and tragic death she was shedding tears for – it was for a lifetime of lies, for her family, her children, for Amelie Fox, *for herself*. If only they knew the real truth about this man they spoke of in such high regard and with so much love and respect; if only they knew what he really was, what he'd done, the secret he'd taken with him to his grave, one she was now left to keep for him. She's sure it would've been a very different script then.

Bob and Julie immediately stop talking as she enters the kitchen, a little unsteady on her feet. She feels drunk, or high, or a bit of both, but still she's compos mentis enough to realise that she's interrupted something of a heated exchange between them. In usual circumstances she might've asked them if everything was OK, but right now she has neither the energy nor the inclination. She's just so exhausted. Her bones feel like they're made of cement and there's a painful ache in her chest like there's a gaping open wound inside her, one you could fit a beach ball through.

'How are you, love? You must be tired.' Bob looks at her with concern.

'I need a cigarette.' Maggie practically falls into the chair, searches the table of wine bottles for one that has something left in it. She pours herself a glass of red, drains the dregs into the glass.

'It was a good service,' Bob says ruefully. 'I was pleased so many people turned out for the old sod in the end.'

She nods, can barely speak. She's been talking – listening to people talk about Len – all day. She really just wants them all to go, to leave her alone so that she no longer has to keep up this charade of the grieving widow. If she has to hear one more bloody word about how 'wonderful' Len was, she thinks she might burst into flames.

'I'll get you a cigarette,' Julie says, searching her handbag. 'Didn't even know you smoked.'

'Ah well, you think you know people, eh, Julie?' Maggie says, tapping her nose as she slurps her wine.

Bob and Julie exchange a sideways glance.

'Well, the buffet was lovely,' Julie says chirpily. 'You'll have to give me the caterer's card in case we ever have a—'

'Funeral?' Maggie interjects, snorts into her wine.

'I was going to say party... an event.'

Bob clears his throat. 'Len would've loved it today, would've enjoyed seeing all the old faces, everyone together... It was wonderful to hear all the stories, everyone's memories about him.'

'It's so hot! Why is it so bloody bastard hot?' Maggie stumbles as she stands and Julie gasps.

'It's OK... I'm OK,' she says, raising a palm as they both jump towards her. 'I'm just opening the French doors, get some air in here... can hardly breathe.'

A rush of warm air hits her as she opens them – it feels like fire in her lungs.

'You really should sit down, love,' Bob says. 'It's been a long day, a tough day for you.'

'You don't know the half of it, Bob,' Maggie slurs, knocking back her empty glass. 'Any more of this?' She waggles it at him. 'Or have the vultures drunk the lot?'

'Come on, Mags – why don't you sit down, eh? Take the weight off. I think you've probably had enough.'

'Oh sod off,' she sneers at him. 'I'm not a bloody child, and it's my house. If I want another ten glasses, I'll have them. I don't need *your* permission.'

She's drunk. She's angry.

Hold it together, Maggie. You're almost over the finish line – don't ruin it now.

'Shall I get Christine?' Julie asks nervously, looking at Bob.

Bob shakes his head, pours her another glass of wine. Maggie lights the cigarette Julie has given her with a lighter from the table. He sits down opposite her.

'I know how difficult this must be for you, Maggie,' he says softly. 'I mean, it's difficult to believe that we were only here the other week, celebrating your twenty-fifth anniversary and—'

'And you weren't speaking to each other,' Maggie says, remembering what Len had told her about them falling out. 'That's right, isn't it?' She puffs on the cigarette, coughs a little. She hasn't smoked in over thirty years.

'What?' He bristles a little, looks uncomfortable.

'Yeah, Len told me you'd fallen out. Didn't say why though. So tell me, Bob, why weren't you two talking that night at the party? What was the argument about?'

'I... I...' Bob's mouth is open but nothing much is coming out.

'C'mon!' Maggie prompts him assertively, fuelled with wine and Valium. 'Must've been a reason.'

She flicks ash onto the kitchen floor. She knows she shouldn't be asking him about this, that it's potentially opening a can of worms – and it hardly matter now she supposes – but she can't help herself. She's genuinely intrigued.

'Well, it wasn't really an argument as such... We just had a few words is all. You know what Len could be like sometimes.'

'Funny!' Maggie's laugh sounds slightly manic. 'He said exactly the same about you! No, tell me, I want to know... what were these "few words" you had? What was it about?'

'Oh, it was nothing. Just some petty squabble over some car business – a load of nonsense.'

'You're lying,' she says, looking directly at him, 'just like you were lying that day I popped by to see you. You remember,

Julie?' She looks over at her standing by the sink. It may be the drink but she's sure she sees panic in Julie's close-set eyes. 'When I dropped by on my way to Savacentre?' She snorts. Savacentre, *as if*.

'I'm... I'm not lying, Maggie...' But his voice sounds disingenuous, no conviction in it.

'So if you're not lying then you can just tell me, tell me exactly why you two weren't speaking at the party and why you were lying that time I—'

'Oh for God's sake, Bob,' Julie interjects, 'just tell her, will you?'

'Tell me what? Let me guess,' Maggie says, almost half enjoying herself now. 'It has something to do with the night you were supposed to stay at the Platinum Inn together, the night of the vintage car fair at Riverdown Park.' The night Amelie Fox was murdered. 'There was no bathroom or kitchen leak or whatever, was there? Len didn't stay at that hotel that night, did he? Or did he lie to you too, ask you to cover for him? Was that it? Was that what the argument was about?'

Julie brings three glasses to the table, pours them all a generous measure of brandy.

'No, it wasn't,' she says quietly.

'Oh, so why was that then?' Maggie's tone is sharp.

Julie sighs resignedly. 'Because it was *us* who lied to *him*.'

32

'What are you talking about, *us* who lied to *him*?' Maggie swigs some more brandy, looks at them both anxiously. 'You're not making any sense.'

Julie sits down at the table now. Her body language is making Maggie nervous, her knees beginning to jiggle manically underneath the table with the influx of adrenalin.

'Bob?' she prompts him again.

He shakes his head. Inhales deeply. 'Julie and I... well... well...' He drops his head into his hand, rubs his forehead. 'Jesus, this is so difficult. Look, we were just trying to help. I really don't know what we were thinking now really...' He takes his glasses off, rubs the bridge of his nose. 'I know you won't probably think so, that you'll be angry, he didn't—'

'Didn't *what*?' Maggie's voice sounds shrill with panic. 'Jesus, Bob, for Christ's sake! Just tell me!'

'He said that you were, well, that you seemed, *distant* from him.'

'Distant?'

'Yes,' Julie attempts to continue, 'not interested in him in that way... you know, *sexually*. He said that since you started going through the change, you'd withdrawn from him, weren't up for it in the... bedroom.' She closes her eyes. 'He confided in Bob – asked his advice I suppose.'

'Yes... yes, he did,' Bob says, quickly adding, 'but he never said anything derogatory about you, Maggie, I swear to you. He was just worried about you, thought that maybe you'd gone off him, that you were no longer attracted to him. He didn't know how to approach the subject with you. He felt awkward; didn't want to make *you* feel awkward. He wasn't sure how to broach it all.'

Maggie swallows dryly. Len had been discussing their sex life, or lack of it, with Bob, and in turn, he'd told Julie? He'd told him intimate details about her, about her menopause, things that were private between them? Things they hadn't even discussed with each other? She feels a little sick, embarrassed, shocked – she'd had no idea Len had been feeling that way, let alone confided in his brother. And she's still none the wiser as to exactly what it is they're trying to tell her.

'So, you know, Bob kind of mentioned it to me, about how Len was feeling a bit... *frustrated,*' Julie says. 'And so I asked a friend of mine – she's a very well respected sex therapist – to come over that night, thought she might be able to have a chat with him, offer him some advice.' She says the last sentence so quickly that Maggie's unsure she's even heard her correctly.

'Wait, *what*?' Maggie shakes her head. 'You... you set Len up to speak to a sex therapist?'

Julie looks down at the table. 'Well, it wasn't one of my best ideas in hindsight, I have to say,' she says quietly, 'I just thought, well, I thought it might help, if he talked it through with a professional. And she's a good friend.'

Maggie shrieks incredulously, gulps back more brandy. Is she really hearing this?

'So, tell me what happened *exactly*?' She demands to know. 'Was this the night of the car fair, on the Wednesday? Did you book a hotel – the Platinum Inn? Did Len *know* about this friend of yours, agree to talk to her?' She can't believe what they're saying to her.

'No, no,' Bob cuts in, finally gaining the courage to speak, the coward.

'You'd better explain to me, Bob, just what the fuck all this is about!'

She's shaking now, visibly, the brandy sloshing around in the glass she's gripping.

'We didn't...' Bob bites his lip, looks down at the table sheepishly. 'We didn't exactly tell him.'

'You didn't *tell* him? You thought you'd simply surprise him with a sex therapist who you'd told his private business to? How could you do that to me, Bob? How could you do that to Len?'

'Like I said,' Julie pipes up, 'it was my idea. Bob told me how miserable he was and I thought... I know she helps people in your situation all the time. I... thought it might help him – help you both.'

'Help him? *Help me*? Ha, huh, my God.' Maggie can barely get the words out. 'Well, I might've expected that from *you*, Julie,' she sneers at her, 'but *you*?' she throws Bob a look of contempt. He has the good grace to look ashamed at least. 'So you're telling me that you were complicit in this... intervention?'

Maggie can't think straight. Had something gone horribly wrong, the night of Amelie's murder? Had Len got into some kind of situation? How did Amelie Fox fit into all of this? It's not making any sense.

'Well, I... Oh Jesus, Jules.' He looks at his wife for help.

Julie rolls her eyes, sighs heavily. 'The plan was that Len and Bob were going to the car fair as usual and then Bob was going to bring Len to ours,' she says. 'Len thought Bob had already booked the hotel, but Bob told him last minute that they were coming back to our house instead. So...'

Maggie is looking at them simultaneously in quick succession, her head shaking so violently she thinks it might come off her shoulders.

'So we went to the car fair – that part is genuinely true,' Bob continues, 'and we came back home, to mine and Jules', together – Len and I and... Well, I mean, he was horrified, you know, when he saw her, when he realised why she was there, at our house, this woman. He was angry, insisted that she leave immediately. He was livid with me, angry that I'd betrayed his confidence and talked to Jules about the conversation we'd had. I was sorry – we thought we were helping. We just thought—'

'Helping?' Maggie spits the word at him. 'You thought that betraying his trust, telling your wife his personal business and her inviting her sex therapist friend over, a woman he'd never met, never asked to meet, to discuss his sex life was *helping*?'

'Oh God.' Julie rolls her eyes and shakes her head. 'I knew we shouldn't have told her the truth – knew she would react like this!'

Bob casts Julie a helpless look. 'But you were the one who insisted we tell her!'

'And what happened after she left, this *friend* of yours? Did Len walk out? Did he get a cab, go to the hotel?' Surely this is what happened? Maggie's thoughts are racing manically. It had to have been because if it wasn't...

'No,' Bob says solemnly. 'He wanted to leave but he'd had too much to drink. We all had. We'd been drinking all day – you know it always gets a bit messy at the car fair... Anyway, he thought about getting a cab back home, back here, but he knew you would ask questions, wonder why we hadn't gone to the hotel like he'd told you, so...'

Maggie's heart is beating so hard and heavy in her chest that she feels lightheaded, like she's going to pass out.

'... so he stayed the night on the sofa, crashed out around 9 o'clock. We both did.'

The words hit Maggie in slow motion, blow by blow, each

one of them a short, sharp impact to her body. She covers her mouth with her hands as she leaps up, the momentum causing the kitchen chair to fall backward, the brandy bottle crashing to the floor and smashing.

She's backing away from them, away from the table, her hands still tightly covering her mouth, preventing her from screaming. Her eyes start to dart around the room; everything is beginning to spin, her vision blurring. She's hyperventilating, her whole body vibrating. She's going into shock. *She's going to collapse.*

Bob is looking at her, sheer panic etched across his features, so similar to his brother's.

'We both stayed on the sofa all night, left the next morning. I drove him back here myself. I'm so sorry, Maggie, please... It was a terrible idea, stupid. I'm just so, so sorry.'

Julie is still shaking her head, her eyes closed as Bob stands and tries to reach out to Maggie, his hands open, imploring with her. He looks tearful.

'He wouldn't even speak to me the next day. We drove back here in silence. I apologised to him profusely. We made a mistake, a bad error of judgement, that's all. Len was as appalled by the idea as you are now, and—'

Maggie's chest is heaving – she's making strange noises, unable to get oxygen into her lungs.

'You... you don't know what you've done. Do you realise... what you've done?' She's crying, gasping for air, her arms outstretched as though she's pushing the words she's just heard away from her, doesn't want them to come close enough to make impact. But they're there, hanging above her like a cele-bratory banner in neon letters, screaming the truth at her. *Len stayed at Bob and Julie's house the night of Amelie Fox's murder.*

33 DAN

I ring the doorbell.

'So, are you going to tell me exactly what it is we're doing here, gov?' Davis says.

'Len Wendover,' I reply.

'What about him? Who is he?'

'I don't know,' I say. 'He's dead.'

'Dead?' She glances sideways at me.

'Yes, he died a week or so ago, of a wasp sting.'

'What?' The glance becomes a stare. 'He was killed by a *wasp sting*?'

'Anaphylactic shock,' I say. 'A severe allergic reaction.'

'Jesus, so... is that why we're here – you think his death was suspicious, maybe?'

'No,' I say. 'I don't. And it's not.'

'OK, so...?'

'I don't know,' I say, 'why we're here exactly, just that I feel as if we should be.'

'That doesn't make any sense, gov,' she says.

'He owns, or rather owned, a Cadillac.'

'I thought Parker was dealing with that side of things – why couldn't he come and check it out?'

'He was, he is, but I wanted to do this one personally,' I say.

It came to me that night, or rather that morning, where I'd heard the name Wendover before. I couldn't place it at first, when Parker had mentioned it to me just after I'd interviewed the delightful Graham Benson, but it had set a bell off somewhere inside me, pressed the search button in my mind's computer. I knew it would only be a matter of time before I remembered. And that time had been the following morning, around 3 a.m. while I'd been in bed next to my heavily pregnant and restless wife who'd spent most of the night tossing and turning in a bid to try and find a comfortable position for more than five minutes.

'You're hogging the bed,' she'd shoved me gently. 'Move up a bit.'

After precariously balancing on the edge of the mattress for what felt like far too long, I'd given up on the idea of sleep as much as she no doubt had. I suppose it's a small price to pay, after all; she's doing all the hard work, so I decided to retreat to the sofa and was making us both a cup of tea in my boxers when it came to me.

Len Wendover! The man at the candlelit vigil!

I'd almost fist-pumped the air in triumph. He'd introduced himself and his family to me that night – his wife, a son and his girlfriend, and a daughter too if I recall, made something of a point of it. Of course this isn't reason enough on its own to arouse any suspicion, and yet I must've logged it in my memory bank for a reason. I'd left it in Parker's capable hands to follow up the list of MG owners in the area. He was going through the list in alphabetical order and hadn't got round to 'W' yet. Plus of course Len Wendover was now deceased thanks to a tragic accident. But still, my intuition has brought me here, to his front door.

'It may be nothing,' I tell Davis. 'Barking up the wrong tree, but let's see, shall we?'

I ring the doorbell again.

Eventually, a woman answers it. 'Yes... can I help you?'

'Detective Chief Inspector Riley,' I say, flashing her my ID. 'And this is DS Davies. Are you Mrs Wendover – Mrs Maggie Wendover?' I know she isn't. The woman I met that night at Amelie Fox's vigil was smaller with dark hair, and this lady is tall and blondish.

'No, I'm her friend, Christine Langford,' she says, looking a little perplexed. 'Is everything OK?'

'Yes, yes, absolutely,' I assure her. 'We'd just like to speak to Mrs Wendover if possible... is she in? Can we come in?'

'Um, yes... yes, she's here, but it's not really a good time – she's resting upstairs.' She turns and points, like we aren't sure where upstairs might be. 'You may not be aware, but her husband has just died. It was his funeral yesterday and she's... well as you can imagine she's...'

I nod. 'I'm sure. We won't take up much of her time, but it would be helpful if we could speak to her.'

'Can I ask what about?' Christine says, opening the door to allow us in.

'Just a couple of routine questions – it's really nothing to worry about,' I say.

She nods, looks concerned. 'Go through to the kitchen. I'll go up and let Maggie know you're here, see if she's up to visitors.'

Davis and I head through to the large kitchen diner. The place is filled with flowers, bouquets and bunches of them perfuming the air, and condolence cards crowd the kitchen table.

I pick one up, read it.

Dear Maggie, Lewis and Remy, sending you

our most heartfelt condolences on the deeply tragic loss of your beloved husband and father, Len. He was a wonderful man who touched the lives of many and was loved by all. He will be sorely missed. With all our love, your neighbours, Brenda and Ron...

I pick up another, and another, and they all say a variation of the same thing, describing Len as a 'legend', 'kind', 'loveable', 'loyal' and noting how much he'll be missed.

'Obviously a well-liked and respected bloke,' Davis comments.

'Yes,' I say, 'and so was Ted Bundy.'

She shoots me a look. 'You think Len Wendover had something to do with Amelie Fox's death?'

I shrug. 'That's why we're here, ostensibly.'

I recognise her instantly as she walks through the kitchen door, marvel at my own ability to have remembered her features so accurately given our very brief encounter, certainly enough to identify that she's Maggie Wendover, the same woman I fleetingly met the night of Amelie's remembrance vigil.

'Maggie... Maggie Wendover?'

'Yes,' she says. Her voice is a soft, low rasp. 'I'm Maggie. Can I help you? Christine says you're police officers...'

'Detective Chief Inspector Riley – Dan Riley.' I hold my hand out and she tentatively shakes it. 'And my colleague, DS Lucy Davis. Perhaps you remember me?' I say, smiling at her.

She looks a little nervous as she gestures for us to sit down. I suppose it's only to be expected.

'I... I'm sorry,' she apologies. 'Have we met before? You'll have to forgive me, it's just that my husband, Len, he...'

'Yes, yes I know,' I say soberly. 'We're very sorry for your loss, Maggie, for you and your family. This must be an incredibly difficult time for you all, and again, I apologise for coming here unannounced, especially since I hear the funeral was only yesterday. I hope it went well – as well as these things can go anyway.'

'Thank you.'

She looks exhausted, like she hasn't slept in weeks, the dark circles underneath her glazed eyes testament to that. A wave of empathy washes over me. I've been there. I know how she feels.

'Has something happened? Please tell me it's not more bad news.' She wraps her kimono dressing gown protectively around her, goes to the sink and fills a glass with water. I notice that her hands are trembling. She opens the fridge.

'Can I get you anything? Tea? Coffee? A soft drink perhaps? Goodness knows we all need it in this heat. Ah, the milk's off.' She sniffs the bottle, turns to her friend. 'Chris, you wouldn't run down the shops for me, would you? We need a few other bits as well: dishwasher tablets, bread and—'

'Of course,' she says. 'Do you want me to go now? Or shall I wait here with you while...' Christine looks over at myself and Davis.

'It's fine, honestly,' Maggie says.

'If you're sure. OK, I'll get my keys.' Christine nods at us with a small smile before leaving the room.

'It goes off so quickly in this heat,' Maggie says, pouring the milk down the waste disposal. 'I can offer you a peppermint tea; something soft instead? Water?'

'Water would be great, thanks,' Davis says.

'Perhaps we can sit down,' I gently suggest.

She does as I ask, brings some glasses to the table and a bottle of Evian from the fridge.

'Ice?'

'No. No really, it's fine.'

She shakily pours the water.

'Thanks. Listen, Maggie, we wanted to talk to you about Len.'

'What about him?' she says. 'He was stung by a wasp, went into anaphylactic shock, he asphyxiated, so the post-mortem report says. I tried to administer his EpiPen but... but I was too late.' She sips her water, looks visibly distressed. 'Is that why you're here, to ask about his death? Because I've been through all of this, told the policeman – the one who came that day – everything, how it all happened... There's no problem, is there?'

'No, no,' I say, 'and we certainly don't want to upset you any further, truly. This must be a dreadful time for you. I know you were married a long time – twenty-five years, wasn't it?'

Her face registers surprise. 'Yes. How do you know that?'

'He told me, your husband... that night at the remembrance vigil for Amelie Fox, he introduced himself – and your family – to me. Do you remember? I saw you there.'

'I'm sorry, yes, now you mention it... I think I do. I'm sorry,' she apologises again, 'my head's all over the place at the moment. It's been such a shock, so difficult to come to terms with, losing him so suddenly that way.'

'I'm sure,' I say softly, pausing for a moment, aware of her fragility. 'He had a car, your husband, Len – a Cadillac, is that right?'

She swallows some water, starts coughing violently.

'Are you OK?' She sounds like she's choking and I'm almost about to start banging her on the back with the palm of my hand.

'Wrong hole,' she says hoarsely, pointing to her throat. 'Sorry, excuse me.' She composes herself. 'Yes... yes, he does. He was a vintage-car fanatic. He bought old American models from the fifties and sixties mainly, and then restored them back to their original glory. It was his passion. He loved his cars, spent hours working on them – a real labour of love it was... Why? Why do you ask?'

'It's strictly routine, you understand,' Davis says. 'We're checking all the GM models in the area, and those who attended the car festival down at Riverdown Park recently.'

'In connection with what?' she asks. 'Not the Amelie Fox murder?'

'If it's OK with you, we'd like to organise conducting a forensic search of the vehicle,' I say, adding, 'strictly for elimination purposes.'

'What?' She looks at us both respectively. 'Why? When? You know the car never even drove. He hadn't got it up and running yet – it wasn't road worthy. It's been sitting in the garage ever since he had it shipped over from the States.'

'Yes, I understand,' I say. 'Like I say, it's just routine.'

She blinks at me rapidly. 'I don't understand. You think Len's car is somehow involved in a murder inquiry?'

'No – no, Maggie.'

'It's a great big bright-pink Cadillac – you can't exactly miss it. It's hardly subtle – certainly not the ideal vehicle to use for transporting a body!'

Davis and I exchange a brief glance. *Who said anything about transporting a body?*

'Could we... could we see it, Maggie? The car, if it's not too much trouble.'

She looks spooked, upset, and admittedly I do feel a touch guilty. The poor woman has just buried her husband of twenty-five years after losing him in a frankly bizarre and tragic accident, and here I am asking to poke around his beloved prize possession the day after his funeral.

'Well, I... I...'

The doorbell rings suddenly.

'That was quick. I thought she took a key.'

Maggie hurries from the room. I hear voices in the hallway, whispers, low and inaudible. She returns a few moments later.

'My son, Lewis, and his girlfriend, Casey,' she introduces us with what I detect to be some reluctance.

'We thought we'd pop by, Mum, see how you're doing. How *are* you doing, Mum?' He looks at her with concern, embraces her.

'We brought you round some shopping, just some basics you know, a few provisions,' Casey says, beginning to unpack the groceries from the bag efficiently. 'Some eggs, milk, pasta, wine... most importantly, wine.'

Maggie looks like she's about to cry. 'That's so thoughtful of you both... thank you, darlings.'

She looks over at me. 'Detective Riley here wants to take a look at your dad's car.'

'Really?' Lewis says, shooting me a puzzled look. 'Why would you want to look at my dad's car?'

Casey sits down. 'God, it's so hot,' she says, fanning her face with a hand and rubbing her belly in an exaggerated way that makes me think – quite sweetly – that she's trying to let me know that she's pregnant.

'Your first?' I say.

'Yes!' She beams proudly. 'Can you tell?'

'My wife's expecting our second – not long to go now.'

'Oh, that's exciting! I'm due in November! Hopefully it will be a bit cooler by then... I can only imagine how your wife must be coping in this heat!'

'She isn't to be honest. I—'

'My dad's car?' Lewis interrupts. 'You want to see my dad's car?'

'Yes.' I smile affably at him. 'We're looking at all GM and Cadillac owners in the area. We'd need to impound it, for forensic purposes. It's just routine,' I reassure him, again, 'providing you give your permission, of course.'

Lewis looks at his mother, shrugs. 'Is this about Amelie's

murder? You can't possibly think that Dad... that Dad had anything to do with that surely?'

'You knew Amelie Fox, didn't you, Lewis?'

He blinks at me, a little taken aback. 'Me? No... yes, well, I knew who she was – we all did. She went to my school; we were at primary school together. I remember her, from back then anyway, but I didn't know her, hadn't seen her in years, only on Instagram anyway.'

I nod.

The kitchen door opens again and a young woman enters. 'What's going on? I heard voices.'

It's the daughter I assume, though she looks different. I suspect she's just woken up – her blonde hair is messy and she's wearing pyjama shorts and a T-shirt that says 'Good vibes only' on it.

'Who are you?' She addresses me outright, looks me up and down.

'Detective Chief Inspector Riley,' I say. 'Dan, and this is DS Davis.'

'Why are you here?'

'Just a routine visit.'

'He wants to look at Dad's car – wants a forensic team to take a look at it,' Lewis tells her.

'Daddy's Caddy? Why on earth would you want to look at that?' She slumps down at the kitchen table next to her mother. 'You OK, Mum?'

Maggie nods silently, squeezes her daughter's arm.

'You knew Amelie Fox, didn't you... um... I'm sorry, I've forgotten your name.'

'Remy,' she says. 'I remember you, from the vigil – you're the detective.'

'Yes.' I smile. 'So, you knew Amelie?'

'Nope,' she says, stifling a yawn. 'I knew her by name, knew that she grew up round here, that we went to the same middle school. I followed her on IG though because she was like, well, she was sort of famous… and no one famous has ever come from round here, but I never saw her out locally, never spoke to her, not even at school I don't think. Lewis did though, didn't you – you knew her?'

He glares at his sister. 'No! I didn't, not really. I mean, I saw her once or twice, out and about you know, here and there over the years, but she didn't know who I was.'

'I suppose you've heard that we're asking all the local men from the area to give an involuntary DNA sample,' I say, knowing fine well he does – he was right there when Len confirmed both he and his son would be willing to take part. 'Would you be prepared to give one, Lewis?'

Maggie is standing now, though she looks a little unsteady on her feet. 'This really isn't the time, Detective – we're all in shock, grieving. Perhaps you could come back another day?'

'Look, I realise my timing is terrible, and I'm genuinely sorry for the inconvenience and any upset this may cause you, but I have to remind you this is a murder inquiry, Maggie.' I'm careful to keep my voice even, friendly. 'We're requesting exactly the same from all GM and Cadillac car owners in the area, and we're currently collating as many DNA samples from locals as possible. It's all just bog standard, elimination-process procedure that's all. We're not singling you out at all – I want to reassure you of that.'

'It's OK, Mum.' Lewis steps forward. 'Of course I'll give a DNA sample. You can take it now if you like. Then I'll show you to the garage, to see the car.'

'Lew…' Maggie looks at him.

'Don't worry, Mum, it's OK.'

'Thank you.' I nod my gratitude at him, remove the DNA kit from my jacket pocket.

'I'm sorry to have to ask you all this, but could you tell me where you were the night of Wednesday the twentieth of May – and your husband, where he was too?'

Maggie's face looks ashen, almost grey. 'Is this really necessary? Can this not be done at a later date, when we're all... when we've all had a chance to come to terms with everything?'

'Well, I was in London,' Remy says, 'I live there. I'm a fashion student – not that you can probably tell right now.' She giggles, rubs a hand through her matted hair.

'Casey and I were at home – we live near Eden Gorge. I got home from work around 7.30 p.m. like I do most nights. We were there all evening.'

'Yes,' Casey says, 'I remember I made Mexican food... I've been craving spicy stuff ever since I've been pregnant – can't get enough of it.'

'Funny, my wife has too.' I smile, turning to Maggie. 'And you... Len...?'

She shakes her head. 'I was here, like I always am. I was making last-minute preparations for the anniversary party... it was on the following Saturday you see. I was double-checking the RSVPs; I think I spoke with my friend, Christine, on the phone at some point. She can tell you when she's back.'

'And Len? He was here too?'

Maggie pauses ever so slightly. 'No. He was with his brother, Bob. They go – they went – to the vintage-car festival every year together, something of a ritual, been doing it for years, ever since it started. Anyway, he stayed over at Bob's house that night, with him and his wife, Julie. You can ask them if you like.'

Davis is frantically scribbling in her notebook.

'Thank you,' I say genuinely. 'Thank you, Maggie. I'm sorry I had to ask – it's my job, I'm afraid.'

'Yes,' she says quietly, 'I understand, of course.'

.   .   .

'Well, that threw up the princely sum of nothing,' Davis says as she drives us back to the nick.

'Don't be too cocksure, Davis,' I say. 'You know what it's like in this game – got to keep an open mind.'

'Yes, but I don't get it, boss. Why the interest in the Wendovers?'

'Did you notice,' I say, distracted by my own thoughts, 'what Maggie said about the Cadillac, something about it not being the most subtle of vehicles to use if you were transporting a body?'

'Yes,' she says, 'but c'mon, gov, it doesn't take a genius to work out that's why we're interested in it, does it?'

'I suppose not, no,' I muse.

'Besides, she says it doesn't even run.'

But the word she'd used, 'transport'... it struck me as odd somehow. Maybe Davis is right and I'm reading too much into this, focusing on instinct instead of cold hard evidence.

'The boot – the carpet was missing from the boot of the Cadillac. It was pristine everywhere else...'

'I get what you're saying, gov, but it doesn't mean much on its own. He was refurbishing it – something could've spilled over it and he ripped it out, anything. Anyway, forensics will take fibres from the remaining carpet and if it's a match – plus we can check the alibis, the son's DNA... but right now there's nothing at all to link Len Wendover to Amelie Fox's murder.'

'Hmmm.'

'*It's a jigsaw puzzle, Danny boy – got to build the outer framework before you can put the final picture together.*' And there's something... *something* about the Wendovers that isn't sitting right with me.

'No,' I agree with her. 'Nothing *yet*.'

34 MAGGIE

She has to leave the house, get out, escape, otherwise she thinks she might actually lose her mind. She's already lost her mind. She doesn't know where to begin, where to start organising her thoughts, how to get them into some kind of rational order. Instead they're simply a tangled mess of twisted wires, woven and knotted up tightly together, like a bag of discarded Christmas tree lights, and they're firing at her like bullets from a machine gun, the thoughts and the questions – fast, unrelenting, in lightning succession, not enough time for her to catch a breath, to process one before another comes right up behind it.

Maggie had thrown up right there on the kitchen floor almost seconds after Bob and Julie had hurriedly left her house the night before, wretched her guts up everywhere until there was nothing left inside her, save for panic and guilt and fear, such paralysing fear that it had threatened to swallow her whole.

'Come on, sweetheart.' Christine had rushed into the kitchen, had physically held her up so she could vomit in the sink. 'It's OK...' She'd made soothing shushing noises as she'd pulled her hair back from her face. 'It's OK, darling. It's been a tough day. You're going to be OK... OK, I'm here. I'm here...'

Christine had tried to put her to bed, but sleep, Maggie had realised, wasn't going to be on the agenda any time soon. Maybe it never would be again – not restful anyway.

'*Julie*... that two-faced fucking bitch!' Maggie hisses underneath her breath as she continues to pound the pavement, unaware of the strange glances she's gleaning from passers-by as she mutters manically to herself. She hasn't even bothered getting dressed properly, had just thrown on an old pair of running shorts and grabbed a dirty T-shirt from the floor before she'd fled. She'd just needed to get out of that house, away from everyone, from everything. From that detective.

'Oops... Hi!'

She almost physically connects with the oncoming woman in front of her, has to stop herself short of bumping right into her.

'Sorry,' Maggie mumbles, 'I didn't see you there. I—' She recognises her. *Oh no*. It's... it's Alex's mum, isn't it? The woman who'd blatantly blanked her in the Savacentre that day she'd gone to visit Bob and Julie.

'It's... it's Maggie, isn't it?' The woman looks at her, affords her a weak smile.

'Yes,' Maggie says, suddenly aware of how she must look – a hot, sweaty, crying dishevelled mess. She pulls at her hair – it's stuck to her face. 'I'm so sorry – forgive me... I've forgotten your name.' Her memory hasn't been good at the best of times lately, but now it feels like a void, a black hole.

'It's Della. Are you... are you OK?' She looks at her with concern. 'I heard about your husband. I'm so sorry. Alex always said what a lovely man he was.'

'Yes... yes he was, thank you.' She wants to carry on walking but is suddenly compelled to ask her about that day. 'I saw you recently, didn't I? In Savacentre. Do you remember? I was standing in the deli queue, waved at you – I thought you must've seen me?'

'I... I...' Della starts to speak, shuffles awkwardly. 'Actually, yes, I did see you.' She sighs resignedly. 'I'm really sorry – I didn't know what to say to you, after what happened between Alex and Remy. I just felt so... awkward.'

Maggie shakes her head. 'I don't follow, I'm sorry,' she says, jiggling on the spot, unable to keep herself still due to all the nervous energy coursing through her. 'Alex and Remy?'

'Yes, the falling-out they had. I'm a terrible coward when it comes to these things. I do apologise – I really didn't mean to be rude.'

'What falling-out?'

Della looks surprised. 'Remy didn't mention anything?'

'No. No she didn't.'

'Oh well... it's a shame an' all, that they won't be living together anymore, but these things happen I guess.'

'They're not sharing a flat anymore?'

'No.' Della blinks at her. 'She didn't mention that either?'

'No! But then... I'm usually the last to know anything where Remy is concerned. I haven't even met her boyfriend yet and she's planning on marrying him!' Maggie's laugh sounds disingenuous and forced. She doesn't want to have this conversation, but the words spill from her mouth automatically, like someone else is in control of them.

Della looks shocked. 'Boyfriend? You mean the boy – that man – they fell out over?'

Maggie's confused already. She can't be dealing with this. 'I didn't know that's why they fell out; I didn't know they'd fallen out at all. Listen, I'm sorry I—'

'She slapped her in the face. It all got a little out of hand.'

'What? Who slapped who in the face?'

'Remy. She slapped Alex in the face, something about her liking this boy's picture on Instagram or something silly like that. Teenage stuff really – they both should know better by now,' she adds, clearly embarrassed. 'It all came to a head when they were driving up from London, up to your place on that Wednesday. She was supposed to come and stay at ours for a couple of days before the party – you were having an anniversary party that weekend, weren't you?' She suddenly looks a little sheepish. 'I'm sorry, I didn't mean to remind you. I... But well, then they got into this terrible fight and—'

'I really can't stop. I'm... I'm on my way to meet someone,' Maggie says. 'I'm really sorry to hear about the girls. I'm sure they'll make it up soon enough. You know what girls that age can be like.'

'Yes. Yes, of course. I understand. This must be a terrible time for you all. I didn't really want to mention anything but... are you sure you're OK?'

Of course I'm not fucking OK. Do I look OK? Would she be OK if she was me right now?

'Yes – yes I'm fine, taking one day at a time...'

One day at a time. That's what people say, isn't it, after a tragedy? *Take one day at a time.*

'It was nice to see you... um...' She shakes her head – she's clean forgotten her name already!

'Della,' she says.

Maggie can't get away fast enough. She can't be dealing with Remy's petty squabbles right now. She'll ask her about it later, when she's had the chance to think, to calm down – *if she could just calm down.*

Her mind returns to the scarf. That's where it had all started, finding that bloody scarf in the loft and— *Hang on!* She's remembered something, something from that night – the night of the anniversary party.

She'd been there, hadn't she? She'd seen her, standing on the landing, hovering awkwardly the night of the anniversary party. It had struck her as odd even at the time. What was she doing upstairs? She'd looked shocked when Maggie had seen her, like she'd been caught red-handed doing something she shouldn't.

'What were you doing in my house?'

Although it's late afternoon, Brenda answers her front door in a dressing gown, her hair wrapped in a towel.

'Mags?' She looks at her, taken aback, like she doesn't recognise her.

'What were you doing in my house?' Her voice is a manic high-pitched shriek. 'Upstairs – that night, at our anniversary party. I caught you on the landing – hovering about looking shifty. I *need* to know, Brenda – you have to tell me!'

Brenda's eyes are wide with shock and confusion. 'Mags, are you OK? You look terrible. Why don't you come in?'

Maggie marches through the front door. 'No. No I'm not OK. I'm *far, far* from OK, Brenda!'

'Come and sit down.' Brenda's voice is laced with concern.

'I'll get you a drink. A cup of tea… some water… You really don't look good.'

She has no choice – if she doesn't sit down, she'll fall down, right here on Brenda's laminate floor.

She carefully leads her through to the kitchen, pulls up a chair and physically places her on it. 'I'll get you a drink. Gosh you're sweating – burning up.'

'Vodka,' Maggie croaks. 'I'll have a vodka.'

Brenda looks at her like vodka isn't a good idea but she says nothing, goes to the fridge.

'Please, have some water first at least,' she says. 'This heat-wave… you must stay hydrated.'

Maggie snorts but accepts a glass of water anyway, gulps it all back without taking a breath.

Brenda places a glass of vodka on the kitchen table and Maggie takes a mouthful, savours the burn at the back of her throat. She lets out a deep 'ahhhh'.

'Perhaps I should call Christine,' Brenda says. 'I'm worried about you – you don't look well. I mean, it's understandable, hardly surprising, what with everything that's happened. You wouldn't be human if you—'

'I just need you to tell me what you were doing upstairs at my house on the night of the party,' she cuts her off sharply. 'I caught you loitering on my landing, you remember? You looked startled – you looked *guilty*.'

'What are you talking about?' Brenda looks confused, bewildered. 'I… I was going to use the loo I think,' she stammers quickly. She slides into the chair next to her, places a hand on her arm.

Maggie snatches it away. 'You'd been up inside my loft, hadn't you? Hiding something. You need to tell me the truth, Brenda! You have no idea how important this is.' She breaks down then, starts sobbing. 'You just have… no idea!'

'Oh, Mags, I—'

'Stop calling me that!' she screams suddenly. 'It's MAGGIE – my name's MAGGIE!' She hiccups into her hands, tears and snot dripping into her palms.

'Let me get you a tissue.'

'I don't want a bloody tissue! I want the truth. You went up into my loft, didn't you? *Didn't you?*'

Brenda blinks at her, opens her mouth to speak. 'Of course I didn't. Why on earth would I do that?'

'Hiding something – you were hiding something.' But her conviction has abandoned her. Clearly Brenda has no idea what she's on about – from her tone of voice, her body language – unless of course she's a convincing liar.

'What could I have possibly been hiding?'

Maggie shakes her head. Her hands are trembling, her vision blurred through crying.

'I'll get you another vodka.' Brenda stands. 'I might have one myself now.'

Suddenly Maggie starts to laugh, causing Brenda to turn around and look at her in alarm.

'You know, I thought— At first I thought that you and Len...' She shakes her head. 'That you and Len were having an affair.'

Brenda's eyes are like saucers. 'An affair! You thought – you thought that Len... *me and Len?*'

Maggie exhales, gulps back the vodka that Brenda hands her. It seems to be helping to calm her at least.

'Why *on earth* would you have ever thought such a thing?'

She shakes her head. 'I saw the way you looked at him at the party – how you danced with him, throwing yourself at him. I mean, take Clive for instance! The man hadn't moved in five minutes before you were sniffing around him like a dog in heat, flaunting yourself...'

A look of hurt flashes across Brenda's face, a face that somehow looks different without all the make-up, softer perhaps. She notices a rash of fine lines around her eyes, a little puffiness like she's been crying or hasn't slept well.

She pauses. 'I can assure you, Maggie, can swear to you, truthfully, there was never *ever* anything going on between Len and me. That's absurd! I hardly even knew him really. I mean, he was always polite, friendly... was always pleasant to me whenever he saw me, gave me a little wave, said good morning, and that's always as far as it ever went, I promise you.' She shakes her head in disbelief. 'An affair! How could you even think such a thing?'

'Where is *your* husband? Where is Ron?' Maggie's tone is bordering on accusatory. 'Now I think of it, I haven't seen him in ages. He didn't show up at the party either. So where is he? Underneath the patio?'

Brenda shakes her head, snorts softly. 'Well, now I've heard it all,' she sighs, pauses. 'Listen, Mags – Maggie. There's something I should probably explain to you.'

Brenda goes to the fridge and brings the bottle of vodka to the table, pours them both another shot.

'Ron and I... well...' She pauses, looks up to the ceiling. 'He left me – about two months ago now. He left me for another woman, a younger woman.' She exhales through her nostrils. 'He came home from work one evening, told me he was leaving me, that he no longer loved me, no longer found me... *attractive*.' She winces slightly. 'Said he'd met someone at work – *Caroline*,' she says bitterly, 'and that he wanted a divorce. I haven't seen him since.'

Now it's Maggie's turn to be shocked. 'What?'

'Thirty-five years we'd been together – longer than you and Len even, and just like that: gone.' She claps her hands together. 'It's been, well, since he disappeared, it's been like he died – like your poor Len, so you know... I understand the pain you must be going through because even though Ron isn't... he isn't dead, more's the pity, it's as if he might as well be.'

Brenda looks visibly upset now, wipes her nose with the back of her hand and sniffs. 'I... I didn't want to tell people at first. Thought the silly old git might come back, even *hoped...*' Her voice trails off into a sad whisper. 'Him and *Caroline* are somewhere in France apparently.' Her voice is dripping with a mix of sadness and resentment. 'Anyway, I felt... well, I've felt so ashamed, so... so discarded, ugly and old, thrown away like an old pair of slippers. I confided in Clive, I suppose because he didn't know me – didn't know us – it was easier to tell him – he was new to the area, and besides, he's had his own tragedies, recently widowed, just as they were about to move into their new house together as well. Now he's rattling around the place all on his own, lonely and grieving for his wife... poor soul. He's been coming here, to see me. I've been trying to contact his wife, you know... her *spirit*. The poor man is desperate for some kind of connection, some sort of message from beyond.'

Maggie is stunned into silence. 'I... Oh God, I had no idea.' She not sure if it's possible to feel any more wretched than she already does – guilt is creeping through her veins, slowly poisoning her, drop by drop. 'I'm so sorry.' Her head falls into her hands. 'Brenda, forgive me, I... I'm not thinking straight right now. So many things... a lot has happened. I just don't know what's what anymore.'

She swallows back the emotion lodged inside her throat, but it's stuck there like a brick, and she wonders if it will ever leave, ever soften. How could she have got so much so wrong? Has she been guilty of listening to idle gossip, believing everything everyone tells her to be the gospel truth? All these assumptions, they couldn't have been further from reality. Len, Brenda, Clive... A wave of shame and self-loathing settles upon her like fresh snow.

'It's OK.' Brenda smiles at her gently, places her hand on top of Maggie's on the kitchen table and taps it. 'Grief does terrible things to a person. It's understandable, why you're so upset. Don't do what I did and try to put on a brave front – it only eats away at you inside. It's good to let it all out – the anger, the pain. God knows it has to go somewhere.'

Fat tears are falling from Maggie's face. Her nose is running, and Brenda pulls another tissue from the box, gently wipes them away before handing it to her.

'You know, I've been meaning to say something to you, was waiting for a good moment but I guess there isn't one, not in these circumstances... It's about Len.'

Len. Just the mention of his name is like a knife through Maggie's guts, a thousand tiny cuts to her conscience.

'He came to me in my special sleep, not long after he passed.'

'Special sleep?'

'Oh.' Brenda waves a hand. 'It's shorthand for my visions. Sometimes they happen at night, when I'm unconscious.'

'Like a dream you mean?' Usually Maggie would dismiss this as nothing more than utter tripe, politely humour her, but so many strange things have taken place – things she could never have imagined – was it such a stretch to believe that Brenda is psychic?

'Sort of. Not exactly. Anyway, I think he was trying to give me a message, or rather send a message to you through me.'

Maggie blinks at her, suddenly hopeful and expectant. 'What did he say? Did he say anything? Tell you anything?'

Brenda nods. 'He wanted you to look for something – something inside a drawer.'

A burst of adrenalin explodes inside her like a bomb and she feels her pelvic floor loosen. *The EpiPen? Oh God.*

'Did he say what it was that he wanted me to look for?'

She shakes her head. 'I think it was more that he wanted you to find something he'd left—'

But before she can finish the sentence, the doorbell rings.

'I won't be a minute.' Brenda goes to answer it, and a few moments later, Clive walks into the kitchen.

'Hello, Maggie,' he says, all arms and legs.

She looks up at him ruefully. Creepy Clive, that's what she's been secretly calling him, and yet now that she knows his story, after what Brenda has told her, he doesn't look creepy at all, just desperately sad and lonely.

'How are you? How are you bearing up? God, don't you just hate it when people ask you that?' he says, flashing her a small smile, which she now recognises as a knowing one.

'I'm OK,' she lies, and he gives her a look that suggests he knows this.

'That good, huh? Well,' he says, holding up a bottle of wine that he's brought with him, 'you're in good company at least.'

Maggie somehow manages to smile at him, poor awkward-looking Clive. And then it comes to her. *Of course,* Clive!

'Actually, I'm glad you're here, Clive, that I've seen you. You might be able to help me with something.'

'Oh?' he says, perking up a little. 'Always happy to be of assistance if I can.'

'Something you mentioned a couple of weeks back, about seeing the Cadillac – about seeing Len driving the Cadillac in the early hours one morning. Do you remember telling me that?'

Clive uncorks the bottle with a satisfying pop, sniffs the rim before decanting it into three glasses.

'To those left behind,' he says. 'To us.'

'To us!' Brenda says spiritedly.

He takes a sip, savours it for a second or two.

Maggie swallows her entire glass whole.

'Yes.' He nods. 'I remember. The Wednesday night – well, Thursday morning actually. I was awake – terrible insomnia you see – looked out of the window. I'd heard a car starting up and I thought... well, that's when I thought I saw it.'

'You *thought* you saw it? You *thought* you saw Len driving the Cadillac?'

'Yes. I did see it – you can't really miss it, can you, great big pink thing? – but then you said... you said it wasn't roadworthy, that it didn't go or something, and I thought I must be going gaga, because I could've sworn, absolutely could've sworn...'

Maggie nods. 'You're sure— I'm sorry.' She shakes her head, a little embarrassed about pressing him. 'You're absolutely sure that you saw the Cadillac, saw Len driving it down the road that morning, the morning of the twenty-first? It's just that, well, it's really quite important.'

'Quite' didn't really cover it.

He looks at her a little curiously. 'I'm absolutely sure,' he says. 'Yes, I saw it backing out of the garage, reverse, then turn and carry on up the road. Oh,' he adds, as though he's suddenly thought of an important detail. 'But it wasn't Len who was driving.'

36 DAN

I'm trying to fit it all together, that jigsaw in my head. Murder cases, at least some of them, aren't always cut and dried like they are on the telly where there's a prime suspect and the motive is clear from the beginning.

Sometimes a murder can take years, decades, even centuries to solve, if they're even solved at all. Often, it's a slow, arduous, painstaking process that involves a huge amount of intelligence, a vast network of people all working collectively: forensics, cyber experts, analysts, pathologists, witnesses, psychologists, all kinds of specialists...

'The Eiffel Tower wasn't built in a day, Danny Boy!'

It's a long game sometimes, a waiting game, yet somehow, as I sit here at my desk, my aching, swollen feet up on it, tapping my teeth with my chewed biro, I feel certain I have all the answers in front of me already, that it's all here somewhere, and I feel it so strongly, it's like there's a clock ticking inside me, a bomb ready to go off, the answers I'm searching for waiting to explode inside of me like confetti at any minute.

I exhale heavily as I look back through some old statements:

the Foxes', Holly Redwood's, Graham Benson's... reread them all in case I've missed something. I *must've* missed something.

'I put a rush on Lewis Wendover's DNA, gov, like you asked,' Davis says, breezing through the door like a breath of fresh air.

Fresh air. Can't recall when I last had any of that. It's stifling in the incident room thanks to the fact that the air conditioning is – of course – currently broken, and even with all the cheap fans running at full blast, it feels hotter than Death Valley. It's been the hottest start to June on record so far, the news full of cracked pavements due to the inclement weather, hosepipe bans, grass fires, and people frying eggs on tarmac. The heat, it really does do strange things to some people.

'Archer's putting pressure on pathology too.' She raises an eyebrow. 'Not like her to stick her oar in so directly,' she adds.

I exhale through my nose, throw my biro onto my desk. 'Maybe she has a vested interest,' I say cryptically.

Davis is nobody's fool though – picks up on it straight away. 'And why would that be?'

I shake my head. 'Some things are best left unsaid, Davis.'

'Well, anyway, we should have something from them imminently. But in the meantime, here.' She places something onto my desk. 'It's hardly been a priority because of his alibi, but here's a copy of the contents of Graham "G" Benson's phone.' She mocks him with finger quotes. 'All his text messages, call history, photos... most of which I'm pretty sure are of himself,' she concludes brightly and, I've no doubt, rightly. 'There could be something in there?' she says, adding, 'You never know.'

'Wonderful,' I say, deadpan.

'Happy viewing, gov – it's gonna be a long night.'

'Why don't you go home, Lucy?' I say as I begin to download it onto my laptop.

She looks at me, her head cocked to one side. 'You sure, gov? It's a bit early, isn't it?'

'Perfectly. It's going to be a beautiful evening – make the most of it. We'll all be back moaning about the cold weather again soon enough.' I'm somewhat surprised though because ordinarily she would object, fight me over it, which makes me wonder if she has plans. A date maybe?

'Well, if you're sure.'

'Perfectly,' I say again.

'Right well, I'll be off then. See you in the morning, gov.'

I nod. 'Hope it's not Graham Benson,' I say.

'Graham Benson?' Her brow furrows.

'That date you're going on tonight,' I reply as she's walking out the door.

'Not in this lifetime, gov.' She winks at me. 'Besides, I only have the one mirror in my apartment anyway.'

There's a mountain of text messages and images on Graham Benson's phone, making me wonder if he ever actually has a conversation with anyone in person or when he gets time in the day to eat or sleep. I can only assume this mere mortal stuff happens when he's not taking selfies or in the gym, which seems to be an awful lot. Every moment of his life appears to be documented on social media, through photos and texts, Snapchat and IG, Facebook, TikTok, Twitter and Telegram. I start with the photos – there's thousands of them stored on his iCloud alone.

I take a sip from the plastic cup of water on my desk and pull a face. It's tepid, so I make my way over to the water cooler for a fresh cup. Davis is right – it's going to be a long night.

I click on the first image of a shirtless, tanned and toned Graham posing in a pair of tight pink chino shorts as he takes a selfie in the mirror... Graham, topless again, working out at the gym... sprawled out on a sun lounger in Mykonos, flexing his well-defined quads and sipping on a cocktail...

I sigh, continuing to scroll through, each one a variation on the one before, the odd image of a fancy plate of haute cuisine or a bottle of champagne surrounded by sparklers in some over-priced swanky restaurant thrown in for good measure.

There's Graham on a rooftop bar in London, flanked by his almost identikit 'bros', all in a uniform of skin-tight shorts and crisp designer polo shirts and slip-on shoes. There's Graham on a jet ski in Ibiza wearing Ray-Bans and flexing his abs, Graham smiling from what looks like a dentist's chair getting a set of what he refers to as 'Turkey teeth' in the caption, a before and after shot where his already neat white smile appears to have been made even neater and whiter, a steal at six thousand euros.

There's a picture of him and his mum, tagged as 'The original G ma' in the post – a small, attractive-looking woman holding a huge balloon within a balloon and who he towers over as he kisses the top of her head...

There are countless images of him with various different women of course, all young, all beautiful, mostly blonde and in varying states of (un)dress, at parties, clubs, on the beach, in a bar, in his bed... and ah! Finally, there she is: Amelie Fox. Posted on IG a little over two months ago, Graham is standing next to her, his arm draped around her small waist, their set of perfectly white smiles simultaneously glowing like neon out at the camera, offset by their matching tans. They're holding champagne flutes up in what looks like celebration. They look happy, easy in each other's company, and, undoubtedly, they do make for a very aesthetically pleasing couple I suppose.

I enlarge the photo on my screen, study it. They appear to be in a bar or club – he's tagged the venue, a place called Vibe. I google it. It's a bar/nightclub in Soho, popular with 'celebrities' by all accounts, the website blurb blatantly name dropping various 'regulars' who all seem to have appeared on some kind of reality TV show that while I've never watched, I know to be extremely popular with today's younger generation.

I try to imagine what it must be like, showcasing your entire life like Graham Benson appears to do – every personal, private moment shared with an audience, no part of your existence hidden.

I've been staring at Graham and Amelie's image for what feels like hours now, waiting for it to tell me something and... *hold on*! A burst of adrenalin hits my stomach and explodes, like confetti. Is this it, the Eureka moment I've been waiting for?

I lean forward closer to the screen, enlarge the image as much as I'm able to, zoom in on the background, on the person standing some way back in the distance, glancing sideways at them as their photo is taken. I rub my dry eyes. I think I recognise them. Yes, yes I'm sure I do, though they look different somehow...

'What the...?' I stare at the screen, unblinking, my heart rate increasing with each breath.

'Good Lord,' I whisper, my mind rewinding back to the interview Davis and I conducted with Graham Benson. I'm just about to pick up the phone and make a call when it rings, startling me.

'Detective Chief Inspector Riley?' the voice on the other end enquires brightly. 'This is Dr Justine Maslen from FSS. The DNA sample, the one you put an urgent rush on. Lewis... Lewis Wendover.'

'You've got a match?' My chest is so tight with adrenalin I can barely project the words.

'No...'

I feel myself inwardly crash, my initial excitement and anticipation dropping rapidly like a descending rollercoaster. 'Oh...'

'Well, no *and* yes actually,' she says.

'I'm sorry, I don't quite follow.'

I can hear her breathing down the line.

'I ran it through the usual channels, which didn't produce anything I'm afraid. As you know, it was a small sample to begin with as it was, but then I conducted a CODIS search...'

'Still not following,' I say, though my spirits are gingerly beginning to rise once again.

'Combined DNA Index System,' she explains.

Still means zip to me.

'*And?*'

'Well, the results clearly show that the forensic profile you gave us is not the source of the crime-scene profile – of the DNA we recovered from underneath Amelie Fox's fingernail.'

'OK.' they fall flat again.

'But...'

Ah, there's a but!

'... there was a partial match, which means a possibility does exist that a close biological relative of the offender might be the source of the crime-scene profile.'

I pause, allow the words to sink in for a second.

'Hello? Detective Inspe—'

'Well, well,' I say, staring at the enlarged image on my computer screen. 'Now that's interesting... very interesting indeed.'

'Is it? Oh jolly good,' she says. 'I hope it can be of help. I'll send you over a copy of our findings.'

I pick up the receiver again as quickly as I express my gratitude to Dr Maslen and replace it. 'Graham Benson?'

'Who is this? If you're a hack, yeah, you gotta go through my agent... How did you even get my personal digits, man?'

'DCI Riley – Dan Riley. We spoke the other day.'

'Oh,' he says, clearly crestfallen that I'm *not* a journalist requesting an interview. 'Yeah, I remember. You calling to tell me the results of my DNA test, because I could've saved you the bother if you have?'

'They came back as expected, Graham,' I say, 'a DNA match on the sperm sample, but no match on the other.'

I'd suspected as much. Graham Benson's story had checked out, and the alibi he'd provided had been fully corroborated.

'Like, I said, I could've told you that. So, what can I do you for then, Dan?' he says – overfamiliar, like I'm one of his 'bros'.

'Something you said, during the interview with myself and my colleague.'

Looking back now, it had been a glib remark, one I think was even interrupted, dismissed as irrelevant at the time, but I'm beginning to wonder now if it was anything but. 'Something about how some girls are difficult to get rid of.' *Harder than herpes* – I'm sure that's how he'd delightfully put it. 'Do you remember?'

'Er, yeah, man.' He sniffs. 'I think so. Why?'

'I need you to come down to the station, Graham,' I say. 'Now if possible.'

'*Now*? You're kidding me? But I'm like— Look, I'm like super busy right now...'

'It's important, Graham,' I say sagely. 'You could even be integral in helping to solve Amelia's murder.'

I'm appealing to his ego, which isn't difficult given it's the size of a small continent. As I'd predicted, Graham's fake forlorn mug has been splashed all over the papers recently, the opportunity to raise his profile on the back of the 'love of his life' Amelie's murder far too big a temptation for him to resist.

'We'll send a car for you, if you like,' I add, hoping the special treatment will swing it.

There's a moment's pause.

'OK,' he says. 'But like, can you at least tell me what for?'

'Yes,' I say. 'There's someone I need you to identify.'

37 MAGGIE

She can see the heat rising up from the tarmac – hazy lines blurring a few inches off the ground as she walks the short distance across the road from Brenda's house back to her own like a zombie in a horror film, her movements jerky and uncoordinated. Adrenalin now acts like an anaesthetic, coating her in a sweat-dazed fog, trying desperately to protect her from the flames of fear that are licking at her feet. She's hyperventilating, her worst fears becoming more and more real with each fateful step she takes towards her house. She tries desperately to stay calm, but trauma is all around her like a forcefield, an electric fence, replacing her blood in liquid form, pulsing through her body, and as much as she tries to think, tries to somehow stop herself from thinking the unimaginable, all she can hear in her mind is the word *no*, over and over and over again.

There's a cool, still, almost eerie silence as she enters her house.

'Remy?' She calls out her daughter's name as she throws her keys onto the console table. They miss – clatter to the floor loudly. She can't physically bend down to pick them up. If she does, she will surely shatter every bone in her body.

'Remy?' She must be in – her car is still here.

She calls her name again, goes through to the kitchen. Her kitchen – the hub of her home – has, she realises in this moment, always been such a safe place, a place where they, the Wendovers, had gathered together to share the day's collective news over the years. It was where they ate, where they talked and laughed and interacted, *where they'd been a family*.

She flashes back to when her children were little, sitting at the large oak table, colouring books and pens sprawled out across it, lids discarded, fighting over the purple felt tip – always the purple. It has seen years of life, this table, a thousand dinner times and parties, Christmases, birthdays, pencil indentations on the wood from the pages and pages of homework that have been completed on it. She'd taught her children to read at this table, had been proud of the fact that they could write their names perfectly even before they went to primary school.

They'd made love on it once too, her and Len, maybe more than once perhaps, drunken balmy summer evenings after too many cocktails when the kids were all tucked up in bed, back when she'd been younger, happier, when she'd felt more like herself. She wonders what it might say, the table, if it could speak. The stories it would recant of all the laughter and tears throughout the years, all the memories.

Remy's phone is on the table – she's definitely here. It's playing music softly, the volume low... She recognises the song – 'Wicked Games' – though it sounds different to the original, a remix. *Nothing is original anymore*, she thinks sadly. Why does everything always have to be messed with, changed and altered... why, when it had already been perfect in the first place?

She recognises it as the same song that had been playing on that awful video, that tawdry home-made sex tape that had featured Amelie Fox.

She picks the phone up with a trembling hand, clicks onto

the messages icon and begins to scroll through them, unsure of what she's looking for while simultaneously knowing that whatever it is, she doesn't want to see it.

Someone called 'Gray'. There are hundreds of exchanges between them, spanning across a few months, from early March to the middle of May. Is Gray the boyfriend she's been talking about all this time, Whatshisface, the one she hasn't yet met, the one whose bloody name she could never remember and who apparently wants to marry her daughter? Does he somehow fit into all of this terrifying mess? If so, how exactly?

Maggie sits down at the table, spots a packet of cigarettes and a lighter. They must belong to that treacherous bitch Julie – she probably left them in haste as Christine had evicted her and Bob from the house in those terrible moments after she'd learned the truth.

Truth. How could she have spent the last three decades of her life being so sure of what it was only for it to vanish like it had never existed at all. Julie had been good for something at least, she thinks bitterly, taking a cigarette from the packet and lighting it.

> Remy: Are you blanking me? U gunna be at Vibe on Sat?

> Remy: Y U not reply? (Cross face emoji)

> Remy: Was it just a ONS?

An ONS? *A one-night stand...*

> G: yh.

> Remy: But that night was special. Was I as good as Angel?

Maggie continues to read, holding her breath. Angel? *What is this?*

> Remy: but u said U liked me.

> G: send nudes (wink emoji)

> Remy: OK (bashful emoji)

Maggie can barely look at the naked images of her daughter through her tears – they're dripping down onto the phone screen. She wipes them away, continues to scroll down with a shaking hand.

> Remy: U like? (Smiley emoji)

> Remy: Hellooo?

She sends more images, more graphic this time.

Maggie stifles a gasp with her hand, her whole body vibrating. She extinguishes her cigarette in an empty glass, instantly lights another. She can't look at them.

> Remy: Happy now?

> Remy: U there?

> Remy: Ur a fking user!

> G: leave me the fck alone weirdo!

> Remy: u making me mad!

> G: I'm blocking ur number freak!

> Remy: I'll tell people U raped me

G: Wot! Your crazy!

Remy: I love you.

G: Blocked.

Soft sobbing noises escape from Maggie's throat as she reads the exchanges, tears spilling from her face down onto the table. Gray. *Oh God.* Was he the man in the sex video – the one she'd seen on Len's laptop?

'Mum?'

Maggie drops the phone in alarm, gasps in shock as she sees her daughter's silhouette in the kitchen doorway. 'What are you doing with my phone?'

'Oh, Remy,' she says, blinking at her through blurry, tear-filled vision. 'What have you done?'

'What are you doing looking on my phone?' Remy moves towards her.

Instinctively, Maggie backs away from her. Is she frightened of *her own child*? She's certainly terrified of what she might've done.

'Sit down, Remy.' Her voice feels remarkably calm as she pulls up a chair. 'I need to talk to you.'

Remy blinks at her. She looks terrified herself now. She knows – she knows that she knows; she can see it on her daughter's face, a sort of scared resignation, a look she recognises, like she used to give her as a child when she'd been caught doing something she shouldn't.

'That's private,' Remy says quietly, but she does as she's told and sits down at the table opposite.

Maggie looks at her, her beloved daughter, her beautiful child, a child she grew inside her, one she'd birthed, nurtured; a child she's taught right from wrong; a loving child, happy, sweet-natured, funny, intelligent, caring... it was inconceivable, just utterly *inconceivable* to think, to believe, even for a moment, that she's capable of killing someone, of murdering another human being, of disposing of their body like trash...

'Remy.' She reaches across the table, takes her daughter's hands in her own. They feel soft, a little clammy to touch, hands she's held since she'd been born, so familiar she could identify them in a million pairs. 'You need to tell me what happened.'

Remy looks at her, her dark eyes a little glassy now. She shakes her head. 'I don't know what you mean, Mum... tell you what happened? Wh-What happened when, to who?'

But her shaky voice betrays her, her body language leaking as she begins to squeeze Maggie's hands with her own in anxiety.

'You know who, Remy.' Tears are dripping down her face now; she can't control them – they're like a faulty tap. 'You need to tell me *everything*.'

She sees her daughter swallow, her gaze lowering to the table.

'I'm a terrible person,' Remy says quietly after a long pause.

Maggie's head is shaking; her whole body is vibrating, like she's white goods on a spin cycle. She tries to stop it, but she can't – it's seized control of her.

'No,' Maggie says, 'no, you're not a terrible person, Remy.' Her voice catches and she takes a sharp intake of breath. 'But you did a terrible thing, didn't you?'

Remy is nodding slowly.

'Oh, Remy...'

Maggie breaks down then, drops her head onto the table with a thud. She's still gripping her daughter's hands.

'Oh, Remy, why? *Why*? How could you? How could you ever do such a terrible, *terrible* thing? Do you realise... do you realise what you've done?'

But she doesn't. How could she possibly know that her actions have directly led to her own father's death? How has Maggie been so stupid, so blind, so convinced of Len's guilt? It's running through her mind, still frames flashing up inside her head: the scarf, the stuff she'd found on Len's laptop, the missing and reappearing suitcase, the black sacks by the kitchen door, her falling-out with Alex, her drastic change in hair colour... Could she have prevented this? She'd been wrong. She'd made a dreadful, *terrible* mistake. And now everything she'd feared happening *is* happening – now all her worst nightmares are present and real. And it's worse – far, far worse than she could've ever imagined.

Maggie heart feels like bone china in her chest, fragile and brittle – any sudden movement and it will surely break, fracture into tiny pieces, turn to ash and dust, like her husband, just like her innocent Len is now. Nothing more than ash and dust...

'I-I didn't... I did-didn't plan it.' Remy's voice is a high-pitched protestation. 'It was – it just – it just *happened*.'

She looks up from the table at her. 'How?' she says. 'How did it just happen, Remy?'

'You hate me, don't you? I hate myself, Mum.'

'I don't hate you, Remy. I'll never ever hate you – you're my child – but I hate what you've done.'

'I just... I just wanted him to like me,' she says. 'I just wanted to be like her. He liked *her*. Everybody liked *her*. She was just... just so... so *perfect*.' She's gripping Maggie's hands tightly, tears spilling down her cheeks onto the kitchen table. 'I thought if I could just be more like her, then he would love me.'

'He? You mean Gray? This Gray character?'

Remy nods. 'I slept with him, had sex with him, in – in a nightclub toilet.' She bows her head again, looks ashamed.

'Oh, Remy...'

'You don't understand,' she says, raising her voice again suddenly. 'That he even *noticed* me... it was like winning a prize, Mum. G Benson wanted to have sex with me – *me*! It made me feel... I felt like somebody, you know? Somebody worth knowing, I had to be if he liked me.'

'I read the text messages, Remy,' Maggie says.

'Oh God.' Remy shakes her head.

'He wasn't your boyfriend, was he? He used you and discarded you. You meant nothing to him.'

'Don't say that!' Her voice is a pained cry. 'Please! Don't say that!'

'He didn't want anything to do with you. All the talk of coming to the party, going on holiday together... of him wanting to *marry* you? None of it was real, was it, Remy? You were fixated on him – it was all in your head, this... this imaginary relationship.'

'No! NO! It wasn't, Mum. It was her – *she* was always there, in the background. If she'd stayed away... if she'd just stayed away from him!' Remy bangs the table with a fist.

Maggie recoils, startled, even a little fearful, but she doesn't let go of her daughter's hand.

'I went to see her. I thought if I could just talk to her...'

'How did you know where she lived?'

Remy rolls her eyes. 'It's all over Instagram, Mum. *Perfect* pictures of her in her *perfect* apartment, wearing her *perfect* clothes with her *perfect* figure. It wasn't hard to find out.'

'And?'

'And so I went there, to see her. I waited outside her apartment building until someone came out and I went in, took the lift to her floor, knocked on her door. I was crying, in a bit of a state. She was a bit freaked out at first, a bit miffed to see me standing there, out of the blue like that, sobbing on her doorstep. At first she thought I must be a neighbour who lived in the block and that I'd locked myself out or something. She asked me if I was OK and if something had happened. That's when she recognised me, from the clubs... asked me how I knew where she lived, and I lied and said I had a friend who lived in the same apartment block, that I'd seen her go into her apartment before. I told her I wanted to talk to her about G. I just wanted to talk to her. She could see I was upset, so she eventually let me in...'

'What did you *do*, Remy?' She doesn't want to hear it, any of it, but she knows she must.

'We talked for a bit... she was getting ready to go out. We talked about her IG, about her career as a model, her OnlyFans followers and how much money she made from it. She told me about the audition she was going to, about *Sex Text Ur Ex*. Gray was doing it – they were going to be on it together, film it together in Marbella. I knew I was losing him...'

But Maggie knows that he'd never been hers to lose. It had all been in her mind, her daughter's clearly damaged mind. Maggie can barely breathe, has to remind herself how. *In through the nose, out through the mouth...*

'I told her,' Remy continues 'about me and G, that I'd slept with him, had sex with him in the nightclub. I told her that I loved him, that I was in love with him and wanted to be his girl-friend, if only she'd stay away from him and – and...'

'And what, Remy?'

'And she *laughed* at me!'

Maggie sees hurt and anger flash across her daughter's face.

'She started laughing at me... told me I was stupid, that G would never love me, that he only really loved himself and that I was a fool for sleeping with him, for allowing him to use me and then throw me away, and I just... I just felt so *angry* – so much anger and rage in that moment, like I wasn't good enough... wasn't good enough to be loved by someone like that, like him, and I just – I just flipped out, picked up a perfume bottle on the dressing table, where she was sitting getting ready, and I hit her with it – hit her on the back of the head.'

'Oh, Remy, Remy... why did you do that? *Why?*' Maggie is pleading with her, her face a mass of tears and mucus. She can't wipe it away, can't let go of her daughter's hands.

'I... was shocked. I saw blood, coming from her head. She

was... she fell sideways off the stool onto the floor, and I... I went to her, kneeled down next to her and... and the scarf – there was a scarf around her neck, and I just... I just started squeezing it, tightening it around her neck.'

'No, no, no, no, no...' Maggie is shaking her head. She can't bear to hear it, can't bear for the words to be real, to be the truth.

'She was making noises – these horrible gurgling sounds – and she put her hands up to her neck. She was reaching out for me with her hands; I think she grabbed hold of my arm at one point, but she was unconscious, drifting in and out...'

Maggie thinks she's going to be sick, vomit all over the table. Her guts are churning manically, somersaulting, flipping over and over and over.

'And then suddenly she stopped. She stopped moving, stopped making those horrible sounds, and I... I just stood up, stood there, looking at her on the floor.'

Remy is sobbing now, her voice a hiccupping rasp as she struggles to expel the words. 'I... didn't know she was dead, not at first. You believe me, don't you? I couldn't breathe. My chest was heaving – I was out of breath, panting. I was in shock, like suddenly everything had stood still around me. And then... then I sat down. I sat down on the bed for... I don't know... It felt like hours. It hadn't sunk in, what I'd done, what had happened, but when it did, when I realised she was dead, that I'd... kill-killed her—' Her sobs are uncontrollable now – hysterical loud anguished cries.

Maggie squeezes her daughter's hands tightly. 'It's OK, Remy, it's OK.' She has to let her finish, let her confess. 'What happened then?'

Remy takes an audible intake of breath, tries to compose herself. 'I left her apartment. Drove back to my own, though I can't remember doing it. I was in a daze, in shock. I couldn't function properly, couldn't think straight. I knew I had to hide the body somehow, but I didn't know what to do, didn't know how to. So I... I went home, I climbed into the loft and got a suitcase, yours and dad's, the one I borrowed when I moved into the flat with Alex.'

The suitcase from the loft.

'I went back to her apartment. I'd left the door unlocked – had to wait until someone came out of the building again. And I cleaned up, tidied up her dressing table, wiped everything down with a cloth, made sure there was no blood visible, on the floor. And then... then I took off her clothes and I... I put her in the suitcase.'

Maggie is rocking back and forth, low groans escaping from her lips involuntarily. 'Ohh... ohhh, Remy, no... Why did you do that? *Whhhhhy?*'

'I wheeled her into the lifts, never even checked to see if anyone had seen me. I wasn't even thinking about that at the time. I had to get her out of there, to get – to get – *to get rid of her*. I put the suitcase into the back of my car. It was so heavy I struggled to lift it. And then I drove here. I don't know why... I don't know why I came here, but it felt safe somehow. It felt safe to be *home*.'

Maggie is nodding through her tears.

'It was late when I arrived. I knew you and Pops would be asleep. I parked my car in the garage, next to Dad's Caddy, and just sat in it for ages, hours it felt like, just thinking, just thinking *what have I done? How can I fix this?* I think I fell asleep for a bit.'

'You – you *fell asleep?*'

Remy's hands feel cold in her own, like all the blood has drained from them.

'I don't know. Fell asleep, blacked out maybe... I knew I had to dispose of the suitcase. I just wanted to pretend it hadn't happened – like if I just got rid of it then it wouldn't be real. And then I thought of Riverdown Park, how you used to take Lew and me when we were little... I've always loved it up there.

It's such a pretty place and I wanted her to be somewhere nice, you know? I wanted to do something nice for her.'

Maggie closes her eyes – they're stinging and sore from crying. She doesn't want to open them again. Wants it all to be some horrific nightmare – just a terrible, dreadful nightmare.

'But then my car wouldn't start again. It was just turning over and over and— Oh God.' Remy's head drops down onto the table and she starts banging it against the wood. 'I couldn't get it to start so I panicked, I just really panicked. I was so scared – terrified. My mind was racing. I took the suitcase out of my boot and put it into Dad's Cadillac.' She looks up at Maggie imploringly. 'I *had* to – I had no choice.'

Maggie thinks of the stuff she'd found then – the porn and the searches on Len's computer.

'Did you come into the house while your dad and I were sleeping?'

Remy nods slowly. 'I didn't want to wake you up, but I was frightened, so scared. I didn't know what to do. I went into Dad's study. I'd borrowed his laptop a while back, when mine wasn't working. He'd told me not to tell you at the time – thought you'd be cross that I'd broken mine again.'

Maggie feels her whole body deflate. Len had never said anything, never told her that he'd loaned his laptop to their daughter. Why? Why hadn't he mentioned anything? They always told each other *everything*.

'I knew his password because he'd given it to me when I'd borrowed it before. I went on it, started searching for stuff – ways to get rid of a dead body. I was freaking out. I had to get the body out of the house.

'I knew he kept the keys to the Cadillac in the garage some-where, so I searched for them, found them hanging up. I mean, I didn't even know if the car even worked, but when I tried, it started up and I was just so relieved. I drove the Cadillac down to Riverdown. Parked it some way back from the river, behind

some bushes, hoping it wouldn't be seen. Then I took the suitcase, wheeled it down the bank. I tossed her clothes into the
river. Then I opened the suitcase. I didn't want to leave her in it
– it was your suitcase; yours and Dad's – so I took her from it,
and then... then I rolled her down the riverbank.'

39 DAN

The car containing Graham Benson turns up an hour or so late.

'He kept us waiting,' PC Slater explains with a raised eyebrow. 'Had to do his hair apparently.'

'Graham!' I say as he wafts into the interview room in a cloud of strong aftershave and hairspray. '*Delighted* to see you again.'

The irony is completely lost on him, however. I can't imagine Graham Benson ever entertaining the idea that seeing him again could ever possibly be anything otherwise.

'No problemo,' he says as I gesture to him to pull up a chair. 'Anything to help Amelie.'

And himself in the process no doubt.

It pains me a little to think that Graham has played quite a pivotal role, albeit unwittingly, in helping to solve Amelie's jigsaw puzzle. I can only imagine the reflected glory he'll dine out on when he realises the part he's played in all of this. He's clearly already a self-styled hero in the production of his own life's performance so this will no doubt send that gargantuan ego of his stratospheric.

'So,' he says, leaning back into the chair and crossing a sockless slip-on-shoed foot over his other knee. 'What can I do you for, Detective? I can't be too long, sorry – got a date.'

I smile, wishing I could open a window and let out fifty quid's worth of the stench of his extremely cloying, yet no doubt expensive, aftershave.

'Who's the lucky lady?' I find myself asking, thinking of the TV interview he'd given on a recent six o'clock news special about Amelie's murder, the crocodile tears he'd cried, how he'd referred to her as 'special'.

'Just some chick who messaged me on IG, saw me on the news. My follow count has almost doubled since I did that interview. Chicks galore, man... all wanting a piece of G.'

He looks so incredibly smug that I'm forced to look away, lest he detected the disgust in my face.

'Every cloud,' I remark, though of course my sarcasm is lost on him once again. 'You mentioned, Graham, during our previous meeting, something about "some women being harder to get rid of than herpes".'

'I did?' he says. 'Oh yeah, herpes...' He grins. 'That's kind of funny.'

'Were you referring to someone in particular, Graham?' I outright refuse to call him 'G' and I think he's wisely accepted this because he hasn't bothered to correct me. 'Someone who'd, I don't know, been pestering you, harassing you maybe, giving you any unwanted attention.' Though I could hardly imagine any attention given to Graham Benson ever being such. It's patently clear that attention is the likes of Graham Benson's lifeblood and that without it – unwanted or otherwise – he would simply wither away, like a glass of water being thrown over the Wicked Witch of the West.

He pauses for a moment before shrugging. 'Yeah, well, some chicks are a real pain in the arse. You sleep with them and they think you belong to them afterwards – that you're, like, an item, you know?'

'And why would they think that?' I ask. 'Obviously you must make it clear to them, these women, before you... before you become intimate with them, that you're not interested in a relationship, so why would they assume otherwise?'

I knew exactly why though because I suspect that he *doesn't* make it clear. I imagine Graham Benson is a consummate *liar* when it comes to getting what he wants – sex and adoration – from all those fawning, fame-hungry, naïve young women. I can only imagine the chat he uses on them to talk them into bed. Some might say it serves them right, that they're desperate to get close to him in a bid to promote their own profiles, the idea of being papped together with this Z-lister out in some tacky, overpriced nightclub an exciting prospect, but still it's ugly, vacuous and shallow.

He shrugs. 'Bitches are crae-crae, man, tapped.' He touches his temple with a finger. 'Some of them anyway.'

I nod. 'Has this happened recently? This "crae-crae" behaviour from a woman? An unwanted... admirer perhaps who may have got the wrong idea after you'd had sex with her?'

'Listen, you ain't no one unless you've had a stalker, man. It's a hazard of the job I suppose – goes with the territory.'

He really does think he's Tom Hardy's better-looking younger brother.

'But yeah... there was this one girl, not long ago. Now she was *proper* nuts.'

'Tell me about her, Graham.'

He shrugs again. 'Met her at Vibe, this club in London that I hang out at sometimes. A lot of my brethren chill there. Sonny from *Date Your Best Mate*, Jonesey from *Fantasy Island*, Pete from the last series of STYX...'

He drops their names like litter. If he's trying to impress me, it isn't working. I haven't a clue who any of them are.

'She was trying to get into the VIP area where we were

hanging out. I'd seen her before, once or twice – she was skulking around me.'

'Skulking?'

'Yeah, you know, trying to get near me, to get up in my space, get my attention.'

'And it worked?'

He shrugs again. 'We have girls around us all the time. It looks good, you know, to have a pussy posse. So I was feeling generous one night, let her into the sacred inner sanctum, invited her to our table. She was all over me like a rash, draping herself around me, getting all up on me.'

'Was Amelie there, that night you invited this girl into your "pussy posse"? Can you remember, Graham?'

He pauses, looks almost thoughtful for a moment, something I imagine is a rarity unless it's for the cameras. 'I dunno... Yeah, maybe... actually yeah, now I think of it, she was there that night. She was flirting with some dude from that DIY programme off the telly, some old bloke, trying to make me jealous.'

'And were you? Jealous I mean?'

'Nah, man. Couldn't have given a shit if she'd wanted to fuck some old grandad.'

'No? Watching the "love of your life" flirting with another man didn't even ignite the teeniest flicker of jealousy in you?'

He realises what I'm trying to say, or rather what *he'd* said about Amelie in the news interview he'd given and had no doubt been paid handsomely for.

'Well...' He bristles slightly. 'We did that kind of shit to each other – tried making each other jealous and that. Anyway, she invited me to the ladies' room, beckoned me to follow her in...'

'Amelie did?'

'No, the crazy chick. So I followed her. I knew what she wanted and I gave it to her.'

'In the toilet? In the ladies' toilet in the club?'

'Yeah.' He says it so nonchalantly, like it's a regular occurrence, which in all fairness it probably is.

'How romantic,' I say, unable to help myself.

He shrugs again. 'She wanted a piece of G and she got it.'

'So you exchanged numbers?'

He nods. 'Big mistake, man, giving that loon my digits.'

'Why?'

'Because she started texting and calling me non-stop, blowing up my phone day and night, claiming she loved me and shit like that.'

I'd been through the messages already, every single one of the hundreds sent, but I needed to hear his version of events.

'Did you reply to any of them?'

'Yeah, a couple. I didn't want to be you know, like, totally rude, man…'

Ever the consummate gentleman.

'But then she got all weird and shit… telling me to fuck off one minute and the next saying she loved me and stuff. She wanted to see me again.'

'And you didn't want to see her?'

'Nah, man. She weren't even my type.'

'But you had sex with her anyway?'

'It ain't a crime, is it? Have you never had sex with someone you didn't really fancy just because it was offered to you on a plate?'

'No,' I reply honestly, 'I haven't.'

He looks at me then like I'm having him on. 'She started saying some dangerous shit, man, like she was gonna tell people I'd raped her – *raped* her, man. If anything, it was the other way round – I couldn't get rid of the mad bitch, so I blocked her in the end. Had to.'

'And you never saw her again?'

He shakes his head. 'Don't think so – not that I remember.'

'This girl, did she know Amelie Fox? Did Amelie ever

mention her, talk about her to you? Did you ever see them together?'

'Everyone knew Foxy, but I never saw them together, never saw them talking or nothing. I can't – *couldn't* – see Foxy being friends with the likes of her anyway.'

'Not cool enough?'

'Exactly,' he says. 'She was a nobody, man, a wannabe, a hanger-on.'

'And did she have a name, this wannabe, this *nobody*?'

'Yeah, it was... wait... shit, man, I can't even remember it now. It was a few months back. I'm really bad with chicks' names.'

'Try and think, Graham,' I say through clenched teeth, my patience wearing thinner with each passing second in his odious company.

He looks up at the ceiling. 'Hmmm, Renee maybe. Jenny. Something like that. Fuck...'

The complete schmuck can't even recall her name.

'Remy?' I prompt him. 'Could her name have been Remy Wendover?'

'Yeah!' He goes to fist-bump me, but I keep my hands firmly on the desk. 'Yeah, like the brandy – Rémy Martin, though I prefer Courvoisier. Smoother.'

Like himself.

'And would this be her?' I ask, sliding the image I'd taken from his phone towards him, the one of him and Amelie Fox together, smiling for the camera like something out of a tooth-paste advert. 'Would this be Remy Wendover, the girl you had sex with in the toilet at the nightclub – the girl standing behind you both?'

He stares down at it, picks it up and inspects it closely. 'Yeah, man. That's her – crazy-ass bitch. I never knew her surname though. She never told me, and I never asked.'

'You don't recall seeing her that night, the night this photo was taken, April thirtieth, only a few weeks before Amelie's murder?'

He shakes his head. 'No. But I guess she must've been stalking me back then as well. I mean, look at her looking at me! Can't keep her eyes off me.'

He continues to look down at the photo, studying it intensely.

'Hold up,' he says after a moment. 'I just noticed something.'

'Yes?' I say expectantly.

'If you look closely, in this light... don't you think I bear a striking resemblance to a darker Ryan Gosling?'

I don't feel good about potentially interrupting Davis's date but duty calls.

'Gov?' She answers the phone a little breathlessly. It sounds like she's been running, or maybe...

'Put your clothes on. I need you to meet me at the Wendovers' house,' I say.

'The Wendovers'? *My clothes!*'

'Yes.'

'Now?' she asks.

'Right now.'

'Has something happened, gov?'

'Pathology came back with a match – a partial match.'

'Partial? A partial match to the son's DNA? To Lewis Wendover?'

'Yes, Davis.'

'But I don't... I don't understand.'

'Neither did I at first,' I say. 'But then I stumbled across something.'

'What, gov?' Davis asks. It sounds like she's getting dressed, and I imagine her holding the phone between her shoulder and ear as she struggles to slip on some trousers.

'Just meet me at the Wendovers', soon as you can, Davis.'

'On my way now, gov,' she says, just as the phone drops to the floor.

Luck. It had been pure luck that I'd spotted her in the background of the photo of Amelie Fox and Graham Benson, nothing more or less. I didn't recognise her at first – her hair colour was different from when we'd met at the Wendovers' house, and I hadn't paid that much attention to her when Len had introduced his family at the remembrance vigil. It was blonde, like Amelie's, and it was dark, much darker in the picture, but it was her, I was sure of it.

40 MAGGIE

'We have to go to the police,' she says. 'Remy, you know we must go to the police – that you must tell them what happened, what you did. You understand that, don't you, Remy? You understand that we have no choice?' She's still clutching her daughter's hands in her own. They feel smaller somehow, like when she was a five-year-old.

She hears Len's voice gently telling her off in her head. *'She's not a child anymore, chickadee.'* He never once raised his voice to her in all the years they'd been together, not that she can ever recall anyway, and certainly never in aggression. The truth is your child never stops being your child, no matter their age, no matter where they are in the journey of life – they always remain *your* child. And right now, in spite of everything she's done, her child needs her.

'I'll come with you, to the police station. We'll ask to speak to Detective Riley. He seems nice. We'll ask to see him and tell him everything.'

Remy is silent.

'I'm in so much trouble, aren't I?' she says eventually, tears continuing to roll down her cheeks.

Maggie finds herself wondering who they're really for. Because no matter how much she loves her daughter – and she does, more than anything in the world – what she's just heard has stunned her to her core.

'Yes,' Maggie says. She isn't going to sugar-coat it. How can she? Her daughter has murdered someone. She is responsible for Amelie Fox's horrible death. And Maggie knows, she understands in all its brutal clarity, that her life, that her daughter's life and the lives of their family, are going to change forever, and that she must never, ever again think that things couldn't ever get any worse than they already are because this, this is living evidence that they *can* and *do*. 'Yes, Remy, you are.'

'Will I go to prison? Will I go to prison for a long time?'

She looks at her mother imploringly, the fear in her pretty dark brown eyes so palpable that it feels like a machete through her heart, slicing it clean in two.

'I... I didn't mean to do it. I wasn't in my right mind. I don't know what came over me. It was just – it was just...'

'We'll get you a lawyer, a good lawyer,' Maggie tells her. 'I'll sell the house if we have to. We'll tell the truth, that you weren't well, that you were suffering from depression, that you were overcome psychologically, having a mental-health breakdown.'

She thinks back to the voice message Remy's college counsellor had left on her phone that time, how she'd only listened to a portion of it. Was she calling her to express concern for Remy's mental well-being, her state of mind? She desperately hopes she hasn't deleted it. It could be crucial evidence to support her diminished responsibility. If only she had listened to it properly!

If only... Somehow, everything came back round to those two words.

'I don't want to go to prison.' Remy finally lets go of Maggie's hands, buries her face in them. 'I don't want to spend my life locked up... locked away. Please, Mum, help me. I'd rather die.'

'We'll go and get cleaned up,' Maggie says, surprised by the calm efficiency in her own voice. She's slipped into autopilot mode. She has to clean up this mess, somehow keep this sinking ship afloat. They'll all go down otherwise. 'We'll get dressed. I'll call Christine. Gary works for a law firm – maybe he'll know someone. A good defence lawyer.'

Remy's face looks pale in the late afternoon light. She wipes the snot from her nose with the back of her hand.

'Everyone will hate me,' she says. 'Lewis, Casey... Christine... Gray.' She sobs into her hands. 'He'll despise me, won't he? I only wanted him to like me, Mum. If he'd just liked me...'

'I know, Remy,' she says, her inflection flat, exhausted, *resigned*.

'Can I take a shower?' Remy asks, looking up at her with wide brown eyes, so much like her father's, so much like Len's. In this moment, she would give anything, *everything*, to have him back, have him here next to her, by her side where he'd always been, where he still *should* be.

'Yes.' She nods, her arms folded tightly across her chest – scaffolding to help keep her upright. 'Have a shower, put on some clean clothes, and then we'll drive down to the police station – we'll drive there together.'

Remy comes to her then, wraps herself around her mother tightly, burying her face into her clavicle. Maggie feels the wetness of her tears against her skin, drops her face onto her daughter's head, breathes her in. She smells of perfume and sweet sweat, that same perfume that Brenda wears, that *Amelie Fox* wore.

'Why, Remy, when you're perfect just as you are? You never needed to be anyone else – you didn't need to be like her, like Amelie. You didn't need him to like you. There are so many others on the planet... someone who would love you for who you are, take care of you, tell you how beautiful you are. It didn't have to happen. You should've talked to me. Why didn't you talk to me, Remy – tell me how you were feeling, what you were thinking? I could've helped you – I *would've* helped you. I could have prevented this, all of it. It's my fault... I've let you down – I've let everyone down so badly.'

She holds her, squeezing her small body, pressing it into her own tightly in the hope that somehow, she will absorb her by osmosis, that her daughter will become part of her once again and that she won't have to face the horror of what she knows is coming, for all of them.

'I love you, Remy,' she says. 'I will always love you.'

Remy looks up at her, her soft cheek stuck against Maggie's chest.

'Promise?' she asks, childlike, as if time has reversed and she's a little girl once again.

She'll always be her little girl.

'I promise.'

Maggie waits statue still in the kitchen while Remy goes upstairs to shower and change. It's late afternoon and the sun is low, a beautiful orange and pink ombre glow uplighting the sky across her garden, casting shadows over the blossom on the apple tree. She steps out onto the patio, looks up at it like a masterful watercolour, hand-painted by God himself.

'The best things in life are free, chickadee!'

It all seems so surreal, so unreal, unfathomable, unjustified, *unfair*. Just a few weeks ago, she'd been standing right here on her terracotta patio – a patio she remembers fondly that Len had laid himself – in the magnificent garden of her wonderful home, their anniversary party in full swing. She hears the sounds of the singer, his smooth, rich tones permeating the air, the happy, animated chatter of her guests, friends, family, neighbours... It had been a celebration of their lives together, of all the beautiful memories, all those years and moments shared, cherished, of the many more they'd hoped were to come.

But they're gone now, those beautiful moments in time. Now they're forever tarnished, coated in an oily black sheen, and they can never again be perfect.

Loss – she feels it like acutely, like the air around her. The sun is still warm in all its dependable glory, refusing to go down without a fight. She must be like the sun; she must fight to rise another day. She cannot give up now; she cannot give in.

Her greying complexion, her summer sandals still on her feet, inches above the floor. Her head, cocked unnaturally to one side, and her tongue, purple and exposed, hanging from her mouth...

Maggie sees her ten-year-old self staring up at her mother, feels the confusion, the fear and shock all over again as her young mind tried to process what was in front of her, what no ten-year-old should ever have to see.

She squeezes her eyes tightly together, willing the vision to vanish, rests her fingers against the apple tree in a bid to stop herself from collapsing. She must just stay upright.

She knows what she must do, what she should've done from the beginning. How can she expect her daughter to tell the truth, to confess to her terrible crimes when she herself is no innocent? She's always taught her children to tell the truth. '*You can't argue with it,*' she would say. '*Have nothing to fear from it. It will always come out – in the end, everything does.*'

Maggie turns back to the kitchen, checks the clock on the wall. Remy is taking her time in the shower.

She makes her way through the kitchen and up the stairs, takes them slowly, one at a time, the effort exhausting her.

'Remy?' she calls out. She can hear the shower running in

the en suite as she walks into the bedroom. 'Remy?' she calls her once more.

Maggie opens her wardrobe, pulls out a clean shirt, some summer shorts, and throws them on the bed. 'Are you going to be much longer?'

Then the doorbell rings.

41 DAN

'I hope you're right about this, gov,' Davis says as I ring the doorbell of the Wendovers' home. 'I can't help feeling sorry for Maggie Wendover if you are,' she adds. 'She's only just lost her husband.'

'I'm aware of that, Davis,' I say with a heavy heart. 'We wouldn't be here if I thought otherwise.'

I ring the doorbell again, keep my finger on it for a few seconds longer.

'Maybe they're out?'

'Their cars are out front. I—'

A look of something flashes across her face as she opens the door but I can't quite place it. Is she expecting us?

'Detective Riley.' Her voice is a reed-thin whisper, almost inaudible.

'Mrs Wendover... Maggie, isn't it?'

She looks different somehow, paler, a ghost of herself. I feel a stab of guilt shoot through my solar plexus as she stands silently back from the door, opens it to allow us in.

She's expecting us.

We follow her through to the kitchen.

'We apologise again, turning up unannounced like this. I know this is a difficult time for you. How are you bearing up?'

But I have the answer already simply by looking at her. Her demeanour is frail and brittle, like if you touched her, she'd shatter into a thousand pieces. I need to tread carefully here. I note the empty vodka bottle on the table, a vase of dying funeral flowers next to it. They seem poignant together somehow.

'Listen, Maggie, can we sit down?'

'Please.' She nods. Her movements seem slow and laboured. 'I'll stand if you don't mind.'

Davis glances sideways at me, gives me a look that tells me she hates this part of the job as much as I do.

'It might be better if you sat down,' she says gently. 'We need to have a chat with you, to talk to you about—'

'I know why you're here,' she interrupts. 'It's about my daughter, isn't it? You're here to talk about Remy.'

I inwardly sigh. 'Yes, Maggie,' I say. She knows. 'Is she... is she here, Remy?'

'She's upstairs, in the shower,' she says, going to the fridge and taking some bottled water from it. She decants the contents into some glasses, begins to slice some lemon.

'We need to speak with her,' Davis says. She'd already requested backup on the way here. They'll be here soon, the cars with their sirens alerting the curtain twitchers and the press in turn, a plethora of people descending upon this poor woman's sanctuary at any moment, a home that's still filled with funeral flowers and condolence cards, and I feel the sadness all around me, palpable and oppressive, dripping like the sweat on my face down the walls.

'You're here to arrest her, aren't you?'

Maggie's voice is eerily calm. I hear the acceptance in it underneath the raw anguish that she's trying her best to suppress.

'For Amelie Fox's murder?' She pushes the glasses of water towards us across the table.

'Did you know, Maggie?' I ask her gently.

But she doesn't answer.

'I must rinse them off first,' she says, turning and busying herself at the kitchen sink with some dirty dishes on the side. 'Before they go in the dishwasher,' she says. 'It gets all clogged up otherwise, all that dirty water being recycled...' She judders a little. 'We were getting ready, were going to come and see you, but, well... here you are! You saved us a journey at least.'

I suspect she's in shock. I've seen it a thousand times before, the strange calmness, the jerky laboured movements, the occupation with something trivial – like washing dishes – a distraction, something to create distance between yourself and the horror of the reality you're staring down the barrel at.

'We really need to speak to her,' Davis says again.

I know what she's thinking because it's exactly what I'm thinking, that maybe having heard us come in, Remy could climb out of a window, abscond, and that's the last thing I want to happen, chasing a young woman through a suburban street on a hot day like today. On any day.

Maggie downs tools. Pauses for a moment.

'Yes, of course. I'll go and get her,' she says, flicking out her wet hands as she leaves the kitchen.

'Do you think she's confessed? Told her mother the truth?' Davis says. 'She didn't look surprised to see us – said she knew why we—'

A scream suddenly startles me – a piercing, sharp, prolonged sound of human distress, causing both Davis and me to jump to our feet instantly.

'Upstairs!' Davis says.

The scene that greets us as we stand in front of the bathroom door is one I know will remain with me forever, one that will come to me in my darkest moments, haunt me, and no doubt everyone else witnessing it too.

She's naked, the shower still running, the scarf around her neck – a scarf I've seen so many times now, in that last photo of Amelie Fox – tied to the light fitting above. Her complexion is greying, slightly bluish, unnatural to the eye. Maggie is hysterical, desperately pulling at the scarf, frantically fumbling with it, her wet hands slipping as she struggled to untie her.

'Oh no, no! Someone help me – please help me! Remy... oh my darling – not my baby. What have you done? *What have you done?*'

'Backup,' I hear Davis shouting into her phone behind me. 'We need an ambulance and backup at 25 Whiteheart Drive, Thorton Vale – we need it NOW!'

'Oh Jesus.' The adrenalin has hit me like a boulder square in my chest as I rush to assist, putting my shoulders underneath her legs to lift her up, looking around for something sharp that we can use to break her loose. There's nothing.

'She never meant to kill her,' she says. 'She isn't evil. She... she isn't well. Oh God, oh please dear God, *help her!*'

The sheer terror I see in Maggie Wendover's eyes is soul destroying, a desperate mother frantically trying to save her child's life – a life I can see is rapidly ebbing away.

Relief fills the room as the knot finally undoes and Remy collapses, her young, naked body limp in my arms.

We lay her on the bathroom floor and Maggie puts a towel underneath her head. She's crying – dreadful, guttural, primeval sounds emanating from her as she touches her daughter's pale face, pulls at her limbs, frantically searching for signs of life.

I try gently to remove her, but she's thrown her whole body almost on top of her, protecting her, sobbing, 'Nooooo, nooo... oh please nooo.'

'Maggie... Maggie please,' I say as I try to prise her away

from her daughter's limp body so that I can begin to administer CPR.

There's no pulse and her lips are cooling against my own. But I try. God help me, with every breath in my body, *I must try.*

42

I race down to the interview room, throw the door open. 'Maggie?'

She's with a friend, I recognise her as the woman who'd answered the door to us once before – Christine somebody.

'I tried telling her,' she says, leaping up from the chair, her tear-stained face covered in anguish, 'I tried telling her that she shouldn't come, that it could wait, that she's in shock and needs to rest, but she wouldn't listen, said she had to come now, that she has to speak to you. She's really not in her right mind, keeps blabbering on about Len, about her mother... some kind of warning.'

'She's asking for her mother?'

'Her mother's been dead for over forty years,' she says. 'She committed suicide when Maggie was ten. She found her... she came home from school one day and found her *hanging*.'

I feel like I've just been winded. 'Oh. Oh Jesus.'

'This is all just so awful... so, so *awful*. I can't believe any of it.' She drags her hands down her face, starts pacing with all the nervous anxiety she's clearly experiencing. 'I mean, Remy... There has to be some mistake surely?' She looks at me for some kind of clarity. 'Remy wouldn't hurt a fly – she's a lovely—' But she can't finish the sentence before she breaks down.

'It's OK.' I put my arm around her. 'It's... Christine, isn't it?'

She nods through the sobs.

'Look, why don't you go home – go home to your family? I'll take care of Maggie here. I promise, OK?'

'Lewis and Casey – her son and his girlfriend – they're at the hospital now. Maggie hasn't left Remy's side all night – and I hadn't left Maggie's – but then she insisted, absolutely insisted that she come here to talk to you, that it couldn't wait. Lewis's girlfriend is pregnant, you know – they were all so looking forward to it, a new baby. Len and Maggie, becoming grandparents, and then he died... and now all of this has happened, and Remy is in hospital clinging to life—'

She's hyperventilating, and I signal for Davis to come and take over, to take her away. I close the door, look at Maggie as she sits in the chair the other side of the table. She's staring down at the floor. She looks so small, like she's somehow shrunk in the past few hours, gradually diminishing with each passing second.

'Maggie,' I say softly, 'we don't have to do this now. You should be at the hospital, with your family.'

She looks up slowly. 'Family. *Family*?' she snorts, gently swaying from side to side. If I didn't know better, I would say she was drunk. I suppose she is sort of – trauma drunk.

'This is not the best time to do this,' I reiterate gently. 'It can wait until tomorrow, Maggie. I can come and see you at home. We can talk then, when you've had some rest, been seen by a doctor.'

'No.' She shakes her head. 'You saved my daughter's life. If it wasn't for you, I'd have lost her too. I wanted – I needed to come here, to thank you. I'm just so... so grateful to you, Detective Riley, I—'

'I was just doing my job, Maggie,' I say gently. 'Have you had any news, from the hospital?'

'A minute longer they said... any longer and she'd almost certainly have died. The CPR you gave her saved her life. She's still in intensive care. They're not sure what damage there'll be, if it'll be lasting, but they hope she'll make a full recovery,' she adds, 'physically at least.'

'That's great news,' I say, though it seems so incongruous to the poor woman's situation that it sounds almost absurd. I look at her and she blinks at me through watery eyes.

'There's something else,' she croaks, 'something else I want you to know.'

'Oh?' I rest my hand on her upper arm. 'Don't you think it could wait until—'

'I need to tell you what happened, what *really* happened. I need to tell you now, before I change my mind and do the wrong thing again, make the wrong decision.'

I pause for a moment. Sigh. I pull up a chair, tentatively sit down opposite her.

'What do you want to tell me, Maggie?' I take her hand in mine across the table. It feels small and warm, and an image of Remy's limp body as we'd freed her from the noose suddenly flashes up in front of me, causing me to take an inward breath.

'I want to tell you everything,' she says, 'from the beginning, and I want you to listen, to try to understand.'

Her face is red raw from crying, her eyes bloodshot and sore, and I want so much to be able to take her in my arms, this broken, traumatised frail-looking human being, and hold her, give her the tiniest morsel of comfort, only I'm forbidden from doing so.

Got to keep the feels at the door, Dan.

But how do you do that in this kind of situation? How would you be human yourself if you could?

'Are you sure, Maggie?'

'Yes,' she says without hesitation. 'Perhaps if I'd done this in the beginning then I wouldn't be sitting here now. I need to right the wrongs somehow, Detective Riley, to restore some kind of balance. The gods, they'll keep punishing me otherwise. Do you believe in God, Detective?'

The question throws me a little. 'In all honesty, I don't know. Sometimes I think there's a higher power, someone we all have to answer to, but then I think about the injustice of life, of how such terrible things happen to good people; I think about the loss some people experience for no apparent reason, how loved ones are taken from them in the most dreadful, cruellest ways, and I think there can't be, that none of it would happen if there was. But I do know that we all have something to answer to at the end of the day – our conscience. So maybe I do believe in God, an inner God, one most of us possess inside us.'

'Hmm.' She nods thoughtfully, pauses for a long moment. 'Karma,' she says. 'Do you believe that if you do something bad, then the cosmos rights the wrongs and something bad comes back to you? Like an eye for an eye, Detective?'

I sigh. 'If only it worked like that, Maggie. Much as I'd like to believe it, I'd be out of a job if it did.'

'Remy thought so,' she says, her eyes glazed in a thousand-yard stare. 'She thought that because she'd killed Amelie Fox, that was the reason her father was taken from her.'

I dip my head. 'So it shows she has a conscience, that whatever terrible crime she committed, she has a conscience.'

There's another long pause and I take her hand again. 'Maggie... you wanted to speak to me, tell me, help me to understand. Where did all of this start?'

She sniffs, shakes herself out of her trance and looks into my eyes. 'It started with a scarf – a scarf I found hidden in my loft...'

I sit patiently as Maggie explains it all to me: the scarf, the perfume, the bin liners by the back door, the pornography and searches on her husband's computer, his lack of alibi on the night of Amelie's murder...

She was suspicious. There were too many coincidences; too many things that were off.

'I thought about coming to the police,' she says. 'I even drove here, to the station, waited outside, thought about what I would say...' But she couldn't go through with it. 'It wasn't hard evidence.' She looks at me imploringly. 'It was all just... circumstantial. I... I wanted to protect my family, my children. I didn't know what to do, what I was going to do. I was frightened, confused. I lost the ability to think clearly, rationally. I made the error of keeping it all to myself, and it all built up, stronger and stronger in my head. Len must've killed her, the scarf, the laptop, the lies about where he was, our neighbour's sighting of the Cadillac, only... I got it wrong, Detective. I got it so, so wrong.'

'Oh, Maggie...' I bury my head in my hands momentarily. 'You should've come to us. I can only imagine what it must've been like, carrying around that kind of burden, those kinds of suspicions about your own husband.'

'I convinced myself that he'd done it,' she says. 'As much as I didn't want to, I truly believed that Len, my Len, had killed Amelie, that he was somehow capable of it, because none of it made any sense, no sense at all. It seemed to be the only conclusion I could draw at the time, the only explanation.'

'So you decided to sit on it?' I say, trying to imagine the absolute trauma she would've been experiencing – the crippling suspicions, the mind-bending pendulum swing between belief and disbelief, the abject terror of what she thought her husband had done, who he really was, a man she'd known most of her adult life. 'Christ, Maggie...' My head is shaking like a puppet on a string.

'Will I be charged?' she asks.

She's stopped crying now – I suspect she has no more tears

left in her. I push a cup of water towards her, tell her to drink some.

'Charged with what?' I say. 'I'm not sure we can charge you with anything. You should've come to us, absolutely, brought the scarf to us, but... I don't know, Maggie. You can't be charged with having suspicions – you didn't *know* it was evidence, even if you suspected it was.'

She nods slowly, looks down into her lap, her hands wringing in them, her knees jiggling.

'What about murder... can I be charged with that?'

I shake my head. 'Murder?' I take hold of her hand once again. 'This isn't your fault – you didn't kill Amelie Fox, did you? I'm so sorry, Maggie. I'm just so sorry...'

She's crying again now, looks like she's about to drop to the floor.

'No,' she says, her voice a hoarse whisper, 'I didn't kill Amelie... but I did kill Len. I did kill my husband.'

At first I think I must have misheard her, this poor wretched woman who's lost both her husband and discovered her only daughter is a killer in a painfully short period of time.

'I... I don't know what you mean, Maggie,' I say gently. 'Len died of anaphylactic shock. He was stung by a wasp – he had a severe allergic reaction and asphyxiated.'

Suddenly I feel sick: nausea hits my empty stomach the same time as a bolt of adrenalin. 'Didn't he?'

She doesn't say anything for a moment – just sits silently, staring.

'Maggie...' My tone has dropped an octave through fear of what I think she's about to tell me.

'Listen to me, Maggie.' I reach for both her hands now, grip them tightly. 'You don't want to do this. You don't know what you're saying. You're in shock. You need to go home; you need to rest, sleep on it. If there's anything you want to tell me tomorrow then you can, with a lawyer present, OK?'

'I killed Len,' she says again. 'I killed the man I love, the man I loved for over thirty years, a wonderful man... an *innocent* man.'

'No, Maggie,' I'm warning her now. 'Why are you telling me this? The post-mortem says it was accidental death. He was killed by a wasp sting!'

'He shouted out to me,' she says, half smiling and crying at the same time, 'from the garage. I was in the kitchen, heard him call my name.' She wipes her eyes with both hands, closes them like the memory is too painful with them open. 'I ran to the garage... I knew straight away what had happened – I'd seen it once before you see, when we'd been courting and he was stung, went into anaphylactic shock. I almost lost him then too. His face was swollen, his lips...' She shivers slightly. 'His eyes were bulging out of their sockets. He... he was reaching out for me... reaching out for my help. I told him to hold on – that I'd go into the kitchen and get an EpiPen. So I ran – ran back to the kitchen and... I knew he needed help quickly, that his organs would start to shut down if I didn't administer the drugs as soon as possible. But instead... when I got to the kitchen and located the EpiPen, I just stood there.'

She lets out an incredulous laugh. 'In those few minutes, I thought about what he'd done, what I *thought* he'd done, how he'd killed that young woman, maybe even raped her. I thought about the stuff on his computer that I'd seen, those disgusting images. I truly believed in that moment that he was a cold-blooded murderer, that I'd been living with a liar, a monster, a psychopath all these years without even knowing it, because it does happen, doesn't it, Detective?' she pleads with me, and I nod.

'Yes, Maggie, it does.'

'I thought of my children, of Lewis and Remy, of Casey and my granddaughter on the way. What would become of them, of all of us, if it came out – and it would've come out – if Len was unmasked as Amelie Fox's murderer, as a sick, twisted pervert who preyed on young women? Their young lives, all our lives, would have been ruined, destroyed forever. There'd be a court case... we'd be vilified as a family. People would've thought, would've believed, that I'd known, that I must've known all along... and I couldn't bear the thought of it, of my children hurting, of the shame and horror they would endure. I thought —' She's trembling so much I fear she might come right out of her seat. 'I thought, if he was... if he was dead then it would solve everything. I could destroy the laptop, forget anything I'd seen and found and that we'd all be OK. He'd be gone, unable to hurt anyone, hurt us again. In that split second, I made a decision, and so... I waited.'

I'm holding my breath now, trying desperately to process what she's telling me. 'How long, Maggie? How long did you wait?'

She visibly swallows, chews her lip manically as she looks at me with terrified eyes. 'A few minutes – four or five or six...' Her head drops. 'Maybe more. I don't know.'

'And then?'

'And then... well, I panicked – sort of shook myself out of it. I grabbed the EpiPen and ran into the garage and administered it in his leg, his thigh. But—' She collapses onto the table, her head thudding against it. 'But I was too late.'

43

The relief is so potent, so powerful that she can't be sure her pelvic floor hasn't given way and that the drenched feeling isn't her own sweat and urine. She feels lighter somehow, like she might just float up off the chair into the ether, like one of those helium balloons her kids used to love when they were little.

Her body, limp in her arms, wet and slippery, her hair, the wrong colour, matted to her pallid skin.

She'd thought she was just taking a shower. Why hadn't she realised? Why hadn't she assumed the worst like she always does? She almost hadn't reached her in time. Oh, the bitter irony of it all! She has to get this over with as quickly as possible, wants desperately to be back by her daughter's bedside right now, holding her hand as she fights for her life, whatever there might be left of it. It was karma.

'You do understand what you've just told me, Maggie?' The detective is looking at her with kind dark eyes. He's held her hand throughout. He's a good man – she feels it with what little senses she has left.

'Yes,' she says. 'The truth. I've told you the truth.'

His head is bowed. He looks distraught.

'Oh, Maggie...' He doesn't know what to say. What could anyone say? She made a mistake. And now she's here, in an airless police interview room, her life imploded, her husband dead, and her daughter a murderer who'll probably spend most of her best years incarcerated if she survives her suicide attempt. Her family is destroyed. Lewis will hate her, will blame her for his father's death, and she'll never get to see her granddaughter. Perhaps it's no more than she deserves.

Life, an intricately stitched patchwork quilt built upon chance, upon fate and luck, decisions and choices. It's a right turn here and wrong turn there. One minute you can be cruising along happily in fifth gear only to miss the sharp ninety-degree-angle turn coming up on your right and end up over a cliff. Maggie understands it now, the absolute fragility of life, how one wrong turn can set off a diabolical chain of events, lead you on a path of destruction – that one last drink that takes you down the road to addiction, that one forbidden kiss that ends in divorce and heartbreak, financial ruin and custody battles. And you never see it coming until it's too late, until what's done is done and can't be undone. It's in the choices you make, those life-altering split-second decisions; it's in the people you meet, the job offers you take, the time you said yes when you really meant to say no; if only you'd waited a few more minutes, if only you'd left sooner, if you'd just spoken out, or kept your mouth shut, listened to advice or chosen not to take it. It's all just a lottery at the end of the day – someone has to win, and others must lose.

A strange sense of peace wraps itself around her like a cashmere robe. She's spent her entire life worrying, thinking about the worst that could happen, always trying to pre-empt it, prevent it, stay one step ahead of it, and now it's finally here. She'd been right to fear it all along.

'Will I be charged?' she asks him. 'Will I go to prison?'

Detective Riley gently squeezes her hand. Empathy is

such an underrated quality in a person, she thinks. Everyone an armchair judge and jury these days, gleefully condemning others and the situations they find themselves in. She knows she could've kept her secret to herself, that she didn't have to confess. No one would've ever known what happened that day in the garage, what she'd done. But *she* would've known. She would have to spend the rest of her life living with the knowledge that she'd let her beloved Len die like an animal on the cold concrete floor of their garage, that she'd believed he was a killer and took it upon herself to be judge and jury, allowing him to die in fear and pain. How could she ever lead a happy, peaceful life knowing she'd let an innocent man she loved die?

There was a horrible irony to her story, that it was in fact her own child who'd committed the murder she'd been convinced her husband had, and that in turn Remy had, she felt sure, believed her father's tragic passing was punishment for what she'd done and ultimately tried to take her own life as a result. Well, it was certainly going to make for great headlines now, wasn't it?

'I... I don't think you can be charged with anything, Maggie.' Detective Riley looks on the brink of tears. 'Legally, there's no duty to rescue law in the UK, unless it's a parent/child situation. Morally, however... well, I guess that's a different matter.'

'Yes,' she says quietly, 'that's the part I'm struggling with.'

She looks at him. 'Would you have done the same thing, if you'd been in my shoes? If you'd believed that your wife, your partner, had betrayed you like that, duped you for all those years, killed another human being in such a terrible way... if the opportunity to erase it, to erase them, to prevent your family – save your children – from the pain of knowing their mother was a monster, if it presented itself to you, like it did to me, like I thought it did, would you have taken it, Detective Riley?'

He's silent for a moment as he looks at her. She sees the

sadness in his eyes, wonders if in fact it's simply her own reflecting back at her. 'Would you?'

'Maybe,' he says after the longest pause. 'Maybe I would.'

She doesn't know if he's simply being kind or if he's really telling the truth, but she's grateful anyway.

'You're not a terrible person, Maggie,' he says, and the words undo her – she can feel herself unravelling, coming apart inside. She wants to be with him, with Len. She wants to be where he is now.

'You have children of your own?' she asks, wondering why she feels so calm. For the first time since she can recall, she feels a stillness inside her, a shift somehow, like she's been stripped of all the trivial, pretentious stuff, of a heavy coat she's been wearing for too long, and underneath, the real Maggie has been laid bare, the person she's perhaps always meant to have been – one unencumbered by constant worry, plagued by impending thoughts of disaster, the fear of not being good enough, successful enough, attractive enough, *just enough*.

'Yes,' he says, 'I have a stepson, a daughter and another on the way – she's due any day now, my wife.'

'How wonderful.' She smiles genuinely. 'They're a gift, really, aren't they, children? A mysterious gift. You can love them, nurture them, guide them, teach them right from wrong, you can do all you can, hope they'll turn out to be good people, lead a happy life... but the truth is, no matter what you do, no matter how much you give to them, you never know, not really, how they'll turn out in the end.'

44 DAN

Vic Leyton examines the pages in front of her. 'Judging by the post-mortem report, I'd say it was quick, that the reaction was severe.'

'Yes, but specifically,' I press her. 'How long *exactly* would it have taken for Len Wendover to die?'

She blinks at me like I've asked her 'how long is a piece of string?'

'Well, Detective Riley, I can't say absolutely *exactly*,' she retorts, bristling slightly as she moves her glasses up the bridge of her nose.

'Your best shot?' I cock my head to one side, give her the puppy-dog eyes Fiona says I do whenever I'm about to tell her something she probably doesn't want to hear. 'I know how good you are – how accurate you are with TOD.'

She sighs. 'Flattery won't get you anywhere, Dan,' she says, but I can tell she's pleased by the comment, maybe just a little, because her cheeks have slightly flushed red. 'Anyway, why is it so important? Is this something to do with a case you're working on?'

'Sort of,' I say ambiguously.

Archer was furious that we couldn't charge Maggie Wendover with a crime – absolutely incandescent, she was.

'She let him die – she let her own husband choke to bloody death, just stood back and watched?'

'She thought he'd murdered Amelie Fox,' I'd said. 'And in all honesty, given how she explained it, it's not so difficult to understand why.'

'Yes, but she said it herself, didn't she, that it was all circumstantial? She couldn't be *sure* he'd done it. By all accounts, Len Wendover was a nice man. He'd never abused her; they were, by her own admission, a happily married couple... he'd never shown any signs of being capable of killing someone!'

'Neither did her daughter,' I'd responded. 'Look, we of all people know how it can sometimes be – killers are cunning, sometimes they're your next-door neighbour, your boss, a family member, a friend, someone you love and trust... they don't all come with a neon sign around their neck.'

'I'm quite aware of that, Riley,' she'd snapped back at me, her face flushed red with frustration. 'Can't we do her for withholding evidence?'

'But you just said yourself, it was circumstantial. The only real piece of evidence was the scarf... and that's still missing.'

I say missing, but I have a fair idea that Maggie has it hidden away somewhere. I know what I saw – I know Remy Wendover used it to hang herself, and that it was an entirely different scarf that was lying there later, when we returned to the scene. But I can't prove it, and I'm not sure how much it really matters now that Remy has confessed.

'She could've taken it – got rid of it like she did the laptop.'

'It won't hold up, ma'am, and you know it. The CPS will laugh it out of court. Besides, I think living with what she did is going to be punishment enough, don't you? She's lost a husband and a daughter, albeit in a different way.'

'I'll reserve my empathy for the Foxes, Riley,' she'd said, slamming the door in my face.

She's right of course: Amelie Fox is the real victim in all of this, and yet I can't seem to shake it, the abject sadness and regret I feel for Maggie Wendover having to spend the rest of her life with it all weighing heavily on her conscience. She made a terrible decision that day, *she made a mistake,* one I'm concerned she won't be able to live with.

'Well.' Vic straightens up. 'From the moment he was stung, he would've immediately experienced difficulty breathing, a tightness in the chest. He may have been coughing, had difficulty swallowing; his skin would've become red, itchy perhaps. He would've experienced confusion, may not have been able to speak or had difficulty speaking – that would've occurred in the first two minutes.'

'Two minutes?'

She nods. 'His blood pressure would've dropped rapidly due to loss of oxygen; there would've been severe swelling of the eyes and face, hives appearing on the skin; he would've gone into shock, his airways becoming blocked... and then, asphyxiation. In severe reactions like this, death can be rapid, usually within fifteen minutes if drugs aren't administered in time. In Len Wendover's case, I would estimate that it took roughly around five or six minutes from when he was stung to his expiration,' she summaries succinctly. 'Like I said, it was extremely quick.'

I throw my arms around her. 'Vic Leyton, I love you! Thank you!' I say, planting a kiss on her left cheek.

She looks shocked, takes a step back as her face blooms crimson.

'Well, I hope I've made someone happy,' she calls out to me with that enigmatic half-smile she does as I practically run through the door.

. . .

'He would've already been dead by the time you would've got to him with the EpiPen,' I say, a little breathless as Maggie finally answers the door.

She blinks at me, a little taken aback.

'Detective Riley, what...? I thought you were a reporter – they've been hounding me, banging on the door day and night.'

I march through the front door, head towards the garage.

'He was close to death – Len was already close to death when you heard him. In the garage, when you heard a noise.'

'He... I don't know,' she stammers. 'His face was swollen, his eyes were bulging, he was wheezing, making these horrible sounds. I...'

'And you ran from here, the garage, into the kitchen to get the EpiPen.'

'Yes, I... What is this, Detective Riley?'

'Show me,' I say, clicking on the timer app on my phone. 'Run to the kitchen, go to where the EpiPen was, take it and run back again.'

She blinks at me with wide eyes and I suddenly notice how tired she looks, how much she appears to have aged over the last few days. She looks tormented. It's not surprising really, after what she's been though, and that's without the added round-the-clock harassment from the press.

'I...'

'Go – go, Maggie!' I say, raising my voice, and, startled, she begins to run.

I watch the timer. Ten seconds... thirty... a minute... two... It's a big house and the kitchen is at the back, all the way over the other side of the building.

'Two minutes and ten,' I say as she returns, panting slightly, holding a spoon. 'It took almost two minutes for you to run from the garage to the kitchen, grab the EpiPen and return.'

'Yes? Did it?' She looks at me blankly. 'What does that mean? What are you trying to say, Detective Riley?'

I shake my head, explain. 'You heard a noise coming from the garage, right? You ran from the kitchen to see what it was. From what the pathology report says, judging by Len's symptoms, by the time you found him, at least three or four minutes had already passed, maybe more.'

'I still don't—'

'It took you maybe one minute to run to the garage, open the door. You saw Len – you saw Len on the floor and you went to him, yes?'

'Yes,' she says. 'I kneeled down next to him.'

I nod. 'You kneeled down next to him, looked at him, saw what had happened... then you searched through the drawers in the garage for an EpiPen, yes?'

'Yes, yes I did. But it wasn't there. I thought there was one in every room, but it wasn't there.'

'So another minute passed, possibly more, a minute thirty perhaps, then you ran back to the kitchen, rifled through the drawers, found the EpiPen and you—'

'I waited. I've told you this already, Detective. I don't understand. I don't understand what you're doing, why you're doing this.'

'He would've already been dead,' I say. 'Even if you'd run back to the kitchen, grabbed the EpiPen and run back and administered it to him without hesitation, he would've already been dead.'

'No. No... But... *would he?*'

'Yes, Maggie,' I say. 'Six minutes the pathologist said. It took Len approximately six minutes from the moment he was stung to his heart stopping. It was quick, the reaction severe – there wouldn't have been anything you could've done to save him. He would already have been dead by the time you got to him.'

She covers her hand with her mouth, stifles the cries coming from it. 'It's... is it true? Is that really true?' She's shaking. 'Oh God. Oh God...'

'Yes, Maggie,' I say, 'it is. You *didn't* let Len die – it wasn't anything you did or didn't do. There was nothing you could've done. I just... I just want you know that. You need to know that. I—'

My phone rings suddenly. It's Fiona.

'The baby is coming,' she says, struggling to get the words out between the 'arrrgh' noises she's making.

'What? When!'

'Now!' she says.

'Quick, Daddy, the baby is coming out of mummy's bum-bum,' I can hear Pip in the background, squealing excitedly.

'I'm coming now,' I say. 'I'll be at the hospital in ten minutes.'

'Noooo... noooo,' Fiona screams down the phone. 'You don't understand, you stupid man. The baby is coming – it's coming NOW!'

Maggie is staring at me. 'I think you'd better go, Detective Riley,' she says, smiling.

I think it's the first time I've seen her do that.

'Your gift awaits.'

'Goodbye, Maggie,' I say, halfway out the door already. 'Look after yourself.'

'Goodbye, Detective Riley,' she calls out after me. 'And thank you – thank you for everything.'

The scene that greets me as I burst through the door to my apartment is like something straight out of *Stranger Things*. Fiona is on the kitchen floor, legs akimbo, our baby's head crowning from— well, I don't need to draw a picture. Pip is holding her mummy's hand and crying. She looks terrified now, and I rush to comfort her.

'It's OK, sweetheart, Daddy's here. Daddy's—'

'Finally!' Fiona gnashes her teeth. 'Ohhhh Godddddddd. It's coming. It's *coming*...'

I walk in a circle for a second, arms flailing as I desperately try and think what to do.

'Have you called an ambulance?' I ask, picking up my phone to dial 999. Oh the irony!

'No, I haven't called a fucking ambulance, you idiot!' she screams at me.

I feel now is probably not a good time to pull her up on her language in front of Pip.

'Where's Leo?' My stepson is the designated man in charge when I'm not here. To be fair, he'd probably do a better job at handling things than I am right now.

'He at AJ house,' Pip sniffs. 'Mummy is upset...'

Towels. I need to get some towels. That's what you do, isn't it? I've seen it on the telly.

I quickly call 999.

'The ambulance is on the way,' I tell her, after I've hung up, and start heading to the bathroom in search of those towels.

'Don't you walk away from me, Daniel Riley! Don't you dare bloody walk away and leave me— Arrggghh. *Argggh-hhhhhhh!*'

But there's no time – I grab her hand.

'Push!' I scream, squeezing it. 'Push!'

And then he's here, on the kitchen floor, covered in blood and white stuff that looks like a thin layer of cream cheese. And I'm laughing and crying at the same time, and Pip is clapping her hands together.

'He has a winkie,' she cries, laughing. 'I can see his winkie!'

I pick him up and place him on Fiona's chest.

'It's a boy!' And I'm crying, fat tears dripping down onto her, mixing with the blood and sweat on her skin. 'We have a son...'

'Well…' My poor Fi is shaking with shock as much as I am as I cradle them both in my arms. 'He's nothing like his father, is he?' she says as she lets her head flop back onto the kitchen floor. 'He's on time for one thing.'

She bends down, arranges the flowers gently on his headstone. Irises and winter roses, from their garden of course. Len had always been so proud of his garden. *'Who needs to fork out for a bunch when you can grow your own, chickadee?'*

Maggie inhales deeply, wraps her coat tightly around her thin frame. It's a bitterly cold December day, a stark contrast to the endlessly long hot summer that has gone before. It seems like a distant memory now.

She comes here, every week without fail, to visit her husband, brushing the icy leaves from the granite, sweeping away the debris, bringing fresh flowers. Sometimes Bob comes with her and they make the sombre journey together. She's long since forgiven him and Julie for their ill-thought-out 'intervention' and his presence – not unlike his brother's – brings her both pain and a strange sort of comfort simultaneously. None of this was Bob's fault; he wasn't to know any of it. None of them were. Today though, she is alone.

'Little Lennie is getting bigger by the day,' she says to the headstone. 'She's an absolute treasure she is, Len, all chunky arms and legs, just like Remy was as a baby. They should be chunky at that age, don't you think? No one likes a skinny baby... She's the image of Lewis to look at when he was her age too – Casey couldn't believe it when I showed her some photos. She has his nose, and eyes just like her grandad, like her auntie's... Anyway, we're all packed up and ready to go. The removal van is coming at 9 a.m. sharp. I know it means I won't be able to come and see you as often as I'd like, but we'll be closer to her there. I know that's what you'd want, Len...'

Maggie dabs at the corners of her eyes with an old dry tissue from her pocket. The statement was true enough – she does want to be closer to Fieldview, a secure psychiatric hospital near Wakefield where her daughter is currently incarcerated. But it was also, if she was completely honest with herself, to escape the hatred and rage that has become her shadow now, the relentless press harassment and intrusion she's endured on a daily basis, the looks of disdain and contempt she sees on the faces of friends and strangers alike, the poison-pen letters and internet trolls who seemed to manage to find her even after she'd wiped her entire family's social-media history.

It caused a public outcry when Remy was convicted of the lesser charge of manslaughter on the grounds of diminished responsibility instead of murder. Three different psychiatrists had found abnormalities in her mental functioning and agreed that her state of mind was substantially impaired at the time of Amelie's killing. As a result, she'd received a sentence of twenty-four years to be served in a secure psychiatric facility, though Maggie had been informed that with ongoing treatment and any closely monitored substantial and subsequent improvement, she could potentially serve as little as twelve.

The Foxes are appealing the sentence and have made no secret of their horror at what they described as 'a blatant miscarriage of justice'. Could Maggie blame them? Not if the shoe were on the other foot, she couldn't. The Foxes will never get to see their daughter again. But in her own truth, neither will

Maggie. The day Remy committed that terrible act was the day she too had died. While she may still be here in the physical sense, the child she grew and knew has all but disappeared, and although she's too scared to make her true feelings public for fear of reprisal, in some way, this is worse, for while we may never stop grieving for loved ones lost, the passing of time can act as a slow and gentle healer, but to grieve for the living... that's a different kind of life sentence altogether.

It had been a wrench to sell the house, the home she and Len had built, had lived and loved in all those years – a family home filled with memories, some too painful to live with now, the walls just open wounds. They were making a new start in Yorkshire – her, Lewis, Casey and little Lennie. Christine still gave her the occasional phone call – she called it 'checking in'. But it wasn't the same as it had been before. Nothing was the same.

People, her friends – they don't know what to say to her anymore. She can't say she blames them – she wouldn't know what to say to herself either. She's known as the mother of the murderer now, and they as a murderer's friends by way of association. People look at her with unconcealed disdain, contempt contorting their features as they cross the street to avoid her. Mud sticks, and she will forever carry the sins of her child with her. As Remy's mother, it's kismet she supposes – the gods had decided.

She takes it from her pocket, stares at it in her hand. The one question that continues to burn in her chest is why Remy never destroyed it, never threw it into the river along with Amelie's other possessions. She'd wanted so much to ask her daughter, to hear an explanation, but in doing so she ran the risk of exposing herself. Remy would wonder why her mother hadn't confronted her, or worse, she'd put two and two together and realise she'd drawn the conclusion she had, question her about Len's death... Maggie can't help but wonder what would be different now if she'd never gone up into the loft and discovered it. Would Len still be here, despite what Detective Riley had told her? Would Remy? Perhaps.

'You mustn't torture yourself,' the counsellor had told her. 'You mustn't torture yourself with what ifs. It's what *is* that matters now. What ifs will keep you stuck in the trauma, but you can't go back and change it. None of us have the luxury of rewriting history, Maggie.'

She'd seen it, wrapped around her daughter's neck that terrible day as she'd hung from the light fitting, had desperately struggled to untie it. When she and Detective Riley had eventually succeeded, she'd stuffed it into her pocket. He'd enquired about it, but no one had come for it, searched the house for it, and so she'd fobbed him off with one of Remy's old scarves as a replacement instead. Did he believe her? She wasn't sure, but no more had come of it. Was it a deliberate oversight on Detective Riley's behalf or had he understood her need to retain it? Allowed it, given that they didn't need the additional evidence in light of Remy's confession.

She stares down at it, feels the pink, expensive-looking fabric between her fingers, those horrible little black skulls... She takes a lighter from her coat pocket and sets it on fire, holding the corner of it until she no longer can, the flames licking against her skin. She watches until it is nothing but ash on the ground. And then she turns and walks away.

Brenda is waiting on her doorstep when she arrives home.

'Oh, there you are! I was ringing the bell. I came to say goodbye, Maggie,' she says a little sadly. Brenda and Clive are perhaps the only two people on the street that seem sad to see her go.

Not so smug now, eh, Maggie!

'I wanted to wish you – wish you all – good luck.'

'That's very kind of you, Brenda,' she says.

'Clive sends you his best too.'

They're an item now, Brenda and Clive, two people who came together and found each other through their respective, collective sorrows. Maggie is happy for them. Despite appearances, they seem suited somehow.

'Thank you – both of you. I wish you a lot of luck too – a happy life together.'

Brenda smiles, looks at her a little tentatively. 'Listen, Maggie, there's something I've been meaning to tell you. I tried telling you a while back, but then, well, then everything happened and I wasn't sure whether to or not, but now that you're going, that I'll probably never see you again...'

Maggie would have usually counteracted this by saying something like, 'Of course you'll see me again, Brenda,' would have fobbed her off with polite platitudes as people always do. But it's different now – *she's* different.

'It's about Len...'

'Oh?'

'He keeps... he keeps coming to me – in one of my special sleeps.'

'Ah, those,' Maggie says, smiling softly.

'He says there's something in the drawer – the bedroom I think. Something he wanted you to have. I think he's trying to send you a message of some sort...'

'Well,' Maggie says softly, 'we're all packed up and ready to go now. I've cleared out all the drawers in the house – they're all empty now.'

Brenda looks a little crestfallen. 'Really? Oh well. Perhaps... perhaps I've got it wrong.'

She steps towards her, embraces her. 'Well, goodbye, Maggie and... I'm so sorry,' she says, 'for everything.'

Maggie swallows back the lump in her throat as she closes

the door behind her. '*Something in the drawer... I think he's trying to send you a message.*'

Perhaps she'll do one last check after all, make sure they haven't forgotten anything.

Maggie makes her way up the stairs and into the bedroom with a heaviness in her chest, perhaps for the last time, and goes to the bedside cabinet. She's sure it's empty – she remembers clearing it out herself.

She opens the drawer, feels inside, her fingers running along the edges and— Hang on, she *can* feel something, something small, there, in the left corner.

She reaches for it, takes it in her hand, the other instinctively shooting up to cover her mouth as she gasps... She looks down at it in the palm of her hand through the tears that have formed in her eyes.

It's a Hershey's Kiss.

A LETTER FROM ANNA-LOU

Thank you so, so much for choosing to read *The Lie in Our Marriage*. It means an incredible amount to me that you picked it, and if you enjoyed it, and want to keep up to date with all my latest and former releases, please sign up at the following link. Your e-mail address will never be shared, and you can unsubscribe at any time.

www.bookouture.com/anna-lou-weatherley

If you enjoyed *The Lie in Our Marriage*, I would be so incredibly grateful if you could spare the time to write a review. It means so much to hear what you, my dear reader, thinks, and it makes such a difference in helping new readers discover one of my books for the first time.

I absolutely love hearing from my readers – you can get in touch on my Facebook page, through Twitter, Instagram, Goodreads or on my website any time.

With love and thanks,

Anna-Lou

facebook.com/annalouweatherleyauthor
twitter.com/annaloulondon
instagram.com/annalouwrites

ACKNOWLEDGEMENTS

Oh gosh, where to begin! I always find acknowledgements difficult to write as there are so many people I want to thank and namecheck, and I'm always mindful of missing someone out! I went through a very tumultuous and difficult time personally while writing this book; it was a time of endings and new beginnings. I even managed to move house, though looking back I'm not entirely sure how! But in among all the chaos, the heartbreak and upheaval, I continued to write this book, for myself, and for my dear readers, who are my support and inspiration. So thank you, firstly, to anyone who has bought my books and has appreciated my work – without you, it couldn't happen, and all the time you enjoy my work, I will continue to write, come what may!

Thank you, as always, to my absolutely incredible mummy. Without your love, support, all the laughs, the tears, the advice, the friendship, the encouragement, the help you selflessly give, the positivity you naturally exude and the hope, I absolutely would not have been able to write this book. The world is a far better place with you in it, and I never want to imagine one where you aren't. You are my guardian angel, and I love you so much.

Thank you to my loyal and wonderful friends, to Sue Traveller, who has overcome her own difficulties with such aplomb, dignity and humour this year and last – another inspirational woman and a kindred spirit. I always laugh so much when we are together, and to me, that's priceless.

Thank you, Kelly Hancock. Again, a truly wonderful friend who has faced difficulties with strength and stoicism, and who has always been there for me regardless. I have learned a lot from you, and your kindness is a gift.

I also want to thank Lorraine Leon for all her incredible support. The world needs more people like you in it. Your altruism and empathy, kindness and understanding (as well as knowledge) makes the world a better, safer place.

My sister and friend, Lisa-Jane, yet another incredibly strong woman (there's a theme going here!) with a heart of gold and inner strength that is inspirational, not to mention an unrivalled sense of style! I wish we got to spend more time together. I treasure the memories we share and all those I hope are to come.

Also, my beautiful boys, 'Lz' and 'Phil', wonderful, challenging, demanding, funny, infuriating – and the loves of my life. Also to LM, DC, B&B, H and Merhan.

Thank you to my exceptional agent, best in the business, the legendary Mr Darley Anderson. I enjoy our conversations (and lunches) so much, and you have been a wonderful and huge source of inspiration, advice, wisdom, support and guidance to me both professionally and personally – I'll have that Conran sofa one day! Thank you also to Rebeka Finch, Roseanna Bellingham and all the team at the wonderful Darley Anderson Agency.

My publishers, Bookouture, what can I say other than the hugest 'thank you, thank you, thank you' for being wonderful, for supporting me, for promoting me, for believing in me and for continuing to do so? Thank you to the inimitable, formidable, unstoppable and beautiful Kim Nash, Noelle Holten and Jenny Geras especially.

I write this in no particular order, but lastly, and importantly, I want to thank my editor, Claire Bord. For over a decade we have worked together, and I am so incredibly proud and grateful for the wonderful, trusting relationship we have built both professionally and personally. Literally, from day one you have believed in me, supported me, guided me and inspired me. You have played such an integral role in my career as an author and any successes thus far. You have been there with me throughout all the ups and downs. I owe so much to you. The words 'thank you' simply aren't enough. I wish you so much happiness and the success you richly deserve moving forward. So, it's befitting then, that I dedicate this book to you, my lovely editor. I'm going to miss you so much.

Made in the USA
Coppell, TX
21 September 2023

21857787R00203